THE MOLE

The Cold War Memoir
of Winston Bates

THE MOLE

The Cold War Memoir
of Winston Bates

PETER WARNER

THOMAS DUNNE BOOKS

St. Martin's Press

New York

THOMAS DUNNE BOOKS.
An imprint of St. Martin's Press.

THE MOLE: THE COLD WAR MEMOIR OF WINSTON BATES. Copyright © 2013 by Peter Warner. All rights reserved. Printed in the United States of America. For information, address St. Martin's Press, 175 Fifth Avenue, New York, N.Y. 10010.

www.thomasdunnebooks.com
www.stmartins.com

THE LIBRARY OF CONGRESS CATALOGING-IN-PUBLICATION DATA IS AVAILABLE UPON REQUEST

ISBN 978-1-250-03479-3 (hardcover)
ISBN 978-1-250-03480-9 (e-book)

St. Martin's Press books may be purchased for educational, business, or promotional use. For information on bulk purchases, please contact Macmillan Corporate and Premium Sales Department at 1-800-221-7945, extension 5442, or write specialmarkets@macmillan.com.

First Edition: October 2013

10 9 8 7 6 5 4 3 2 1

For Cynthia, Emily, Jill, and Nick
Each in your own way

CONTENTS

THE MOLE

This animal, destined to seek its food and provide for its subsistence under the surface of the earth, is wonderfully adapted, by the all-wise Author of nature, to its peculiar mode of living. It enjoys the senses of hearing and smelling in a very eminent degree: The former gives notice of every approach of danger; whilst the latter enables it to find its prey in the midst of darkness, and compensates in a great measure for an almost total want of sight.

—A GENERAL HISTORY OF QUADRUPEDS
by Thomas Bewick and Ralph Beilby

DRAMATIS PERSONAE

This selective list *includes the dates and job descriptions that are relevant to my account.*

Dean Acheson: U.S. secretary of state, 1949–1953.

Joseph W. Alsop: Journalist and syndicated newspaper columnist; his column Matter of Fact, written with his brother Stewart from 1945 to 1958 and then solely by Joseph until 1974, appeared three times a week in more than three hundred newspapers.

Tracy Barnes: Assistant deputy director for Plans, CIA, 1960–1962.

Alice Bates: Sister of Winston Bates.

Simon Bates: Father of Winston Bates.

Richard Bissell: Deputy director for Plans, CIA, 1955–1962.

Elizabeth Boudreau: Hostess, Washington, D.C., 1946–1986.

Lawrence Boyer: Pentagon procurement officer, 1952–1961. Governmental Relations director, Autonomic Devices, Inc., 1967–1972.

Dramatis Personae

Deborah Boyer: Housewife, Washington, D.C., 1952–1961. Client Services associate, Ashford, Abelow, Marcy & Cannon LLP, 1971–1974.

McGeorge Bundy: National Security advisor, 1961–1966.

William Bundy: CIA analyst, 1950–1959; assistant to secretary of Navy, then secretary of Navy, 1960–1964; assistant secretary of state for the Far East, 1964–1969.

Robert Cage: Library assistant, Library of Congress, 1951–1955.

Roy Cohn: Chief counsel, 1953–1954, Senate Permanent Subcommittee on Investigations under Senator Joseph McCarthy.

Gardner Denby: American Foreign Service officer, 1946–1964.

Cathy Dieter: Call girl, Washington, D.C., 1970–1972.

Allen Dulles: Director of Central Intelligence, 1953–1961.

James E. Flannery: CIA officer; assistant to Richard Bissell, 1955–1961.

J. William Fulbright: United States senator from Arkansas, 1944–1974; chairman Senate Foreign Relations Committee, 1959–1974.

Richard Helms: CIA chief of Operations in the Directorate of Plans, under first Frank Wisner and then Richard Bissell, 1952–1962; head of Plans (DDP) CIA, 1962–1965; director of Central Intelligence of CIA, 1966–1973.

Henry Hess: Colonel, U.S. Army; counterinsurgency expert; attached to the Joint Subsidiary Activities Committee of the Joint Chiefs of Staff, 1958–1961.

E. Howard Hunt: CIA officer; chief of Covert Action, Domestic Operations Division, CIA, 1962–1966; president's Special Investigations Unit under Richard Nixon, 1971–1972.

Lyndon B. Johnson: Thirty-sixth president of the United States, 1963–1969.

Curtis E. LeMay: Air Force general, commanded firebombing of Tokyo; head of Strategic Air Command, 1948–1957; Air Force chief of staff, 1961–1965.

Walter Lippmann: Writer and journalist; his influential, widely syndicated newspaper column, Today and Tomorrow, appeared from 1930 until 1967.

John (Jack) J. McGowan: Officer, Canadian Security Intelligence Service, 1948–1964.

Matthew Mason: Major, later colonel, U.S. Army Intelligence, 1942–1961.

Ayn Rand: Russian-American screenwriter, novelist, and philosopher.

Richard Brevard Russell Jr.: United States senator from Georgia, 1933–1971; chairman Armed Services Committee, 1951–1953, 1955–1969; chairman Senate Appropriations Committee, 1969–1971.

Leverett A. Saltonstall: United States senator from Massachusetts, 1945–1967.

Sergei Striganov: Political counselor, Soviet embassy, Washington, D.C., 1954–1957.

PART ONE

THE SLEEPER

1

On April 28, 1953, I quit my job as a cataloguer in the map collection of the Library of Congress. After work, I met Robert Cage, my only friend at the Library, at a dreary bar on the other side of Folger Park. Robert had first acknowledged my existence three years before, a month after I started at the Library, when I came to work wearing my baggy Parisian flea market suit with a plaid flannel shirt and a tie. "What are you supposed to be?" he said in a flat, expressionless tone. "A poet manqué?" He was right; it was the poet's outfit, circa 1950. But Robert was dressed almost identically, and if he had smiled I would have taken his challenge for a bit of ironic humor. But he just stared at me so I said, "Manqué see, manqué do." I was rather pleased with myself but I got no reaction from him. I must have made some impression, however, because the next time we ran into each other he asked me to sleep with him. When I told him that I wasn't homosexual, he said: "If *I* made this mistake, imagine what everyone else must think."

"Let them," I said indifferently, though of course I cared. Robert didn't care what anyone thought of him. We were both marginal people but I was frustrated with my status while he cultivated his nondescript quality. He had dead-white skin, drab brown hair, and bland, impassive features. He wore heavy-soled black work shoes and brought his lunch to the Library in a metal lunch pail. A brief twitch at the corner of his mouth sufficed for his rare smile or frown. A trace of snide insinuation in his voice was his only inflection. I was jealous of his deadpan style though I was too self-conscious to emulate it. We would sometimes take the train together to New York for a weekend. My twin sister, Alice, had moved to New York at about the same time I moved to Washington and I would stay with her and go to the opera and museums. Robert would spend the weekend drinking and going to jazz clubs. During the return trip he would mock my taste for mandarin culture.

"What did Burnson say when you quit?" Robert asked. He was referring to our supervisor, whose attachment to his collections of fire maps and Colonial America maps was pathological.

"It took him a while to realize that I was quitting," I said. "He couldn't believe that anyone would choose to leave his little world of maps. The only thing he cared about was whether he would be allowed to replace me."

I hadn't actually told Robert what I was going to be doing. He was staring at me in his disconcerting way: his face frozen, his pale eyes fixed intently on mine. It was a look that often impelled people to babble on until he gave some enigmatic hint of approval. But I was immune today.

Finally Robert said: "I imagine they won't let him replace you for a while. You'll be good for the budget." He ordered another whiskey. "And you're going to be . . ."

"I'm going to be on Senator Saltonstall's staff."

There was a long pause while Robert gathered his imperturbability. I could read his mind: This was a big step for me.*

"Onwards and upwards," Robert said drily. "That project of yours on the Massachusetts Bay settlement maps seems to have been opportune."

For a moment I felt exposed: Had my motives been so obvious? "It's mainly research and some speech writing. Are you surprised?"

"Mildly. I had assumed you were on your way to becoming a Li-

---

* For the first time in a generation there was a Republican majority in the Senate and Leverett Saltonstall, senator from Massachusetts and patrician man of the people, had become chairman of the Senate Armed Services Committee.

brary lifer." Robert's disappointment in himself for underestimating me was probably as close to congratulations as I would get from him. "Does Saltonstall know that you're still a Canadian citizen?"

"Of course. He even promised to expedite the citizenship process. He can put through a private bill for me."

"It's just as well that you're out of here. Once they root all the lefties and perverts out of the State Department, who knows where they'll turn? They'll probably start in on the Library. And they'll have a field day here. Like shooting fish in a barrel. Not that you'd have been in any danger—despite Burnson's suspicions—but they could get me on both counts."

"Don't worry. Nobody cares about the Library."

Robert regarded me with sour contempt. "Oh you're a fool and you're leaving a fool's paradise." Robert ran his hand through his hair, as emphatic a gesture as he allowed himself. "They'll go after the Library too. It doesn't matter where you work. Like that poor sucker Harris from the *Voice of America*. And you read those stories about Cohn and Schine in Europe." Roy Cohn and David Schine had just concluded a faultfinding trip across Europe, which mostly consisted of holding press conferences in various foreign capitals to cavil about how few copies of *The American Legion Magazine* there were in American embassy libraries.

"At least I won't have to worry about being threatened by Cohn on the sex front," Cage said. "Since I'd have no qualms about threatening back."

It was the first allusion I had ever heard to Cohn's homosexuality. "You and Cohn? Are you serious?"

"A poignant encounter in Rock Creek Park. Memorable only for the fact that it was Cohn."

"I think I'm going to meet them tonight. Or Cohn anyway. I'm going to a party at Elizabeth Boudreau's home. Cohn is supposed to be there."

At this he raised his eyebrows, which felt to me like a triumph. "And I took you for a silly boy. All this time you have been calculating your future. And now you're not only off to the Senate, but also entering sophisticated Washington society. All those questions you had about her . . . you weren't so casually curious after all."

Robert was quite drunk. I had been careful to have only one drink because I wanted to be alert at the party later. I stood up and said good night. "Keep in touch," Robert said and waved to me with his hand high above his head, as if I were sailing away. And I was. It was the first time in three years that I believed I was fulfilling my purpose in Washington. I had felt helpless until now, unsure how to move to some useful vantage point. But when Saltonstall asked my map division to do a favor for the Massachusetts Historical Society, I leaped at the chance and contrived a couple of personal encounters with the senator. He took a shine to me, especially after I showed off my amazing memory by naming all the ships and their captains of the Great Migration, which had carried Saltonstall's ancestors to the Bay Colony.

After leaving Robert, I took a trolley to Dupont Circle and then walked across the P Street Bridge to my little garret apartment in Georgetown, which was only six blocks away from Elizabeth Boudreau's mansion.

A lot of shameless maneuvering had gone into my invitation from Elizabeth—almost as much as had gone into my new job. I met Elizabeth at St. Thomas Episcopal Church of Georgetown, in whose chorus I had volunteered to sing with the very intention of meeting someone like her, as well as some of the government and military figures who seemed to be active at the church.

Elizabeth Boudreau stood out in the chorus. She had a tinny voice and a propensity for missing entrances and singing the wrong words, but she underwrote the choral director's salary. After some research, I decided to cultivate her. She was a girl from a destitute but "good" southern family who had married Bob "Butch" Boudreau, a Louisiana lawyer. Though not rich or well bred, Boudreau's avaricious drive promised to revive her sapless family tree. He was an advisor/sidekick to Huey Long, and he and Elizabeth had arrived in Washington in 1933, when she was eighteen. After Long was assassinated two years later, Boudreau stayed on in Washington as a lobbyist for Standard Oil until

1942, when he went off to war. A year later, Boudreau was killed in Italy. Back in Washington, Elizabeth discovered that her estate included several thousand acres of prime oil-producing land in Louisiana. Soon it included a magnificent house in Georgetown.

I did what I could to make Elizabeth notice me. I became the choral director's favorite because we shared a mutual contempt for the Metropolitan Opera's ragged chorus. Once the director began holding me up to the others as an example of error-free singing, I plotted to run into Elizabeth in Georgetown. The first time I said hello to her, in a florist's shop, she didn't recognize me. But the second time, when I just happened to be passing by as she was leaving her home one morning, occurred the day after a rehearsal during which I had ruined her solo by loudly launching into her part. Again she didn't recognize me, but this time I approached her and apologized for my blunder. After that we began to chat occasionally during rehearsal breaks. I doubt if I made much of an impression. Although Elizabeth was hardly an A-list hostess in 1953, I was a drone for the Library of Congress and of less than even passing interest. My break came when I mentioned my research on the Bay Colony settlement maps, which I was doing for the Massachusetts Historical Society at Senator Saltonstall's request. She seemed uninterested, but a few days later she ran into Saltonstall, dropped my name for want of anything better to say, and learned that I was soon going to be a member of his staff. When she called to invite me, I thought at first it was Robert Cage, in drawling falsetto, playing a practical joke.

For the next thirty-five years I would prepare my agenda for the evening as I walked to Elizabeth's great house in Georgetown. I would decide whom I wanted to meet, what I wanted to learn, what gossip I wished to catalyze at the party. This first night my plans were modest: I hoped to elicit at least one minor indiscretion to pass on to my undeclared watcher, should I ever be asked. As I walked, I rehearsed little speeches—clever things to say about the Library and self-deprecating remarks about my life, which I hoped would be mistaken for false modesty.

I was greeted at the door by a butler and conveyed to Elizabeth in the drawing room, which was decorated then in a clunky version of veranda colonial. Some thirty guests had arranged themselves in small groups. Elizabeth was seated on a large sofa; with her dress splayed in a circle about her she looked like a taffeta water lily. When she saw me, she motioned assertively for me to approach her. She was small boned and blond, with delicate features and piercing blue eyes. A pale flight of freckles softened her sharp features and gave her a girlish appearance. Standing before her was a fat man with a blotchy face whom she introduced in her gentle southern accent as Arthur Barker, a fellow southerner and a member of the new administration. I recognized the name: He was a protégé of Charles Wilson, the secretary of Defense. "Arthur, Winston sings in the chorus . . ." She paused waiting for Barker to nod. ". . . at St. Thomas, you know, the church? . . . And he just about knows more about music than anyone." Elizabeth spoke in a fluent succession of semi-queries; by the time you had nodded politely three or four times, she would assume you agreed with whatever she was saying. "Arthur has just rented a house in Georgetown . . . on O Street? . . . not far from the university. Arthur was just asking me . . . you know of course they're trying to desegregate the public swimming pool over on Twenty-ninth Street?"

Barker, encouraged by their mutual southernness, shook his head in disgust at the prospect, but I was pretty sure Elizabeth had reasonably liberal ideas about these issues. I decided that Elizabeth and I would gang up on stuffy Mr. Barker. "I don't swim myself, but I do think it is about time for us to let little white children and little dark children inhabit the same water," I ventured.

Elizabeth continued as if I had not uttered a word. "I can't tell you how important it is that they get the Georgetown pool desegregated immediately." Barker looked baffled and I smiled complicitly. "You know they just desegregated the Rosedale pool?" she went on. "That leaves Georgetown as the only white pool. This neighborhood is going to be crawling with white riffraff all summer. The pool will be a magnet. But if they desegregate the Georgetown pool, hardly anyone will come—Negroes can't swim and the white trash will stay away." She looked from me to Barker fiercely, her piercing blue eyes and sharp features challenging us, and then she chortled, delighted to have enmeshed us in her unique logic.

I sensed I had failed my first trial of socializing but Elizabeth appeared not to notice. We went on to discuss other aspects of Georgetown life at which I was more successful. When drinks arrived, Elizabeth used the interruption to introduce me to an obtuse woman who managed Oveta Culp Hobby's office. We discussed *Call Me Madam* though I was unable to tell her what Perle Mesta was really like.

Almost everyone at the party was someone else's assistant or aide. I didn't know why Robert had referred to Elizabeth's salon as sophisticated, though I soon learned she was trying to live that reputation down, playing it safe with a new administration in town. By the end of the Eisenhower years Elizabeth would be enshrined as an A-list hostess and there would be no more invitations for B- and C-list types except for her biannual Thanksgiving Day buffet party. Elizabeth approached me again with a proud smile on her face and a small spidery woman on her arm. "Winston, my literary friend, I have a surprise for you. I want you to meet Ayn Rand."

"You are a writer too," Rand declared. She had one of those gruff, metronomic middle-European accents.

I had rehearsed an amusing little speech about becoming a failed poet in Paris in my foolish youth three years before. But some residual literary pride prevented me from trotting my failure out before another writer. "Actually, Miss Rand, I really think of you as a writer-philosopher."

"Like Burke," she said.

I took that as an invitation to explore her ideas but I was spared by the arrival of Roy Cohn. Rand spotted him across the room. "He's here. I have so much I must tell him." She deserted me without another word.

Cohn too was somebody's assistant, but his arrival riveted the party. His European boondoggle with Schine had gotten a lot of bad press though I had the feeling Cohn didn't care. He was sleek and dark and his baggy baleful eyes measured us with sour expectation. The other guests half turned to glance at him surreptitiously as he spoke to Elizabeth, who was in a state of hostess apotheosis at his presence. I watched

Rand zero in on Cohn across the room. She didn't waste any time; she grabbed at his jacket and Cohn flinched. At that moment dinner was announced and Elizabeth led Cohn into the dining room while Rand scuttled along trying to keep Cohn's attention. As we were sorting out our assigned places, I saw Rand corner Elizabeth. Later I learned she had prevailed upon Elizabeth to change the seating so she could sit with Cohn. There were four tables of eight and Cohn and Rand wound up at my table. I was seated next to Oveta Culp Hobby's executive assistant.

Rand didn't waste a minute of Cohn's time with small talk. "I have wanted to meet you for such a very long time. Have you heard about the work we have been accomplishing in Hollywood?" She pawed at Cohn's arm again. "We have had many serious meetings with studio heads. We have a newsletter that—"

"Who's 'we'?" Cohn asked while he looked around the table.

Rand looked startled. "You have had a brochure from me. With a letter. That is why I am in Washington. We are the Motion Picture Alliance for the Preservation of American Ideals. Within a year there will be no films made that do not present a positive depiction of capitalism."

"Not even *Salome*?" I murmured.

Cohn jerked his head in my direction. For someone who was essentially humorless, this amounted to a guffaw. But Rand plowed right on. "Tell me about your boss, your Mr. McCarthy. Are you sure he is committed to the fight?"

We hadn't even sighted the soup and she was putting Cohn on the spot. Rand's tiny hands were always fidgeting; when they weren't creeping up Cohn's sleeve, she held them in a prayerlike position, her fingertips dancing against each other.

"He's committed," Cohn said. He cocked his head quizzically at her, slightly bemused yet wary.

"There is something weak about his face. He likes to drink I have heard. This could be exploited by the Communists if you are not careful."

The rest of us were studiously breaking our bread and arranging our napkins on our laps while we listened intently.

Cohn pursed his lips; she was beginning to annoy him. "Look,

Mamie Eisenhower drinks too. You think the Communists are going to get to her?"

That shut her up. It shut everyone else up too for the next five minutes. Since no one smirked or smiled or even became indignant, I was sure Mamie's dipsomania was a fresh piece of gossip for most of us. Then, with the arrival of the soup, we introduced ourselves to our neighbors and began to converse as if nothing had happened. Cohn was seated to the right of Oveta Culp Hobby's assistant and I was able to observe him as I made small talk with her. He was bored and restless; his impatient glower made it clear the party wasn't worth his time or his importance. I was enjoying myself, however. The small talk I made was very small indeed, but my private sense of duplicity, of performing under an invisible spotlight, was immensely pleasurable.

"You have a funny kind of accent. Where are you from?"

It took me a moment to realize that Cohn was speaking to me. "Accent? What did I say? Oh, I must have said 'aboot' instead of 'about.' I'm Canadian actually."

"What are you doing here?"

"Here? You mean Washington?"

"No I mean Paris," he snorted. He looked around the table as if he expected gales of laughter at this sally.

"I'm just about to start working for Senator Saltonstall."

"You can do that if you're not American?"

"There's no legal problem as long as Saltonstall wants me. Besides, my American citizenship is in the works. Speaking of Paris, did you enjoy your visit there?"

His eyes narrowed. I had touched a raw nerve.

"I mean it's such a wonderful city. I lived there for three years before coming to Washington. Did you see *Moulin Rouge*? That made me miss Paris. I lived in Paris for three years before moving here. Washington is very beautiful too." I was blathering uncontrollably. Suddenly I didn't feel quite so comfortable with my duplicitous self.

"What were you doing there for three years?" Cohn asked. "Working?"

"I worked on and off. It was really a postcollege fling." To my relief,

Ayn Rand interrupted us and Cohn appeared to lose interest in me. But as the party was breaking up, Cohn came over to me.

"What was your name again? I'll put in a good word for you with Saltonstall."

I walked home in a panic. How stupid to have engaged Cohn enough to pique his interest in me! Even worse, I had mentioned Paris, where my dubious adventure in Washington first began. . . .

2

Paris, 1948

On a splendid morning in early May, I sat with my coffee and croissant at a café on the rue Marbeuf, directly across the street from the apartment building where I rented a large room in a cavernous apartment owned by a World War I widow. Now that spring was firmly in place, Parisians had eagerly shed the dark shabby wool coats that had lasted many of them through four years of occupation and four more years of clothing shortages. I too was emerging from a gloomy period. For almost a year since my arrival in Paris, I had furtively haunted the artistic world I hoped to inhabit. Without ever meeting Cocteau, Picasso, Camus, or any of the other stars of Left Bank culture, I knew them by sight and knew the boulevards and cafés where they could be seen. And now this world, on whose outskirts I hovered in solitary yearning, had wonderfully come to seem within my reach, thanks to my new friends, Viktor and Mara Gregory.

I came upon Viktor and Mara one frigid afternoon in January at the Musée du Jeu de Paume as they stood before a Pissarro landscape. Their excited mix of heavily accented English and French seemed familiar to me and I realized I had seen them several days before at the Café de Flore where they were sitting with the sculptor Alberto Giacometti. Naturally, I had eavesdropped on their conversation but the disappointing subject was real estate. Now I saw my chance. With shocking boldness I lurched into their conversation like a demented tour guide, spouting biographical details and secondhand artistic assessments about Pissarro. The bemused Gregorys had never met a Canadian poet before, certainly not one so eager to relate (almost verbatim) every fact about Camille Pissarro he had gleaned from the museum's official catalog. They let me attach myself to them for the next hour and when we parted they politely asked for my address. When I asked for their address, Viktor demurred and I was sure I would never hear from them again. But one evening three weeks later, as I sat huddled under a blanket in my room, my landlady summoned me to the front door. Standing in the stairwell outside the apartment was a short, pudgy man in a heavy overcoat. An astrakhan hat perched on his head. He had a sallow complexion and the loose jowls of someone who had once been quite fat. I stared at him uncomprehendingly.

He made a little bow. "Winston Bates, it is I, Viktor Gregory. Look at you, shivering like a wretch. You must be fed. Come. Mara awaits us." I grabbed my coat and Viktor took me by the arm. As we headed down the stairs, Viktor turned on my landlady. "If you do not provide more heat, I shall report you. The deputy mayor is a personal friend of mine."

He guided me to a nearby brasserie and led me to a table. "Here is Mara," he announced, grandly waving his arms as if unveiling her. Mara was dark and sensually handsome, with a compact, muscular figure. She rose from the table and returned the gesture to Viktor. I desperately tried to impress the Gregorys that evening, presenting myself as a sophisticated, au courant young poet, who was escaping the bonds of his well-to-do but philistine family in Winnipeg. To my delight, the Gregorys took me up. Soon they were inviting me to meet them at cafés, gallery exhibitions, and recitals. They never gave much notice; Mara or Viktor would come by for me at lunchtime with a plan for the afternoon. I finally worked my way up to an invitation to one of their "evenings." From the way Mara first described these parties, coyly hinting that someday I might be given the honor of an invitation, I assumed they represented some sort of quintessence of advanced Left Bank culture. But when I began to frequent the Gregorys' disordered, underfurnished apartment near the Place Maubert, I was taken aback at the way they threw people and food together without much planning before the event or intercession during it. Sometimes there was lots of good humor and laughter; other times everybody stared at each other, stupefied with boredom.

Viktor dropped names shamelessly and I just as shamelessly scooped them up. There was hardly a personality in Paris about whom he did not have a comment or anecdote that demonstrated Viktor's personal relation to them. I suspected Viktor of exaggerating his range of acquaintances, but he did have some sort of access to the Left Bank world of artists and writers. I had actually met Jean Arp at dinner at Viktor's. Another time, as Viktor and I walked on the rue de Seine, we encountered Giacometti, looking almost as anorexic as one of his sculptures. Without bothering to introduce me, Viktor made some casual conversation with him. And one morning Viktor waved to me from a crowded table as I entered the Café de Flore; there was André Malraux sitting right next to Viktor. I paused awkwardly before them and Viktor waved again, this time inviting me to walk on.

As we became friendlier, Viktor occasionally insisted on my accompanying Mara on her social rounds while he was engaged in his business affairs, which involved entrepreneurial projects in publishing and theater. He was currently attempting to raise money to produce the work of a Romanian playwright Mara had discovered. According to Viktor, Mara's grandmother was the illegitimate daughter of the king of Romania. Viktor's own ethnic identity was a little harder to discern. When I told him I was half Jewish he delightedly embraced me. "Wonderful. I am too." But other times he variously claimed to be half Greek, half Russian, and half Lebanese.

By the time I finished two coffees and two croissants on this beautiful spring morning, I had less than an hour to kill before meeting Viktor and Mara in the bar at the Hotel Pont Royal. It was a perfect day to walk to the Left Bank. As I crossed the Seine, I felt my usual sense of inadequacy as I approached the world of Saint-Germain-des-Prés. One reason I had located in the Eighth Arrondissement was because the Sixth, with its expectations of creative self-aggrandizement, was too daunting for me; though there were some nights lately, as I labored on my poems in my room, when my writing seemed inspired and powerful enough for me to contemplate my assault on the Left Bank. I actually hadn't written many new poems since coming to Paris; mostly I had worked at elevating my college poems, which had won a student prize at McGill, to a new, commanding level of mature ambition.

Some time ago Mara had asked to read my work. I wavered for a while but then realized how my refusal would seem childish to someone who was on familiar terms with so many artists and writers. I had finally handed her some poems a few weeks ago, entreating her, in a voice plummy with feigned nonchalance, to find them diverting. Neither Mara nor Viktor had mentioned my poems since. I didn't know how to bring the subject up nor was I sure I wanted to. But my writing couldn't have been too much of a disaster because the Gregorys continued to invite me to their soirees and to meet me for drinks, en passant, as they whizzed industriously about Paris.

I found Viktor in the Pont Royal's dark, clubby bar. He was exchanging a word with a man who was slouched in one of the stuffed leather sofas. Even on a warm day in May, Viktor was fully turned out in a dark, rumpled suit with vest and watch chain. When he saw me, Viktor held up his hand, cautioning me not to interrupt him. A minute later Viktor hurried over and led me to the opposite corner of the room. As Viktor walked he leaned forward and his stubby arms swung as loosely as a rag doll's from his hunched shoulders; he kept his gaze down and his heavy brows furrowed, as if too preoccupied to watch where he was going. We sank into our armchairs. "You see everybody here, Winston. Absolutely everybody. Before the war that man I chat with was a publisher in Austria. Such a distinguished person! Seeing him in Vienna was like having an audience with the Pope of middle-European literature. Now he tells me he has started a new publishing house in Geneva. I suspect the new house is his home. But he says he wants to publish art books. So who knows? Could be we'll do some business maybe."

"You mean he might help you to start your press?" Viktor had occasionally announced his intention of launching a publishing venture. But since he had never described it to me in any detail, I had assumed it was no more serious than his other interests.

"I have mentioned it to you? Well it is getting closer. I have been making plans to publish limited editions. Very fine printing and paper. Small select audience. Not for my friend in Switzerland. On the other hand, maybe I will do business with him." Viktor pointed to a tall, pale man who was standing at the entrance to the bar and peering into the dark depths where we sat. "One of the most important art dealers in London. His father too, and his father before him." Viktor waved and the man waved back tentatively. Viktor continued: "The whole thing starts again. Europe I mean. Art. Books. Music. And they all come here. Those of us who sort out culture as well as the ones who create it. You know who was just here and you missed? Sartre. Yet Mara has told me this bar is already passé among Existentialists. Now tell me everywhere you have been going and everything you have seen."

I started to tell him about an exhibit at the Bibliothèque but he quickly interrupted.

"Look, Winston. Mara arrives."

Mara specialized in breathless entrances, always rushing from one exciting moment to the next. She cloaked her solid figure in flowing, robelike dresses and richly embroidered jackets and kept her long black hair in braided piles or buns on top of her head with the aid of elaborate pins and brooches. Her makeup was overt, her perfume strong, and she draped herself in costume jewelry that flashed and jangled with her spirited gestures. She greeted me with a kiss, then dipped a napkin in Viktor's glass of water and scrubbed away at the lipstick mark she had left on my cheek.

"Mara, Mara," Viktor said. "Do we have good news for Winston?"

"We always have good news for Winston but today is especially good news."

We all waited expectantly.

"So Mara, tell the young man. He is too shy to ask."

"Winston, you are a very fine poet."

Viktor sat back and beamed at me. "You feel good, no? You should. Mara knows many poets. Éluard had a crush on her. He asked her to run away with him."

I did feel good. After all, Mara was the first person to whom I had shown my work in Paris, though an unseized opportunity with Paul Éluard did not seem to me to be the strongest of critical credentials. On the other hand, if she did know Éluard and other poets, and she did like my work, she might help it to get read in serious circles. I decided to be pleased with Mara's endorsement.

"Before the war, Winston," Viktor continued, "I am instrumental in helping a number of artists to publish their work in limited editions, *éditions luxes*. We help them to produce and sell artists' books and sometimes portfolios of etchings. Next time you are at my home, ask me to show you the book I made with Max Ernst. Sometimes I introduce my friends who are writers to my artists so they can make books together. So it is time for me to start again." Viktor reached across the table. "Shake my hand, Winston."

I grasped his hand uncomprehendingly.

"You have shaken the hand of your publisher."

I was suddenly weak with eagerness and confusion. I had only recently begun to think of sending my work to one or another of the small badly printed literary magazines that littered serious bookstores. I saw the publication of my work in almost any form as a passport to the Left Bank, where my new confrères and I would practice art and literature in a state of hectic ecstasy. The thought was on my mind almost constantly now, as if I were poised to dive into very chilly waters. Now someone was ready to push me in.

"Viktor, tell our young man what you have in mind," Mara said.

"What I have in mind is that the poems of Winston Bates will be published in a very fine limited edition and they will be illustrated by one of the most famous of modern artists. What I have in mind is that someday this will be a famous publication, very rare and very valuable. Collectors will prize it because it is beautiful, because a famous artist has been inspired to do some of his finest work, and because that inspiration comes from the first published work of the famous poet Winston Bates. Now we drink to our book together." He summoned a waiter and ordered champagne.

"I can't believe this news," I said. "I never expected anything like this. How are you going to find the artist to illustrate the book? Won't he have to speak English?"

"We have found one." Viktor grasped his lapels and proudly inflated his stout, little chest. "I have spoken to Picabia. He is interested."

I must have looked as I felt, bewildered and distressed. What did Picabia's art have in common with the bitter elegance of my poetry?

"I cannot understand . . . you look disappointed. I have tried to make for you a wonderful surprise." Viktor rapidly deflated, and looked as if he were on the verge of tears. He looked helplessly to Mara for reassurance.

"It is a big surprise for Winston. Perhaps he has not seen very much of Picabia's work."

"I haven't. I've seen very little." My passport to the Left Bank floated tantalizingly before me. "But I like it. I've always liked it . . . what little I've seen." Mara and I had just seen an exhibit of Picabia's paintings: The work was interesting but rarely pleasing, with strange biomorphic shapes on monochromatic backgrounds. "Do you think he understands my work?"

"When you see what he does, you will understand your own work better. This is how it is done. Picabia takes you under his wing, gives you a profile, an introduction." Viktor searched my face eagerly for a sign of assent and nodded encouragingly.

"It does sound wonderful . . . but it seems so strange. Everything is all arranged and I haven't done a thing."

Viktor cleared his throat. "A few arrangements are still to be made. I will need to line up investors who will subscribe to the edition. Not so easy these days."

3

Late one afternoon in November 1954, my train from Washington, *The Senator,* pulled into South Station in Boston. I had set out very early in the day from Washington on the *Morning Congressional.* Outside the station, the newsboys' cries filled the unseasonably tepid air. They were shouting something about Joe McCarthy being hospitalized. I bought a *Herald* and scanned it anxiously in the taxi. I was relieved to learn that McCarthy had merely injured his elbow; I would not have to alter his brief but distasteful appearance in the speech I had written for Senator Saltonstall. I gave the speech a final, nervous review. If Saltonstall liked it, I hoped it would lead to more trips to Boston, more escapes from Washington. In the year and a half I had worked for the senator, I had been to Boston only twice. My job was confined to Washington, to supporting Saltonstall with research on policy and committee work. I blamed Pennie Gouzoule, Saltonstall's personal secretary in Washington, who had taken an instant dislike to me and convinced Saltonstall that I lacked the common touch necessary for political speech writing. But in the aftermath of the grueling 1954 election, in which Saltonstall had barely survived the national Democratic retrenchment, I was supposed to give Saltonstall a fresh voice.

The taxi left me off at Devonshire Street. The first time I visited these offices, from which the Saltonstall and Co. interests were run, I was quite excited. I had imagined some sort of High Wasp time warp, full of ancestral portraits, framed documents, and Windsor chairs. Instead I found a miscellaneous collection of battered desks, woebegone rugs, and filing cabinets representing several generations of office furniture.

"There he is," Saltonstall said to no one in particular as I entered, "the man with the speech. Sorry to make you come all the way up here, but this one is going to be covered nationally. I trust you had a good trip, Mr. Bates." Calling me Mr. Bates, with a paternal twinkle in his eye, was Saltonstall's way of showing he was fond of me. He took a good deal of pleasure in his persona—the laconic Salty with his twinkle, his fortitude, his crusty propriety.

We went over the speech for about an hour. Saltonstall removed my snide aspersions on McCarthy. "I know the election is over but let's see if we can't restrain ourselves. Roy Cohn was up here the week before last and he filled Faneuil Hall."

"I'm sure you've heard that McCarthy is in the hospital."

Saltonstall laughed derisively. "I spoke to someone who knows Joe's doctor at Walter Reed. The man has a bruised elbow. My goodness, what a weakling!" He closed his eyes for a moment, then looked directly into my eyes and cleared his throat, announcing a serious turn in the conversation. "As you know, Winston," he began, using my given name for the first time, "there are going to be some changes in my office when the new term begins."

"You're staying on Armed Services, aren't you?"

"Yes, but since I'm no longer chairman, less of the Armed Services business is going to go through my office. I know you have been eager to work on defense and foreign affairs and I wonder if I can keep you interested."

Had I been so transparent? I had tried to wiggle my way into the committee's legislative agenda. But Saltonstall's other assistants resisted me, arguing that my Canadian citizenship disqualified me. I was given little to do with policy matters unless Saltonstall needed some research for one of his less influential committees. I kept hinting that I was ready for more responsibility but now Saltonstall appeared ready to fire me. I had a dismaying vision of crawling back to the Library of Congress. "I'm sure I'll still be able to help you. Perhaps there are some other areas of responsibility I could develop."

"I'm sure there's more you could do. But you've made a very good impression on several other members of Armed Services." He chuckled. "I'll never forget how you helped us work over those dunderheads from the Pentagon during the NATO hearings. One senator who was especially impressed with you was Dick Russell. And he's going to be chairman now. There's a position on Russell's staff opening up and I'd like to do Russell a favor. Not that this won't be a good deal for you as well."

The recent NATO hearings had finally given me a chance to show off. Saltonstall's private bill for my American citizenship had just passed and Saltonstall felt comfortable about giving me more access to military plans and projections. At first, all the senators were grateful that I had more information at hand than any of their assistants. Gradually it dawned on them that I wasn't consulting notes as I darted from senator to senator, whispering relevant facts about treaties and troop strengths. At the conclusion of the hearings, Lyndon Johnson came up to me and said, "I don't know what you've got inside that head, boy, but you just keep it in good shape."

"You mean you want me to go to work for Richard Russell?" I asked Saltonstall.

"Even though it's on his staff, your primary duties will be with the Armed Services Committee, so we'll still see quite a lot of each other. It would have been inappropriate for you to work on defense and intelligence issues while you were still a Canadian citizen, but now that my bill has gone through, there's no problem. You'll be going where the power is. With Russell in the Senate and Vinson running House Armed Services, Georgia is going to become one big military base. Think it over. You don't have to give me an answer today."

I arrived back at my home in Georgetown in the early evening the next day, after a stop at the office. My next-door neighbor was arriving at the same time. He glanced at my bag. "Good trip?"

"Very good. I was in Boston."

"Boston! That's a great city," he said emphatically. I thought he was going to explain Boston's particular attraction to me, but he gave me a vehement thumbs-up and entered his home.

I knew his name, Larry Boyer, and his wife's, Deborah, though they didn't seem to know mine. They had arrived with the new administration in the spring of 1952 and had purchased the narrow whitewashed brick house that was adjacent to the wider brick house whose top floor I rented on our street of brick row houses. An extension to the back of my house had been topped off at my floor with a small porch just large enough for a table and a couple of chairs. It was the most satisfactory feature of my apartment. For nearly seven months of the year I drank my coffee, read my newspaper, and minded my neighbors' business on the porch. From my vantage point, I surveyed the interior quiltlike compound of yards with proprietary alertness, as if they formed a crossword puzzle whose solution earned me their secrets. I knew, for instance, that my neighbors Larry and Deborah were newlyweds when they arrived in Washington, married just after Larry's graduation from USC. Several wedding presents were unpacked beneath my gaze, including a fondue pot that Larry put on his head while he crooned, "I'm fond a' you." He was a tall, ill-proportioned young man with long arms and legs and a short torso. He had an attractive though scrunched-together little face, with a turned-up nose and an eager smile. He always seemed to be dancing about his "Deb," tendering his boyish enthusiasm, which she accepted with affectionate indulgence.

My immediate neighbor on the other side of my house, who rented the ground-floor apartment, was an English journalist named Malcolm Stanley, a stocky man who thrust his belly forward aggressively as he walked. I never saw him during the week, but he spent all of Saturday and Sunday sitting on his patio, no matter how intense the heat, a small canvas hat perched above his red face, drinking himself into a stupor as he pored over a vast array of newspapers. As night fell he would be passed out in his chaise, floating on a lake of newsprint. At the far end of our interior compound, obscured by a large linden tree, was a Negro rooming house, of which there were still several in Georgetown. An extremely elderly, rail-thin black man maintained a small vegetable garden beneath the linden tree. Directly abutting the backyard of my house was the backyard of the Clearys, a CIA man and his family who had moved into an ungainly pseudo-Georgian house. According to my landlady the previous resident, also CIA, had committed suicide. There was plenty of room in their backyard for the Clearys' bomb shelter, which they installed within months of their arrival. After many months passed without a nuclear holocaust, they began to use the shelter for storage, producing from it on weekends rakes, tools, toys. Theirs was a large family, four children, and as the weekend went by, the yard gradually filled with interrupted and abandoned projects. As darkness fell on Sunday evening, Mr. Cleary would scurry about, picking up the pieces of a bicycle, cleaning paintbrushes, closing bags of fertilizer, disassembling the half-assembled Seven Dwarfs Play Cottage, and shoving everything down into the shelter.

During my first year in Washington, I had frequent episodes of extreme, trembling fear. I couldn't believe that, in my urgent need to escape Paris, I had allowed myself to be recruited and then dumped, helpless and untrained, into Washington. My recruiter in Paris had referred to my role as a kind of consultant or informant, but I wasn't fooled—or rather the euphemisms allowed me to fool myself until I resurfaced in Washington and realized I was trapped. Sometimes on a late spring Saturday afternoon, when the air was hot and dense, I would bring my small radio out onto the porch and listen to the opera. As de los Ángeles's or Schwarzkopf's voice drifted into the cloying humidity with that squashy, pre-hi-fi tone of strangled yearning, I would wish that *this,* this fishbowl world of innocent circumstance in which my neighbors and I were suspended, could be enough to satisfy my elusive masters. I would imagine developing Mr. Cleary and the English journalist as sources of information, or at least getting to know them well enough to convince whoever was watching me that I had such sources. The longer I went without being contacted, the more I wondered if my value to my watcher was waning. The entity that efficiently and anonymously slipped five hundred dollars into my bank account every month had every right to feel disappointed. But five years had passed without so much as a tap on the shoulder, and it is only natural that the longer

an unrealized threat hangs over one, the more time one has to rational-
ize and excuse the source of that threat. It was a kind of Stockholm
syndrome: After feeling like a hostage for a long time, I began to identify with my oppressors. My putative "watcher" in Washington became
in my mind rather like an imaginary friend who was pleased, *really
pleased,* with my job on Saltonstall's staff. In hindsight, it would have
been better if I had never taken the job with Saltonstall and remained a
worthless Library staffer. But when Saltonstall told me that my primary
duties for the new job would be with the Armed Services Committee
itself, I realized it was too perfect: Armed Services not only oversaw the
military, the CIA fell within its purview too. My reticent masters would
be so proud of me if I took this job. When I was recruited in Paris I was
told: "Someone will be watching you." Recalled in Washington, this had
a vaguely menacing aspect at first. But as I grew comfortable with my
role, it became in my mind more like a promise: *Don't worry, someone
will be watching out for you.*

4

On rainy days the old Senate Office Building had a musty odor, as if in a far recess a huge accumulation of books and documents were slowly yellowing and mildewing its way into oblivion. As I hurried back and forth between the Armed Services Committee offices on the first floor and Senator Russell's office on the second floor, I was encouraged by this stale intimation of forgetfulness. Surely there was a place for someone who didn't forget, someone whose extraordinary memory could range freely over the billowing tide of information. During my early weeks on the new job, Russell was extremely generous with his time and accessibility. With the new Democratic majority in the Senate, he was at the height of his power, a level he was to sustain for over twenty years. I found his diffidence puzzling at first. He never told me how he wanted anything done; rather his account of how the committee functioned had an impersonal, descriptive quality. "The committee needs to be briefed by memo on the witnesses and their testimony no later than the day before the witness appears," was almost the first thing he said to me, matter-of-factly, in his gentle but pronounced southern accent. "That memo is the result of discussions with the chair several days before the appearance. The chair should always know exactly what the witness is going to say." At about midnight that night, I sat up in bed with the sudden realization that Russell was actually saying, "I want *you* to brief the committee . . . I want *you* to discuss with me . . ."

Russell was so passionless, so austere and unapologetically direct in the exercise of his authority that his power took on an abstract quality. If he had a grand plan for the future of America, I never saw it. Neither the trappings nor the perks of power interested him. He was unswayed and unamused by the foibles of the lobbyists and defense contractors who tap-danced about the committee in ardent supplication. I came to realize how reassuring his blandness was to his colleagues. A man with no cynicism, not even irony, was a man who could be trusted. People described him as brilliant, but it was not in the sense of having a radiant intellect; it was his ability to speak precisely to any point that compelled assent. His contentment with his sober directness was a measure of his absolute self-confidence. About the only time he had misjudged himself was his abortive bid for the presidential nomination in 1952. He found he lacked the histrionic talents required for popular leadership, and his racial politics marked him indelibly as a regional politician.

He was slightly homely, yet not unattractive, and his usual countenance was one of earnest determination. Unmarried, he lived alone in

The powerful senator from Georgia, Richard B. Russell Jr., was my boss from 1954 to 1971, except for a brief interlude in 1964 when I worked at the White House. *LBJ Library photo by Yoichi Okamoto*

hotels, first at the Mayflower and later at the Woodner. He worked constantly and quietly. He avoided the social circuit in Washington, turning over the many invitations that came his way to his staff. His one hobby was reading history, with an emphasis on military history. Despite his interest in history—or perhaps because of it—his expectations of the human race were limited and so he was rarely disappointed. He assumed that people behaved according to type—personality, race, gender, class, appearance.

The only time I heard Russell express any anger during my first months on the job was after one of his private lunches with Allen Dulles. In those days, Armed Services was the nominal oversight committee for the CIA. I say nominal because according to the general consensus in the Senate, any agency that enabled such efficient transitions in government for the peoples of Guatemala and Iran ought to be exempt from tedious legislative reservations. Eisenhower had always backed Dulles up on this. The few occasions on which Dulles condescended to speak to the whole committee were always in executive session, though nothing much was ever said. Saltonstall had once told me that as a matter of policy neither he nor the committee ought to know what the CIA was up to. Russell too had announced that the activities of the CIA needed to be taken on faith. The difference between the two men was that Saltonstall actually believed what he said while Russell was privately frustrated with the CIA's autonomy.

I was approaching Russell's office just as the gray-haired gentleman-spy emerged from their lunch. I was too far off to overhear the conversation, but Dulles was waving his pipe like a baton, as if serenely conducting the Cold War. They shook hands and Russell stood in the doorway watching Dulles depart. When Russell noticed me approaching he twisted his mouth in a little frown and motioned for me to follow him into the office. His inner office had the pleasant, informal look of a successful country lawyer, with wooden filing cabinets and bookcases, botanical prints on the walls, and a few small plants. His crowded but orderly desk was placed on a low platform close to the head of a large conference table, which filled most of the office. Sometimes Russell would work at his desk while members of his staff or the committee sat around the table. Though his manner was anything but magisterial, Russell's distance and slight elevation from the table—he was almost hidden behind the stacks of files on his desk—gave his remarks an irrevocable force. On this day he directed me to a seat at the conference table not far from the remains of his and Dulles's lunch. Russell remained standing with his hands in his pants pockets. I could see his fists were clenched.

"That man seems to think I'm somebody's fool. 'Now Dick, the world's too complex and ugly for you little boys. Just give us the money to take care of things and don't ask questions.'"

"He actually said that?"

"'Course not. Not in so many words. He just sat there sucking on his lips and telling me how Ike gets all starry-eyed when he hears about the agency's stunts, their wires inside the Kremlin, their double agents, as if to say 'I've got Ike wrapped around my little finger so you should be glad I'm even polite to you.' The man honest-to-God winked at me. He better watch out. Ike's onto him, and not just because he runs the agency like a glorified prep school."

"So Eisenhower is going to rein Dulles in."

"That Dulles is slippery. He appears to give the Armed Services Committee lots of attention because he doesn't want some special intelligence committee to be established in the Senate. And I don't either. But all we get from Allen is lip service. I told Ike, if Allen comes over here and occasionally tosses a few crumbs our way, Allen will have to take the heat all by himself when the agency gets in trouble."

While Russell spoke I tried to think of impressive things to say to enlarge my stature in his regard. I began to wonder if I shouldn't interpret this conversation as a suggestion that I increase my grasp of intelligence issues.

Russell snorted. "And then, after Dulles gets through letting me know I'm about as important to him as a buzzing mosquito, he gets around to his war with J. Edgar Hoover. Suddenly, I'm his indispensable chairman, and supposed to back him up. Now we do both agree that Mr. Hoover is selfish, shortsighted, and about as mean as a wild hog. 'Course, I always remind Allen that as wild hogs go, Hoover is a brilliant administrator. He gets the point." Russell chuckled thoughtfully. "I told Dulles a little about my bright, new assistant."

"Who?"

"You. Winston Bates, the one-man memory bank."

I shrugged sheepishly.

"Don't you mind. A memory like yours is a real asset in our business." Russell looked at me appraisingly. "Now I hope you don't object but I volunteered your services."

"To Dulles?"

"Yup. He could use someone to go to a reception at the Russian embassy. There's a whole bunch of Russian writers who are on a tour of the U.S. You're going to meet them. I'll wangle an invitation for you. Hope you like vodka."

"Sure, but why me? Dulles must have . . . oh I get it—the Russian embassy is FBI territory."

"You got it. Hoover would raise high holy hell if a CIA person was in contact with the Russians here in the U.S. Hoover's sure to have his own person keeping an eye on them, but all he cares about is that Communists don't infect America. Dulles wants to know if there are any likely prospects who could be useful to him back in Russia. All you have to do is talk to as many of them as you can and then give someone from the agency your impressions."

I felt a kind of claustrophobia about the layers of deception involved in this assignment, but I couldn't see how I could get out of it. "I'll be glad to, though I can't imagine what he thinks he can learn from a bunch of writers."

"Not much, probably. Then again, son, if they were rocket scientists, you wouldn't be the one going to the party."

I cautiously felt my way into the Armed Services Committee. My position was on Russell's staff, not the committee's, and I had no specific assignment aside from my obligation to brief the members of the committee and its subcommittees. To write my memos I had to first interview the committee staff and then the relevant staff members of the senators on the committee. Though all of them knew me from Salton-stall's staff, I was now perceived as Russell's person, and my job was an implicit criticism of the way they had informed the senators and each other of what was going on. I was beginning to understand that I was the sort of person who would never be popular with his peers. Thanks to my extra source of income, my clothes were nicer than my colleagues', and my interests—opera, art—more frivolous. Thanks to my memory, what was work for them seemed effortless for me. And finally, I was extremely deft at impressing their bosses, the godlike senators. William Darden, the chief of staff for the committee, was especially suspicious of me. Most of the others tolerated me but none of them gave me any more information than I absolutely needed. They zealously guarded their little boroughs of responsibility, all of which fell within a larger territory that was circumscribed by the Pentagon on one side, the defense industry on another, and, on the third border, a horde of legislators with a ravenous interest in harvesting the defense budget for their districts.

My first rite of passage was my security clearance. I was given a form to submit that required only the most skeletal details of my past, and then I waited for my interview. I spent hours rehearsing my story in an attempt to make it seem dull and ordinary. Yet I was hardly tested at all. The man who interviewed me—a dyspeptic, retired Treasury agent—was barely interested in my life in Canada, and only slightly more in my time in Paris. Had I been hitched to a modern lie detector, the little inward start that accompanied my denial of ever having traveled outside of France would have sent the needle scratching furiously. When he asked to see my Canadian passport I told him I had torn it up when I got my American citizenship. But with my security clearance under my belt, I was ready to explore Fortress America.

The military-industrial complex could not have been more eager to embrace me. As awareness of my new job spread among the defense contractors and lobbyists, I was wined and lunched in a merry round of importunate conviviality. I was almost always taken to the Rib Room at the Mayflower Hotel where the food was dull and the drinks strong. If my host had been in the business for a while, the meal would begin with a fond recollection of the feverish atmosphere during World War II, when all the defense contractors used the Mayflower as their base of operations. There was plenty of money to be made then but they also believed they were part of a noble cause. The Cold War for them was more like a fortuitous circumstance. By the time the war stories were over, J. Edgar Hoover would make his entrance and I would be informed, as if I were a wide-eyed tourist, that Hoover lunched at the Mayflower every day.

It didn't matter to these benevolent hosts that I had no power and no experience; a lunch was an investment in my future. I looked on my time with them as an investment too. I had only to demonstrate the slightest intimacy with some aspect of a contractor's business in order to receive several confidences that I could use with another contractor to prompt still more confidences to use with other contractors. I selected the invitation of the man from General Electric for my first industry lunch. He was an incredibly handsome man and well aware of it, with a square jaw, square shoulders, and bloodshot blue eyes that crinkled reassuringly at the corners. He explained to me how he wasn't simply a lobbyist but an upper tier GE corporate executive whose presence in Washington demonstrated the importance and sophistication of GE's defense effort. Over his third martini, which he consumed between the soup and the entrée, he enlisted me in GE's war with Pratt & Whitney, a war they would be losing but for Saltonstall's intercession on behalf of their manifestly better engines for the F-104 fighter. He implied there was some dark alliance between Pratt and Lockheed, who was building the F-104. We also had interesting discussions about GE's nuclear submarine reactors, which would help get me started in my lunch with Electric Boat, and about radar systems, which would help me with Bendix.

The man from Bendix was a sturdy bundle of energy who twisted and twitched as he spoke. He had a solemn, squirrelly face and a small beard—unusual for Washington in those days—that he tugged vigorously as he considered the limitless possibilities of defense. He explained that he wasn't really a lobbyist: Bendix took its defense responsibilities so seriously they had placed him, a genuine scientist, in charge of their Washington office. He enjoyed coercing my awed assent to his visionary leaps: "You must see, Winston, the extraordinary implications of the DEW Line.* We are translating warfare into information. Global information."

The man from Electric Boat wasn't a lobbyist either; he was a retired admiral, who attempted to enlist me in his war with Admiral Rickover, the father of the nuclear submarine.

It took about two months for me to eat and drink my way through most of the major defense suppliers. I was aware the whole time that this anecdotal education in defense defined the subject from an extremely one-sided point of view. But as my experience grew, I could listen to the man from Lockheed rattle on about the F-104 while I imagined the Air Force commanders who were already making noises about the need for a new, improved generation of fighters, and I would picture the gleam in the eyes of Lockheed's competitors, a gleam they would fix on the legislators in whose districts these new fighters might be built.

During my first round of lunches I was constantly aware of being on display. My eyes would sweep the restaurant while I wondered if anyone there was watching me with special interest. The man from Bendix had mentioned the DEW Line, and he went on to joke that despite all the technology, there was one weak link in the Distant Early Warning shield: the corps of Eskimos and drunken fur trappers who had been enlisted to search the northern skies for a Russian nuclear attack. This was the sort of secret that made me quiver with deceitful pleasure, especially with J. Edgar Hoover seated across the room. I sat up alertly, preening for my anonymous watcher who would want to hear about this glaring vulnerability. The idea that trappers and Eskimos could be enlisted to prevent a Russian air strike made me wonder about my watcher. Was an amateur like me watching me?

---

* The Distant Early Warning (DEW) system was a joint U.S.-Canadian project to build a network of radar stations along the northern perimeter of North America and Greenland to warn of a Soviet attack.

*

I tried to imagine the reaction of my watcher if he observed me as I entered the Soviet embassy to meet the delegation of the Union of Soviet Writers—shock, consternation, or perhaps he would be impressed by my ability to get places. One of the doormen walked me into the reception area and handed my invitation to a man at a table who found my name on a list. He raised his head, took a quick mental snapshot of me, and passed me on to another escort, with the pronouncement: "Librarian Bates."

My invitation had been routed through the Library of Congress since my position on the Armed Services Committee would be considered provocative. My escort, a tall, lean man, shook my hand firmly and said, "Striganov. I am political advisor for the Russian embassy. Vodka is to your liking?"

I discovered I did like vodka. It was served very cold, in tiny glasses. We stood together and surveyed the party, which was filled mostly with other men who were standing awkwardly together and surveying the party. The room was overheated. A choking haze of cigarette smoke hung in the air. Two huge portraits of Stalin and Lenin glared down on us with solemn indignation. Striganov's intense eyes darted here and there with lupine vigilance. His high-strung impatience seemed barely under control. His cigarette rose to his mouth and retreated with sinuous rapidity.

"What does a political advisor advise about?" I asked.

Grateful for an excuse to converse, he spoke quickly: "I am here to assist in understanding America. To help Russian leaders understand America. Here is example: Your president Eisenhower declares intention to cut four hundred thousand soldiers from army. I help to decide, is he making peace-loving statement or saving money to spend on bombs? Do we like or do we worry?"

I was taken aback by a question that implied my real job. Russell had recently told me how little he liked Ike's idea of cutting the military. Had I been identified already? I shrugged my shoulders. Striganov grimaced, disappointed with my reluctance to join the issue.

"And what does librarian do?" he asked dutifully.

I described my old job at the Library, doing my best to make it sound as boring as possible. I wanted to get rid of this man and meet some writers. Striganov felt the same way; he nodded distractedly while he looked for help. "Comrade Polevoy!" he called. A stocky, flushed man with an amiable smile approached us, his hand extended. "Librarian Bates is from the Library of Congress. Comrade Polevoy is secretary of Union of Soviet Writers." Striganov slipped away, disappearing into the party like a hot knife through butter.

Polevoy had an explosive laugh that he uncorked at the slightest provocation. Soon a little band of Russian writers had gathered about us and we were all laughing determinedly. Between shots of vodka, we snared smoked fish and scooped caviar from trays that circled us on the shoulders of sour-faced waiters. What with the jokes and the toasts, it took some effort to remember all the writers' names. They lived in either Moscow or Leningrad. The ones from Moscow teased the ones from Leningrad and vice versa. They teased me about American television while they puffed on their Marlboros. Polevoy, a big smile on his face, nudged me. "You can explain perhaps one television show? *I Love Lucy*?" They must have watched it all together for as soon as Polevoy mentioned the name all the writers began to laugh, even the ones who didn't speak English.

"I'll be glad to try but I don't watch much television." I had purchased a television during the Army-McCarthy hearings, mainly because no one in Washington talked about anything else, but aside from watching old movies late in the evening, I hardly used it.

"Lucy seems to me bourgeois Little Tramp," Polevoy declared.

I didn't understand until he performed a jerky imitation of Charlie Chaplin.

"She don't ever get what she wants, like the Little Tramp," Polevoy explained, "but she has big apartment, rich husband. No pathos."

A writer urged Polevoy to do his Chaplin imitation again. He went tottering about the room, screwing his hand around as if he were twirling his cane. The second time was more hilarious than the first time. Gradually the writers wound each other up in a cacophony of challenges and ripostes and volleys of laughter, like the frantic silliness of children when the end of playtime draws near.

Several days after the party, a young man from the CIA came to my office to debrief me. His name was Roger Bennett and he had recently graduated from Yale. He was fair, fat, and fumbling, with a puppylike eagerness to please. I was sure I was one of his very first official encounters as a CIA employee. He showed off his training in clandestine techniques with giddy delight. "Of course, though I am not going to be *in the field,* as we say, I still must understand *humint*—that's what we call human intelligence gathering." As he ran through the vocabulary of tradecraft, I realized just how inadequately equipped I was to be a spy in Washington. As far as I knew, I had no *principal* or *handler* who was the person who controlled my watcher, and my watcher was really called a *contact,* though he appeared not be interested in contacting me. More importantly, I had no idea if I even had a *control,* the puppet master who controlled my handler's strings. I had been given no *recognition signals* or *dead drops.* I didn't even have an *emergency exfiltration signal.* "That's when you think your cover has been blown and you need to get word to control to get you out. Or vice versa, if your control needs to warn you to get out. Of course, control will have had a *safe house* set up in advance where you can hide until the exfiltration route is operative." Roger giggled at the silliness of it.

When we finally got around to my episode of clandestine fieldwork at the Russian embassy, I described all the writers as either devoted Communists or too comfortably lodged in their state-supported dachas to be vulnerable. Roger accepted my apologies for not obtaining more useful information.

"It's okay. Really. I mean no one is going to walk up to you at a party and whisper that they're ready to turn over the Russian order of battle for Western Europe."

"I did speak to a man called Striganov. He wasn't one of the writers but he did seem quite full of himself. He said he was a political advisor. Have you ever approached him?"

"Striganov?" Roger was amused. "Even I know who he is. He's a big deal. He's probably the top KGB guy at the embassy now. Not a likely candidate."

In my desire to appear constructive I recalled another man at the party who joined no group or conversation for very long but circulated among the writers, an unctuous, unconvincing smile on his face. I had first seen him in conversation with Striganov. As he sidled up to my group of jolly Russians, they edged cliquishly closer to each other and smirked. He hovered for a few moments before departing with a shrug. I guessed he was some sort of bureaucrat who was watching over the writers. I made an effort later to engage him in conversation. He was surprisingly friendly. All he wanted to talk about were America's burgeoning suburbs. He couldn't believe that Americans could afford to buy all those big new houses. To please Roger, I described this man as the one writer who seemed to me restless and dissatisfied, someone who didn't appear to share the other writers' values.

"You didn't get his name?" Roger was scribbling rapidly.

"Not his name, but he should be easy to pick out. Like many of them, he had dirty blond hair, which was rather long and unkempt. But there was an oriental cast to his features and his skin was darker than you would expect. Also, he was the only person there who wasn't smoking."

Roger was quite glad to have something to discuss with his boss. We agreed to keep in touch. After Roger left I realized that I was beginning to enjoy myself. When he had mentioned another tradecraft term, *sleeper*, my shock of self-recognition was a little titillating. So *that* was what I was! No wonder my contact wasn't making contact; as a sleeper I would not be awakened until I could be useful. So what if I didn't have an emergency exfiltration signal. So what if I had no safe house, no dead drops. Perhaps that was the counterintuitive point to my invention as a spy: I was not a trained professional; I would not be caught because I was not one of them. My recruiter had promised that I would not be expected to provide secrets about weapons systems or rockets. I didn't exactly believe this, but I couldn't imagine that I would ever know such secrets. Now I knew these secrets yet I had been left alone. Was control saving me for something special? As a newly minted U.S.

citizen, I realized that what I was doing was treason, at least technically. But with my reassuring moral agility, I rationalized that I was only technically American. I had no bad intentions; nor did I have any good intentions. I was essentially stateless and, except for my belief in the existence of my control, I was faithless. My only true friends in Washington were my several selves whose public presentation I was beginning to find such a compelling activity. There I was at the Russian embassy, an aide to Senator Russell pretending to be a librarian while spying for the CIA—Winston Bates, the great dissembler, showing off for his control.

5

Paris, 1948

A few weeks after Viktor unveiled his plan for my *édition luxe*, I went to a dinner party at Viktor and Mara's apartment on rue de Bièvre. Their ancient building had settled unevenly over several centuries, leaving none of the floors level and none of the walls vertical. I had become accustomed to the formula for Viktor's parties. There were usually about sixteen people crowded into two small, low-ceilinged rooms. I would know about half of them, who were drawn from a pool of regular guests. The rest were first-timers, swept up by Viktor from his ceaseless migrations about Paris. Occasionally there would be a semi-luminary from the intellectual and artistic world of Saint-Germain-des-Prés—Jean Arp; Pierre Prévert, the film director and brother of Jacques; the painter Denise Colomb. Not one of them, as far as I knew, ever came to a second party. This was not so surprising since the dismaying collection of Viktor and Mara's regular guests included Bruno Cassini, a sad-faced man with spidery arms and legs who needed no persuasion aside from a lot of wine to declaim his incomprehensible poetry. There was also Maximov, a White Russian with an imperial manner, and a profession as a picture framer, who usually came to blows with Paul Renan, a proofreader for *l'Humanité* and a fervent Marxist. Other regulars included a painter of cloying Parisian street scenes, and a sclerotic archivist who worked at the Bibliothèque nationale. Viktor's special guest this evening was the manager of the Théâtre du Vieux-Colombier, where Viktor hoped to stage his Romanian playwright's work. The little playwright, thin to the point of emaciation, spent the entire evening skulking in a corner, a look of hollow-eyed awe fixed on the theater manager.

The one subject on which all of the regulars agreed was the genius of Viktor. At some point in every party they would exclaim over Viktor's wide knowledge of artistic life, his business acumen, his beautiful wife. At a previous party, Cassini had taken me aside to show me an edition of lithographs by Max Ernst. "You have no idea how much money Viktor made for Ernst with this portfolio. Yet Ernst was barely grateful." I looked at the lithographs longingly; Ernst's work would surely grace my poetry more aptly than Picabia's.

On this night in June, Viktor greeted me with eager expectation. I had told him a few weeks ago that I had written to my uncle Maurice, the well-known Montreal art collector and patron, about my book. Tonight, at my triumphant grin, Viktor clapped his hands together and exulted. "You have heard from Montreal? Wonderful!"

"Yes, my uncle Maurice is going to help us."

Viktor clapped his hands together. "We have to make plans quickly. Choose a printer. Buy paper. I will introduce you to Picabia. By the way . . ."

I took a deep breath. "Five thousand. For fifty books."

"Dollars? U.S. dollars?"

"Yes. I'm sure we can get a good rate. Is it enough?"

"Not as much as we hoped for but we will be fine. We will have to work a little harder to get advance orders but Picabia is a wonderful name. Very important figure again after the war."

"I can't get the money all at once. Maurice wants to send it in stages."

"Don't worry. I can't spend it all at once!"

Viktor laughed and laughed and so did I. We took our leave of each other with an embrace. Back in my room, I read Maurice's letter again.

June 1, 1948

My dear Winston:

Lois and I were so glad to hear from you. It sounds very much as if you are becoming a man of the world. Here in Canada everyone is working hard to put the terrible war behind us. France seems very far away. I worry for you sometimes when we read about the Communists taking power in Europe. The U.S. will never permit it. For better or worse, we all march to Washington's tune. Does everyone in Paris think there will be another war?

But life must go on. I am proud that you have insinuated yourself into French culture because it seems to me that I have had an influence on you in that regard. And I am impressed that you are going to collaborate with Picabia. I have seen pictures of his new work in a magazine. So I have enclosed a cheque for $100 for one of the books. And I am sure that when I see the finished work I will be inspired to buy another.

> *With great affection,*
> *Maurice Levy*

This was at least the tenth time I had read the letter, searching for an opening, an implied promise of more money to come or a hidden invitation for me to ask for more. Maurice was my mother's wealthy Montreal brother and my summer jobs in his dress factory had helped to finance my trip to Paris. When I was first trying to impress Viktor and Mara, I had portrayed Maurice as Canada's most adventurous collector of twentieth-century art, though he really was a collector only in the sense that he owned a book about Chagall. So it was natural, when addressing the sticky subject of financing the Bates-Picabia *édition luxe,* that Viktor proposed we ask Maurice to purchase seventy-five copies at $100 each, which Maurice in turn could sell to a Canadian gallery. I had inflated Maurice's offer of $100 to $5,000 because I feared any lower amount would discourage Viktor. Now I was at an impasse. I couldn't touch the remaining $2,768 in my bank account; that was supposed to support me in Paris for at least two more years.

And there was nothing to be gained by appealing to my parents, whose futile little importing business had been bailed out by Maurice on several occasions. My book now seemed as remote as the world of the Left Bank.

I thought about paying a visit to the Canadian embassy, where I had become something of a fixture. Perhaps I could find a patron there, even the ambassador himself. I had never mentioned this possibility to Viktor or Mara because I was a little embarrassed about having placed myself on the guest list for events at the Canadian embassy. I was not invited to formal state dinners of course, but the embassy had lots of modest receptions designed to celebrate and extend Canadian culture and business. A letter from Uncle Maurice to a functionary at the Department for External Affairs in Ottawa, plus my own persistence at the embassy, had put me on the list for cultural events. My motive in going to these receptions was hardly a need to keep in touch with Canadian arts; rather, a reception every other week or so amounted to a free meal every other week or so if I diligently stuffed myself with appetizers.

Because I didn't really care about the impression I made at the embassy, I was utterly unlike the awkward aspirant I was on the Left Bank. With almost spontaneous facility, I exercised the particular blend of formality, resolute enthusiasm, and effortless banter that marks the effective guest. There was not a large contingent of Canadians in Paris and pretty much the same expats always turned up. I kept my poetry ambitions to myself and let them regard me as an amiable young man who had chosen Paris as the place to enjoy a happy interlude between university and serious life. I had begun to wonder how this persona would be adjusted in the eyes of the embassy crowd when the Bates-Picabia limited edition was published. I pictured myself at an embassy reception in my honor, modestly receiving everyone's surprised congratulations.

I usually tried to wind up these receptions by consuming a third course of appetizers with Gardner Denby, a young American Foreign Service officer. Gardner was the only person from the embassy world to whom I had confessed my literary ambitions. He was a cultural attaché who had been assigned the Canadian embassy as part of his beat. He was thirty, just old enough to be somewhat of a mentor to me but young enough to make it enjoyable. I had never met anyone even close to my age who made a social relationship so easy. He was about my height, shortish, but trimly sturdy in contrast to my slightly rounded physique. He held himself with an athletic confidence and always greeted me with an eager, wide-eyed gaze that implied everything I said was of great interest. Perhaps my artistic self-absorption was a relief from his job. He professed to be charmed by my complete lack of interest in political and diplomatic issues. I skimmed *The Herald Tribune* just enough to keep up with the concerns of my embassy acquaintances, but in truth events such as the Berlin Blockade only concerned me because World War III might break out before my poems were published. He was from Cincinnati, and his positive, generous nature, which seemed to me to reflect well-to-do provincial America, had been refined with a European fluency acquired during his two years of service in Paris. For all his easy charm, Gardner had also made his ambition clear to me; his star was rising in the diplomatic corps.

One interest Gardner and I shared was a love for American films of a certain jejune trashiness. Paris was full of such films from the last ten years, and part of the amusement Gardner and I took in *Black Angel, Humoresque,* or *Kings Row* was the intense, almost spiritual devotion with which French audiences worshipped the flickering absurdities before them. At certain moments of transcendent twaddle— Bogart lighting a cigarette, Bette Davis throwing her head back—a murmur of assent would run through the audience at the Cinema Favart as if they were in the presence of some deeply urgent working of the cinematic art.

In early August, still in search of a patron for my *édition luxe,* I attended a reception on a hot, squally day. I scanned the gathering for my only official Canadian contact at the embassy, a cultural officer named Albert Dubois. The vacation exodus had reduced the usual crowd and I found Gardner looking disconsolate. He ignored my greeting. I tried to make small talk.

"Sorry, Winston, I've lost the point. Where were we?" He looked at me apologetically and then smiled helplessly. I had never seen Gardner in any mood but genial good spirits and I wondered if our relationship was close enough for him to confess his problems to me.

"Is everything all right?" Given my limited interpersonal skills, I asked the question with some trepidation. What would I do if he said no?

I was saved by the appearance of a tall, broad-shouldered man who planted himself between Gardner and me. He had a full head of vivid red hair above a big, raw face. His features were grossly masculine except for his small dark eyes, which glared resentfully. I thought the man was angry about something until I saw he had extended his hand to Gardner.

"Gordon, my lad. We meet again."

"Gardner, but don't apologize—except for the 'my lad' part."

The man laughed heartily and insincerely. He looked at me curiously. His heavily lined face looked bleary in contrast to the muscular energy that seemed to radiate from his body. I remembered noticing him once before, a few months ago, at another reception.

"Winston Bates," said Gardner, "I'd like you to meet Jack McGowan."

My hand vanished in McGowan's grip. I felt tiny and weak next to him.

"Jack is my new opposite number here at the Canadian embassy," Gardner said drily.

"So you flog Canadian culture?" I said. My interest was rising. It would be good to get to know him. "Did you organize today's reception? Are you especially interested in the performing arts?" Today we happened to be snacking and drinking in honor of two French Canadian women who were members of Roland Petit's Les Ballets de Paris.

McGowan winced. "Ballet's not exactly my cup of tea. Dubois arranged this before he was transferred back to Ottawa."

My heart sank: Dubois, my only embassy contact, was gone.

"What is your cup of tea, Jack?" Gardner said sarcastically. "Art? Literature? The exquisite intensity of chamber music?"

"I like jazz," McGowan said tentatively.

"Well *tout* Paris is eager to learn more about Canadian jazz."

I tried to deflect Gardner from his harsh chafing. "I was quite friendly with Dubois."

McGowan furrowed his brow. "Bates? The name is kind of familiar . . ."

"Perhaps when you went over the invitation list for today's event, it leaped out at you."

"Never looked at it. Some twit does that stuff for me."

I was quite desperate to make an impression, yet McGowan seemed inaccessible. I tried again. "I actually saw you once before here, at the LeBlanc reception before the Milhaud premiere."

He nodded.

"If you've forgotten the reception perhaps I can refresh your memory . . ." And in my eagerness to impress McGowan, I performed one of my memory stunts: I began to name all the guests who had attended the party. Along with some names I provided a thumbnail description: "Robert Bogeart, dark eyes, big ears, works for Bank of Montreal. Georgina Smight, blond, about twenty-six, studying with Nadia Boulanger . . ."

It wasn't such a difficult feat. I already knew about forty of the regular crowd; and at the reception I had energetically introduced myself to a great number of new faces and I had overheard quite a few other introductions. McGowan stared at me, a tentative smile on his face. Gardner appeared to be more puzzled than amused; until now I had managed to hide my unique memory.

McGowan finally cut me off. "How do you do that? Is it a trick or something?"

"I've always been able to remember anything I read. But once you have the ability, you develop techniques for other situations."

"I see. Where did you say you're from?"

"Winnipeg."

"So you're Canadian," McGowan said, beaming. "I'm glad you're on our side. I was afraid you might be of Gardner's persuasion—part of the U.S. threat to world peace and stability."

McGowan looked at us expectantly until we realized this was supposed to be a joke. I prudently laughed while Gardner sighed. General

Vanier, the Canadian ambassador, presented himself. He shook hands with Gardner and McGowan and was introduced to me. After a few perfunctory remarks, Vanier took McGowan off to meet someone.

"Quite a performance, Winston," Gardner said.

"Do you think I went too far? Sometimes I can't resist. I must say, that McGowan person seems to be an unlikely choice for a cultural attaché."

"Oh for God's sake!" Gardner snapped. "You've got the strangest combination of sophistication and dimness of any person I've ever met. Don't you get it? The man doesn't give a damn about culture. He's an intelligence officer. A spook."

"Do you know that for a fact?"

"If I can't spot them by now I should go into another line of work. We've got plenty at our embassy too. Half the trade advisors are really intelligence officers of one kind or another. Spying is a growth industry these days." He laughed bitterly.

I recalled a conversation we had over a month ago. "Are you so out of sorts because that job didn't come through?"

Gardner regarded me with a mixture of disbelief and exasperation. "You still don't get it, do you? Haven't you read a newspaper lately? Let's go someplace where we can talk."

A sudden spasm of rain flung itself from the swirling clouds as we left the embassy. We ran into the first café we came to, a nondescript neighborhood place populated by a few dour drinkers. We sat by a window and Gardner stared at the street for several moments, deliberating on what he would say to me. Finally he spoke. "There's no good way to explain this but I need your help. I'm sure you remember everything I told you about the job."

"You didn't tell me much. Just that you didn't expect the offer. It surprised you. But you said you really weren't sure if you wanted to leave the Foreign Service to work for the Carnegie Endowment and for that man, the one you worked with at the UN charter conference in San Francisco."

"That man?" Gardner beckoned, encouraging me to remember more.

"Are we playing a game? Let's see . . . he had a funny name, a ticket name. Snake? No. Hiss. Is that right?"

"That's right, Alger Hiss. And you still don't get it? I suppose if you're Canadian there's really no reason to pay attention to the news from America. Hiss has just been accused of being a Communist, a traitor, a *spy*!"*

"Is he?"

"How would I know? I don't even know him very well. I was just about the most junior person at San Francisco, a glorified secretary. He was head of the State Department delegation. We became friendly but he left the State Department to take over the Carnegie Endowment. We've exchanged a couple of pleasant notes since then. He wrote to congratulate me when I came to Paris. But that's all until he offered me the job."

"So why are you worried?"

"Oh dear, Winston. You really are all wound up in your own little world of books and art and music. The thing is, I told you about the offer because you're outside my diplomatic orbit. You're just about my only friend in Paris who isn't connected to the embassy in some way. I probably wouldn't have taken the job anyway, but I didn't want the State Department to know about the offer until I decided."

"And now you're afraid that this contact with Hiss will somehow harm you?"

"Of course. For all I know this will blow over soon. Hiss has denied everything. But unless he is completely vindicated, some odor will linger anyway. And if anyone finds out he tried to recruit me, the odor will stick to me. You don't know what it's like in the U.S. now."

"Well don't worry. You could be the spy of the century and it wouldn't bother me."

It was the wrong thing to say. Gardner looked at me plaintively and

---

* I should explain for those who have forgotten or were born too late to care: Alger Hiss was a State Department official until 1946, a member of the delegations at Yalta and at the UN charter conference in San Francisco. In 1948 he was accused first of being a Communist and subsequently of being a spy by Whittaker Chambers, an ex-Communist.

made a sort of whimpering exhalation. "It's nice that it wouldn't bother you but all I want is for you not to mention Hiss's job offer to anyone again, *ever*. Is that something you could do for me?"

"Don't worry. I won't say a word."

"Well . . ." Gardner breathed deeply several times in an effort to relax.

"Seriously. I won't say anything. I'm sure it will be all right."

Gardner studiously shredded his napkin. I ran my finger around the rim of my Pernod glass. The rain started up again.

"I should be going," Gardner said. He stood up. "I appreciate your discretion, Winston. I really do."

I watched him leave. He walked quickly, occasionally swerving abruptly to avoid puddles. It began to pour and Gardner began to run, sprinting and leaping until he was out of sight. I ordered another Pernod. I felt extremely satisfied. From fallacious gossip to clandestine truths, the discovery of secrets gave me a thrilling, selfish sense of gratification. Even where there was no special reason for secretiveness, I derived a peculiar pleasure from not telling Viktor and Mara about my friendship with Gardner or about my embassy parties, or not telling the embassy crowd about my identity as a poet. I did once make the mistake of bringing Gardner to one of Viktor and Mara's soirees in an effort to impress him and was mortified to discover that he had met them on his own. He confided to me that they had a reputation for crashing parties at the U.S. embassy and said he had been warned off them because of some murky Eastern European political connections. I was careful to describe my relationship to Viktor and Mara as a slightly distasteful social obligation I had inherited from my Canadian uncle. The very effort of keeping anyone who knew me separated from anyone else who knew me was a compulsively absorbing activity. I was a person who found it easy to absorb information, but creating, discovering, and keeping secrets was tantamount to being inducted into the mysteries of adult life.

And there was yet another secret to my life in Paris. All during that rainy afternoon in August, and during many previous afternoons and mornings as I went about my activities in Paris, there was something else on my mind, a destination so utterly personal and compelling that, as I talked to Viktor or strolled with Mara or rewrote one of my undergraduate poems for the seventeenth time, or even while I listened today to Gardner Denby's confession, its anticipation would seize me so insistently that I would catch my breath.

The rain was stopping. Though I had plenty of time, my secret made me impatient. I took the Metro and sat mesmerized among the gently swaying passengers until I exited at Châtelet. I didn't have far to walk now, and I was pleased to see that with the rain gone, the neighborhood was coming to life. The first time I wandered into the area was two months after I arrived in Paris, when I visited Les Halles in the darkness of early dawn to see the day's supply of food get crammed into the maw of Paris. It was hard to believe the reports of food shortages when the gross abundance of raw meat and vegetables packed on carts and trucks, stacked in the stalls, or scattered negligently in the gutters was enough to make me gag. I wandered aimlessly through the narrow streets until, some distance from Les Halles, I heard shouting. I glanced across the street where two women were yelling angrily and pulling at an elderly man who simply stood by, sheepishly passive. It took several minutes before it dawned on me that the two women were prostitutes arguing over a customer. Before my freshly opened eyes, the street scene reclarified itself into a full-fledged red-light district. I now noticed women in every doorway, women of every age, size, and in every variety of dress. Several of them called to me, pleading and then clutching their hearts in mock desolation as I hurried by. I didn't return for at least two weeks.

Today, I wandered up the street, inspecting the women from a careful distance, never pausing long enough to be accosted, and slowly approached the intersection with the vacant *blanchisserie* on one corner, the fly-specked Tunisian couscous restaurant on another, and, on the corner diagonally across from me, Paulette in her convent school uniform with her girlish braids and her small face as white and round as a plate.

She arched her eyebrows and smiled at me fondly but professionally. "Monsieur?"

A fellow professional by now, I nodded and followed her. Need I say Paulette was not a schoolgirl? She was in her midtwenties at least. But the uniform and her slim figure made her seem less experienced, which had allayed my anxiety enough to approach her the first time. And though there was no hesitance in any of her actions, she had a kind of naïve solemnity, an almost studious concern for my fragile innocence. We had come a long way since then. I followed her up the stairs and into her spare, functional room. She undressed me as I stood before her, her hands stroking my neck and cheeks, my chest, as she unbuttoned my shirt, still stroking as she unbuckled my belt, pulling down my pants and shorts, stooping to remove my shoes as I stepped out of my pants. She didn't bother with murmurs of endearment, though I suppose if I had needed them she would have. I had grown used to listening to the cries and shouts that floated in through her window on an interior courtyard. When I was naked, I lay down on her bed and watched her undress. Then she knelt beside me and began to lightly stroke my entire body, periodically bending to take my penis in her mouth, then rising to stroke me some more. Sometimes she would sprinkle a lilac-scented talc on my body so that her hands traveled over me with exquisite smoothness. She kneaded the arches of my feet and slipped her fingers between my toes. She caressed my nipples. Gradually she focused her hands and then her mouth on my penis. Usually I came in her mouth, though today she mounted me, buried her face in my neck and slowly squirmed until I came.

It had taken two months, perhaps seven visits, for us to bring our encounters to their full elaboration. I used to wonder how she worked it all out. Did she consult with other prostitutes? Or were my desires so patently obvious that even a child, or rather a woman pretending to be a child, could figure me out? Possibly the only specific request I ever made of her was that she tie her braids back so they wouldn't dance ticklishly on my groin. I asked hesitantly, fearing I would break the spell of her uncanny excavation of my desires. She nodded thoughtfully as she accepted my pathetic little demand.

On that warm October afternoon when Paulette first introduced the talc, I sighed with grateful resignation. It all seemed complete to me. I lay beneath her mouth and hands, feeling as if I were on an ocean, drifting through her ministrations. As I was about to come I heard the distant sound of music and the faint wail of a child.

6

Elizabeth Boudreau was practically the first person I told about my appointment to Senator Richard Russell's staff. Not that we were particularly close then. After my first dinner at her home, when I met Roy Cohn, I was invited three more times over the next eighteen months: first to a crowded cocktail party in celebration of the publication of Chester Bowles's *Ambassador's Report*; then to a late-night reception in honor of Igor Stravinsky after the premiere of his Septet at Dumbarton Oaks, which Elizabeth hosted as a favor to Mildred and Robert Bliss, who had owned Dumbarton; and finally to her biennial, postelection, Thanksgiving Day buffet in 1954. None of these events were very exclusive and it was clear to me I had been selected to fill a slot. I dressed well, spoke well, and knew something about music. I was a dependable background detail, a daub of mise-en-scène. From the frequent descriptions of Elizabeth's parties in *The Post* and *The Star,* I knew the tempo of her entertaining had quickened. She probably had an extensive collection of slot fillers. Now when you called Elizabeth to RSVP, a secretary answered and pulled your name from a file.

Elizabeth's Thanksgiving brunch buffet was a week after Saltonstall offered me the job working for Russell on Armed Services. As I arrived I saw Elizabeth Boudreau speaking to Arthur Barker, the Defense Department official I had met on my first dinner at her house. A short, chesty man, he was by now so swollen with self-regard he resembled a huge pouter pigeon. I planted myself before them and was ignored as

Barker, in a display of ritual obsequy, overgraciously thanked Elizabeth for inviting him after his family had left him alone in Washington for the holiday. After five minutes or so had passed, attention turned to me. Elizabeth reintroduced us but Barker didn't remember me. "Where do you work again?" he asked impatiently, as if the only reason he could have forgotten me was due to my inconsequence.

"Most recently for Senator Saltonstall. But Senator Russell has just taken me on to his staff. I'm spending most of my time on Armed Services Committee business."

"Well! Wouldn't exactly think of you as the military type. But hell, if Dick Russell does that's good enough for me. I guess we're going to be seeing a bit of each other. Banging heads maybe. And I've got a hard one, so watch out! Just a little joke, Bates. We all get on fine with Dick Russell. He's a good friend of the department." Barker chucked me affectionately on the shoulder and I swore to myself that if he ever showed up as a witness before the committee I would have him eviscerated.

Elizabeth took the announcement of my new job in silence, without so much as a congratulatory smile. A glazed, distant look had come over her. She was in the grip of some complex assessment that, I abruptly realized, had to do with *me*. I saw my life, such as she knew it, flash before her scheming eyes: my devoted membership in the St. Thomas choir; a clever but nasty remark I made nearly a year ago about Chester Bowles's wife who was wearing a gaudy sari; my tastefully selected clothes; and my proximity in Georgetown, which had begun its irresistible spiral into impeccable smartness. She refocused her gaze on me. "Winston, do you play bridge?"

"Of course," I lied.

"Next Thursday? Here? At seven thirty? You'll be my partner."

By the time I presented myself at Elizabeth's house the following Thursday evening, I had memorized Charles Goren's *Winning Bridge Made Easy*. Our opponents were an owlish admiral, whose father had been an admiral too, and his wife. I held my own, though I was rattled by Elizabeth's occasional abandonment of the accepted bidding conventions for intuitive flights of inspiration. "Oh come on, Winston," she would urge with a sly smile while I paged frantically through Goren's book in my mind, looking for a rationale for her bid. During a break for drinks and snacks she took me aside. "I like to throw folks off the scent sometimes. Just loosen up and go with me."

A week later I accompanied Elizabeth to an evening with eight hands in Cleveland Park. By then I had fortified myself with two advanced bridge books and the growing conviction that this was a game made for a mind like mine. Even this second time out, I found the people we played with to be transparent. I remembered every aspect of the play while Elizabeth was too busy socializing to remember anything. Over the next several bridge events, I took control and Elizabeth acceded, grateful to be winning more often. Though she still launched outlandish bids every so often, smiling sweetly as our opponents groaned, I learned to tolerate her impulsive notions.

So I carried Elizabeth in bridge and she carried me to a level of social Washington I had barely glimpsed until then. All at once we were a couple on parade at cocktail parties, theater openings, charity dinner dances in overheated hotel ballrooms. And from then on, my life in Washington was set on the busily humdrum course it would follow for decades: from home to office; from office to home; from home to social event. Elizabeth and I were out four times a week and she entertained at home at least once a week. Given the alacrity with which she swept me up, Elizabeth must have been looking for a presentable man for some time. There were a number of events to which she wouldn't go unaccompanied, and there were a number of others to which she would never be invited alone. Of course men, men of power, were commonly invited alone in Washington.

I wondered if people assumed that Elizabeth and I were lovers or saw us for what we really were. She occasionally spoke fondly of her late husband's rough-and-ready style and I assumed she still wasn't prepared, a decade after his death, to let another man into her intimate life, especially someone like me, who was anything but rough and ready. Six months into the relationship, the evidence indicated she didn't find me sexually attractive. I can't say I found her girlish southern charm particularly attractive either, which was a relief because it seemed to me that a condition of my secret identity was the absence of intimacy. I didn't have a very precise idea of what, exactly, I was protecting, but I was always on my guard.

Aside from Washington parties, my only social life consisted of going to New York to attend the opera and visit my twin sister Alice, who had moved there two years ago. She had a job as a secretary for New York University's Sociology Department and she lived in a shabby, underfurnished floor-through on East Fifth Street off Second Avenue. She looked gaunt and distracted most of the time, and she regarded her several lovers as tiresome afflictions, useful mainly as fodder for her therapist. Our mother, Lillian, had written to me asking if there wasn't something I could do about Alice, but it seemed to me Alice took a certain mordant pleasure in her carelessly devolving life.

My visits after I moved to Washington were the first occasions Alice and I had spent any time together without one or another parent present. Though we were twins, we had emerged from our family life as strangers who had inadvertently shared a unique experience. Until we were eleven, Alice and I enjoyed a special twinnish relationship that was a nurturing refuge from our parents. With furious ambition, Lillian had force-marched Alice and me through academic accomplishment and cultural nourishment while our father, Simon, murmured encouragement from the sidelines. Beginning when we were seven, she dragged us to every touring company of musicians who came to Winnipeg. From Yehudi Menuhin to the Hart House String Quartet, Alice and I were there, scrubbed and rigidly attentive on either side of the supremely pleased Lillian. At intermission, I would be invited to show off for Lillian's friends from the Women's Musical Club by reciting the number and key of each of the Beethoven quartets in chronological order. As time went on, my fabulous memory became an irresistible source of public satisfaction to Lillian. Though Alice and I professed mutual disdain for Lillian's overweening pride in me, I secretly delighted in her approval. When we were eleven Lillian determined with her usual maladroit decisiveness that Alice should be held back a year in school so she wouldn't have to compete with me. Selfishly, I didn't mind. Alice had recently become quite a bit taller than me, for which I had been teased by my classmates. Lillian convinced herself it was all for Alice's benefit but as Alice saw it Lillian's only objective was to make me the center of attention. Once we were separated at school, Alice refused to go to another cultural event with Lillian and I became the entire focus of my mother's insatiable expectations.

On the day that Lillian announced our separation, Alice came into my room and hissed at me in a tone I had never heard from her before: "You think you're so smart. I'm taller than you and smarter than you. All you do is remember things."

I could see how Alice might believe this. I was an unworldly child, almost infantile in my infatuation with my memory, while Alice was the perceptive one who figured out what was going on in the real world and helped me to navigate it. But from the moment Lillian held Alice back in school, there were no more supportive insights from Alice. Instead, there was a tone of hostile triumph as she took every opportunity to remind me just how dense I really was. Most memorably, when we were sixteen, she pointed out that our parents' marriage had been tacitly over for at least a year. "You idiot, don't you see anything? Dad is almost never home and when he does show up he sleeps in the cellar. And he only shows up because Lillian makes him pretend for our sake, which really means for your sake." It was true; my mother had become such a hegemonic presence in my life that I had barely noticed my father's fading one.

Now I was trying to reconnect with Alice, who was still taller than me, still all elbows and knees. Our visions of our life together were like two flashlights, narrowly illuminating different features of the same large dark room. Alice, incited by her therapist, saw our family life as tragic, with our father, Simon, as the failed and banished hero, Lillian as the evil witch, and me as the lucky, favored son. What my flashlight garishly revealed in that dark room was an excruciatingly hapless family. My sense that secrecy and concealment lay at the heart of adult life came no doubt from Lillian and Simon's unfathomable relationship. It was a Depression marriage, joined in the belief that any two people are better off together than alone. To say they had nothing in common except their size—a tiny, short-tempered Jewish woman from Montreal and a slight, mild-mannered English immigrant—is to say everything about them. I could never get my mother to elaborate on any aspect of her life: what it was like to be orphaned at thirteen and raised in semi-poverty by her brother; why she became a bookkeeper; why she moved to Winnipeg; or why she married my father. In her view, there was nothing to be gained by reflecting on the setbacks and compromises in her life; she just pushed heedlessly forward. My father, clearly one of those compromises (or possibly a setback) was equally unforthcoming about his life in Canada, though to Alice and me he would ruminate sentimentally about the England he had left behind. Any emotional connection between Lillian and Simon—aside from irritated impatience on her part and stoic endurance on his—was invisible to me. As a child, I became a spy in my own home. I would rummage through my parents' papers and old photographs. If they were together in a room, I would pause before entering in the hope of overhearing some evidence of a relationship. Even when I overheard them having sex, their grunts and sighs sounded separate and solitary. My curiosity about them became a larger confusion as I grew older and discovered I had no idea of what people do to, for, and with each other when their needs and desires are openly shared.

If the enigma of my parents' bond trained me as a spy, the effort to conceal my amazing memory was my primary experience as an impostor. From grammar school on, my so-called photographic memory enabled me to be first in any class I took. As a young child, I never thought my talent was special; it was just a game I played with myself. To me, my brain was a labyrinthine honeycomb; the fun was to stash any fact, image, or incident in its own little chamber and then locate it again. At first my memory was an attention-getting talent, on the order of tap dancing and magic tricks. But as I grew older, the academic benefits of remembering almost everything became obvious and my envious classmates began to dismiss me as a freak. I tried to disguise my ability. When I was called on in class, I would deploy a repertory of puzzled looks and confused hesitations before supplying the correct answer. If I stuttered a little and wrinkled my brow as I declined in Latin, I always managed to get through it perfectly. During a test I would chew on my pencil and squirm in my seat in an agony of indecision, and I always took all the allotted time to complete it. I didn't have as much need to hide my gift at McGill, but even there my professors were sometimes overwhelmed by the sheer amount of information I could disgorge on tests. Occasionally, a professor suggested that less information and more original thinking would be helpful. That seemed like jealous carping to me, but it was the real reason I took up poetry in college: I wanted to refashion myself as an intuitive and talented artist, a creative person rather than an intellectual automaton.

The vexed and anxious young Winston, whom Alice recalled so clearly, was to me only notionally myself now. My connection to my childhood had been stretched almost to the breaking point by my life in Washington; only the early intimacy between Alice and me seemed like a true loss. I doubted we could ever recover our childhood paradise, but I couldn't let go of the connection. Though her therapeutic interest in the Bates family drama could get tedious, she was my only link to the world outside of Washington and I found her louche life a refreshing contrast to the conventionality of the capital.

One evening at Alice's, I had just finished dressing for the opera. She was sprawled comfortably among a collection of pillows on a cheap imitation oriental rug, a glass of wine in her hand. "I like watching you get ready to go out, the way you tug your cuffs, straighten your tie and check yourself in the mirror. You're like Father that way, about clothes and appearances."

"But he was such a dandy. Remember that ridiculous Borsalino hat he had?"

Alice sighed. "I thought he looked elegant."

"I'm not dandyish, am I?"

"Really you're not. You're a just a bit fastidious about the way you look." She smiled gently. We had adopted a tone of affectionate amusement for personal observations. "It's too bad you're going alone when you look so nice."

"Any time you want to come with me, let me know. I'll get another ticket."

"That wasn't exactly what I had in mind."

"Aha! Lillian's been at you about my lonely life. But why don't you come with me sometime?"

Abruptly she switched the family discourse. "You know he'd like to hear from you."

"Who?"

"Come on. Father, of course. He's coming for his annual visit in the fall. Will you come then too? You have no idea how much he wants to connect with you."

"I really don't."

"You're blind."

There was often a plan for me to come to New York when Simon visited Alice but some complication always came up. Lillian had forced me to invite her to Washington earlier in the spring and Alice had come down and stayed overnight. Crowding my mother and sister into my small apartment had been claustrophobic. Simon's predictable attempts to stay out of my way would be even more oppressive. I knew I would be unable to get to New York.

As far as Elizabeth Boudreau was concerned, the crowning event of our first social season together was Helen and Walter Lippmann's cocktail party in April 1955. It was the first time she had been to the columnist's home, a rambling Tudor near the National Cathedral. Lippmann was at the very top of the social food chain because he behaved as if he had transcended it. His newspaper column was a monument on which he inscribed his Olympian corrections of the national mood and his projection of himself as a senior consultant to the course of history. His dinner parties were reputed to be demanding affairs. Guests were expected not only to hold forth on the major issues of the day, but also to place them in the context of the great historical issues. If one were comfortable with French and Russian literature, so much the better. Elizabeth's knowledge of history began and ended with the Civil War; she was as grateful not to be invited for dinner as she was to be invited for cocktails.

Walter Lippmann's column, Today and Tomorrow, was essential reading in Washington. I knew I had arrived in Washington when I began to be invited to his home. *Photo by Alfred Eisenstaedt//Time Life Pictures/Getty Images*

As cocktail parties go, the Lippmanns' was fairly sedate. Elizabeth and I milled about industriously in the large sunken living room until we came upon Lippmann, stationed unavoidably before us. Elizabeth quickly reversed direction and abandoned me. He was standing with Senator Saltonstall, listening with his brow furrowed soberly. Occasionally he would shake his head with stately despondency. His strong dark features would have been called sensual were it not for a certain delicacy, a refined self-absorption in his manner. I hovered nearby until Saltonstall noticed me and drew me into the conversation with a fond pat on the back. I told Lippmann how much I had admired his new book, from which I quoted extensively after having paged through it the night before. He was grateful for the compliment; the reviews had not been particularly good.

"Winston's our new star on Armed Services," Saltonstall said. "Got his own little subcommittee last month. He's so smart we had to invent one just for him."

I had recently been given some responsibility for a new subcommittee on the CIA, consisting of Harry Byrd, Saltonstall, and Russell. It was a very Russell-like initiative: since the CIA regarded his committee as a tedious formality, Russell had created a special subcommittee. It didn't increase our control, but the illusion of activity warded off the Foreign Relations Committee's attempts to pry CIA oversight, such as it was, out of Russell's hands.

Lippmann frowned as Saltonstall innocently described his pleasure in an unfettered CIA. Lippmann had recently served on an oversight committee that examined an unfortunate episode of CIA malfeasance in Greece.

"Maybe your attitude is the best one, Senator," Lippmann said. "If you don't care what they do, you can't be disappointed. Their hands were dirty in the Polk affair. I knew it. But I did my duty. I insisted we had to look the other way. But that was a squalid little war. What I can't abide is their assumption that history is malleable, that it can be shaped without the hard patient work of policy and diplomacy." People joked about Lippmann's tendency to pronounce instead of converse, but there was an undertone of shrill exigency in his voice, and his gestures were oddly disconnected, almost eccentric. He fixed me with a direct stare. "Do you think Nasser wants to have anything to do with that pompous little shah the CIA installed in Iran? Foster Dulles's Baghdad Pact is farcical. Nasser will flirt with us, dance with the Russians, and taunt the British and the French—who are the only ones who might be said to have genuine interests in the region. Meanwhile Dulles, Allen that is, doesn't think Suez is worth much concern compared to the fun of playing cat and mouse with the Russians in Europe."

Saltonstall surreptitiously nudged me with his elbow; he found Lippmann's pontifical tone humorous. But I was transfixed. An idea, a premonition, had seized me and shaken me. I was lost for a moment, as if I had briefly fainted and then come to. Lippmann was looking at me expectantly. It was my turn to expound. I blurted out something about Suez being a long way from London before coming to my senses. I recalled a few paragraphs from an old piece in *Le Monde* about how Britain and France had gone from colonial competitors to comrades in the Middle East. I more or less plagiarized the piece, translating as I went along, though I accidentally lapsed into French as I quoted Mendès France. Lippmann nodded approvingly. When I had spoken for a sufficiently long time, I stopped, declared my pleasure in meeting Lippmann, and walked abruptly away.

I wanted to be alone. Lippmann's description of the Middle East had set me off, unlocking a kind of code or sequence in my mind. Suddenly the countries, the competing interests, had appeared before me just like a bridge game, a game in which I knew not only who held which cards, but also the intentions and capabilities of the players. It wasn't merely the day-to-day accounts of sporadic fighting between Egypt and Israel, or Britain's negotiations with Egypt over the Suez Canal, or France's difficulties in Algeria. There was also the discussion I had with Senator Russell when Churchill resigned and Anthony Eden became prime minister. "Maybe I'm just a dumb country boy," Russell said, "but that Eden's about the sorriest excuse for a leader I've ever seen. Who's he preening for? He never stops. The sun is setting on the British Empire and that man wouldn't know how to turn on a light." Russell was referring to Eden's languidly effete style, which had seemed rather overt on his last visit to Washington.

It may seem like convenient hindsight to say I foresaw the Suez Crisis at that early date based on those flimsy clues, but my flash of intuition was even more detailed: I projected that war in the Middle East was just the sort of crisis to lead to my awakening. Where else could control turn but to the brilliant Winston Bates, who had positioned himself at the intersection of the CIA and the Pentagon? Wasn't this the kind of information that a clandestine "consultant" could provide? It was merely a plausible scenario, but each of these possibilities—the Suez Crisis and my awakening—reinforced my certainty about the other to the point that they became for me an inescapable reality.

Mesmerized by my vision, I wandered out into the garden with its resplendent magnolia tree and rankly fragrant air, then back into the house, exchanging only bland pleasantries with anyone I encountered. A hand was on my arm, a voice whispered in my ear: "Shouldn't we be going, Winnie?" The limousine was waiting outside and Elizabeth sidled into it with a contented chortle.

I was still lost in the Middle East when Elizabeth spoke. "Winston, are you there? I'm trying to get your attention."

"Good party, Elizabeth?"

Her sharp face was alive with greedy satisfaction. "Very good. And you had a good party too. I ran into Lev Saltonstall. Such a nice, stupid man! He said you made a real impression on Lippmann."

The limousine turned a corner and I saw the National Cathedral looming above us. "We had quite a long talk. Lippmann was considerably odder than I had expected."

"Well he's been gaga for months. Helen says he's much better. You heard about the hospital? They actually put him away for a short time. Then he and Helen went out west to cure in the sun. They just got back. It's all because of some book he just published. It took a lot out of him, she said."

"So did the reviews. You know, we managed to talk about the Mideast for fifteen minutes without once mentioning Israel."

"What do you expect? He's about as Jewish as you are, Winston."

"Or as anti-Semitic as you. A tiny little bit in either case."

"The last thing he wants is to be known as some sort of spokesman for the Jews. You know he's the only Jewish member of the Metropolitan Club? So he's not going to be very Jewish. He's even thought about becoming Catholic. Helen told me she put a quick stop to that. She's a lapsed Catholic and the idea horrified her."

"You and Helen seem to have become fast friends." I was impressed at her ability to worm our way into the Lippmann orbit.

"That's how the invitation came about. But if we want to go to any of the really important Lippmann parties . . . that big New Year's Eve party? . . . or the spring and fall cocktail parties? . . . you'll have to go on making an impression on Walter. Because she's really working for Walter when she entertains. You have no idea how I had to hint just to get invited to this little thing. I finally had to appeal to her romantic side."

"It's nice to know she has one."

"Oh she does. She and Walter were married, but not to each other, when they met. They had an excruciatingly secret affair. It's hard to imagine him as a lover. He's *so* serious. But he is attractive isn't he? Those dark eyes . . ."

"How did you get to Mrs. Lippmann's romantic side?"

"I told her about us."

"Us?" My voice cracked. Where was this conversation going?

The limousine was slowing down. Usually her chauffeur let Elizabeth off at her home and then dropped me at my place. Elizabeth rapped on the window. "Bud, why don't you drive along Rock Creek for a while. It's a pleasant evening isn't it, Winston?"

"Us?"

"You can't pretend, Winnie, can you, that people don't wonder about us? I merely told Helen about the difficulties we've had to overcome. She was so sympathetic."

"I hadn't been aware of the difficulties. Not to mention the over-coming."

"You know what I mean . . . our differences? I'm a bit older than you. I'm established here in Washington and you're just beginning to make your mark. I'm rich and you're smart." Elizabeth was enjoying herself.

"So now, instead of suspecting we're having an affair, people will be sure of it."

"Oh relax, Winnie. Neither of us has anyone else in our lives. This works. We'll probably still be seeing each other long after every couple I know is divorced. And it's not necessarily so bad for you to have people think you're having an affair with me." She leaned forward and tapped on the window. "Time to go home."

I suppose it was good for people to think of callow me as a worldly man. As for her, I doubted she needed a lover. She embraced her social life with carnal avidity. When she gossiped about politicians, it was with a lascivious titter. At parties she floated from person to person, gathering them up and working on them until they burst into laughter. Then onto another group, slipping up to someone to whisper intimately, a knowing smile welling across her confidant's face. Sometimes we would meet midway through an occasion to compare notes. If things were going well, she would be breathless, her cheeks flushed, her eyes gleaming. Tonight in the car, she appeared relaxed and content in the sporadic sweep of headlights, suffused with a postcoital glow.

"Well?" Elizabeth said impatiently.

"Well what?" I said.

"How hard does a girl have to hint?"

I was speechless with shock. She *was* suggesting we have an affair, a *real* affair, not a simulated one. Why was she now attracted to me? I didn't know what to say, though I felt some gesture was called for. I leaned toward her.

"Not now," she said impatiently and pushed me away. "I just need to know . . . to know . . . ?" She looked at me sharply.

I finally caught on. "Of course I find you very attractive. And would love to—"

"Good," she said quickly.

I could see I wasn't supposed to name what we were going to do.

"Next Tuesday . . . we have that State Department reception? Perhaps you could get away from work and come by for me a bit earlier than usual?"

And that was how it began, and in a sense ended. For the next ten years or so, we only made love in the late afternoon at her house before social occasions. We never went to a hotel or to my apartment, nor did we ever travel together. And there wasn't that much sex: once every couple of weeks during the first year, then gradually falling off to ten or twelve times a year. Elizabeth's sense of southern propriety required us to hide any public sign of intimacy; it was okay if we were assumed to be having an affair, but not to be thought of as *lovers*. If there was a dinner party at her house, I never lingered, always leaving with the other guests. When headed to her house in the late afternoon for a sexual interlude, I had to be on the lookout for mutual acquaintances; sometimes I took an extra walk around the block before the coast was clear. Yet it was perfect in its way. Though the sex itself was not that remarkable, its infrequency helped to keep it fresh and prevented the affair from becoming burdensome. We were an ingenious social construct.

There were other pleasures in Washington now as well. My work for Russell had made me more professionally confident, and that confidence was reaffirmed by my new job with the CIA subcommittee. At the office or out with Elizabeth, the idea of knowing something about myself that no one else knew intoxicated me. My detachment became exquisitely vigilant, my conversation more arch, my gestures a touch dramatic. I could see that people responded to this quality in me—at least I had a presence if not an essential identity. If you were seated next to me at dinner you would find me attentive and clever, an inexhaustible fount of knowledge about Senate business, a source of gossip that always stopped short of indiscretion, and an appreciative recipient of the same from you—no matter if I had heard it many times before. My mantle of implied power, worn with such confident modesty, would put you at ease: your initial prick of disgruntlement at being seated next to a senator's *assistant*—important *you*!—was soon replaced by the satisfaction that you were next to the indispensable *aide* to the third or fourth most powerful man in Washington. Relieved, your gossip might just stray over the edge of discretion. I did wonder whether hidden within me there was a secret, embryonic identity that, when circumstances finally permitted, would hatch as a fully evolved and integrated Winston Bates. But I was too pleased with my socially constructed self to feel unfulfilled.

My social life began to produce professional benefits. Russell's staff and the committee staff couldn't help but notice that one or another of the senators would often greet me with a reference to some social encounter. Once, as I was preparing a memo on Eisenhower's intention to cut manpower in the military, I repeated a remark to a colleague that Lippmann had made to me at his party. My colleague was a plodder from the Midwest who managed the Subcommittee on Manpower and Personnel. He looked at me peevishly. "So Walter just took you aside and whispered into your ear his opinion about how serious Ike is about peace. I guess he thought telling the right person would be the way to influence the lives of countless future generations."

I took this resentment of my social access as an affirmation of my presence, an acknowledgment that I was a success. My ability to remember everything on Russell's agenda, including his calendar and extensive sections of his correspondence and legislation, had inexorably made him dependent on me. I was his shortcut; rather than wait for some question to be researched by the appropriate secretary or aide, he often turned to me and the answer was usually on the tip of my tongue. There was some calculation to all this; I tried to anticipate his needs by checking his calendar a week in advance. Russell's gratitude was genuine, though it was hardly shared by the rest of his staff.

*

My photographic memory had been of huge advantage to me in school and in my career. But I had always been nagged by the sense that I was nothing more than a warehouse of facts. Now I had had an insight, a shock of intuition about Suez, and it seemed to me so profound that I couldn't imagine that my patient control wouldn't find it as compelling as I did.

Gripped by the idea of contact, I tried to stay abreast of Suez developments. Though Armed Services did not formally have much to do with diplomacy except to anticipate its failure, I hoped my new CIA duties would help. To show Russell just how importantly he regarded my subcommittee, Dulles told Russell that his deputy, Richard Bissell, would liaise directly with me. Bissell, to show how importantly he regarded me, appointed his assistant to actually be the liaison. This assistant, an ex-GI named Jim Flannery, never spontaneously replied to a single question I put to him. He would come to the office, make a note of everything I asked or said, promise to check with Bissell and get back to me. At the next meeting he would produce his little pad and go over the minutes of the previous meeting, with comments by Bissell. "Laos . . . not too much to say about that. Saigon . . . Lansdale just giving advice . . . good relations with Diem. Lhasa . . . watch and wait. Personnel . . . current levels adequate . . . number classified. Egypt . . . Nasser not too stable. We're relying here on Israeli intelligence and State Department. As for Europe . . ." Here he would smile. Europe was going well. The CIA had great hopes for Eastern and Central Europe. There were rumblings of dissent in Poland; Hungary looked to be an opportunity as well. The CIA was ready to roll back the tides of Communism. On the one hand, I was frustrated by the focus on Europe and the lack of information about Suez. On the other hand, if Suez was being left to stew on its own, there was a greater likelihood of its boiling over.

Russell too was mainly interested in Europe. He wanted to know more about Soviet troop levels in Eastern Europe because he was opposed to Eisenhower's plan to cut manpower in the armed forces. Fewer troops, according to Russell, would make the United States too dependent on sophisticated technology and nuclear weapons. And dependent on the black arts of the CIA as well. He thought Eisenhower was doing it principally to convince the Soviets he was sincere about peace. Only a president who had won World War II could have gotten away with defense cuts in the middle of the Cold War. To put pressure on Eisenhower, Russell decided to hold hearings on manpower levels and the armed forces and I was put to work getting the committee up to speed on the hearings. The plan was to drag the Joint Chiefs before the full committee and exploit their disagreements. Since the Air Force was getting half the defense budget and the fewest cuts, Russell organized the Army and Navy to declare their opposition to the president's plan. It was the kind of thing I was good at handling since it cut across so many issues.

The hearings became a modest circus, with each of the Joint Chiefs arriving in full uniform, surrounded by a small flotilla of officers and

At a hearing of the Senate Preparedness Subcommittee of the Senate Armed Services Committee. Senator Lyndon Johnson (second from right), who chaired this subcommittee, was appointed by Senator Russell to give him some military credentials as Johnson prepared to run for president. My first mentor in Washington, Senator Leverett Saltonstall, is on the far left.
Library of Congress, Prints & Photographs Division, U.S. News & World Report Magazine Collection, LC-U9-1186-16

civilian aides from the Pentagon. I had written the committee's script in collaboration with Russell and I seated myself behind the senators, ready to reinforce them with suggestions for penetrating, newsworthy questions. Everything I had absorbed in my first year with Russell came into play. Without consulting any notes, I prompted the senators with the facts, figures, and thoughtful speculations that made them look like lords of defense. Russell, a man of few compliments, was extremely pleased with my performance.

On the last day of hearings, we faced off against the Air Force and its leader, General Twining. As the hearings drew to a close, a skinny young man in civilian dress standing behind Twining began to wave his arms wildly, pointing to himself and then to us. Senator Saltonstall leaned back and said over his shoulder to me, "Who is that guy?"

"I have no idea."

"He sure thinks he knows you."

"Me?" I looked more closely. It was my neighbor Larry Boyer. When he saw the recognition on my face he grinned and lifted his arms skyward, as if thanking God for the extraordinary circumstance of the two of us meeting each other here.

7

When the manpower hearings recessed late in the afternoon, I quickly slipped out of the hearing room. From the corner of my eye I saw Larry Boyer fighting his way through the scrum of reporters and senators. I made it to my office without being intercepted but an hour later the phone rang.

"I can't believe it, Winston. We're in the same business! Sorry I missed you at the end but my boss introduced me to Senator Russell. Well actually General Twining's not my boss, Trevor Gardner's my boss, but Twining's his boss. Well not exactly his boss, Wilson's his boss, but you know. Anyway Senator Russell told me all about you. This is great. Just great! Wait till I tell Deb. She'll die. Listen, it's real late today and I'll bet you're tired. But tomorrow is Friday. How about dinner at our place? Just the three of us. Real casual."

I didn't see any way out of it. For the first Friday in two months, I had no plans with Elizabeth. If I didn't accept this invitation, I would be making excuses for the next two months. I said I was looking forward to the evening.

"Deb's going to be real excited."

When I presented myself on Friday, Larry greeted me at the door. "Hey, didn't I say this was a casual dinner?" he said. I was wearing a tie and a blazer. He was dressed collegiately, in a white shirt, khaki pants, and white suede shoes. He took me up to something he called the "family room," which he proudly told me he had constructed himself. I had heard the hammering and banging every weekend lately. The walls were now covered with dark wood paneling, and jutting from the paneling at odd intervals were shelves on which were displayed various trophies, clocks, and plaques. One shelf displayed a collection of beer mugs embellished with fraternity emblems and university seals. Pinned to the wall above the mugs was a USC pennant. On another shelf were gathered most of the Walt Disney cartoon characters, exuberantly realized in colorful plastic. On the floor was a red and purple shag rug. A black Naugahyde easy chair and a black Naugahyde couch faced the television set, its small sea-green screen set in a hulking wood cabinet.

I complimented Larry on his decorations and renovations.

"I had to get it finished. Deb's father bought the house for us, you know. He's coming to Washington on a business trip next month and whenever he comes he always complains about how old the place is. He wanted us to find a house in the suburbs. Deb will be right up with the dip and the drinks. Amazing, huh? We've lived next door how long? Three years? Almost four. And now we finally find out we're in the same business."

"It's not really that amazing," I said. "I've only had this job for a few months."

Deborah arrived with the dip, a large bowl filled with thick creamy glop with little bits of something suspended in it.

"Onion dip," Larry murmured in satisfaction as he plunged a potato chip into the bowl. "Deb made it from scratch. What do you think?"

"It's delicious," I said, obediently swiping at it with a chip. Deborah winked at me and, without our having exchanged a word, we seemed to be complicitly connected on a plane just above Larry's head. She was long limbed, an inch taller than me, and she moved with a flowing, self-contained grace. Her features were at once perfect yet ordinary in their unexceptional evenness and the rather expressionless regard with which she greeted the world. Her most striking feature was her hair, a wide, wheat-colored carpet that hung down below her shoulders.

Next to the bowl of dip was a large glass pitcher filled with a purple liquid in which floated ice cubes and pieces of fruit. I eyed it sadly, canceling my silent prayer for a martini. Larry hoisted the pitcher like a trophy. "Hey, sangria! Deb makes great sangria."

"So Winston . . . ," Larry began, and then fell silent while he tried to think of something appropriate to say. Suddenly he brightened. "So what did you think of the Academy Award nominations?"

"Oh Larry, Winston doesn't want to talk about the movies."

I was disappointed. Movies had seemed like a productive area.

"I'm going to be fixing some food downstairs," Deborah said. "Why don't you talk shop and get that all out of the way before I come back."

"Careful on the stairs," Larry called out as she left. He turned to me. "She's . . . you know, pregnant."

He looked to me eagerly, for approval I suppose. "How nice. What do you do for Trevor Gardner?"

"Procurement mainly. You know, keep tabs on the suppliers. Approve specification changes."

"Do you have a background in this? An engineering degree?"

"Nope. Just experience. After I graduated college I went to work for Deb's father. He manufactures these neat little electronic gizmos that go into navigation systems in military jets. You've probably heard of the company, Autonomic Devices, Inc., ADI, they—" He broke off and looked at me in alarm.

"Don't worry. I've got full security clearance."

"Hey, you read my mind! These components—"

"But don't take my word for it."

"Good idea, Winston. Good idea. Anyway, working for your father-in-law isn't always such a good idea. Don't get me wrong—we got along great. But both of Deb's brothers were already in the business. And one of them was giving me a real hard time. Deb didn't think there was enough room for me so she got her father to get me a job in Washington. And here we are."

His life continued to spill out of his mouth without caution or restraint until Deborah returned with a tray of plates and silver.

"So when is the baby due?" I asked.

Deborah's mouth dropped open. "Oh, Larry! You didn't! I mean we only just found out." She turned to me. "Like yesterday we found out. I didn't want to say anything. I haven't even told my family yet."

Larry hung his head. "Sorry, Debs. I thought it was only our families we weren't going to tell right away."

"Never mind," she said. "Let's just drop the subject. Please."

We all dutifully sipped and dipped without speaking for several uncomfortable moments. Larry sprang up. "I just remembered: I've got something to show you. I'll be right back." He dashed out of the room.

I turned to Deborah. "Sorry."

"It's not your fault. And Larry really means well. It's just that he's so . . . so . . ."

"Guileless," I suggested.

"That's it, guileless. Guileless," she repeated happily, relieved to have a good excuse for Larry.

Larry returned with a handful of photographs. "My dad, my mom, and my sister all went to Disneyland last week. It just opened. These pictures just came today. Dad owns the six biggest drugstores in the Valley."

Deborah stood up. "We're going to eat here. Larry wants to watch TV. I'll be right back with the food."

When Deborah was out of sight, Larry gave me a sheepish grin. "Guess I should of kept my mouth shut. Deb's okay. She just gets a little excited sometimes. That's why I'm good for her, she says. I can get her to relax. Most of the time. Oh great!" he exclaimed as Deborah returned. "Hawaiian chicken."

Larry was amazed I didn't watch television. Seizing the opportunity for a conversion, he eagerly filled me in on the family history of Ozzie and Harriet Nelson. Later in the evening we came to a craven little piece of Cold War paranoia called *I Led Three Lives*. The hero was a member of the American Communist Party, an FBI counterspy, and an average citizen. It hit close enough to home to expel me from my Naugahyded comfort. As I made my good-byes, Larry whispered: "I'll call you on Monday. At your office. There's something I want to ask you. Business."

He called at ten on Monday morning. "Can we meet some time soon?" His voice was low and tense.

"Do you want to come over here? I'll give you lunch."

"Your office isn't a good idea. Somewhere else maybe, like a park or something."

For just the briefest instant my skin crawled. *No, this can't be contact. Not Larry Boyer.* "Why don't you just drop by this evening at my apartment?"

"Your place . . . I never thought about that but why not? I mean we're neighbors. There's no reason we shouldn't visit each other."

"I'm going out at about seven thirty, but if you can come earlier . . ."

Larry rang my bell at a quarter of seven. I stood on my landing, listening to him thunder up the stairs two at a time. When he entered the apartment he turned slowly around. "Neat place! Look at all those mirrors and stuff on the walls. How many rooms do you have?"

"This is it, except for the kitchen and bath. Behind that screen is an alcove where I sleep."

Though the praise came from Larry Boyer, family-room designer, I was pleased. I had tried to make the place look like a well-to-do Bohemian studio in Paris, with oriental screens and draped textiles.

"It's a pleasant evening. Let's sit out on my porch while we talk," I suggested. I led him through the kitchen and out on the porch.

"Everything looks different from up here. Look, there's my barbecue!"

I offered him a seat. He sat on its edge, nervous and uncomfortable. Suddenly he affected a look of relaxed composure, settling back in his seat and allowing his arms to flop down casually. "So Winston, we're colleagues."

"I suppose that means you checked out my security clearance."

He flushed. "I had to be sure I could speak to you in confidence."

"Did you actually read my file?"

He shook his head and sighed resignedly. This wasn't going the way he planned. "No. I don't have enough authority to read other people's files; just enough to find out if you're cleared. I have something to tell you. But you've got to believe that I'm doing this all on my own. Nobody asked me to make contact with you. Nobody even knows that I'm speaking privately to you. This is all my idea, if you know what I mean."

"You mean you'd like me to keep our conversation a secret."

He nodded unhappily.

"There's no problem. I know you'd never put me in a position in which I was compromised. And I'd never put you in such a position."

"Thanks, Winston. You can count on me. Here's the story. Do you know anything about a spy plane project? A plane that will fly over Russia so high that it can't be shot down, with a camera that can photograph military installations on the ground." He gulped and his eyes widened; he couldn't believe he had finally blurted it out; if he could stuff the cat back in the bag he would.

"I don't know a thing about it."

"I see." He leaned forward. "I'm going to go one step further. But if it makes you uncomfortable just stop me. Senator Russell—his committee that is—keeps track of both the CIA and the Pentagon, right?"

"Right."

"So don't you think it's strange that you don't know anything about a collaboration between the Air Force and the CIA to build a plane to spy on the Russians that's going to cost more than twenty million dollars?" His secret finally out, Larry smiled in triumph. His eyes fixed on me as he awaited my astonished reaction.

"Why are you telling me this?" I demanded sharply.

He started as if he had been caught stealing. "Oh God, why did I do this? I knew it was a mistake. I never should have opened my mouth."

"I just want to know where this conversation is going."

"It doesn't have to go anywhere. Really. We could stop right now." He cast his eyes wistfully in the direction of his barbecue. "Let's stop. Just forget I ever said anything."

Now I was sure Larry hadn't been put up to leak this to me. "Tell me what this project is called."

"It's called Aquatone. And they've almost got a prototype built."

"Who are they?"

"I told you. The CIA and the Air Force. And we've got these

concerns . . . you know, joint operations and all . . ." His small face twisted with the distress of getting himself in deeper and deeper.

"*Concerns!* You're trying to tell me the Air Force is concerned that the CIA is going to control the operation."

He looked at me in amazement; I had read his mind.

Senator Russell was quite pleased to find out something about the CIA that we weren't supposed to know. It gave him considerable satisfaction to mention the spy plane to Dulles at their next lunch. "I thought he was going to swallow his pipe," Russell reported. " 'Course, the first thing he wanted to know was how I knew. I think I protected your source pretty well. I let Dulles believe that Ike told me. He said Ike only knows a few details. In fact Ike threatened to kill the project if there were any leaks. Dulles even took himself out of the loop, though the money is being channeled through the director's reserve fund. It's Richard Bissell's show and he's set up the operation outside agency headquarters in a secure building. I told Allen I understood the need for secrecy, but an operation involving both the Air Force and the CIA is about the best example of why his oversight committee is Armed Services and not Foreign Relations. But if he doesn't cooperate with us he'll have to play with them. And there are some real tough nuts over there—like Fulbright. Bill may be lazy but he stinks of ambition. Your Pentagon source is going to have to accept that the CIA is in control. When these planes start flying over Russia, they're going to be called U-2 weather planes, 'U' stands for 'utility.' Ike wants only civilians involved. Otherwise we've got an act of war on our hands if one of them goes down in Russia."

"And if a pilot's captured, do you think he'll be able to stick with the story that he's a weatherman?"

"The thing is, the plane flies so high the pilot's not going to survive if it goes down."

"Are we for the plane?"

"We are. It's the only way we'll know if the Russian missile program is really so far ahead of ours."

"Will Bissell brief the committee about his plane?"

"He briefs you, then you brief the committee, but don't tell them much. Dulles doesn't even want it known that Bissell is the guy in charge of the project. Bissell didn't like that—he wants to do the briefing and get all the credit—but Dulles insisted. He likes you. You must have done a good job at that Russian party you went to. I told Dulles that I would trust you to tell me anything that I needed to know, but otherwise you keep it all to yourself. You're in the loop now."

"So if there is a leak, I'll be blamed."

"I wouldn't lose much sleep. Sooner or later word will get out. But you'll probably get a pretty good dog and pony show from Bissell. And maybe a trip out there to see the plane."

"Out where?"

"Beats me."

Out there turned out to be Burbank, California, where they were building the prototype at the Lockheed plant, as I learned a day later from Richard Bissell himself, Dulles's deputy director, who made me come to his office and wait for twenty minutes before he saw me. He was a tall man with pale skin, short-cropped hair, and an awkwardly vigorous manner. Originally an academic economist, he worked for the OSS during the war and then the Marshall Plan. Bissell's professorial quality struck me at first—the impersonal clarity and precision of his thinking. But there was a subtle ostentation to the way he invited you to admire his perceptions, as if each idea were skewered and displayed on a little pin. And, as I was to discover, he had a testy impatience with other people's ideas.

Bissell filled in the background of the Aquatone project. Edwin Land of Polaroid had convinced everyone that the technology now existed to take useful photographs at an altitude higher than Soviet missiles could reach. Lockheed was the most advanced jet designer around and the plane was conceived of as a stripped-down version of their F-104 design, with wider wings and fewer features, such as the ability to defend itself. "Can you imagine, the Air Force wanted cannons on the plane!" Bissell shook his head. "They had this fantasy that their cowboys would be able to shoot their way through Russia while taking pictures. The only person over there who understands anything is Trevor Gardner.

Twining's a military-type idiot. LeMay thinks he's a Hollywood hero. And that Secretary Talbott . . . Where does Ike dig up these hacks? The only hope is to make the plane light enough to fly above the defenses while using very little fuel. It's really a glider with an engine. But it's not going to be very fast or very maneuverable."

I knew enough about the specifications for the F-104 to quiz Bissell in some detail. By the time I finished, I had Bissell's respect. He invited me to come with him to Burbank when the prototype was finished and he hinted I might be invited out to the desert when they tested it. He leaned close to me, his eyes gleaming. "When we get this plane up in the air we're going to have the Soviets in a lock as far as intelligence goes. We'll be both in their heads and over their heads. They won't be able to make a move without our knowing about it. It will drive them crazy."

When Bissell shifted into speculation he displayed an aggressive bluster that seemed false to me, the overcompensation of an academic. I hadn't missed the fleeting reference to being *in* the Soviets' heads; he was hinting at something, but at the flicker of interest in my eyes he imperceptibly shook his head.

I had to tell Larry there was little I could do for the Air Force at the present juncture. If he kept me informed, I suggested, I might be able to do something later on. He was almost relieved that his little scheme was going nowhere. But since we shared a secret, Larry decided we were bound together. Larry figured out that I was usually accessible between six and seven o'clock, between work and social life, and he would knock at my door as I was dressing and then sit with me on my porch while I had a drink. Larry had a great, aching affection for his own childhood. He had grown up on the suburban frontier of the San Fernando Valley and he couldn't imagine that anyone wouldn't be interested in this most wonderful, sunny, carefree existence.

Larry was a junior at USC when he laid eyes on Deborah, who was a freshman. He pursued her indefatigably until, just before his graduation, she surrendered and left school without finishing her degree. Sometimes when he was well into one of his stories, his gaze transfixed and shining, I wondered if he wasn't wrapping himself in the past to protect himself from an ever more demanding present. I knew what the Pentagon was like; Larry had neither the self-importance nor the cynicism necessary to navigate the bureaucracy. I could hear the worry in his voice when he asked me if there wasn't anything more I had learned about the spy plane, if there wasn't some advantage over the CIA I could secure for him to bring to his masters as a trophy.

There wasn't much satisfaction for me in accumulating the kind of defense secrets that simply came to me as a result of my job, such as the specifications of every weapons system in development. But to have discovered Aquatone, something I was *not* supposed to know, and to have developed Larry as a source in the Pentagon, that was the kind of covert activity I found personally satisfying. I didn't see precisely where Aquatone would lead, as I did with the Mideast, but I sensed it was worth keeping up with the project.

8

The C-47 did not so much land as settle onto the landing strip, descending in a series of gentle shudders. It was August, 1955, and when the door was opened the heat hit me like an assault. It had been hot enough in Burbank when I arrived there yesterday, but the California air had had a faintly aromatic quality, a promise that the heat could be mastered if only you surrendered yourself to it. Here in the Nevada desert no human accommodation was possible; you simply suffered. The plane taxied over to a ramshackle collection of corrugated Quonset huts and small hangars that appeared to have been tossed negligently on the desert floor. The landing strip stretched off into a vast, barren terrain punctuated only by small piles of rocks. In the far distance, a range of mountains was faintly visible.

An officious young man with a crew cut greeted me at the foot of the ladder. "Mr. Bates? I'm Sam Miller. Welcome to Paradise Ranch. Mr. Bissell asked me to look after you. He's in Colorado Springs, at the Air Defense Command, but he expects to be here tomorrow." The young man described himself as the assistant to Kelly Johnson, Lockheed's engineering genius. He escorted me to a jeep and we drove a short distance to a hut. "Drop your bag off and let's go straight out to the runway. We've got a flight scheduled this morning. The U-2's seventh flight ever, actually."

We waited near the runway with a small knot of casually dressed engineers and test pilots. Sam pointed out the four or five CIA officers

Over the years, the U-2 spy plane touched down in a number of my activities in Washington.
NASA

who must have visited the company wardrobe department before coming to the desert; they were tricked out for the Sahara with their boots,
flap hats, and water bottles.

There was nothing for me to do here except observe. Bissell had been
scrupulous about the letter of his agreement with Russell: He had kept
me abreast of the plane's schedule and had even flown me out to Burbank in July to see the first finished prototype; yet I was told nothing
about the plane's specifications, technical problems, or even the eventual
scope of the program. In its small hangar in Burbank the plane seemed
large, swollen with all the hope and effort that had been put into it. Here
in Nevada, it looked vulnerable when it was towed out on the runway.
Its wide wings were so frail they had to be supported at the tips by
wheeled supports. Beneath the endless sky it appeared diminished and
toylike, the product of boyish enthusiasm rather than technology.

There was a long delay while the pilot and several engineers had a
discussion. The dry heat was unrelenting. My perspiration evaporated
instantaneously, leaving a thin film of salt on my arms as I was sucked
dry. The plane finally took off, rising buoyantly as the wing supports
fell away. It disappeared in a few moments. "Moscow, here we come,"
murmured Sam. He grinned sheepishly at me.

My earlier visit to Burbank in July had coincided with the first summit conference in Geneva.* When Eisenhower announced his Open Skies proposal for verifying arms control, all the engineers in Burbank had groaned. If each country permitted the other to use aerial surveillance, there was no need for the U-2. Bissell had shrugged. "We've been put on hold until after the summit. But the Russians will never agree to it." I had replied that Bulganin had sounded fairly positive. "Wait till Khrushchev gets his teeth into it," Bissell said smugly. "We're quite confident that he's got the power these days." Bissell had been correct. The Russians denounced the proposal and Eisenhower, to everyone's surprise except his, emerged from the conference as a hero of peace. Before we'd returned to Washington, Bissell assembled the Aquatone staff for a chest-thumping speech. "Let's open up their skies for them, boys!" he'd concluded, flailing his fists and grinning heroically as cheers rained over him.

The worst part of watching the test flight was waiting in the desert for the plane's return. What difference could it make if I didn't see it land? But everyone else who had witnessed the takeoff stayed out near the runway, chatting and kidding around while they pretended to ignore the heat. An absurd sense of pride kept me from fleeing the scene as I expired in the desert. Finally a shout went up as the U-2 appeared again, a tiny silent speck in the horizon.

Bissell arrived the next day. He was all over the compound, meeting separately with the test pilots, the engineers, and his agency cohort. An Air Force major had arrived with Bissell, but he just trotted after Bissell from meeting to meeting. There wasn't any doubt that Bissell was running the show; he reveled in his authority, which, he made clear, was derived from his being smarter than everyone else. I didn't have much to do. I wasn't invited to attend any meetings and there was only one more test flight for me to witness.

I was scheduled to fly back to Burbank late in the day. An hour before my departure Bissell found me. "Are you satisfied now?" he asked

---

* This was the first Cold War summit, to which Eisenhower had to practically drag the reluctant John Foster Dulles.

me, as if my presence was a tiresome obligation. But before I could reply he said: "War broke out in Colorado Springs. Between the agency and the Air Force that is. Allen Dulles was there and so was General LeMay. LeMay made his big pitch to take over the project, now that we've designed the plane. Luckily I had warned Allen that this was coming. Curtis LeMay never quits. He tried to steal the Polaris from the Navy. Imagine, SAC subs! Ha! Ha!" Bissell had one of those rhetorical laughs, more a sign of amusement than a symptom. "LeMay doesn't realize we've already got Ike sewed up. Ike is scared stiff this will look like a military operation."

"But you're going to need the Air Force. Who's going to fly the planes? Whose airfields are you going to use?"

Bissell nodded. "I know. We'll have to come to some sort of agreement. But on our terms. I've already worked out what I'll offer them. What we'll do is let them recruit and train the pilots. And if they want to appoint a deputy director of the project—reporting to me of course—I won't object too much. Since the pilots have to be whitewashed, they become CIA personnel anyway. The important thing is that we set the agenda. The Air Force's idea of intelligence is laughable."

"Are you telling me this so I can stick up for you in Washington?"

"I'm sharing our point of view with you. I'm trying to keep Senator Russell happy. But I don't imagine we'll need your help. Allen seems to have a fine relationship with the president. And of course there's Allen's brother Foster, God help us. But if I should need your assistance, I'll ask."

If I had been fully invested in my Washington career, I would have been concerned about Bissell's contempt for me. But what satisfying compensation it was to know that the deputy director of the CIA was obliviously face-to-face with a sleeper who knew just about every closely held defense secret.

A day later, when I was back in Washington in my office, I returned the five phone calls from Larry Boyer. "I would guess you've been calling me about the spy plane wars."

"How did you know? And where've you been?"

"I've been to the desert to see the plane fly. And I know there was a big blowup in Colorado Springs between Bissell and LeMay."

"You know everything! General LeMay flew in yesterday and was he steamed! Uh, I'm not sure I . . ."

"There's no need to talk on the phone. Why don't you drop by this evening? I think I can help you."

Larry must have waited at his window for me to return home. By the time I had unlocked my front door he was opening his. He followed me up the stairs to my apartment, peppering me with questions that I deflected calmly. I deposited Larry on the deck with a drink and in-sisted he wait until I was changed and dressed for the evening. On the way back to the deck I discovered Larry in the kitchen, helping himself to another drink. We sat down outside. It was early evening. In the steamy air, the leafy trees, thick vines and bushes blurred into dense green heaps.

Larry's small face glistened with sweat. He looked to me desperately. "Do you think you can really help me? I kind of made a mistake a while back and told a few people in the office that I had some pull over in the Senate. So yesterday we're in a meeting and LeMay is screaming at us to do something about the CIA, and this snotty colonel who works for Twining and pretends he's a real egghead turns to me and says, 'Maybe Mr. Boyer's connections on the Hill can solve the problem. Would you consider bringing the weight of your influence to bear on Allen Dulles? We'd be forever in your debt.' Big joke!"

"You didn't mention that I was your pull in the Senate?"

"Oh no. No names. I'm sorry I ever said anything now."

"Good. Now if you promise never to mention my name, I'm going to tell you what to do. You're going to go back to your office tomorrow and call a meeting with the same people. You'll tell them that you've managed to arrange a deal. You'll say that they should approach Bissell directly with the following specific demands. One, that the Air Force recruits and trains the pilots. Two, that the Air Force gets to appoint the second in command to Bissell. And of course that the Air Force provides all the logistical support the project needs. You'll also have to tell them that Bissell will be in command."

"I don't know. I don't think LeMay will be satisfied." He was right to be afraid of LeMay.

"He probably won't. But right now he's up against Ike and both Dulleses. You people don't have enough clout. You've got to sell this to them on the basis that they should take what they can get now and be in a position to take over when and if the CIA screws it up."

"That's what LeMay thinks—that they can't run such a large operation. Are you sure the CIA will buy this?"

"Trust me. And your people will buy it too. Except for LeMay, they're all bureaucrats. They should know when to compromise."

Larry looked doubtful. He ran his hands through his hair and massaged his neck. "I just don't know." He glanced forlornly over his shoulder, down toward his patio. I could see Deborah sitting there in the gathering darkness, calm and immobile.

"Larry, you've got to go in there and really sell this to them or it won't work. But I know you can do it. I've set it all up for you."

"I know you have, Winston. I honestly appreciate it. It's just . . . Oh damn! I'll try."

We fell silent. In the gloom I saw a white, ghostlike figure standing in the backyard that faced my house. A cigarette periodically glowed and dimmed as he inhaled. "There's Mr. Cleary," I said. "Did you know he works for the CIA?"

"What?" Larry was suddenly panicky. "How do you know he's CIA?"

"My landlady told me years ago."

"He's watching us!"

"He's not watching us. He's having a smoke. And he is not an operative. I checked him out. He's in Scientific Intelligence, supposedly a mad genius. He makes tiny cameras and microphones. You don't have to worry." The doorbell rang. It was my ride. Larry followed me down the stairs. A limousine was waiting.

"Look at this car!" Larry exclaimed. "Where are you going?"

Usually I walked over to Elizabeth's house but I had been away. This was a gift. "I've got a bridge game tonight."

9
***

Paris, Frankfurt, 1948

After lunch, I packed the beaten-up suitcase that Jack Mc-Gowan had given me and took a taxi to the Gare du Nord. There was not a busy schedule of international trains in 1948; all I had to do was follow the general flow of people in the station until I found the correct track. I was disappointed when I saw the train that was to bear me into darkest Europe. My expectations came from a decade of films featuring suspenseful and romantic train passages. But this motley collection of cars had been crabbed together from many decades of railroad history. I found an empty seating compartment in one of the older second-class cars. As we pulled out of the station, I felt a stab of apprehension: Was I on the right train? This modest and groundless worry was a stand-in for my colossal sense of fear about the whole trip.

For some time the train moved slowly but steadily. After an hour a pair of conductors entered the compartment. They scrutinized my papers and tickets, giving me an extra glance or two as they unfolded my letter from *The Winnipeg Free Press*, which had commissioned me to write an article on the Canadian battalion in Soest and its role in occupied Germany. When they left the compartment I took several deep breaths. I leaned back and closed my eyes. If I pretended to be asleep, perhaps I would fall asleep. . . .

This terrifying trip had been set in motion ten days before, when I was virtually abducted from a Canadian embassy party. I was vulnerable. I had recently dipped into my own savings to give Viktor five hundred dollars as a sign of good faith from Uncle Maurice. Viktor had become impatient with my excuses for Uncle Maurice, to whom I had written again, asking him to buy just twenty-five books. There had been no reply for weeks and as I handed Viktor my money, I knew it was lost; my book would never happen and I was handing away half a year in Paris or half a year of visits with Paulette. So when Jack McGowan, alleged intelligence agent, sidled up to me at the embassy and said, "I've got the chance for you to earn a spot of money," I was completely in his power.

McGowan escorted me from the ballroom and out into the street. He paused for a moment beneath the tall chestnut trees on Avenue Foch. "We'll go to my place," he decided. As I scrambled to keep up with his authoritative pace, he grilled me about how long I had been in Paris and why I was there, whether I had traveled in Europe, where I had gone to school. After fifteen minutes we came to a small, shabby hotel called the Spontini. Ignoring the halfhearted greeting of the woman at the desk, he snatched the key from her without breaking stride and mounted the steps two at a time up to the fifth floor.

McGowan had a dark, smelly little room with a round garret window and ceilings so low he could barely stand erect. He made space for me to sit on the one comfortable chair by removing a pile of laundry from the chair and dropping it on the floor. Beside the unmade bed was an open suitcase with underwear spilling out and a shirt draped over the raised lid.

"Drink?" He lifted a bottle of scotch and disappeared into the bathroom, returning with two glasses.

"No thank you," I said, but McGowan poured me half a glass anyway. He sat on the bed.

"Here's the deal," McGowan said. "I need someone to make a delivery for me."

"I don't drive, I'm afraid."

"No, no," he said impatiently. "I don't want a driver. It's very simple. I give you a package. You take an overnight train to Frankfurt. You meet an American CIA officer in Frankfurt who will teach you the routine. You spend a night in Frankfurt and return to Paris the next day. Not too challenging, eh? Someone with a memory like yours should be able to follow a few simple instructions." He joked in the patronizingly hostile tone that men who fancy they are men of action often adopt with men like me.

"What's the CIA?"

"Used to be OSS."

I nodded as if I understood what he was saying. "What's in the package?"

"Just some papers I need to get to Frankfurt safely."

"Are they valuable papers?"

"Let's put it this way. It wouldn't be good if you lost them but no one's going to try to take them away from you either."

"Am I supposed to tell anyone who asks that I'm making a delivery for the embassy?"

His black eyes darted at me. "What you tell anyone who asks is that you're a journalist. I'll get you a letter that says you're a journalist on assignment. And you're not working for External Affairs. No one at the embassy must know you're working for me. That includes your American friend too. This has to be our secret." He thumped his chest emphatically.

"Then who do you work for?"

"You really want to know everything, don't you?" There was a note of self-pity in McGowan's sigh. He shook his head slowly. "It's amazing. That huge embassy is filled with twits who have nothing to do but wring their hands and pretend that Canada has a role to play in the postwar world. And what role is that? We make the tea when the Russians, the Brits, and the Americans get together. Lester Pearson!" He spat out the name of Canada's new undersecretary for External Affairs as if he were expelling a rotten piece of meat. "But I'm expected to actually *do* something, so where does that get me? In a ratty little hotel begging a fucking poet to be a courier." He drained his glass. "Sorry, Bates. No offense."

"None taken. You know of course I have no German."

"Not a problem. I expect you'll have half the language memorized by the time you leave. Three hundred dollars plus expenses for one trip. No more questions. What do you say?"

He loomed toward me. I found him compelling and a little frightening. I was in his grasp. "Just one question: Canadian dollars?"

"U.S., actually. That's not a problem I take it?"

"Of course not," I said trying to appear nonchalant.

I arrived at the Frankfurt Hauptbahnhof in the late afternoon. My body felt cramped and buffeted when I stood to gather my belongings. The station appeared to have suffered only modest damage during the war. The waiting room was filled with American soldiers.

McGowan had given me a map and the address of a hotel. "You can walk," he said. "It's near the Opernplatz, where the opera house used to be."

Outside the station I blinked in the extremely warm sun. It was Indian summer in Frankfurt. Soldiers lounged indolently against their jeeps and trucks. Compared to Paris, Frankfurt was eerily quiet. I approached a GI who was sitting on the running board of a jeep. "Can you tell me how to get to Opernplatz?"

"Take a taxi," he said aggressively, as if I were asking him for a ride.

"Really, I'd rather walk. Which way is Opernplatz?"

He waved in a manner that indicated at least a third of the city. I set off. The map McGowan had given me, an out-of-date Baedeker, bore little resemblance to postwar Frankfurt. Because so many buildings had been obliterated it was hard to tell where the streets were. A prewar map! What kind of intelligence service was I working for? I passed a bulldozer organizing bricks and charred timbers into neat piles. Occasionally enough of a building's façade remained for me to approximate the general direction of the street but there were no street signs. I asked several German passersby for directions to the Opernplatz, which usually prompted a brief resentful stare until the offer of a cigarette inspired a more helpful attitude. After I had distributed nearly half a pack, I waved down an Army jeep. The chubby, crew-cut corporal at the wheel laughed when I asked him for directions.

"You're here," he said. "This is Opernplatz. Or this was it."

I looked around. There was no opera house to be seen; just a large open space dotted with scattered piles of timbers, brick, and stone. On the far side of the area I saw a relatively intact area of older buildings.

"Do you know where the Hotel Prague is?"

The soldier smirked. "I just found out myself. Get in."

He drove around the square, made two quick turns, and stopped in front of a dowdy six-story pension sandwiched between two commercial buildings. "You're a little early, but you'll enjoy yourself," said the corporal.

The small lobby was uncarpeted and unfurnished except for a dumpy sofa and a desk. The elderly clerk shook his head gravely when I gave him my name. I had a sinking feeling; McGowan was supposed to have booked the room. I offered the clerk U.S. dollars and dangled a pack of cigarettes before him. He motioned toward the sofa. "You wait, please." Half an hour later, a stocky woman descended the staircase behind the counter. She was dressed for the weather in what appeared to be a white lace slip; a fringed black shawl was draped over her shoulders and a thick black belt circled her waist. Her high heels echoed in the still afternoon. She was trailed by an American soldier who paused on the stairs to hitch up his pants and grunt.

"Ah good," said the clerk. "We have the room ready for you in so few minutes. The very best room."

While I waited, another prostitute came in with a soldier. The soldier paid, the clerk gave them a key, and they disappeared upstairs. The clerk smiled at me reassuringly. "Not to worry, gentleman. We save the best room for you."

I hunched down in the chair, imagining McGowan laughing at me back in Paris. I felt the helpless, furious anger I used to experience when my schoolmates bullied me. A voice called from upstairs. My room was ready.

There was no telephone in the best room, just a mirror, a lamp, a dresser, and a bed. The clerk downstairs directed me to a nearby *Bier-stube* where a few cigarettes got me the semiprivate use of their telephone. In my rudimentary German, I gave the number McGowan had given me to the operator. There were lots of clicks and other background noises before the telephone rang. A man answered in German but as soon as I said I was calling at the suggestion of Jack McGowan he switched to English and transferred me to another man.

"Yes, right, McGowan. Let's see . . . I know I've got something here about you . . . Here it is." There was a pause while he read his instructions. "Right. I suppose you want to deliver . . . the goods." He giggled self-consciously. "It's very simple. We will meet tomorrow, and together we will go to the I. G. Farben Building, at Grüneburgplatz. Where are you staying?"

"The Prague."

"Oh dear. Well let's meet at the *Bahnhof*. About ten? We can get a taxi from there. By the way, my name is George."

After frankfurters and boiled potatoes at the *Bierstube,* I returned to the Prague. I could hear music pouring out into the warm evening, a thick, clumsy braying of American pop music with an oompah-pah tuba beat. The lobby was smoky and tumultuous. Soldiers shouted hoarsely at each other and pawed the outnumbered women who slapped at their hands and laughed. I locked my door behind me and braced a chair against it.

In the morning I attempted to remove the manila envelope from the hidden compartment in the lid of the suitcase. As I fumbled with the frame, I muttered to myself that it served McGowan right to have hired someone as incompetent as me. It finally snapped open just as I was contemplating the humiliation of carrying the entire suitcase with me to the meeting with George.

I didn't know what to do when I got to the train station so I strolled about advertising myself until a young man approached me with his hand outstretched. "You seem to fit the description. Winston?"

"George?"

"That's me." George seemed an unlikely spy and not just because he was shorter than me. With protuberant eyes behind thick glasses, and a large, down-turned mouth, he looked almost professorial. He examined me with mild curiosity, no doubt wondering how McGowan had come up with such an unlikely courier. "Was the Prague everything it was cracked up to be?" he asked with a smile.

"I didn't know what to expect."

He shook his head. "I suppose McGowan wanted you to experience some local color. Shall we commence the training mission?" He gave a little ironic laugh, as if it were all a big joke.

He marched me out of the station where we found a taxi. I was vaguely disappointed by the absence of any surreptitious behavior. "Tell me about McGowan," he said as we rode. "What's he like?"

"He's all right," I said carefully. "He seems quite competent."

"Competent! Overcompetent from what I've heard. There are a couple of guys at our station who were at that camp in Canada during the war, where the British and Canadians trained the OSS. McGowan taught the art of knife fighting. They called him the Killer Boy Scout."

At the huge I. G. Farben Building, the headquarters for the Supreme Allied Command, George took me through the steps that would soon become my routine. We made our way to an office called Technical Support, and there I handed the package to Major Matthew Mason, a taut, wiry man who jerked his head pugnaciously at George and took the package off to another room. Ten minutes later he returned. "Everything's in order." He sized me up while taking a deep drag on his cigarette. "Where're you staying?"

"At the Prague last night. But I'm on the way back to Paris this afternoon."

"The Prague! You! Where does McGowan dig you guys up?"

"What's with the guys who had this job before me?" I asked George when we were back in the taxi.

"Don't mind Mason. Those Army Intelligence guys tend to be jerks."

When we pulled up at the station, George gave another of his self-conscious laughs and said, "Welcome to the exciting world of spying."

*

"You mean to say you didn't sample the delights of the Prague?" McGowan grinned roguishly. My night at the Prague appeared to have been a hazing ritual.

We were in McGowan's gloomy little room. I had taken him step-by-step through my trip to Germany. In revenge for the Prague, I repeated George's description of him.

"'Killer Boy Scout,' I like that. I was pretty gung ho in those days." He fished his bottle of scotch out of the pile of clothes in his suitcase, which still lay open on the floor. He offered me a drink, which I accepted.

"Well you passed the test, Bates. There was nothing in that package you delivered. It was just a dummy."

"I wondered why no one seemed very concerned about the package. I could have delivered it the day I arrived in Frankfurt. I also can't imagine that you would have put me into the Prague if you really cared about the security of the package."

"Just a little inconvenience to see how you'd react. Next time we can arrange for nicer surroundings."

"I think you better tell me what I'm really going to be doing."

He stared at me for several seconds, and then looked off in space, trying to decide if I was worth his trust.

"Here's the story: Every couple of weeks we deliver a package to the U.S. Command in the I. G. Farben Building in Frankfurt. Mostly it contains cash, sometimes a lot of cash, and some coded instructions about what to do with the money. The money is from a huge hoard of cash, hundreds of thousands of U.S. dollars. Real money, not counterfeit, that the Germans had stockpiled and hidden away here in Paris. They must have liberated it from French banks. British intelligence found it just a step ahead of OSS, who was onto its existence too. OSS and MI5 decided to keep the discovery a secret and share the cash. A private endowment for intelligence you might say. And to eliminate interagency suspicion, Canadian intelligence was selected as the custodian, the banker for the money. We just have to ensure that both agencies agree to any disbursement. When the money gets to Frankfurt, U.S. Army Intelligence, who has no idea of its origins, washes the money, so to speak. If needed, they convert it to other currencies. Then it's distributed to various operations in Frankfurt and Berlin run by MI5 and the CIA. So we were trying you out, to see if you'd be an acceptable courier to the CIA, to see if you could follow instructions, to see if you peeked at the package. The last courier peeked. I also need someone who can at least pretend to be semiprofessional so the Americans' opinion of Canadian intelligence doesn't sink any lower than it already is. Maybe the next time you go you can show off your fabulous memory."

He stood up abruptly and clenched his fists. "Christ! I can't believe it. I'm wasting my time running a messenger service while Canada's diplomatic corps makes the world nice for democracy." He sat down again and buried his face in his hands. He shook his head slowly and massaged his face. "You know, I trained half the OSS in Canada during the war. They all went off and saw action but not me. Now look what I'm doing." He sighed and counted out three hundred dollars in U.S. currency on the bed. "Next time we do this it will be for real."

"How soon? And never again at the Prague, please."

"In two weeks. I promise we'll find better accommodations."

Now that I was assured of a flow of money, I was willing to dip further into my nest egg. When I gave the next five hundred dollars to Viktor, I told him that Maurice would keep sending the money in stages as long as I assured him we were making progress toward publication. Viktor launched himself into a frenzy of activity. Publishing the book did not seem to be so much a systematic process as a frenzied summoning of it into existence. He insisted I accompany him all over Paris. We bustled through a paper merchant's warehouse in Belleville, fingering samples and discussing absorbency and reflectivity, as if I knew what I was talking about. At a bindery in Saint-Denis we examined cloth samples; a distinguished maroon seemed appropriate. Every so often I would hand Viktor another installment, usually on the order of two or three hundred dollars. I was quite pleased with Viktor's openness, his willingness to involve me in all the details and decisions, but whenever I inquired about Picabia's work he put me off, saying it was Mara who had to deal with Picabia. One day, at a letterpress printer in Montparnasse, we were quoted an astonishing amount of money to print my book. I finally decided to be assertive.

"Maurice has told me he won't send any more money until I meet Picabia and see some of the images."

"I must tell you, Winston, Picabia is being difficult. He told me he has no time to make the work."

"Oh no!"

"But he said he has a drawing that might be appropriate for a frontispiece. It's a drawing of an upside-down man."

"Frontispiece? No one will pay hundreds of dollars for just a frontispiece. And what does an upside-down man have to do with my poems?"

"Don't be upset. I told you he might be difficult. He is bargaining. He wants us to offer more money."

"No more money!" I startled myself with my outburst.

Viktor took a deep breath and sighed. His fat little face was cherubic with tender sympathy for me. "I know how much you want your poems to be published well. Tell me this, Winston, you brought the next payment with you?"

I nodded.

"We must find a way to keep Maurice from withdrawing his support. I have an idea perhaps. You know, if we just use Picabia's frontispiece, twenty-five hundred dollars will be almost enough money to make the book, since we won't have to print any other images. Just the one picture from Picabia. The rest the poems of Winston Bates. Wouldn't Maurice approve? It is you he wishes to support."

"I think so. If it really requires less money he won't need to pay as much for his copies. It's all relative isn't it?"

"It's always relative with relatives," Viktor proclaimed. "With the money you give today plus a small last amount—very small I promise—I will have enough to buy the paper, that beautiful maroon cloth, and have enough left over for the printer."

I handed the money to Maurice, six hundred dollars this time, which included an advance of five hundred from McGowan and the hundred dollars my mother had sent me for a new winter coat and a watch.

Once Viktor actually decided on a printer, and introduced me to him, my sense of embarrassment at paying for my own publication began to turn into blithe optimism. After all, the book would appear. My work would be read and mostly praised. I would laugh off the occasional vituperative review as the revenge of an enemy. Why, even having enemies would be a kind of affirmation. My writing flowed now. With my new self-assurance, I became impatient with Paulette. On some afternoons her efforts seemed interminably predictable. I took it upon myself to suggest new variations, lying there on my back, a fretful naked little pasha, peevishly ordering her tongue here, her hands there. As she dutifully complied with my instructions, I would become exasperated and occasionally impotent, for which I would castigate her with a quick sneer. You would think I would have stopped seeing her, but I took it to be part of my new entitlement as a nearly published poet to have the satisfaction of treating someone badly, even if I had to pay for it.

10

On one of my New York visits, I went to the Five Spot Bar to listen to jazz with my sister, her new boyfriend Stanley Wright, and Robert Cage. Robert had left the Library of Congress and moved to New York six months before. I had introduced him to Alice and they had become quite friendly. The three of them smoked marijuana before we left, which I refused out of fear of losing control. I probably would have bowed out of the evening except for the intercession of Stanley, a man for whom thoughtfulness was a form of art. He was the first Negro with whom I had ever had an extended conversation. Washington in the midfifties was a segregated southern city in which the races were separated by an impenetrable wall of genial courtesy. *The Washington Post* supported civil rights on its editorial pages but its classified sections still declared which jobs and apartments were or weren't colored. My Canadian origins conveniently exempted me from guilt over America's racial problems, but I was apprehensive about how Stanley would react to my association with Senator Russell. He put me at ease with an enveloping concern for me, as if working in Washington could only be an affliction from which New York was a reprieve. Stanley was tall and angular, with thin, bony shoulders hunched over a shallow chest. Above his high cheekbones, his large, liquid eyes welled with compassion. His voice was utterly persuasive, a rich velvety flow of encouragement and reassurance. He worked as a special events coordinator for an obscure New York City bureaucratic entity, which required him to spend a great deal of time going to jazz clubs—"to stay abreast of the talent" as he put it.

I took in the smoky panorama. There was one other interracial couple in addition to Alice and Stanley, a few dressed-up black couples on dates, a table of four white businessmen who had shed their jackets and loosened their ties, a couple of professorial types, and several white hipsters, as they were called then—altogether a motley group yet all quite at ease here. When the music began I sat up alertly, aware of Robert's amused glances; he thought my mandarin tastes would be offended by jazz. But I surrendered to the experience, happy for a brief time to be so far removed, figuratively speaking, from Washington and Suez.

Ten minutes after we returned to Alice's apartment, at about two thirty in the morning, the telephone rang. It was Jim Flannery, Bissell's assistant. With my new job, the CIA insisted on knowing where I could be reached at any time in case they couldn't locate Russell.

"I've been calling you all night. Are you alone?"

There was one phone and no privacy in Alice's apartment but I told him I was alone.

"Dulles is trying to get hold of Russell. Do you know where he is?" I tried to worm the story out of Flannery, but he was evasive. Finally Bissell grabbed the phone. He was in a fury.

"We have to move the whole U-2 operation from England!" he exploded. "Eden's gone nuts. Because *his* Secret Service screwed up an operation while Khrushchev was visiting England, *we* have to get out. I want you to talk to Russell. It's going to take some money to set up somewhere else." The first U-2 squadron was currently poised and waiting for orders in Lakenheath, England, while Eisenhower fretted about Russia's potential reaction to the violation of their airspace. "You can say to Russell that most of our intelligence about Soviet missile and rocketry research has come from that goddamn tunnel in Berlin.* Now that operation has been blown and we need to get the U-2 up in the air."

---

* The Berlin tunnel operation, which for two years had tapped into East German communications with Moscow, had been uncovered by the Soviets only a few days earlier.

"Where do you want to set up?" I asked.

"Germany, probably. Adenauer's eager to be helpful. I'm flying to Bonn in the morning. We want to use the Air Force base at Wiesbaden."

I finally located Russell in Georgia. While I briefed him, I turned away and cupped my hand over the mouthpiece. When I was done, I turned back to my companions, plunging through a hole in the great world of powerful men and ignorant armies to resurface in a desolate railroad flat on the edge of the Lower East Side. Alice, Robert, and Stanley were sprawled on pillows on the floor, drinking scotch.

U-2 flights over Russia began on July 4, 1956, from their new base in Germany. Georgi Zaroubin, the Soviet ambassador, immediately objected to "pirate flights" and John Foster Dulles replied that no *military* aircraft had strayed over Russian borders. According to Larry, Eisenhower marveled over the first U-2 photos. When I told this to Russell, he scowled in his tight-lipped manner and picked up the phone. Allen Dulles himself was in the office in an hour with his portfolio of photos, brandishing them before us with apologies. "You're Dick Bissell's person, aren't you?" he said, looking me up and down.

"He's *my* person," Russell said.

"Dick has been very helpful to us," I replied. I followed them into the inner office where Dulles unveiled his photo treasures one by one, like precious

Allen Dulles was quite fond of his nickname at the CIA, "The Great White Case Officer," although it suggested, accurately, that he was more interested in clandestine operations than in actually managing the Agency. *National Archives, 306-PS-59-17740*

Fabergé eggs. "Look at that circle. Now here it is enlarged. You recognize it, don't you? No? Then here it is enlarged again. Can you guess what it is?" Dulles enjoyed playing the showman.

"That's the Winter Palace," I said. It was a clever guess; to me the photo was a collage of blurry shadows, but I could tell by the river that we were looking at Leningrad. Next we moved on to Moscow, where the bulbous towers of the Kremlin were actually discernible; in blurry black-and-white it looked like a toy house.

"How about a military site?" Russell suggested impatiently. "Isn't that the point?"

Dulles obliged, showing us an airfield where, using his pipe as a pointer, he identified various types of Russian fighters and bombers. When we were through Russell said, "I surely never imagined it would work so well. I'm surprised they didn't try to shoot the plane down."

"If they could have, they would have," Dulles chortled. He rubbed his hands together gleefully and then winked at us. He had gotten by on his charm for so long it had become a reflex.

"What's next?" Russell wanted to know.

"Ike has grounded us. Temporarily. Until the Russians calm down. We can't have too many 'weather planes' that go astray. The White House has to approve each flight."

"Ike himself?" Russell asked in surprise.

"Yes, but the order comes from Goodpaster so that Ike can deny he knew about the flight in case something goes wrong. In the meantime we're setting up another U-2 unit in Turkey." Dulles jerked his head in my direction. "He's the one?"

"He's the one," Russell said. "Our memory machine. Go ahead, Allen, you can tell him."

"Do you remember identifying for us a Russian writer about a year and a half ago whom you thought might be sympathetic?"

"The one from the writers' party at the Russian embassy?"

"Yes. I'm afraid he didn't turn out to be a writer. He was actually a KGB agent who was assigned to baby-sit the writers on their trip." Dulles scowled and pulled on his pipe.

"I'm sorry," I said nervously, hoping Russell would come to my aid. "But I hardly spoke to him. He just seemed . . ."

"But he did turn out to be rather taken with America. As soon as we approached him he told us that he was KGB and that he was eager to return to the U.S. permanently." Dulles's scowl had turned into a mischievous grin. Russell too was smiling. "It's always a coup to turn a KGB agent, and though he was young, he was on the way up. Rarely do you find someone whose motives for betrayal are so uncomplicated. He just wanted a new life here, an American wife and a house in the suburbs. We even had to pick a location and have his handler show him photographs of his future home in Arizona. We're very grateful to you."

"I think it was mostly a lucky guess," I said.

"Inspired luck, let's call it," Dulles said.

"And he's been helpful?"

"Extremely. You know, we heard about Khrushchev's denunciation of Stalin in February, and we got a copy of the Polish transcript of the speech from Israeli intelligence in April. But it was your man in Moscow who was the final confirmation that our copy was the real thing and not a fabrication. It's too bad really."

"What's too bad?"

"That we've lost him."

Dulles looked downcast and Russell shook his head in disappointment.

"What happened to him?" I said hesitantly, fearing I was going to be blamed for something.

"We don't know exactly. About a month ago he quite abruptly signaled his handler for a meeting. He didn't indicate that it was an emergency or he was in danger—we had an emergency exfiltration signal set up—but he never showed up, and as far as we know he's disappeared. We've assumed the worst."

"You mean he's dead."

Dulles nodded and puffed at his pipe authoritatively. He was doing his best to sound coldly professional about the whole thing. "I wouldn't be able to tell you this if he were still in place. Our guess is that he overreached himself. Not because we were pressing him. We wanted him in place as long as possible. But he was always after us to set a time-table for his defection. These things are tricky, but one always hopes. He was on the way up. In a few years, who knows. . . . We think he tried to force our hand by obtaining information so important that we would have to bring him in. He probably made a mistake and got burned. We watch KGB headquarters. As far as we know he went to work one day and never emerged. Still, all in all, a success for us, and you."

"Can you point out the headquarters?" I indicated the photographs on the table.

Dulles looked startled, but I didn't think it was such a bizarre re-quest. His pipe stem wavered like a divining rod over Moscow. "There, that's Dzerzhinsky Square and there's KGB headquarters. Nice and close to the Kremlin. Lubyanka Prison's right there too, which is where your man was probably tortured."

My man? Was I connected to his death? I stared at the picture. I tried to imagine him in the dark, conspiratorial corridors of the Krem-lin, risking everything for a ranch house in Scottsdale.

In July, Elizabeth and I were invited for a weekend at Spindrift, the grand Eastern Shore estate of the Honorable and Mrs. George H. S. Ferver, whose bountiful donations to the Republican Party had snared George a minor appointment to an obscure UN committee. The Fervers were at the peak of their campaign to insinuate themselves into the up-per tier of the State Department social circuit by giving the most rigidly formal dinners of anyone in Washington. The weekend promised to be a stuffy, faux-English country manor event, where everyone dresses formally for dinner and speaks archly; just the sort of thing that Eliza-beth detested. But when I heard that the new British ambassador, Roger Makins, would be present, I persuaded Elizabeth to accept. With Ma-kins there, I knew Suez would be on the agenda.

As it happened William Macomber, Foster Dulles's chief of staff, was also a guest. At dinner on Saturday he revealed there had been a breach in U.S. relations with Egypt. Just the day before, the Egyptian ambassador had met with Dulles to discuss a U.S.-British offer to underwrite the construction of the Aswan Dam. The ambassador told Dulles that Egypt had received a competing Russian offer. The idea that the Egyptians might expect the United States to improve the offer so affronted the stiff-necked Dulles that he unilaterally withdrew the U.S.-British offer. This seemed to be news to Makins, who looked ashen.

After dinner Elizabeth cornered me. "What's going on? Everyone kept nudging each other with their elbows and glancing at Makins and his poor wife. But nobody ever *said* anything. I knew I didn't want to come here."

"The Aswan Dam loan was Eden's idea. The U.S. would put up the lion's share of the money for the dam, but the British would sell a lot of the construction equipment to Egypt and keep their influence over Nasser alive. Now the Russians will loan the money to Egypt."

"Oh who cares!" she said impatiently. "I can't believe we're stuck here until tomorrow."

Makins had disappeared by the time we awoke the next morning. I imagined he was back in his office and on the phone to Downing Street, working up a new strategic approach—one of hundreds of similar episodes in the waning of the British Empire. As for me, I had learned enough to predict the next step, which occurred two weeks later when Nasser nationalized the canal and tossed out the French and British. Had my watcher contacted me earlier the course of history might have been changed; instead, self-satisfaction was my only reward.

In those days, Washington went into a state of suspension for much of the summer. Russell spent most of July in Georgia and Elizabeth retreated to her Gulf Coast summer home without so much as an insincere invitation for me to visit. In her absence there wasn't much for me to do. I couldn't think of a single person I would call for a casual afternoon at the National Gallery nor did anyone think of calling me. Was it my status as an appendage to Elizabeth that fixed my social contacts at the formal level? Or was it *me*? Perhaps some ineffable odor of my divided identity kept every acquaintance at a wary distance from me.

Would I even recognize a potential friendship as long as I was looking over my shoulder, awaiting my control? Of course there was my alternate universe in New York, but Alice had taken a share in a small cottage on Fire Island, where there was no extra room.

With no social entanglements, I enjoyed my own company. I would leave the office in the late afternoon to drift through the faintly cool corridors of the Corcoran or the National Gallery. Weekend afternoons were spent in empty, air-conditioned movie theaters or at home on my porch.

In the latter half of August, the Democratic and Republican national conventions for the 1956 presidential election depopulated Washington. Larry and Deborah invited me to watch the conventions on their latest television set, an immense Philco. We kept the lights turned low, partly to encourage the baby to fall asleep and partly because the darkness promoted the illusion of coolness. A small fan had been placed on the floor where it whirred at us quietly. Deborah sat on the couch, utterly engaged with little Mark, who chortled happily, the only one of us not drenched in sweat. Larry was far more interested in which television network did the best job than which candidate the Democrats nominated. He sat on the floor before the television, bathed in its quivering, acidic luminescence, switching channels in a frenzied determination to miss no moment of the competition between Walter Cronkite and the *Huntley-Brinkley* team. I sat in the soft Naugahyde easy chair, damp and sticky, and attempted to peer around Larry's head. Every so often, I would beg Larry to pause in his ceaseless switching and move aside when there was something of interest to me, such as a news report in which the French premier, Guy Mollet, blamed Foster Dulles for Egypt's nationalization of the canal and implied if Dulles didn't back the use of force against Egypt, Algeria would be Nasser's next target.

"Mollet? He's a Socialist, right?" Larry said. "And Eden's an upper-class type. They should hate each other."

"They probably do. But they understand each other. The one they don't understand is Dulles."

"Larry, would you warm up a bottle for Mark?" Deborah asked.

Larry dashed away.

"Larry just loves politics," Deborah said. I responded with a raised eyebrow, as if we shared a secret about Larry, but she was too busy with the baby to notice. Soon Larry returned and we switched back to the Democratic convention in Chicago. There was Senator Russell, wincing sourly at the camera. It had been three weeks since I had last seen him and he looked oddly unfamiliar as he defended his tortuous attempt to keep the southern delegations united against the proposed civil rights platform.

"Would you mind going back to CBS?" I asked. "They were about to do a news wrap-up."

"Oh all right." Larry deepened his voice to the stentorian resonance of an announcer: "And now presenting . . ."—he switched the channels—". . . Robert Trout with the news."

This was an excellent newscast from the Suez point of view. There was a report on John Foster Dulles's departure to London for an important conference on what had now acquired the default appellation of the Suez Crisis. Larry sidled closer to me and murmured, "You should know this—we've got standby plans for U-2 flights over the Mideast. LeMay says Ike doesn't trust the British or the French to tell Dulles what's going on."

Trying to appear casual, I said: "Let me know if you see any pictures . . ."

Larry nodded obediently and slid back to the television. He no longer seemed nervous about confiding in me, and even enjoyed our surreptitious moments. His hand, possessed of a mind of its own, darted for the dial and switched us back to Chicago.

A week later we watched the Republican convention in San Francisco. Here, the big issue for Larry was Eisenhower's reluctance to unequivocally embrace Nixon as his VP again. "Doesn't Ike understand?" Larry asked with real uneasiness. "He's the father. Everybody thinks of him as the father. He shouldn't treat his son like this. Look at Nixon. He's trying hard to show he doesn't care but you can see he does."

Though he adored Eisenhower, Larry was quite fond of Nixon, mainly because of the California connection but also because Larry was attracted to the dogged underdog quality in Nixon that would become so manifest later. When the convention drew to its end, with Eisenhower and Nixon standing together on the podium, Larry was delighted. "That's great. Just great. Look how happy he's made Nixon. They're going to win all right. Everybody loves the good, strong father." He clapped along with the delegates.

"Can't you see *anything*? It's because he's *not* a good, strong father that he's going to win," Deborah blurted out. Larry and I stared at her; she had barely spoken, except to the baby, for two weeks. "Don't you get it? He's just a kind of ordinary father, well-meaning but not really there. He does okay with the day-to-day things—the lawn gets mowed, we learn how to ride bikes—but on the big stuff we're not too sure of him." She was changing the baby's diaper as she spoke, leaning over him and speaking almost to herself. "We just tell ourselves that he's strong, and we hope he'll be pleased enough with our votes to show us his hidden strength and understanding. But he won't. He won't let anything really bad happen to us, if he can help it, but nothing wonderful is going to happen either."

"You're so cynical, Deborah," I said, "I never imagined."

"It's not cynicism. We do believe that strength is there inside him, and we know it makes him happy that we feel that way about him, but he just gets too fumbling and embarrassed to show it. And we love him for it! Maybe it is all for the best. Who wants the kind of father who can't resist bewitching his daughters and overwhelming his sons? Better to settle for someone who doesn't give us that much, someone we can trust to fail us just enough while we know he means to do better."

Larry and I stared at each other. He shrugged, as if to say, "What's with her?" But I was delighted. Over the past year, Deborah and I had forged an unspoken connection based on our fond but patronizing indulgence of Larry's enthusiastic banality. I began to sense a more exacting person beneath her easy blandness. But once her baby consumed her, she seemed to forget our special rapport and no longer responded to the private smiles and nods that sustain such things. Larry was perplexed by her outburst but I was relieved to know the appealing person I had discerned was really there.

*

The Western world was lurching toward a collision in Suez. Although a brilliant feat of diplomacy might have headed things off, diplomacy was in short supply. Eisenhower occasionally voiced his disapproval of Britain and France's threats and military posturing, but he strangely avoided taking a tough stand with Eden or Mollet. Meanwhile, Foster Dulles tried to create an international agency to run the canal, as if Nasser, having nationalized it, would simply turn it over to Dulles's agency. While Eisenhower fussed and Dulles flailed, there wasn't a day I didn't believe that my contact was about to make himself known to me. Yet what would I tell him? All my latest intelligence came from television. Would control be satisfied to know that I *believed* a war was imminent?

Late one afternoon near the end of September, Larry dropped by to see me. He was carrying a manila folder and grinning proudly. "I saw you sitting out on the porch. You're home early."

"I have a cocktail party to go to. And what is your excuse?"

"Booteefool pictures." Now that his son was beginning to speak, Larry frequently lapsed into baby talk. "I couldn't leave them sitting in my desk so I just picked them up and went home with them. Did you see *Huntley-Brinkley* last night? They did a piece on Suez. But they didn't have pictures like these U-2 pictures." He waved his folder seductively.

Though I was dying to see them, I was irritated with myself for making my interest in Suez so apparent. "Really, Larry, considering the risk to you and how little I can help you, I don't know why you bring me your little curiosities." Larry stuck out his jaw stubbornly and waved his folder more deliberately. I felt a small, guilty ache for this clunk, beset by detachment from Deborah, disdain from his colleagues at the Pentagon, and impatience from me. I paused a moment to gather myself, guilt being a somewhat uncommon emotion for me. I didn't realize it at the time, but a pattern was being set: most of the very few twinges of guilt I would ever experience in Washington, or in my life, would be twinged by Larry.

"I'm sorry, Larry. I'm sure these are real treasures."

"You're going to love them." He lined a little frieze of photos on the porch floor.

"What am I looking at?" I asked.

"Malta, there and there. And that one and the one next to it show Cyprus."

"And what do I see?"

"You see what could be the beginning of a British fleet assembling. Look closely. That's a destroyer and there's a cruiser. Now look at these." He dealt out another line of photos on top of the first. "Now we're looking at Marseilles and Toulon. And here we see a couple of French naval vessels taking on supplies."

"Have these photographs been seen at the White House?"

"I'm pretty sure. Bissell and Dulles always bring the U-2 photos over to the White House themselves so they get to tell Ike what they mean before anyone else can. Of course, the only pictures that get everybody excited are the ones of Russia."

"And the State Department?"

"You'd think Dulles would show them to his brother too, but I don't know."

"Well, Larry, this is all very informative. Now I need to find out whether Allen Dulles thinks an invasion is about to happen."

Larry's eyes widened. "Now just a sec. You're not going to let him know . . ." He gestured awkwardly at the photographs.

"Calm down, Larry. Haven't I done my best to help you?" It was true. Larry's stock had soared at the Pentagon since his successful plan for compromise with the CIA over the U-2. "Don't worry, Larry. Isn't this a lovely afternoon? There's a touch of coolness in the air. Fall is coming."

I was very excited: My two special secrets, Suez and the U-2, had been miraculously joined. This was how a gambler must feel when he has a lucky run—anointed and then unconstrained by good sense.

I spoke to Russell the next day. "You know, I've had a hard time connecting with Bissell lately. But you might find an update on U-2 activities quite useful."

Russell stared at me thoughtfully. "Communication a little difficult these days? I'll see what I can do."

Two days later Dulles arrived at the office with Bissell in tow. A few minutes after they vanished into Russell's private office, Russell stuck his head out and invited me in.

"You again!" I said to Bissell, who glowered at the presence of lowly me.

"Mr. Bates, I presume," Dulles said. Though his hair was nearly white, his face was unlined and soft, boyishly appealing behind his mustache. "I've been so busy lately I'm afraid I've neglected you boys in Room 205."

"We live in hope of another dog and pony show. The senator and I were quite taken with your photographs."

"Well you know . . ." He leaned closer to Russell, as if imparting a great secret. "What with setting up new U-2 bases in Germany, and now Turkey, we just haven't gotten enough high-quality missions off the ground lately."

"It occurred to me," I blurted out, "now that your U-2s have been thrown out of Britain, you don't have to feel reluctant to use the planes to see what the British are up to in Egypt."

He made a little show of relighting his pipe and puffed away thoughtfully, no doubt debating whether Russell and I were worth the confidence. "We haven't been reluctant. It's . . ." Dulles stabbed his pipe at the door to the outer office, which was ajar behind me. I closed it and approached them.

Dulles lifted his pipe, as if saluting me. "Mr. Bates's powers of divination are always impressive. We did send a U-2 on a Mediterranean mission recently but the results were inconclusive. Certainly the French and British must take some steps to convince Nasser of their seriousness."

"Like assembling an invasion fleet?"

Bissell and Dulles exchanged a startled glance.

"As rumor has it," I hurriedly added.

"Really, they haven't gone that far. Besides, the real action right now is in Europe. We actually have a chance to roll back the Iron Curtain in Poland and Hungary. We can't let Suez distract us so the Russians think they have a free hand in Europe. The players in the Middle East are all our allies. Nasser only flirted with the Russians in order to extort us a little. If only Foster hadn't been so damned inflexible he could have strung Hussein along."

"What about the Israelis?" I said. "Surely they'll be happy to encourage the British and the French."

"No, they're staying out of it. Jim Angleton has very good contacts with the Mossad, he assures me. If anything, it's Jordan that is in their sights." He looked at Bissell who gave an emphatic nod in agreement. Then Dulles nodded back at Bissell and Bissell raised his eyebrows. I was wondering how long this silent repartee could go on when Russell said impatiently, "Well show us something."

One more nod from Dulles did the trick. Bissell opened a small box on the conference table and took out a stack of photographs. He spread out a few of them and stepped back from the table, his arms folded, waiting for me to embarrass myself. Finally I said, "I'm pretty sure we're not looking at the Middle East."

"No, these are Russian airfields."

"And what do they show?"

"Nothing. Or almost nothing."

"That couldn't have made Ike very happy," I said.

Bissell smiled patronizingly. "If *you* were worried about the vast fleet of Bison-class long-range bombers the Russians claim to have, you'd be extremely happy to find out there's almost nothing to see. You see, in our game, nothing can be really something."

He spread another group of images on the table and I realized we were looking at the same set of images Larry had shown to me. I was unable to restrain myself: "Oh, isn't that Malta and Cyprus? Could those be warships? I don't suppose you photographed any French ports as well."

"Why you're thinking just like an CIA analyst," Dulles said. "Maybe we should lure you away from Senator Russell." As Russell smiled proudly, Bissell spread out the images of Marseilles and Toulon. I professed astonishment and indignation at the sneaky preparations of the British and the French.

"And look at this picture," Bissell said. "Those are new French Mystère jets in Israel. That's a violation of the Tripartite Pact, our so-called family agreement not to upset the military balance over there."

"So they're violating our agreement and we're spying on them. Aren't they supposed to be our allies?" I said.

"The British know we have the U-2. The Israelis too. I'm sure they expect us to peek. It's all in the family. This is a lot less scary than spying on the Russians."

"But what difference does it make if we don't *do* something?" I said. "We're like one of those families that go along pretending some glaring fact doesn't exist. Mother's drinking, for instance. Everybody knows it's happening—her eyes are glazed, dinner is overcooked, the car keeps getting dented—but no one ever acknowledges the situation."

"We're in the middle of an election. No one will face anything until it's over. You can't believe they are actually going to go to war?" He motioned to the photos. "This is all bluster."

That evening Elizabeth Boudreau and I finally earned the sanction of attending Walter Lippmann's annual fall cocktail party, which inaugurated the Washington social season. Within ten minutes of our arrival, Sir Roger Makins, the almost new British ambassador grasped my elbow and told me he had become the old ambassador. He said he had been recalled to Britain to become permanent secretary of the Treasury. He had no idea who his replacement would be. "No ambassador?" I said to Makins. "Is that useful at a time like this?"

"Well it was rather sudden. With all this Suez business going on, I was needed immediately. Macmillan is so involved with policy, someone's got to protect the pound."

Something very unpleasant was in the works if the pound needed protection. The U.S. secretary of Treasury, George Humphrey, was known to be an Anglophobe and had encouraged Dulles to cancel the Aswan Dam loan. A new British secretary of Treasury who had U.S. connections suggested to me that the relationship was going to be tested.

Elizabeth and I had recently been promoted to the social calendar of the other major newspaper columnist of the day, Joseph Alsop. The

I enjoyed Joe Alsop's bombastic personality. I became an occasional source for his widely syndicated, disingenuously named column, Matter of Fact. *Photo by Francis Miller/Time & Life Pictures/ Getty Images*

degree to which Alsop and Lippmann were negative reflections of each other's personalities made one wonder if they had invented themselves in response to each other, like grotesquely competitive siblings. A small, sharp-faced man, Alsop was secure enough in his social position not to care what anyone thought about him. He flaunted his self-confidence by forcing his irascible, imperious manner on you at the slightest excuse. I enjoyed seeing Alsop because he could be depended on to say exactly what was on his mind. All you had to do was push the right buttons and he would begin to sputter. Elizabeth felt relaxed with Alsop because he was more interested in what he thought than in what she thought. He patronized her terribly, but she gave as good as she got, letting him know she thought he was an ill-tempered, pompous blowhard who drank too many martinis. They got on well, though she was disappointed that Alsop never brought us into his Georgetown inner social circle, a tight group of friends that included Allen Dulles, Richard Bissell, Kay and Philip Graham, and Frank Wisner, head of Covert Operations for the CIA.

Alsop had pretensions as a connoisseur and his Georgetown town house on Twenty-sixth Street was dense with artifacts and antiques, mainly French and oriental, which seemed to vibrate in their eccentric enjambments. Our fourth time in Alsop's house came at the end of September, and whom should I see but Richard Bissell, propped up awkwardly against an ornate, eighteenth-century marble fireplace, aloof and alone in the midst of the party, nursing his drink with both hands. He started when I approached him, recognizing me as a familiar face before he remembered who I was. Before I could say a word, Alsop descended on us. "You know, Dick, you're standing exactly where Guy Burgess stood just two months before he flew the coop. Ever meet him?" He thrust his gnomic face at Bissell, his bulging eyes blinking furiously.

Bissell shook his head. He had a wary half smile as he awaited Alsop's twitting.

"Like hell you never met him! Do you remember Guy Burgess, Elizabeth?"

Elizabeth was nowhere near us. Alsop simply bellowed her name without even turning his head.

"Remember him?" Elizabeth scurried over to us. "My dear, he peed into my potted palm. He passed out in my garden. And when I had Bud drive him home, he vomited all over the backseat."

Bissell winked. "Now you know why we let him slip away. It was the worst thing we could wish on the Russians."

"Very funny," Alsop said. "Mark my words, there's one more still out there with a ticket to Moscow in his pocket. It was scandalous to let Philby go back to Britain."

"It wasn't us. We were onto him. It was that oaf Hoover who forced the issue, which is why the Brits recalled him. But even the Brits have left him in limbo."

"'Onto him'? Please! Our mutual friend Frank Wisner was his drinking buddy for years before any of you had the slightest inkling. Angleton too. They drank a thousand Albanians into their graves. But Philby gets to waltz back to Britain where they officially cleared him. So much for being in limbo! He'll be back in business in no time. A source of mine in Britain says he's been posted to the Middle East. Don't say I didn't warn you." Alsop waggled his finger at Bissell with theatrical indignation.

I should have kept my mouth shut, especially since Philby was more or less in the same business as me, but I couldn't resist showing off a little. "Philby knew he'd be safe in the land of Eden," I ventured.

Alsop raised his eyebrows. "You think it was Anthony Eden who let him off the hook?"

"Look at it this way," I said. "Eden went to the Geneva Summit thinking he was going to show Ike the ropes. But Ike's Open Skies proposal stole the show, even from the Russians. And they all treated Eden like some infirm, slightly senile acquaintance whom everyone affectionately patronizes but no one takes seriously. Now he's losing his grip on Suez but he's trying to pretend *we* need *his* help. Do you think he wants to officially announce that Philby, his liaison with American intelligence, has been feeding everything he knows to the Russians?"

"I would say we are losing our grip on Egypt as well," Alsop said drily.

I had hoped Alsop might respond that way. Alsop and I waited expectantly, giving Bissell every opportunity to supply the agency's latest thinking on the Middle East. "I'm sure it will sort itself out," Bissell said, looking down at Alsop and me with his lips pursed, reticently amused by our feeble speculations.

Alsop snorted. "The CIA's idea of sorting out the Middle East usually relies on assassination. The only place you're fully engaged these days is Eastern Europe. That's all Wisner can talk about. You've left the Middle East to the State Department."

Bissell reddened. "You'd like America to be in the thick of things, wouldn't you, Joe? Just wade in with the bombs whenever things don't go your way."

"Walter Lippmann tells me he is now quite afraid that the British and French will get together to do something rash in Egypt," I said.

"Of course he's afraid," Alsop said. "He's afraid of his own shadow. What a perfect alliance. France, Britain, and Israel all hate each other. But somebody will have to kick that tin-pot Nasser in the ass. He's now buying arms from Russia."

"He tried to buy them from us first," Bissell said. "And we agreed. Then Foster reneged. Allen tried to warn his brother he'd be giving the Russians a foothold in Egypt. The more trouble the Russians can make for us in Egypt, the freer their hand will be in Eastern Europe. If we want to put any pressure on the Soviets in Europe, we better keep them out of Egypt."

"Maybe Canada can solve the whole thing for us," Alsop said sarcastically. "Britain, France, and the U.S., their three closest allies, are headed for big trouble and they have no idea how to play it. But they think Lester Pearson ended the Korean War."

"Winston's Canadian," Elizabeth said helpfully. "Originally, that is."

Alsop and Bissell looked at me curiously, as if some odd little aspect of my identity had been revealed.

"Aha. Your countrymen—" Alsop began.

"*Ex*-countrymen," I interjected, sensing the need to put some distance between me and Canada. "I am fully and proudly naturalized."

"Your ex-countrymen are about to appoint a Russian spy as their ambassador to Egypt," Alsop declared.

"I wouldn't go that far, Joe," Bissell said.

"Oh come off it. Herbert Norman's another Philby. We've been onto him since 1942. We dug up the evidence, lots of evidence, but his own people cleared him. Then they warehoused him in New Zealand for the last few years. But now Egypt!"

"All it means is that Canada will be out of the loop as far as our intelligence goes," Bissell said.

Though no one else appeared to notice, I felt I was bathed in a brilliant spotlight. I stood there blinking stupidly for a few moments and then, before more attention came my way, I said, "I think I need another drink." I moved away, the spotlight still glaring hotly on my back.

11

Paris, Frankfurt 1949

I was leaving a cinema early one evening after seeing *The Best Years of Our Lives*, when I met Gardner Denby on his way in. I hadn't seen him in at least two months. We greeted each other enthusiastically but now Alger Hiss lay between us like a gulf. Even I couldn't miss Hiss's frequent appearances in *The Herald Tribune* as the accusations that he had been a Soviet spy transfixed America.

"I hardly go to the embassy anymore," I said apologetically. "I've been incredibly busy." McGowan had suggested that I drop the embassy from my social calendar while I was working for him.

"I haven't been there either, or to my own embassy. I've got a new job. I'm working for the Marshall Plan. For Harriman. We're over by the Place de la Concorde, refinancing Europe out of offices in a mansion where Talleyrand lived with one of his mistresses. Lots of hard work but also lots of fun since we're giving away money. And I'm engaged to be married! To a French girl, no less. Very good family. Or at least it was until she met me." He laughed, at once embarrassed yet extremely pleased with his outpouring of good fortune.

"I've got some news of my own. A volume of my poems is going to be published soon. Illustrated by Francis Picabia!"

"Winston! That's wonderful news, sport." He was so pleased for me that he embraced me, then stood back and took his measure of me, as if I had grown in his eyes. "I can't tell you how happy I am for you. Let me know when it comes out. I'll talk it up."

We congratulated each other on our fine prospects and went our separate ways. Gardner was the first person, aside from Maurice, whom I had told about the publication. It felt good to exercise my new persona as a successful poet.

I now reveled in my competence as a spy. Not that I ever was more than a courier, but it seemed to me I went about my missions with a certain élan. Occasionally McGowan would meet with me to review the schedule. It was an aspect of clandestine professionalism to alter the routine periodically. I always took advantage of the meeting to impress McGowan with my incredible memory of every detail of every trip. I even reminded him to have my credentials from *The Winnipeg Free Press* updated, which appeared to protect me from customs inspections. The other variable in the routine was the pickup of the package. I would receive a note from McGowan, instructing me to be at some café or public place where he would hand it to me. Or instead of a note I would find the name of a hotel and a baggage check.

Upon arrival in Frankfurt, I would take a taxi to Grüneburgplatz, instructing the driver in my rapidly improving German to wait for me. I would enter the huge I. G. Farben Building and make my way through the long halls streaming with soldiers to the Technical Support office where I would hand my package to Major Matthew Mason. After my third trip, Mason became familiar enough to ask, "Nice trip, kid?" Mason smoked incessantly, cupping his hand around his cigarette and dragging on it in tough-guy style. McGowan warned me to be very straight and proper with Mason. "If you get into trouble, he's your only contact there. But don't drop your guard. Those Army Intelligence guys have a chip on their shoulder because the CIA is running the show." Mason's office was run by a hulking NCO, who disliked me because I insisted on handing the package directly to Mason. One time Mason was out of the office and I sat there for an hour while the NCO glared at me. When Mason finally arrived he assessed the situation with a sardonic grin.

"Way to follow those orders, kid." After the delivery my taxi would take me to a quiet hotel called the Schwille. The hotel had a small restaurant and I almost never went out. After dinner I would read, sleep, and return to the train station the next morning. I was an efficient cog in a machine.

One day early in March, just as I was preparing my suitcase for a trip to Frankfurt, my landlady knocked on my door. There was a telephone call for me. Without her knowledge, I had given my landlady's number to a very few people. "It must be an emergency."

"I hope so," she said sourly.

It was Gardner. "I'm sorry to disturb you, Winston. I got this number from your embassy. Is there a chance we could meet? Soon? Today even?"

"Of course," I said. "Are you available for lunch? How about La Capoulade."

I was excited. I had sent Gardner a note after our last encounter, suggesting he might introduce me to the chief cultural officer at the American embassy. All sorts of U.S. literary figures were passing through Paris these days and I wanted to meet them. Just a week ago, Viktor told me the Picabia drawing was on its way and he was planning on publishing the volume in June.

Gardner was waiting for me. We made small talk about his impending wedding and my impending publication. As I had hoped, he offered to send my book to his successor at the embassy, who often dealt with visiting art and literary figures.

As we were having our coffee I glanced at my watch.

"You have an appointment?"

"I must be at Gare du Nord in two hours. I'm going to Germany for a couple of days." I couldn't believe I was telling him. "I have a boring assignment for a Canadian newspaper," I added.

"I see. By the way, have you spoken to your friends Viktor and Mara lately?"

"Not recently. I see them only occasionally. Viktor has some business with my uncle in Montreal. I have offered to help."

"Art business?"

"Yes, as a matter of fact. Why?"

Gardner twisted uneasily in his seat. "Something a bit unpleasant has happened. After that party you took me to at Viktor's place, he began to call me at the embassy. He was quite persistent."

I saw the need to distance myself from the Gregorys. "I'm so sorry. Viktor can be a bit of a pest, I suppose."

"It gets worse. He wanted to be put in touch with American visitors to Paris who were interested in buying art. He said he had access to art that had been liberated from the Nazis but had not been claimed. Masterpieces he said. Is that true?"

"I don't know about the quality, but yes I think he is well connected."

"Each time Viktor called, I put him off, mainly because I didn't have any responsibility for the care and handling of tourists. But then this couple from Florida arrived on the scene with pots of money and minor political connections. Their demands for special favors pissed off everyone at the embassy. A friend of mine at the embassy begged me to find someone who could help them buy art. They were totally suspicious of the reputable dealers he had suggested. They wanted bargains, though almost anything is a bargain these days if you have dollars to spend. So the next time Viktor called I gave him their names. This was just before I left to work on the Marshall Plan and I guess I didn't think it through very carefully."

"Did Viktor exaggerate his connections? He does boast but he also knows a lot of people."

"I'm afraid this went beyond boasting. My friend from the embassy called me this morning. He said it went well at first. Viktor showed the couple some paintings at a run-down warehouse. And they advanced him a good deal of money. But then things seemed to bog down. There were all these formalities. He said he needed more money to grease certain bureaucratic palms and they gave it to him. But still, no Watteau to take home to Florida. Then Viktor began to press them to invest in a play he was producing."

"Oh God, not that Romanian playwright!" Inwardly, I was feeling indignant: Why hadn't Viktor asked them to invest in *my* project?

"The couple finally complained to the embassy and someone made some inquiries. Luckily for me, it seems that Viktor dropped the ambassador's name instead of mine when he introduced himself to the couple. And my friend will cover for me since he was happy to see the couple get screwed."

"Screwed? Viktor may be a bit vague about the details, but I'm sure he'll come through in the end. You just have to be very firm with him."

Gardner looked at me in exasperation. "It's hard to be firm when he can't be found."

"Can't be found?"

"Disappeared. Viktor and his wife seem to have left Paris sometime in the last two or three days. They must have gotten wind of our inquiries. Evidently this has happened before: promises, difficulties, lawsuits. They'll probably turn up here again in a couple of years and act as if nothing happened. I hope you haven't done any business with him."

"Oh no. We talked about something, but there was no money . . . yet . . . I think." My head was swimming.

"That's why I wanted to see you right away, in case I could help you. And of course, to ask your discretion. I'm no longer at the embassy but it wouldn't be good if I were connected to Viktor." He smiled sadly. "Now you have two secrets to keep for me."

I don't remember paying the bill or even waiting for it. I just left Gardner at the café, and when I was out of his sight I began to run. With my suitcase in hand, I scrambled through the narrow streets to the Place Maubert. In the courtyard of Viktor and Mara's building I found a small pile of their furniture. A woman was picking through it, clucking indignantly at the many scratches, nicks, and tears. She had never heard of the Gregorys.

For once it didn't matter to me that I had to share my compartment on the way to Frankfurt. I was locked in my private world of bitter disappointment. My life in Paris so far seemed to have been lived solely in anticipation of the publication of my poems. I huddled next to the window and watched the landscape rush past. I awoke the next morning without any memory of falling asleep. An hour later we were in Frankfurt. I had the sense of moving in slow motion as I delivered my package to Major Mason and got back to the station in time to catch the return train that afternoon. I fell asleep again as soon as the train left Frankfurt. I woke up in the middle of the night. The train had stopped and was just beginning to move again, jerking forward noisily as it picked up speed. I recalled Mara's praise for my poems. How I could have been so oblivious? I had been Viktor and Mara's prey the whole time I knew them.

I had a moment of deep, sighing disappointment before I plunged, pushed over an edge, falling through space, falling from the last comfort I had. In an instant my poems became to me as spurious and contemptible as Mara had said they were good. I desperately tried to recall them but my wonderful memory played a cruel trick. The poems appeared now in my mind as the sum of all their versions and revisions, as shapeless heaps of meters, conceits, and epigrams. I rummaged through these jumbled piles, grasping at phrases and flinching at their pretension, at the lofty inspiration that summoned them and the swollen pride I took in their invention. As my train rattled across Europe, I mentally cast my poems away, phrase after phrase, leaves fluttering away into the night that swept past me like a black wind outside my window.

On that return trip from Frankfurt to Paris, as I discarded forever the vanity of my art, I realized that my future in Paris had become untenable, for there I would see pity and amusement in the eyes of everyone I knew. And what a pathetic little band that was. So few friends, so little experience; how desperately shallow was my grip on my Paris world. Even Gardner now suspected my arrangement with Viktor. *No*, I decided, as the train pulled into Gare du Nord, *I will never attend another cocktail party at the Canadian embassy. And I will never again walk to the Left Bank, for even the sleek gray-green Seine would disdainfully reflect my shame as I crossed it.*

From Gare du Nord, I headed straight to McGowan's hotel. He wasn't there. I flopped into a dilapidated chair in the hotel's sitting room where I remained for three hours, ignoring the curious glances of the chambermaid. It was evening when McGowan finally appeared. He took one look at my face and said: "Seems we have a problem." But he wasn't upset; he looked eager for action.

McGowan bounded up the stairs. I stumbled behind him. About halfway up he stopped abruptly and turned to look down at me. He loomed in the narrow stairwell as I cowered below him. "Didn't lose the package, did you?"

I shook my head and we continued. His room was pitch-black, and I stood by the door while McGowan fumbled and swore in the dark. Finally he found a little night table light on the floor and our elongated shadows danced around the walls and ceiling. McGowan and I moved various piles of clothes and suitcases to make a space to sit. The room smelled of stale cigarettes and unwashed laundry.

"Drink?" McGowan thrust a bottle toward me.

I waved it off. I had to say my piece quickly. "I've got to get out of Paris. I can't stay here anymore. It's come to an end. I've got to leave."

He stared at me and then shook his huge head slowly. "It's a woman. Some tart's got under your skin. Sorry, not a tart. Not you. You poetic ones go for complicated types. And you always get yourselves in too far." He sighed. "So you're quitting on me. Just when everything was clicking. I was beginning to think there was a future for you in the business. When do you leave? And where are you going? I bet you don't fancy crawling back to Mum and Dad in Canada."

I was glad to let McGowan believe I was unhappy in love; I could never have explained the truth to him. "I was thinking you might be able to help me."

"I can get a little extra money for you, if that will help. A bonus, so to speak. I've liked our arrangement. You're a gutsy little guy. Don't worry, you'll land on your feet."

McGowan reached out and patted me awkwardly on the shoulder. It wasn't much of a gesture, but it was the only consolation I would get from anyone. I choked up for a moment. "I'll have that drink now, if you don't mind." He poured me a solicitously large glass of scotch. I gulped at it and attempted to compose myself. "I wasn't thinking of the money, though I do appreciate the offer. I had this idea I might be able to do something for you. Somewhere else, I mean."

"What did you have in mind?"

A lonely, anonymous existence as a secret courier seemed to fit in well with my mood. "Isn't there some way I could work for you in another city? Another country?"

"Canadian intelligence doesn't cast a very wide net." He cocked his head. I intrigued him. A sensual smile spread across his garishly shadowed face. "I want you to do something for me right now. Name all the streets on the route between the Hauptbahnhof and the U.S. Army Headquarters."

"Do you mean the streets one actually takes or the cross streets?" I named both sets—going and returning to the station. McGowan toasted me and I toasted him back.

"Here's another one for you. Read *The Trib* today?"

"Downstairs while I was waiting for you."

"Then this should be easy for you. What was the lead story?"

I repeated the Berlin blockade story word for word. I was in such distress as I waited for McGowan that I couldn't remember actually reading the story; but there it was in my mind, like mail that had been delivered while I was out. McGowan went on to request several other stunts, including the SCNF schedule for all trains out of Gare du Nord; all the Canadian prime ministers as well as all the provincial premiers from 1867 on, along with their party affiliations; and all the stops on various Metro lines in Paris. After each feat, McGowan would refill our glasses. We became quite jolly—McGowan with the sort of pleasure a child takes in magic, and me with a desperate need to show off. Finally I said, "And now I'm going to tell you something you haven't asked for." I began to detail for McGowan the contents, or such contents as were visible, of a fascinating document that I had seen on Colonel Matthew Mason's desktop on my previous visit to his office. It took real work to memorize this material since it was upside down. The document described a number of East European Nazi supporters who had been captured by the Americans and whose future usefulness to U.S. intelligence in East Germany, Poland, and Hungary was under discussion.

When I was finished, McGowan made a low whistle. "Full of surprises, aren't you? I like that about you—easy to underestimate. They'll like this information in Ottawa. Not that they'll do anything with it; it just makes them feel good to know what the Americans are up to."

Boosted by the scotch, my emotions yo-yoed. McGowan's praise lifted me. I felt I had fought my way back from deepest mortification to redemption. I blinked back my tears of joy.

"You play cards? Poker?"

I shook my head.

"You're the type who's a sandbagger. That's a—"

"I know the word."

"Of course you do. You know everything."

"I know everything and I know nothing." I giggled. We were both getting drunk. I was, weirdly, more at ease than I had been since I arrived in Paris. With the anxiety of literary success gone, it was a relief to drink with McGowan. Despite his limited sensibilities, his physical self-confidence made him an easy companion.

"I'm good at collecting secrets," I said. "You know that couple who sometimes come to the parties at the embassy? The ones who are studying at École des Beaux-Arts? Well the husband is having an affair with the thin French-Canadian woman who always gets drunk."

McGowan laughed. Encouraged, I told him a bit more about the affairs and indiscretions at the embassy. At one point, in my eagerness to please, I mentioned Gardner Denby and McGowan pricked up his ears.

"I wouldn't want to *hiss* and tell, but when Gardner was in San Francisco . . ." Before I could blurt out his Alger Hiss secret, Gardner's imploring face loomed up in my mind and I hurriedly changed the subject. "I've heard you're a great expert on knife fighting."

"Oh I am, boy. I can make you a killer in ten minutes. Here, hold this." He gave me a small ruler. "Now the thing to remember is that the odds of your facing off against somebody who also has a knife are practically nil. If he has a knife and you don't, run. If you have a knife and he doesn't, make a first feint with the knife and then stick it in his gut, repeatedly if possible. In the unlikely event you both have knives, remember it's not a duel. Your big advantage is that you are almost certain to be underestimated. You still have to make the first feint, but with the hand that doesn't have the knife, as if you're trying to grab his knife. When he reacts, you take a superficial wound on your arm as you go in for the kill with your knife."

He used a hairbrush as his knife and we practiced killing each other for a few minutes. Even allowing for the scotch, my lack of physical prowess was obvious.

"Let me think about another job for you," McGowan said. "You're too smart to be a courier. Maybe there's something I can set up especially for your talents."

It took him a week, a week in which I more or less hid in my room, emerging only to grab furtive meals at the most dismal restaurants in the neighborhood to eliminate the possibility of encountering anyone who might recognize me. Twice during the week my landlady called me to her telephone to speak to Gardner and each time I refused. The third call was a summons from McGowan. After I hung up, my landlady suggested my life had become too complicated for her and perhaps I should look for quarters elsewhere.

"I'll be out in a week," I shouted over my shoulder as I raced out the door, desperately hopeful.

McGowan lay stretched out on the floor of his hotel room, his head pillowed on a rolled-up raincoat. He outlined his plan fluently, as if he hired people like me all the time.

I interrupted his proposal four times, each time with the same word: "Washington?" I was bewildered by McGowan's proposal.

"Washington, D.C."

"And all I have to do is live there?"

"Live and learn." McGowan seemed very comfortable with his proposal.

"Learn what? Just say it. You want me to spy for you."

"Definitely not. If you think of yourself as a spy, you'll behave like a spy. The Americans are our friends, right? No two countries could be closer. We don't want to know how they build their bombs or where their secret bases are. But they're a little bit nuts, our friends. We need to know what they *think* about Canada—that is if they ever think about us—and what they *know* about their enemies. Their enemies are our enemies, but they're often reluctant to tell us what they know about our enemies. Things haven't been the same between us since that madman Gouzenko defected and blew up the Russian operation in Ottawa."

It all sounded very benign. I had almost no specific instructions except to move to Washington, find a job, and see to it that I got into a position to be helpful. To me, this meant having a wide circle of acquaintances in Washington who would occasionally be indiscreet. I wasn't even required to make regular contact with anyone from Canadian intelligence.

"We'll be in touch with you when we think it's necessary. And we'll decide when it's necessary. Think of yourself as a kind of thermometer, taking the temperature of Washington. Every so often, we'll ask you for a reading."

"Will you be the one who contacts me?"

"Very unlikely. Though, to protect your identity, only a very few of my colleagues will know what you're doing."

"And what if it doesn't work out? What if I'm not useful to you?"

"Someone with your talents will get ahead. And we can be helpful. You may not even be aware of our intercession. We'll be offstage, so to speak."

"But still, what if I'm no use to you?"

"In that case we go our separate ways. It is possible you won't turn out to be useful to us."

"How will you know?"

"We'll know."

"How will I know?"

"The money will stop."

The money was five hundred dollars per month—a very substantial stipend in 1949. But still, just a stipend; McGowan was very definite about that. I had to find a job, preferably working for the U.S. government, and live my life like any other person. Aside from the money, only an occasional conversation with someone about the United States and Canada would acknowledge this unique aspect of my life.

"I'll promise you this, Bates. Some time will pass before anyone contacts you in Washington. Maybe a year or two." He handed me an envelope. "Here's enough cash to get you to the U.S. and get you started in Washington. You'll also find the name and address of a bank in Washington. Open an account there. Your monthly sum will be deposited automatically."

"What if I get into trouble or someone figures me out? What if I get sick?"

"Nobody's going to figure you out because there's not going to be anything to figure out. And don't spend a lot of time looking over your shoulder. When we need you we'll let you know. Someone will be watching you."

12

During my first two years in Washington, the sense that I had trapped myself would sometimes overwhelm me. My heart would pound and I would shake with frustration as I tried to think of a way out of my situation before the FBI discovered me. But in time, my recruitment in Paris took on a remote, attenuated quality, like a fading dream. The very implausibility of my situation—a spy for *Canada?*—became a kind of reassurance: If I could barely believe it, no one else would either. The longer that Canada had no use for me, the less likely it seemed that I would ever be useful. Of course there was the five hundred dollars that appeared magically in my bank account each month. But thanks to time's gift of equivocation, the stipend came to seem symbolic, like the tiny socks and bunting an abandoned baby holds on to for the rest of his life as evidence that he has come from *somewhere*.

All my rationalizations vanished that evening in Walter Lippmann's garden when I intuited the procession to Suez. For I saw Britain's and France's grasping after their vanishing colonial influence in the Middle East coming into conflict with the United States' fumbling but stubborn assertion of its own interests. And there of course was Canada, torn between England, France, and America, the three progenitors of its ambiguous identity. Canada would be desperate to defuse the situation, or at least know with whom they should align themselves. At last the astonishing foresight of having a Canadian sleeper in Washington was clear to me and I became possessed by a sense of personal destiny.

At first my vision of Suez had an abstract quality in my mind, like the inexorable working out of a musical theme. But then I saw the photographs, observed Allen Dulles's odd willingness to let his brother go on with his ineffectual diplomacy, heard about the recall of the current British ambassador, learned of the need to protect the pound. Disparate details perhaps, but they added depth and color to the daily black-and-white record of diplomatic posturing. As each evolving step of the Suez Crisis confirmed my expectations, I began to think of myself as the author of this disaster, whose final, triumphant chapter would be a meeting with my handler. After eight years of sleeping, I had dreamed my awakening. What life would be like for me after awakening was conveniently unimaginable.

So far, my watcher had declined to contact me. But Canada was now shut out of the intelligence loop in the Mideast. Why didn't my handler realize that I could loop him back in? Allen Dulles's account of my unfortunate KGB turncoat ought to have made me cautious about leaping into the fray. There he was, probably dead—in all likelihood tortured to death—while I was trotting around Washington stuffing my cheeks with crudités and swilling martinis. But in a splendid feat of denial, I had equated the consequences of my intercession in the poor man's life with the consequences of almost any other event in his life: his joining the KGB; his assignment in America; his willingness to be turned. By this line of reckoning, his birth was as responsible for his death as I was. No, I didn't feel vulnerable or even guilty; I actually envied him. After all, he had had a control and I didn't.

And so on the morning of October 19, 1956, I set off on a mission that any professional intelligence officer would have called ridiculous, improbable, and potentially disastrous. But in the grip of my sense of destiny, professionalism and prudence were not my strong suits. I was on my way to a diplomatic event at the Canadian chancery. The invitation, which had been sent to Senator Russell, requested his presence at a ceremony celebrating a treaty between the United States and Canada. It had been sent on behalf of the Canadian premier, Louis St. Laurent, which implied quite a high-level event. Security and intelligence officers would accompany the premier; they would certainly notice my name on the guest list. My plan, if you could call it a plan, was to circulate ostentatiously, offering myself to my clients, a whore for acknowledgment. I even fantasized meeting McGowan there and imagined his shock of recognition when he saw me, his beady, obsidian eyes suddenly piercingly intense, then a subtle, compliant bow in my direction.

The Canadian chancery, an imposing Beaux-Arts pile on Massachusetts Avenue, reminded me of the embassy I had entered nine years before in Paris. Fall was in the air; the first cool weather in four months had arrived. What with the convergence of the election, the Suez Crisis, and the Hungarian uprising, Washington was in one of its rare states of collective urgency. I wouldn't have to force the conversation to bring up the latest volley of Suez threats, counterthreats, insinuations, and evasions.

The first familiar face I spotted was George Ferver, my host at the Eastern Shore estate where I had first learned of Foster Dulles's contribution to the folly of Suez. He was standing in the vestibule with two other men. His face lit up at the sight of me. "Winston, so glad to see you here. And did, uh . . . ?" He searched behind me.

"I'm sorry. Senator Russell couldn't make it."

"No matter. Ambassador Heeney, this is Winston Bates, Senator Richard Russell's amanuensis, if I may say. Winston is one of those unrecognized insiders who make Washington work. And this gentleman, Winston, this is Paul Francis, Canada's assistant undersecretary for trade and business. He came all the way from Ottawa for this."

Unrecognized insider . . . was that how people perceived me? I couldn't have asked for a more inviting introduction to Canada. I began to scheme an allusion to my Canadian origins.

"Such an historic occasion!" Francis said. "I can't describe to you the sense of accomplishment we all feel."

I agreed the occasion was indeed important. In my obsession with making contact, I had neglected to inquire about the nature of the treaty we were celebrating today. I suddenly wondered if Ferver's connection might cast its importance in a dubious light. "Is it historic enough for the prime minister to show up? Or Pearson?" I asked hopefully.

"I know they wanted to be here," Francis said. "The prime minister sends his apologies, along with an extremely heartfelt congratulatory message that I will read. As for the foreign minister, this Suez thing is taking a lot of his time. Canada, it seems to me, is so ideally placed to balance the positions of the U.S. and Britain. And France too, for that matter. After Pearson's triumph in Korea, I'm sure they'll turn to him."

My own prescience about Canada's Suez role no longer seemed so exceptional. "Let us hope the U.S. *has* a position," I said sourly.

"Well, I'm sure we do," George interjected hurriedly, embarrassed by my cynicism. "But these things are tricky. One needs to create a mood of accommodation before approaching the sources of contention. If I may say, that was my modest contribution to the treaty we're honoring tonight. I brought both sides down to Spindrift, away from the distractions of Washington, and soon they were speaking frankly."

"You were the social director, you mean? By the way, just what treaty are we honoring?"

"You mean you don't know?" He looked at me with bewilderment while the assistant undersecretary frowned.

"I go to so many events. It slipped my mind."

"But this is in honor of the Salmon Fishing Pact."

"The fish? You mean this is all about a fish?" I had never heard of the Salmon Fishing Pact. No wonder St. Laurent or Pearson couldn't bother to show up for this obscure episode in diplomatic history. Frustrated and upset, I started to plot my escape, but George grabbed me firmly by the elbow and steered me into a large reception room filled with perhaps thirty chairs, less than half of which were occupied. My disappointment turned to dismay when I saw a podium and a long table on which several microphones had been placed.

"This setup is for today?"

"Do sit down. We've assembled quite a distinguished panel, Winston. We have Professor Larson, the maritime law expert from Georgetown, along with an economist from the Department of Commerce and his opposite number from Canada." Ferver looked about. "I am somewhat disappointed. I expected a somewhat larger turnout. Looks like mainly Canadian journalists and Canadian staffers. Americans are so parochial. If only they understood how this issue threatened the unique relationship between—Say! Aren't *you* originally Canadian, Winston? I should have told the ambassador."

As the speakers shuffled onto the stage and seated themselves behind the microphones, Ferver exclaimed how wonderful it was to settle a huge festering discord between the United States and Canada. The ambassador took the podium first to praise this major step in international law as well as U.S.–Canadian relations. The ambassador introduced the assistant undersecretary who repeated the ambassador's pleasantries and proceeded to fulsomely introduce a U.S. State Department official: "I give you the man who patiently, doggedly persevered to ensure the success of this treaty, the man who, when negotiations were at an impasse, brought everyone back to the bargaining table, the man who . . ." He went on in this vein until he was sure we were all poised on the edge of our seats in anticipation: "Ladies and gentlemen, Gardner Denby."

In frantic confusion I jerked my head about wildly. My world had flown out of control. Why had this happened? *What* had happened? From which direction would the next assault come?

When I returned to some sort of equilibrium, Denby was standing at the podium. He seemed remarkably unchanged, still attentive and engaging. He held himself tautly, as if alert to any nuance or implication that might float by. I was sitting three rows back from the podium. I kept my head down, hoping I was hidden behind the two men in front of me. After Gardner's brief remarks, everyone on the panel said his piece and then the undersecretary called for questions, most of which came from the Canadian journalists. Finally the undersecretary said: "Lest anyone think this is a dry exercise in diplomacy, you are all invited to stay for refreshments."

At the rear of the room several tables had been set up with a display of salmon in separate incarnations of poached, smoked, and cured; a giant bas-relief fish had been molded out of salmon pâté. Shining flutes of champagne bubbled invitingly. Afraid to leave, in case Gardner had spotted me, I downed three glasses of champagne, three slices of smoked salmon, and two spreads of salmon pâté. I was about to dig into the poached salmon when I felt an ominous tap on my shoulder.

"It's not possible," Gardner said as I turned. "Winston Bates. Here! Of all places!"

He attempted to embrace me but I had clutched my champagne glass to my chest in a self-protective reflex.

"Are you working here at the Canadian legation?" Gardner asked. "I can't believe I haven't run into you before. I've been in and out of this place constantly over the last month or two working on this damned fishing agreement. But you, sport, what would *you* of all people be doing working for the Canadian government?"

Three days after our encounter, Gardner and I met for a drink at the bar at the Hay-Adams Hotel. As I was explaining my job in Washington and my shift in national identities, the chief lobbyist for Lockheed lumbered up to our table, made a crude joke, chucked me affectionately on the shoulder, and departed. When the waiter came to take our order for another round of drinks, he informed us that Lockheed was picking up our bill.

Gardner was openly amazed. Periodically he would strike his head with the heel of his hand in a mock attempt to dislodge his previous conception of me: "And you've actually become . . . a powerful person!" My highly edited account of my years in Washington appeared to be the most interesting story he had ever heard. He kept his eyes fixed on mine, his mouth agape.

Then it was his turn. Thanks to his Marshall Plan experience he had been slotted as an economics specialist. After working in Paris for two years, he was sent to the U.S. consular office in Lyons as a business development aide. "Very boring, but oh the food, the food." He had arrived recently in Washington to await a new Foreign Service posting, but in Washington his career had stalled in a series of special assignments, the latest being the salmon treaty. "I hope to get posted back to Europe, France of course, but I'm afraid having a French wife has become something of an impediment to my career. This Suez thing has made people at State rather uneasy about my divided loyalties, even though Françoise has become a citizen. They know Françoise's family is quite highly placed in France. We have two children now, Antoine and Solange. Tell me Winston, do you still love terrible movies? I miss those evenings. We should do it again, just for old time's sake. One drops that sort of thing when children come along."

I listened to Gardner with half my attention while the other half was poised in nervous anticipation of a reference to McGowan. He started to recall the odd characters who would show up at the Canadian embassy receptions. There was no pause in Gardner's outpouring of happy memories. Sooner or later he would come to McGowan. I wondered if he was toying with me. Why hadn't Gardner mentioned that huge, striking man already, with his red hair and his irate little eyes?

"You don't really think your wife's French birth has made things difficult, Suezwise?" I asked to change the subject.

"Let's just say that I've felt pretty much like a pariah ever since Mollet started laying into Dulles. And you know, if I didn't feel a need to keep a low profile, I could be very helpful to the State Department."

I was taken aback; we had barely reestablished our relationship and here he was proffering gossip. "You mean helpful in assessing French intentions in the Suez?"

"Assessing French intentions! Everybody knows what their intentions are. It's whether they're going to act on those intentions. No, not whether, *when*."

"And you know?"

"Put it this way, what I know is that even as we speak—"He giggled at himself, rolled his eyes and repeated in a low, foreboding voice, "Even as we speak, the French, the Israelis, and the British are secretly meeting in a safe house outside of Paris. One can only assume they are plotting a joint strategy."

"The Israelis too? You're joking!"

"Absolutely no joke. Distant cousins of Françoise own the house. We've actually been there. It's in Sèvres. Really, Winston, I'm not joking."

"And no one in State knows?"

"Not yet."

"The CIA will find out."

"Eventually. Too late probably. But I'm not going to tell anyone. I just think that my motives would be suspect. Some sort of suspicion will fall on me, some sort of shadow, no matter what happens. I'll bet a few of my friends at the chancery would love to know what's happening in Paris."

"Haven't you been tempted to tell one of your Canadian contacts? You know, we're keeping them in the dark because Herbert Norman, their ambassador to Egypt, has a pink past. But Lester Pearson is aching to play peacemaker."

"Tell the Canadians? You have to be kidding, Winston. That borders on treason, more or less. But they'll be especially furious to discover they have been kept in the dark by Britain. So much for the Commonwealth."

"But you have told someone," I said.

"I have, haven't I?" he said. "You're a *someone* now, aren't you? And you're an American, so it's not really treason, just a gossipy secret. And where secrets are concerned, I'm sure I can still count on your discretion."

When he sat up and faced me with an odd, stubborn look I realized he was implicitly asking if his connection to Alger Hiss was still safe. Was that what this was all about, showing me how useful he could be to me as long as I kept his Hiss secret safe?* But was he also asking me to tell the CIA or the State Department about Sèvres? Perhaps, but then there was *my* secret. Could he be dangling some distant memory of me as a threat: "What about those mysterious trips to Frankfurt?" It was unlikely, but a man with his own secret might be sensitive to the secret in me.

"No need to worry, Gardner," I assured him.

We took our leave of each other with avowals of many future meetings and encounters. It was a relief to get away from him. Until Gardner

---

* Poor Gardner! Alger Hiss never went away. He kept asserting his innocence for decades. Any time Gardner might have thought it was all behind him, a new book or article would appear and once more the issue would be debated.

told me about Sèvres, I had been steeling myself to ask, ever so off-handedly, "And that red-faced, red-haired man . . . What was his name again?" And if Gardner had no current news of McGowan, I planned to delicately maneuver our conversation around to asking him if he knew McGowan's intelligence counterpart at the chancery in Washington. But once Gardner told me about Sèvres, I was staggered by the uncanny serendipity of possessing the crucial fact Canada would need in order to act before Suez ignited. Until my drink with Gardner, all I had for my watcher was my certainty of the inevitable conflict, but now I had a genuine secret to offer.

Over the next several days, events came to a head. Egypt, Syria, and Jordan placed their forces under a unified command. Israel began a massive mobilization of its citizen army. (Allen Dulles assured Eisenhower that Israel was going after Jordan.) In Malta, the British fleet now included three aircraft carriers, two cruisers, and sixteen destroyers, and shore leave for all officers had been canceled. The world's attention was also on Hungary, where a new, rebellious government was in place and the Russian army had pulled back. When John Foster Dulles said he "did not anticipate" sending forces to Eastern Europe, it sounded to me like an implied warning to the Russians to stay out. As far as I was concerned, it was all about me.

Late Sunday afternoon, October 29, I walked home from the trolley stop at Wisconsin and M Street on a cool, blustery evening. A negligently dropped newspaper had been scattered by the wind, some of its sheets swirling on the sidewalk in front of my house, the rest blown up against hedges or impaled on the prongs of the low, wrought-iron fences that surrounded nearby flower beds. I scurried about, muttering as I gathered the newspaper. Soon an ungainly clump of pages was tucked under one arm as I fumbled for the remaining pages. When I got my hands on the sports page, with its extensive coverage of the Maple Leafs, I realized I had been collecting the previous day's *Toronto Globe and Mail*.

Canada calling.

I tried to think of an innocent explanation. I walked to the next house and rang the bell of Malcolm Stanley, my English journalist neighbor. He came to the door looking blowsy and bloated, standing in his socks with his shirt half tucked into his pants. I must have made an odd appearance with crumpled sheets of paper sticking out from my armpits while my hands frantically waggled the sports page of *The Globe and Mail.*

"I'm afraid the postman must have dropped one of your newspapers. It's been blown all over the neighborhood."

He leaned closer. "What on earth would I want with a Canadian newspaper?"

"I have no idea. I just thought—"

"Not mine. Bad enough I have to read American newspapers. Sorry." He closed the door.

I went back to my house and rang my landlady's buzzer. Mrs. Trinker came to the door. A tiny, skittish woman, she was a landlady in name only; her brother, who lived in Chevy Chase, actually owned the building, collected the rents, and handled all the repairs. I showed her the newspaper. She thanked me for picking it up.

"Do you have any idea how it got here?"

"No. Unless . . . I wonder if it was that man! The one from the taxi who rang your bell. At least I think he rang your bell. He did ring your bell—I heard it. He could have dropped the newspaper."

"Can you remember what he looked like? It's important."

"He didn't steal anything, did he?" she gasped. "I really didn't get a good look at him. The taxi was waiting there on the street, three houses up from ours. Right by that linden tree. I noticed it when I came back from the market, about two o'clock. The man in the back was slumped over, like he was reading something, so I didn't see his face. I didn't think a thing about it until I heard your buzzer ring about half an hour later. I looked out the window and saw the man walking away from our door—he got back in the taxi and it drove away."

"Think carefully. What did you notice about him?"

"I only saw him from the back as he walked away. And from the side when he turned at the sidewalk. He was wearing a blue scarf—I remember the scarf. And a hat. A normal-looking man I'd say." She sounded tremulous and defensive.

"Anything else you can think of? Anything."

"I don't know. Was he a little shorter than you?"

"Was he?"

"I mean he was. But I don't . . . Is everything all right?"

"It's all right, Mrs. Trinker."

In my apartment I sat down to catch my breath and then sprang up again: The paper must contain a sign or a signal! I flattened the pages on my dining table and attempted to reconstruct the newspaper. When I found the front page of *The Globe,* I noticed a three-digit number in the upper right corner: 426. My first thought was that it was a date, but April 26 seemed very remote. Was it a code of some kind? Had some instruction to me gone awry? I walked back outside to the linden tree where Mrs. Trinker had spotted the taxi. At the base of the tree I found a small manila card sticking invitingly out of the mud. The number "87" had been rubber-stamped on it in large red numerals; at the top of the card "The Willard Hotel" was printed. The card was slightly soiled but it did not appear to have been sitting out in the weather for very long.

By the time I got to the Willard, it was seven o'clock. I repeated to the desk clerk the story I had given over the phone about emergency plumbing repairs at home, which explained my local address and why I had arrived so late and why I couldn't say, exactly, how many days I would be there. My story still sounded contrived and when I asked for a room on the fourth floor the desk clerk looked at me a little strangely. He assessed me in a quick, professional way—probably deciding if I was there for adultery or suicide.

As the bellboy escorted me to my room, I fiercely scrutinized everyone we passed, hoping for an affirmative scrutiny in reply. The Willard was a serious, old-fashioned hotel, with spare but correct furnishings. I sat in my room on my bed and took several deep breaths. From my suitcase I removed a smaller leather case that contained three heavy books. I took the case back down to the lobby and asked a bellboy to check it for me. He took a manila card, separated it in half, wrote my room number on the part of the card that he attached to the suitcase, and handed the other half to me. The card he handed to me was identical to the one I had found by the linden tree except for its different number. On a house phone I dialed Room 426 but there was no answer. I took a seat in the bar and checked the lobby every fifteen minutes. Two drinks later, a new bellboy had arrived at the station. I slipped out of the hotel, walked around the block, entered the lobby again and presented the check I had found by the linden tree to the bellboy. He disappeared into a storeroom. I could hear some discussion. He returned and said: "You must be the gentleman who couldn't find his check this morning. Wilson tells me we located your bag and sent it to your room." He looked at me suspiciously.

I let him see my key while covering the room number. "I was out most of the day. Just returning now. The bag must be waiting for me in the room. I found the check in my pocket."

I went back to my room, walking as slowly as I dared past Room 426, but I heard nothing. Now what? I had expected to receive something, a set of instructions or directions to a meeting place. I had the self-conscious sense of performing an imitation of a spy. I recalled the tradecraft terms that Roger Bennett used to sling about—cipher pads, dead drops, and Trojan horse operations. It had all sounded foolish to me, a pseudoprofessional game for overgrown boys. But it also provided a vocabulary for communicating with other players in the same game. I had entered a foreign country. The newspaper, the taxi, the checkroom receipt: together they constituted some sort of message. How could I write a sentence of my own in this language, an answer or countermessage?

I had breakfast in the hotel's restaurant, once more advertising my presence to my control. I dialed Room 426 again but there was no answer. At the office, I had the out-of-body sensation of hovering above my desk, watching myself pretend that I wasn't a spy. At midmorning, I called Larry. "Can you get your hands on those U-2 Mideast photos again?"

"Sure. There might even be a few new ones by now. Do you want to come over and look at them tonight?"

"I want to borrow them this afternoon."

"Hey now, hang on," Larry said, immediately suspicious. "I'm not so sure. I mean these pictures are like secrets."

"But I have clearance."

"What are you going to do with them?"

"Make sure that the right people see them. This could be good for you. But you can't let anyone know you've taken the photos. You didn't have any trouble the last time you borrowed them, did you?"

"Nope. Our job is to corroborate what the CIA thinks it sees. We don't do any independent analysis because no one cares what we think. We just file our copies away and nobody looks at them again. Nobody will know they are missing. Now that Trevor Gardner has resigned, there's nobody left at the Pentagon that Bissell will even talk to. We're just waiting for the CIA to screw up somehow. LeMay actually said that the other day. Still, I don't know if I can let the pictures—"

"It'll be okay, I promise. Why don't you meet me at the Willard Hotel at lunchtime? I'll be in the lobby."

"The Willard? Everybody goes there. What's wrong with your office?"

"Larry, you have to get it out of your head that you're doing anything wrong. I'm a security-cleared staff member of the committee that oversees the Pentagon. You're *supposed* to do favors for me."

"I guess."

I was too caught up in my connivance to worry about putting Larry in jeopardy. The next person I called was Elizabeth Boudreau. I mentioned my unforeseen unavailability this evening.

"Winston! You can't do this to me. I refuse to go to Dean Acheson's by myself. I can't stand those events. All they do is whine about the way they would do things if they were still running things. And Felix Frankfurter is going to be there. I've never been able to bear him. The dinner is in honor of some English newspaper editor who just arrived. Frankfurter's such a Brit sniffer he'll be drooling all over him. Acheson's the same way. Have you ever been to that little farmhouse of his in Sandy Springs? It's filled with more rustic chintz than all of Sussex. And all they'll talk about is Suez—as if that amounted to a hill of beans—and we'll have to listen to Frankfurter go on about Israel, which is even more tedious than his English obsession. Foreign policy all night. Your kind of party, not mine. The *best* thing about Acheson's dinners is that they ignore the women. If you stand me up, I'll never forgive you."

The possibility of a serious Suez discussion swayed me. Elizabeth agreed to pick me up at the Willard and to have her chauffeur at my disposal for the evening in case I had to leave Acheson's abruptly. I refused to explain, which only excited Elizabeth. I left the office at eleven thirty and took a taxi to Union Station. The newsstand had sold out of *The Globe and Mail* but I bought a day-old copy of *The Montreal Star*. Back at the Willard, I settled myself in the busy lobby and made a show of reading *The Star*, rattling the pages and muttering about the news. After half an hour, I spotted Larry striding determinedly through the lobby. I waved and he rushed over to me.

"I've got them. Let's go somewhere and I'll give them to you. Right away, okay?" He looked around nervously.

I was as nervous as Larry, but I was determined to receive the photographs in public. Larry feared everybody was watching; I hoped *somebody* was watching. Following my display of *The Montreal Star*, this delivery would be the decisive signal to my handler; not exactly a masterstroke of tradecraft, but I didn't know what else to do.

"Sit down and calm down," I told Larry. "You and I have every reason to be meeting. Now smile at me and make conversation. Talk to me about little Mark. Would you like coffee, a sandwich?"

"Just coffee. I don't have much time."

We sat facing each other across a low coffee table. Larry placed a flat cardboard box on the table from which he was unable to avert his eyes for more than a few seconds. He gulped his coffee and gabbed about Mark, Deborah, and the weather in California. In the midst of his stream of small talk he leaned forward, lowered his voice, and said, "There are new ones of Israel in there. We just got them back a few hours ago from Bissell's lab. The place went crazy when they saw them. We made copies for all the Joint Chiefs. I'm crazy to be doing this." He could stand it no longer. He slid the box across the table to me and stood up quickly, banging the table with his shins and rattling our coffee cups. He took a deep breath and spoke loudly, with affected aplomb. "I must be getting back to the office. Call me if you have any questions."

I went back to my room and called the front desk. I asked to be connected to Room 426.

"I'm sorry," the operator told me, "the party in that room has checked out."

I was stunned. I tried to visualize all my actions from my watcher's point of view. Had I scared him off? None of the clues and events that had brought me to this room seemed coincidental yet nothing would make any sense if there were no contact.

Larry had mentioned there were some new images. I bolted the door and sifted through the photographs. I didn't see any new ones of Israel, but there appeared to be several new ones of the Sinai Peninsula. In blurry black-and-white, they resembled images of distressed concrete walls. I couldn't tell what all the excitement was about until I came to one that had a big crayon circle around one area. After staring at it for some time I made out a thin dotted line snaking across the Negev Desert. It was the Israeli army advancing toward Egypt.

I had the ultimate secret now, and I could see Canada's interest in it clearly. With Israel on the march, Britain and France were about to attack as well. If Pearson knew what was going on, he could swoop in with a preemptive diplomatic strike. But there could be no more than forty-eight hours in which my information would be fresh and useful to Canada. Yet my contact had checked out. For the first time I wondered if I had it all wrong. Or to put it another way: What if it wasn't all about me? Perhaps I was just a little cog of tradecraft in some vast conspiracy. Was Gardner another little cog? I tried to fit his appearance in my life and the secret he imparted into some larger scheme. What if Foster Dulles's apparent ineptitude and rigidity was a highly evolved form of dissimulation, while his brother's detachment was similarly meant to disguise a great global coup for the United States in which Britain, France, and Israel swooped in and secured the canal while the United States simultaneously liberated Hungary? It seemed a rather radical gamble for someone of Eisenhower's stolid temperament but I was lost in a sea of supposition.

It occurred to me to sound out Senator Russell. He would certainly have been consulted if there were a great intrigue afoot. And if nothing else, he would be a reality check for me. When I got to the office he was gone, but he took my call at his apartment in the Woodner. I must have sounded frantic because he invited me to come by right away. He greeted me with a shy smile; he wasn't used to entertaining guests. The light in the parlor room was subdued. He had adapted a dining table as a desk and it was weighted with stacks of files and official papers. A brass banker's lamp cast a pool of warm light over the tools of his trade: a pen, his glasses upside down on a pad of writing paper, and a bottle of Jack Daniel's next to a small, half-full glass. He looked tired. His eyes were runny and red, his skin was pallid, and he coughed frequently. His secretary had told me recently that his doctor had advised him to cut back to half a pack of cigarettes a day. He sat me at a coffee table and fetched the Jack Daniel's along with a glass for me. He nodded firmly as he offered me a drink so I accepted. "This'll make a southerner of you," he said.

"I already am. Winnipeg's in southern Canada. We call it Jock MacDaniel's."

It was the sort of heavy-handed humor he liked; he laughed until he coughed. When he recovered, he said: "What are Allen and his boys up to now?"

"I guess that's what you'd assume since I asked to speak to you privately."

"It's something else? You're not in some kind of trouble, son? Is there some way I can help you?"

The genuine concern in his voice startled me; nobody in Washington had expressed sympathy for me in years. A momentary confessional urge whispered to me, but I shook it off. "No, it's Allen and his boys all right. The CIA should know that Israel is going to act against Egypt."

"Should?"

"They've been fooled, I suspect. The Israelis have led them to believe they are acting against Jordan and they still haven't caught on."

He looked at me incisively. "Did Allen or Bissell ask you to brief me?"

"Nobody asked me to. I'm not sure they see the problem in quite such a pressing way as I do." I kept waiting for him to tell me to back off, that this was a big strike by the big boys and it would all be clear to me in a short time.

"What makes it so pressing?"

"Well the Tripartite Pact says that Britain and France can act to protect Israel."

"I see. If they go into Egypt along with Israel, that will make things very difficult for Ike. You don't have any actual knowledge about Israel?"

"No," I said. "No knowledge." The box of photographs was in my briefcase next to me. If I took it out now, things could be very different.

"Or about Britain and France?"

"No. I'm just speculating that if Eisenhower seems indifferent, Britain and France will get the wrong idea and feel free to act."

"Well Ike's got a lot on his plate. He's in the middle of an election and things are heating up in Hungary, where Dulles promised to roll back Communism." Russell closed his eyes as if peering into the future. "It's true the Russians would love it if the old colonial powers tried to take back Suez. If we get tied up in the Middle East, it will give the Russians a free hand in Hungary."

As usual, Russell saw right to the heart of things and put me back in touch with reality: There was no great unfolding strategy; just slow motion dysfunction. But if Eisenhower knew about Sèvres, and put it together with the new U-2 images, he wouldn't be so phlegmatic. He would feel betrayed. And if Ike jumped on Britain and France right now, Canada would have little use for my special information.

"Besides, what leverage does Ike have over the British?" Russell asked.

"The British economy is pretty shaky. If the Brits start a war, they'll need Ike to support the pound. I don't think Macmillan, their chancellor of the Exchequer, has done anything to protect the pound and George Humphrey won't help unless Ike tells him to. He hates the British."

"Eden's useless but that Macmillan . . . there's a foxy one," Russell said cryptically.* He thoughtfully swirled his drink in his glass. "I appreciate your bringing me your concerns. I trust you're right. Winston Bates is usually right. But you can't expect me to go to Ike with just a theory. It's not my place. But if you should come up with any evidence you can come back to me. I'm happy to pick up the phone. I'm pretty sure Ike would take the call. But otherwise, as long as his hand isn't forced, Ike's gonna do nothin' nowhere."

I got back to the Willard with about thirty minutes to spare. I showered and whipped on my fresh clothes. I was beginning to feel frantic. Yesterday at this time, on the basis of a little manila card, I was sure I was on my way to contact my handler; now I sensed it was slipping from my grasp. But what if my handler came for me this evening? Maybe that was control's plan. I spread the images in a quiltlike pattern on my bed. My handler would know how to break into my hotel room. But how would I know if he had been there? If they wanted tradecraft, I would give them tradecraft. I plucked several hairs from my head and carefully placed them on the photograph of the Israeli invasion. I hesitated at the door. There was nothing of value to me in the room except for the photographs. I left the door unlocked and hung my DO NOT DISTURB sign on the door.

At an Acheson dinner, one was expected to offer well-informed conversation in a serious but spirited style. Tonight Suez and Hungary were staring us in the face and no one but I had an inkling that Suez had precipitated into an actual event. As for Hungary, I knew no less than anyone else. So there we were, excited and agitated, bravely launching our conversational gambits in the dark. Acheson had been out of office for nearly four years and his sources were not always dependable. But he still had complete confidence in his opinions, which he dispensed with forceful authority. When Suez came up, Acheson assured us that

---

* Harold Macmillan, chancellor of the Exchequer and an architect of Britain's Suez misadventure, neglected to protect the pound. Yet he was one of the few Conservative politicians to benefit, rising from the rubble of British foreign policy to become prime minister.

Eden would do nothing so exceptionally stupid as try to take the canal by force. The guest of honor was the editor of *The Sunday Times* of London, H. V. Hobson. Acheson was dismayed when Hobson's wife described Southampton Harbor as they embarked for America. It was teeming with warships and troop carriers of every size; she had no doubt that Britain was heading belligerently for the Suez. I was surely the only guest to know of Israel's involvement. Despite the urge to show off, I wanted to reserve my inside information for Canada.

The conversation kept lurching back and forth from Egypt to Hungary, where it appeared the anti-Soviet rebels were ascendant. Though he had little hard information, Acheson had no reluctance to size up the situation. When someone declared that the United States was obliged to support the Hungarian rebellion if Russia attempted to squash it, he shook his head sadly. "If we want Russia to stay away from Nasser, we'll have to concede the Soviets some autonomy in Eastern Europe."

Every time the conversation swung back to Suez, I pictured my bed in the Willard Hotel, the box of U-2 photographs resting on it seductively just in case my control decided to drop by for a peek. It was a reckless act but I was gripped by the breathless vertigo of a runner near the end of his marathon.

I had been suppressing the urge to speak all evening; and with each unexpressed thought, I took another gulp of wine. By now I was a little drunk and becoming angry: They were defacing *my* Suez with their blind speculations. Dinner was almost over yet Hobson and Acheson were still going at it. Acheson had begun by saying how he thought the Suez Canal was not worth a battle, much less a breach between America and Britain; he thought Britain should back off. Hobson, who was a strong supporter of Eden, attacked Acheson's position vehemently. To my amazement, Acheson began to give ground, finally conceding that Britain probably had some legitimate interest in securing the canal and the United States should back Britain.

We had all just risen from the dining table and were milling about before proceeding into the living room when I lost control and attempted to recapture Suez for myself. The effect of my standing and speaking loudly across the table in order to get Acheson's and Hobson's attention was to make my rhetorical question sound like an accusation: "And what would you say if it turns out that Britain and France have secretly colluded with Israel to manufacture an unstable situation in Egypt that they will together exploit?" Hobson turned red and began to sputter about the outrageousness of my suggestion. Acheson looked startled, pursing his lips so his mustache stood up like an array of porcupine quills. "Not only that," I went on, "what if Eden has steadily lied to Eisenhower and Dulles because he has all along intended to betray them?"

Acheson gazed at me thoughtfully and then glanced about the room until he caught the eye of his son-in-law, William Bundy, who worked for the CIA. They both knew where I worked. I was, in fact, a guest of Acheson's only so he could pretend his intellectual influence was extended through me to Russell. Hobson was demanding some shred of evidence for my views and Felix Frankfurter, who first had to ask Mary Bundy what I had said, joined in. If I was going to look like a prophet rather than a gossip I should offer some proof. I drew myself up. "Why, I'd like to know, when relations are tense, is there still no British ambassador present in Washington unless they have intended to dissemble all along?" It wasn't the most definitive piece of evidence but it was something Acheson would understand. There was a nervous silence. Most of the guests had turned to regard me from the other side of the table. I saw myself in their eyes: my concisely rounded body, my tailored suit, my eyes searching them sharply, demandingly, my hands clasped fervently before me. As we began to filter into the living room, Acheson and Hobson edged toward me, eager to pin me down. As soon as Acheson was close enough I shook his hand, thanked him for a delightful evening, and said how sorry I was to leave early, adding, "I've been summoned." I promised Elizabeth I would send Bud back with the car to take her home and hurried out into the cold and windy night.

My feet clattered through the nearly deserted lobby of the Willard. When the elevator let me off at the fourth floor, I rushed to my door and slipped into the room. I ran to the bed. The hairs I had positioned on Kuntilla and Ras al Naqb were missing!

Now what? I flopped down on a chair and tried to make sense of what had happened. On the one hand I was elated. I had accomplished my mission. On the other hand, what had changed for me? This was, to put it mildly, a tenuous contact. I suddenly felt alone and abandoned in this spotless, anonymous hotel room. I wasn't a professional spy; I was an inadvertent spy who had tried his best. I wanted someone to shake my hand and tell me I had done well.

I wrenched myself awake three hours later, blinking in the brightly lit room, my head thick and aching. With the grim clarity that a hangover affords, the futility of my presence here was overwhelming. I stuffed my belongings back into my suitcase and called the reception desk and told them to find a taxi for me.

It was nearly two o'clock when I arrived home. As I fumbled for my key, my phone began to ring. Of course! Home is where they would contact me. I reached the phone before it stopped ringing.

"Where have you been?" my sister Alice said. "I've been calling all night."

"Yes?"

"Lillian's dead. She died yesterday morning. She had a stroke. Dad's here with me and we're heading for Canada in the morning."

PART TWO

THE ARTIST

13

By the time I landed at Stevenson Airport in Winnipeg, the Canadian newspapers were proudly recounting the alacrity with which Lester Pearson had leaped into the Suez fray, ready to broker a ceasefire and a withdrawal. Surely this was my doing. Didn't I deserve some thanks? Or had I scared off control with this abrupt trip to Winnipeg? Perhaps they thought I wanted to come in out of the cold, to resign as a spy and live openly in Canada, as Burgess and Maclean were living in the Soviet Union. The Russians greeted Burgess and Maclean as heroes; my defection would have horrified the Canadians.

It was my father who really wanted to come in out of the cold; more specifically, out of my cool reserve. After Lillian's cremation, I endured three days in Winnipeg with Simon at Alice's request. Simon seemed to think that Lillian's death had annulled our unfortunate family history and he hovered over me hopefully while Alice did her best to abet a reconciliation. But I was immune to my father's aura of humble entreaty, which came to him all too easily. Simon Bates was a member of the mild-mannered English clerical class. His features were so perfect that were it not for his apologetic stoop and his watery eyes, one would have noticed his beauty before his meekness. When I was a child, he couldn't bear to argue with me, which only encouraged me to provoke him. If I made a pronouncement with which I hoped he would disagree— the obsolescence of the royal family for instance—he would surrender immediately, murmuring softly, "Ah, there you go," as if he never could have imagined such a compelling idea. Along with his desire never to oppose, never to offend, went a need to make the best of any circumstance, from the weather to my mother Lillian's volcanic temper. When she set upon my sister or me—a tiny red-faced dervish, spraying spittle and flailing at us—we would retreat to our rooms, fending off her fury as we mumbled apologies. Afterward, Simon would slip into our rooms, a plaintive smile on his face, and begin a supplicating patter of obscure ditties, pointless puns, and fatuous banter, sometimes capering before me in quasi music hall style. When one of us required an exceptional level of consolation, he would employ his repertory of hackneyed practical jokes—shorting my sheets, putting rubber bugs under our pillows, calling Alice on the phone and pretending that her order for one hundred badminton sets had arrived. This role endeared him to Alice. When Simon was the object of Lillian's wrath, he stood before her impassively as she frothed and slapped at him ineffectually, which made him a hero to Alice. I would have much preferred to be protected from my mother than cajoled out of my misery. To me, his japery and jokes were just pathetic bids for approval, as if he were the needy one, not me.

Now, back in Winnipeg, I tried to be civil to my father because I didn't want to disappoint Alice. With my mother dead and my father consigned to my arctic indifference, Alice was the only seminal connection I cared to maintain, but with Simon lurking over us, there wasn't much connecting to be done with Alice. The main thing that occupied my thoughts during my stay in Canada was my situation in Washington. I fixated on a montage of images: the scattered newspaper; the lobby of the Willard Hotel; me, brandishing the baggage claim check in my hand as if it were a talisman; the U-2 photographs splayed out on my bed. I would scour these images for the code or clue I had missed. The procession of Suez episodes and events, followed by my control's signal, had fallen inextricably into place, shackling me to my destiny. But without the last link, the chain I forged seemed a hopeless tangle of credulity and misinterpretation. What reason could there be for Canada to leave me in this position?

It is reasonable to ask why I didn't leave Washington, just quit my job, and reconstitute myself somewhere else. For one thing, I wasn't really unhappy, just disconcerted. For another, an abrupt departure might have called attention to my unrealized life as a sleeper. But as I look back on my distant self, I suspect the tiny, puzzled creature I see there at the end of my inwardly inverted telescope simply lacked a galvanizing vision of who Winston Bates might be in some other incarnation. In that failing, at least, I was not so different from a substantial part of the human race, those who stay in their deadening jobs or their miserable marriages out of inertia, out of the inability to imagine a more satisfactory life. Besides, my life as a sleeper rather suited me. The only way forward it appeared was to make the best of my abandonment. I couldn't exactly be an agnostic about control—after all someone had checked my images—but I would go forward *as if* my contact would never appear.

I returned to Washington to find I was a minor celebrity. In the leafy precincts of Georgetown, Chevy Chase, and Arlington, tales of my dramatically prophetic pronouncement at Acheson's dinner table were told and retold. My equally insightful appearance at Russell's suite had raised his respect for me. Others found the aftermath of Suez quite difficult. After laying triumphant historical claim to Sinai, Ben-Gurion was forced by Eisenhower to pull Israel's troops out. Eisenhower also led the United Nations condemnation of Britain and France and finally, as the pound was ready to collapse, forced them to withdraw from Suez. Anthony Eden resigned as prime minister. And in Hungary, within hours of the beginning of the Suez invasion, Russian troops and tanks moved into Budapest and crushed the short-lived revolution. Despite pleas from the Nagy government and from the CIA, Eisenhower refused to get involved. Only Canada came off well, as the acclaim for the way Lester Pearson defused the Suez Crisis resounded.*

Though Allen Dulles was hardly raked over the coals, his failure to nose out the plot hatched by France, Britain, and Israel contributed to a faint sense of unease with the CIA's performance. Ever alert to the bureaucratic climate, Dulles became unusually attentive to my CIA

---

* When Pearson was awarded the 1957 Nobel Peace Prize for his Suez accomplishments, I wondered if my early warning had made a contribution.

subcommittee, bombarding me daily with documents, queries, and invitations to exclusive CIA briefings. He even invited me to lunch along with Richard Bissell at La Niçoise, a dark little bistro in George-town with the right sort of reputation for indifferent food but attentive service.

The point of this lunch was quite obscure to me. No one had declared an agenda, though it was difficult to imagine both Bissell and Dulles tak-ing the time to casually chat me up. But there was an agenda, I decided, after noting the suave efficiency with which Dulles steered us through our choices of wine, food, and the first round of gossip. He was *being* Allen Dulles, flaunting his persona for a purpose as he had many times before while Bissell played an adroit second fiddle. I perked up immedi-ately. It was the first time since Suez that I felt the exciting sense of du-plicity that had buoyed me during my first few years in Washington.

Dulles and Bissell kept coming back to Russell. "Dick was tough on us over Suez," Dulles said after drinks. "But fair. We deserved some criticism."

"But he didn't go too far," Bissell added and we all nodded solemnly, agreeing that one more proof of Russell's genius was to let the agency off the hook at the right moment.

"How is your brother?" I asked Dulles. Foster Dulles had recently returned to work after being hospitalized for a cancer operation.

"Better, much better. But working harder than ever. We're sure that Khrushchev is under a great deal of pressure from the old Stalinists. A good crisis would fend them off. But Ike is yearning for some peace process to get started." Dulles smiled mischievously. "Thank goodness Foster's back in action. He'll piss off everyone and save us from peace."

There was a pause. Dulles tended his pipe musingly. Bissell folded and refolded his napkin. "Speaking of Khrushchev," I said, "aren't you afraid the U-2 embarrasses him before his generals? They could be a bigger threat than the old Stalinists."

"It's something we think about all the time," Bissell said flatly, im-plying that I wasn't supposed to think about it. "But it's not our job to keep him in power. Besides, a single U-2 flight offers more useful infor-mation than the entire clandestine service turns up in a year."

Whenever Bissell made one of his self-esteeming pronouncements I bristled inwardly. I didn't expect then that I would find an opportunity to amend Bissell's opinion, but looking back, I think that was when the U-2 seed was planted.

"He's very busy these days, isn't he?" Dulles finally said. "Russell, I mean. That civil rights bill must be a nightmare."

"He's always busy but this is something else—the South's last stand. The worst part is that Lyndon Johnson is in the office constantly, always working on another deal." I rolled my eyes and Dulles and Bissell chuckled.

Bissell looked to Dulles as if for permission and then said, "Russell didn't look well the last time I saw him."

Dulles and Bissell shook their heads sadly.

"I must say, Winston, you've done a terrific job of shouldering the burden while he's been preoccupied," Dulles said.

"First rate," Bissell agreed. "We appreciate the way you've seen our business through Armed Services. And of course your little subcommittee too." He grimaced.

"It's really not that difficult once you get the hang of it," I said. "Just a matter of keeping the rubber stamp clean and ready."

Before the moment of silence became awkward, I winked at Dulles and he burst into laughter. Bissell followed. They looked relieved.

"May I speak frankly, Winston?" Dulles said. "As you know, so far we've managed to fend off any attempts to wrest the CIA from the purview, the *sensible* purview, of Armed Services and give it to some other committee."

Bissell interjected one of his barking laughs at the absurdity of the idea. "Foreign Relations. Or worse!"

Dulles went on. "But we're concerned, what with all the demands on Russell's time—"

"And energy—" Bissell added.

"That such an initiative might achieve a serious level of momentum before we could do anything about it. We wouldn't want that, now would we?" Dulles smiled winsomely. He was really turning on the charm.

"Not us," I said.

"Your subcommittee seems to work so well. It would be a pity to have it . . . disrupted. For you too, I imagine."

"If we work together, we can help Russell through this difficult patch," Bissell said. "And we can help you. If we have confidence in each other, I'm sure your subcommittee can be an extremely powerful entity. As it should be."

"But we need to stay in touch. Informally. Even more than we have. We could take a great burden off Russell. Your very prudent concerns about the U-2, for instance, could be voiced in a more . . . shall we say *resonant* manner." Dulles leaned forward and grasped my forearm with great conviction. "And what a pleasure it will be to see more of you. I shouldn't wonder that you would feel more appreciated by us than by those dull southern boys in Russell's office. We understand that special gifts and proclivities need to be indulged."

So this is how it's done, I thought. I was being recruited to look after the CIA's interests in the Senate. They weren't asking for some profound transgression—just a subtle shift in my sense of obligation. I would be a bit franker with them about where they stood with certain senators and I would ensure that Dulles's pet projects, buried anonymously in appropriations bills, slipped through without undue attention. At first I was quite taken with the idea of adding another layer of fraudulence to my life. In this role, at least, I would know my handlers. I would also know a few more CIA secrets and my subcommittee would appear to have the agency a little further under its thumb. On the other hand, as the years stretched on, the agency's thumbprint on me would become indelible. As Dulles studiously broke his bread and sipped his wine and Bissell glanced about everywhere but in my direction, I considered my options: I could serve Dulles and Bissell; I could agree to serve them but not be helpful; I could agree to serve them and cover myself by telling Russell of the overture and then either help them or not. Russell was the problem. The other senators on the intelligence subcommittee were content to have me point them in the direction of their thoughts, but Russell's sanction only gave me freedom to do what he would have wanted done anyway. And covering myself by telling Russell about this proposal would make him suspicious of my close relations with the CIA no matter how little I did for them.

I thought carefully about my choice of words. "I know Senator Russell will appreciate your concern," I said as blandly as I could. "And in the event, should you need my support, I know I can be very helpful. I'm sure such opportunities will present themselves. But let's see what happens . . . in the event."

Dulles responded with a casual "as you wish" wave of his hand, acceding with a gentle hint of impatience. An hour later I sat at my desk in the Old Senate Office Building and reviewed my cautious evasion. I was pretty sure I had made myself clear. I had tried to say I would accept an understanding but not an undertaking: though I was not averse to going out of the way for our mutual interests, we would have to deal with such issues on a case by case basis. And I had allowed us all to pretend that nothing untoward had even been implied. I was pleased with my talent for being oblique and inexplicit. Another person might simply have said: "So gentlemen, we have an understanding but not an undertaking." But I was not that person. By speaking indirectly, allusively, I left myself room to maneuver. Someone like me, who did not know his purpose in this world, needed a buffer, a bulwark of nuance and implication. Another person—I imagined my counter-person, a gruff, hearty man with bushy eyebrows—might have grinned back in the face of Dulles's onslaught of charm and said: "You old rascal, Allen. You're not going to sucker me down the garden path with an offer like that." Is that not how such men speak to each other? But I was not such a man.

I took the offer from Dulles and Bissell as an affirmation of my post-Suez "as if" strategy. I had defended myself and emerged with their respect; but any advantage gained was for me, not for control, who would have been pleased to know the CIA thought of me as an asset. I would continue to look out for myself. Canada had used me and left me to founder; now, like a shipwrecked Robinson Crusoe, I would make ingenious use of the flora and flotsam of my desert island to survive and flourish. I took stock of my little island: my relationships with Elizabeth and Alice were thriving; my standing with Russell was higher than ever; my social circle was expanding; the defense industry respected me; and, thanks to Larry Boyer, I had a fish-eye view into the Pentagon. Finally, I possessed the essential tool that enabled me to cultivate this raw material: my indispensable memory. But what was in it for me? More than simple survival I hoped. At certain moments during the Suez episode, I was thrilled to hold history in my hands. It was only the prospect of contact with control that kept me from making what I would call a "creative" use of my secret knowledge. For instance, I could have told Allen Dulles about Sèvres. A little later in the process I could have shown the U-2 images of Israel's invasion to Russell and persuaded Russell to contact Ike. In either case, I would have changed the way the event unfolded. The prospect of intervening in the meandering course of history was an irresistible challenge to an isolated castaway. I didn't want to act with godlike powers to "own" the event or to judiciously save the world from folly. Nor was I interested in being a malign force simply for the sake of being malicious. It was more the idea that my own little daubs could indelibly color the canvas of history.

It was at that time, as I became comfortable with my new way forward, that a threat to me and to my future in Washington arose. It came from such an unexpected direction that I did not at first recognize it as a threat. My relationship with Elizabeth Boudreau had seemed to be evolving into something closer to friendship. And that was fine with me since I didn't have any other friends in Washington. The sex had become less frequent and, to tell the truth, my performance was no longer so dependable, though Elizabeth didn't seem to mind as long as her own pleasure was attended to in some manner. But at least twice a week, after attending an event together, one of us would call the other and we would have a hilarious session gossiping about the flaws and foibles of our fellow guests. I wouldn't say the relationship had deepened but it had become more casually familiar. I anticipated more intimate confidences would follow. There had to be a hidden neediness, some pain or emptiness in her life that I could address. But Elizabeth was perfect in her restraint. When we did have sex, it felt like a light aperitif before the main meal, which was always a social event. Yet I found myself oddly attracted to her mysterious circumspection and looked for some way to move the relationship to a more meaningful level. All I needed would be a sign from Elizabeth to let my ardor flow and I remained on hopeful alert.

On the phone one evening, after we had ripped apart Paul and Phyllis Nitze, Elizabeth said, "Winnie, you know Evangeline Bruce is having a dinner next week . . . ?"

"I didn't know. Are we invited?"

"No but Oatsie is and you know we all love her . . . ? Well her husband is unavailable and she asked if she could borrow you. I know it's somewhat late . . . but as a favor to me . . . ?"

That put me in my place. So much for imagining I could be anything but a useful appendage to Elizabeth. I could have refused, but good soldier that I was, I escorted the wealthy and socially top-drawer Oatsie Charles to Evangeline Bruce's dinner. Oatsie's unavailable husband, Thomas Leiter, was a CIA operative, which at least offered the prospect of some indiscreet gossip. Most of Oatsie's tedious conversation was about her Newport home, but she kept coming back to my work for Russell and whether I had much to do with Lyndon Johnson as well. Johnson, by then majority leader, regarded Russell as his mentor and was extremely close to him. Though I saw a good deal of Johnson, I didn't have anything to supply of a personal nature and would have been very careful even if I had. Oatsie was either after something or was trying to hint at something. The next morning I phoned Elizabeth to review the party. I mentioned Oatsie's interest in Johnson and suggested, suggestively, that Oatsie might have some personal interest in Johnson.

Elizabeth giggled. "That Oatsie! She just couldn't resist probing, could she?"

"What was she probing about?"

"About you, me, and Lyndon, of course."

"What do we have to do with Lyndon Johnson?"

There was a long pause. "Do you mean that you have never . . . ?

That no one has ever . . . ? After all this time, I thought you understood. Lyndon and I have been seeing each other for several years now.
Winnie . . . Winnie . . . ?"

"I'm here . . . more or less. '*Seeing* each other'?" It wasn't exactly
"seeing" that I pictured but rather the delicate, small-boned Elizabeth
quivering like an expiring insect beneath the huge grossness of Johnson. "And he's married."

"Really Winnie! What does that have to do with it? Once or twice a
month he comes over when he can get away. And I don't flatter myself
that little me is enough for Lyndon. That man is all appetite." She giggled again. "But seriously, Winnie, everything has fallen into place.
With you and Lyndon my life is perfect."

Now I had really been put into my place. I did not recognize this as
a threat, yet, but it seemed rather bold of Oatsie to speak to me in this
knowing way about Johnson. What did she imagine my relationship
with Elizabeth was like?

Then came the penultimate threat. Dulles called me to ask a favor, a
little extra money moved into the director's discretionary fund. He spoke
to me in a preemptory tone, as if I *had* agreed to do his bidding. When
I said I wanted to check with Russell he became annoyed. "Really, Bates,
I'm merely asking you to move a few dollars from one account to another. No need to disturb Russell." He hung up abruptly.

What had I missed? I went over our lunch in my mind. I had taken
Dulles's facile sympathy for my isolated position in Russell's office as
an offer of institutional camaraderie, an encouragement to identify
with a CIA that had more room to "indulge" people like me, people
with my "gifts"—by which I understood he meant my memory. And
then there were my "proclivities"; what did he mean by that? I pictured
the way he had paused, his lips pursed fastidiously, before saying "proclivities." A key turned in a little drawer in my brain—the drawer labeled
"Denial"—and out popped the memory of several incidents whose implications I had preferred to ignore. There was, for instance, Elizabeth,
after Walter Lippmann's party, remarking that it was not necessarily
bad for me to have people think that she and I were having an affair.
More explicitly, there was the time I rejected Robert Cage's invitation

to sleep with him and he said: "If *I* made this mistake, imagine what everyone else must think."

I had not recognized Dulles's allusion to my proclivities as black-mail because, of course, I wasn't homosexual—though given the attenuated nature of my sexual life, having any sexual identity was a rather technical definition.

I wondered if this view of me was widespread. In those days, especially in Washington, speculation about sexual identities wasn't an appropriate subject of dinner table gossip. The insinuation would more likely spread as a kind of shared assumption, a raised eyebrow, a veiled intimation, which the knowing would recognize. For some people, my life as a bachelor who squired a wealthy woman around town was evidence enough. I'm sure that's what Oatsie Charles assumed. But there were probably plenty of other people who, if they were not directly confronted with an accusation, would never imagine that I could be capable of such behavior. I was pretty sure that Russell would never make such an assumption, nor even understand the subtle innuendos of others. Dulles, having let the innuendo out, probably figured I was in his grip despite my equivocal response.

And then, a few weeks later, came another attack. One day at the office, one of Russell's moronic legislative assistants was exclaiming over some astonishing gridiron triumph of the University of Georgia. He dismissed my barely polite show of interest by saying "I guess football isn't your cup of tea." He made a fey charade of drinking a cup of tea, pinky extended. Now I knew I had to take the threat seriously. Sooner or later someone who had it in for me, or saw some advantage to bracing Russell with "the facts," would speak to him man to man. Russell would be appalled and disgusted. Russell was himself a bachelor, but he was an old-fashioned southern *man,* the sort you could never imagine as homosexual, while, I had to admit to myself, it was at least imaginable for someone with . . . well, with my gifts and proclivities.

Yet I wasn't dismayed. With my island refuge under attack came a nervous yet eager sense of anticipation. I was facing a creative problem: how to socially reconstruct myself to fit within the conventional definition of 1950s American manhood. Clearly Elizabeth and I had failed to convince anyone we were lovers, including ourselves. Successful sex with Elizabeth had sometimes required me to close my eyes and pretend she was Paulette, my "schoolgirl" prostitute. But lately, when I closed my eyes with Elizabeth, it was Johnson who lurched into view and whose priapic presence unmanned me. As I turned the problem over in my mind, I attended my cocktail parties and receptions in a state of detached hypersensitivity, acutely aware that now I was not what people took me for *twice over*. Yet in that excited state of self-consciousness, I exercised my social talents with an ostentatious fluency that could only draw more attention to my ambiguous identity.

A few days after the teacup assault, I took a call from Merrill Appleton, the chief lobbyist for Convair, and agreed to bury seventeen new words in the depths of the Air Force appropriation bill, a benefit to his employers of about two million dollars per word. Appleton had been expecting a much more difficult and perhaps fifty percent less successful process.

"I was sure you saw it our way, Winston, but to cut through the ridiculous red tape this way . . . I can't tell you how grateful we all are. I promise you this, the Atlas program will move along a lot faster than anybody imagines. I can't express how much I value our productive, productive relationship. And please, if there's anything I can do for you . . ."

At that moment I saw my opportunity. "You know, Merrill, just because I didn't accept your first six invitations, you shouldn't assume I *never* wanted to visit your hospitality suite. As it happens, my plans have fallen through for this weekend."

For a moment he paused, measuring the thirty-four million dollars against whatever personal or family plans he had made for the weekend. "This weekend? Absolutely! Friday? Saturday? Saturday can be a very . . . shall I say *entertaining* evening at the suite. When can I pick you up?"

Every important business or trade group had a hospitality suite tucked away somewhere in Washington to entertain those of us with our hands on the money spigots or the regulatory levers. The lobbyists were constantly offering me invitations, which I almost never accepted.

Most of these places were just hotel suites that were pressed into service for occasional parties or to host important guests for a very private drink. Others were more permanent and elaborate, dressed up like nightclubs and elegant salons. The clubs and suites drew on the huge abundance of young single women who came to Washington to work. As invited guests or paid hostesses, they were there to set an entertaining tone for the powerful men of Washington. The well-prepared lobbyist always knew which of the hostesses would accept special assignments for extra pay. The testosterone-fragrant money jungles of Washington would be the perfect place to begin to refashion my identity. At that first night at the Convair hospitality suite, I managed to give a good imitation of being one of the boys, though I hardly believed that I was going to change any perceptions about me in a single night.

Proving my heterosexuality became a rather isolating and discouraging venture as I went from suite to suite, from the faux English pub of the American Tool and Die Association to the cocktail lounge of Ashford and Abelow, the powerful law firm. Though I swaggered and swore, I realized I would not become one of the boys until I went home with a few of the girls. It would have been easier if my goal was just sexual satisfaction instead of its signification, but I was too self-conscious. No matter how I swaggered, there was something about me that didn't encourage even the slimiest of lobbyists to offer me special favors. Nor was I adept at seduction. On my rounds with Elizabeth Boudreau I was a gushing fountain of banter and charm. But face-to-face with a breathless government grade-two assistant, I retreated behind awkward small talk. Inevitably her eyes began to wander. On the other side of the room she could see the rollicking duo of Senators Kennedy and Smathers, trolling for playful young women. Soon I was alone.

It was little wonder I was diffident: my sexual experience was so limited. It was Paulette, with her knowing hands and mouth, who defined most of what I found compelling about sex. I feared I had been so sexually imprinted by Paulette that I could not perform normally. There was something un-American about asking a pert blond secretary to the assistant attorney general for Labor Relations, three years removed from her high school choir, to coat my body with talcum powder, much less don a convent school uniform while she was at it. And what if she gossiped about these decadent desires?

And then I met Fay at a sedate event at the Cotton Growers Association. Or rather she met me, because she came right up to me and said, "You a cotton guy?"

"No, I'm an Armed Services guy. But my senator has Agriculture in his portfolio."

"I could tell you were different," she said.

When she did not immediately ask the name of my senator, I knew she hadn't been around Washington very long. She wore a slightly gaudy party dress, which seemed to hang on her tall, lanky figure. She had a narrow, sharp-featured face and circles under her dark, expressive eyes. She worked as a waitress at a downtown luncheonette on Sixteenth Street.

"You mean I'm not like all the others," I said, trying clumsily to get things to a suggestive level.

She shrugged. "Sort of. Wouldn't know much about the others. This is the first party in Washington that I've gone to. One of my regulars at the luncheonette told me to come. What's it for?"

"We're celebrating the passage of the Agriculture Appropriation Bill. What's different about me?"

"Don't get me started on something like that or I'm gonna say the wrong thing for sure." She looked at me thoughtfully. "All right, you're not smoking a cigar. That's different."

Not that I had ever refused a cigar at one of these events, then strutted around with the reeking monstrosity clenched in my teeth. "Don't ever go to the Tobacco Institute's suite. It's a forest of cigars there."

"At least no one's got a wad in his mouth," she said, which turned out to be high praise. Fay was more or less in flight from chewing tobacco, as it defined most of the men in the small West Virginia town she had fled, including the one she had been married to before she picked up and left. She was working at the luncheonette while trying to study for a Civil Service exam.

"Now I understand why I'm different," I said.

"You're a cute little thing. I saw you standing there looking like you didn't really want to be here."

"I didn't know it showed."

"Well I knew soon as I walked in that I didn't want to be here. So I thought I'd talk to you. You're not here with anyone are you?"

"No. So why did you come here?"

She looked at me with amused annoyance. "Hey you, don't make this hard. You're supposed to say, 'Let's get out of here.'"

"I was going to get around to that," I said defensively. Because this was happening *to* me, I was momentarily flummoxed. Did she really intend to go home with me?

Fay gestured impatiently. "We going?"

I looked around. Among the celebrants were three people I knew reasonably well including Fred Breamer, a legislative assistant to Senator Byrd, who was standing near the door. He was as important a specialist in farm price supports as I was in intelligence, and he was a close friend of a couple of my nemeses in Russell's office.

"Okay, we're on our way." I took her by the elbow and sauntered to the door, pausing by each of my acquaintances to bid farewell. When we got to Breamer I could see the surprise in his eyes.

In the elevator Fay said, "What was that about, mister? You don't believe in getting out on the sly?"

I still didn't quite believe this was happening to me and we stood on the street until she finally said: "So where do you live?"

"In Georgetown."

"I've only been there once."

A taxi pulled up. It disgorged Robert Kerr and Bobby Baker and we got in.

Fifteen minutes later we were at my place and fifteen minutes later we were in bed. Fifteen minutes later she said: "You know, I went to that party because I was horny. It's been over four months, but one look at those men and I knew I didn't want to go home with any of them. I never saw so many fat men in one place. Then I saw you," she said proudly, as if she had bagged me. "I like it that you're smaller than me. You're also kind of hairy and you're real energetic. It was like being fucked by an animal of some kind." She patted my arm. "A *nice* animal. It was different, it was . . ."

"Exotic?" I suggested hopefully.

"That's it."

"You want exotic, I'm also Jewish," I said.

Her eyes widened. "No kidding! Let me see that dick. You didn't give me much time to check it out before." She nodded thoughtfully as she inspected my penis. "Not many Jews where I come from."

"To be honest, I'm actually half Jewish."

"Well it's a good thing they didn't do half a job on your dick."

I glanced at her in surprise and she grinned. Emboldened, I said: "You want more exotic?"

She looked puzzled as I handed her a container of talcum powder.

"That was fun," she said later, without much conviction.

"Let me take you home. Or you can stay."

"You don't have to. Call me a cab."

Over the next three months Fay and I left together from the Tool and Die Association, the Trucking Association, and the American Bankers Association, among others. It didn't take long for the innuendos at the office to stop. I worried sometimes about word of my doings getting back to Elizabeth, but there seemed to be an implicit pact of discretion in which you enlisted when you attended these places. But the news of my ascendant heterosexuality must have filtered back to Dulles, for he never alluded to my proclivities again. As for my proclivities, it seems churlish to complain about the sex with Fay. It was satisfactory enough, better than with Elizabeth, but never as plangent as my memories of Paulette. Fay had a wiry strength; her hands seemed to squeeze rather than stroke, and when she wrapped her arms and legs around me I felt enveloped. Three years later, when Fay got a Civil Service job and a steady boyfriend, we stopped seeing each other. By then my reconstructed sexual identity had been secured.

14

In the summer of 1957, I engineered a move from my pleasant office near the other legislative assistants to a tiny, windowless space off the outer office in Russell's suite. With my door open, I had a view of Russell's two secretaries. The legislative assistants teased me about my new location, suggesting I was now an adjunct to the secretarial staff. The office's high ceiling gave it the feeling of a generously proportioned telephone booth. I had the walls painted a deep rich maroon and decorated them with architectural prints of Washington in its formative years: a copy of L'Enfant's original plans for the city and several of Latrobe's drawings and sketches of the Capitol, including his three-domed version.

One day Gardner Denby dropped by the office and surveyed my embellishments with an amused smile. "Do you think the effect is too antique?" I asked. "Too antic, if you ask me, sport," he replied. Clever Gardner saw the thread of irony twisting through my display of unrealized plans from Washington's past. The advantage of my new office was my view of everything and everyone passing through Russell's office. Russell's office was the most important one in the Senate in the waning years of the Eisenhower administration and Russell increasingly relied on me to keep him oriented. His trust in me had increased in the aftermath of Suez.

"Suez happened just the way you called it," Russell had complimented me.

"Thanks, but everybody should have known what was going to happen. It's just that no one acted."

"Except the Russians," he grumbled.

"You were the one who saw how they could exploit Suez to squash the Hungarian Revolution while the West got blamed for being colonial aggressors in Egypt."

Russell scowled. "If Ike had been quicker on his feet we might have had more leverage in Hungary. But the Russians were too fast for us. What was Allen doing? Next time, son, you push me to call Ike."

"Fighting and food, that's what it's all about," he once said to me. That was what he got out of his interest in history: simple, efficient precepts for setting the events of the day in context. If they cohered into a grand vision at all, it was in his dispassionate acceptance of human nature as base and brutish—except of course for the tragic nobility of the Confederacy. For all his power in the Senate, Russell would never have a national audience; his unswerving support of segregation made him seem a regional figure. Though he wouldn't abandon his views, he recognized he was a dinosaur; and so he had designated Lyndon Johnson as the hope of the South and took every opportunity to promote him. He and Johnson engineered the Civil Rights Act of 1957. Russell received credit in the South for rendering it toothless while Johnson took credit in the North for passing the first general civil rights legislation since Reconstruction.

Gardner's latest assignment was as the State Department liaison to the International Geophysical Year, which left him with a good deal of free time to drop by my office as well as climb his way up the social ladder. There I would be, nattering away with Elizabeth Boudreau at a numbing reception for the new head of the USIA, and suddenly Gardner would be in my face, smiling and chattering with his ever more pliant charm. I didn't regard him as a threat, exactly, but I was always on the alert, expecting him to bring up our cocktail days in Paris, to say ever so nonchalantly, "And do you remember that tall, stupid man, the one with the red hair? What was his name?" But since our reunion in the Canadian chancery, Gardner had not mentioned Paris. No doubt Gardner was waiting apprehensively for me to mention Alger Hiss, who still surfaced periodically in the news as he continued his pyrrhic quest to clear his name.

Russell's response to the current national mood of indecision and meandering optimism, which he blamed on Eisenhower, was to work harder, as if he could carry the country on his shoulders. After long hours of committee hearings, he would often wander into my office when I worked late and let me catch him up on the doings of the day. And that is why he happened to be standing in my office when the phone rang on Friday evening, October 4, 1957.

"You're there," said Gardner Denby. "I was afraid this was one of your Spindrift Farm weekends with the Fervers."

"It is. But I had some work to do with Senator Russell. I'm catching a train first thing in the morning."

"*Senator* Russell? How formal! He must be standing right there in your office."

"He is."

"Perfect. It will save you the trouble of calling him after you hear what I have to say. I'm calling you from a phone outside the Russian embassy." Gardner paused for dramatic effect.

"You're defecting," I said, "taking with you all the secrets of the U.S.-Canadian salmon pact."

"Marvelous, Winston. I was invited to the embassy because of my assignment with the Geophysical Year. The Russians are honoring all the major scientists involved. And barely ten minutes ago, we raised our little vodka glasses on high and toasted the Soviet Union's amazing feat of launching a satellite in orbit around the earth. Whatever that means."

"It means it's going to be a long weekend in Washington. Thanks for calling me." I hung up and gave the news to Russell.

"They beat us to it. Damn it! Goddamn it!" This was as expressively angry as Russell ever got. "I give those Pentagon imbeciles all the money they ask for. I support them when they screw up. But that fool Charlie Wilson couldn't feed the horses in the cavalry. I've never been so glad to see someone leave government service in my life. There must be half a dozen separate rocket and missile projects going on. And the missile people don't talk to the rocket people and the Air Force missile people don't talk to the Navy missile people. Just because he ran General Motors, Wilson thinks he can run the Defense Department as if it's a collection of car divisions."

"When we do get a satellite launched it will probably have chrome trim and automatic windshield wipers."

Russell snorted. "That's a good one. You don't mind if I use it when I get asked for a statement?"

"That's what I'm here for. It's all yours."

"Oh, we're going to really hear it now from Khrushchev. You just wait. He hasn't said a word about the U-2 because he can't do anything about it. But now he's put one over on us and he's going to crow. I can't believe Allen Dulles and his boys didn't know this was coming. As I recollect, it takes a pretty big rocket to get a satellite up in the air. If the CIA had warned us, we might have had a chance to jump-start our own satellite."

"They did warn us . . . sort of. When the U-2 spotted that rocket on a launchpad in Tyuratam last summer, they suggested that it might be part of a satellite program, but no one could believe the Russians were capable of launching one, even with the evidence staring us in the face. It wouldn't have made any difference. The Navy's Vanguard program isn't even close. And that's the one we've been counting on."

Russell winced in disgust. "Get hold of Bissell and see what he knows about the satellite. This should take him off his high horse. I hope you're available this weekend in case I need you."

I tried to call Bissell but the night operator at the CIA couldn't or wouldn't find him for me. I canceled my weekend plans with the Fervers. Of all weekends, this was one that I had been particularly interested in being somewhere other than Washington. A big U.S.-Canadian trade parley was slated to begin on Sunday. The new prime minister, John Diefenbaker, and his retinue would be swarming all over Washington. Elizabeth Boudreau had landed Diefenbaker for a dinner tomorrow night. She had assumed my eagerness to take my Canadian identity out for a spin, but I was doing my best to ignore it these days. When I declined her invitation, she was indignant.

On Saturday morning, Russell called and sounded impatient with me when I told him Bissell hadn't returned any of my calls. I decided to get around Bissell by cornering Dulles, who was on Elizabeth's guest list tonight along with Diefenbaker. I begged Elizabeth to reinvite me.

"Oh you Washington men and your mysterious emergencies," she twittered sarcastically. "But of course you can come for dinner."

"Are you sure you don't mind?"

"Not at all. There will be at least one extra place. Allen Dulles has canceled."

At the party, everyone was delighted to have the satellite to talk about, though a bit nonplussed by the thing itself. I heard Joe Alsop blurt out: "But what keeps the damn ball up in the air?" I noticed Gardner Denby waving to me from the other side of the room. It had taken just two months after I introduced Gardner to Elizabeth for him to insinuate himself onto her regular guest list. He was at my side in fifteen seconds. "Winston, my dear, you owe me one now. I gave you at least a half-hour lead on the satellite story. Wasn't your senator impressed with you?"

"It's not the sort of thing that impresses Russell. But I was impressed and grateful for the effort. You must know that phone booth outside the Russian embassy is tapped and watched."

"Then it's a good thing I called you and not some journalist." He waved to a tall man who came over to us. "This imposing man standing next to me would love to be introduced to you. John Bowen is in Washington with the Canadian trade delegation. John, this is Winston Bates, the éminence grise of America's defense arsenal, and a Canadian to boot."

"*Ex*-Canadian," I added helpfully.

We shook hands in the abrupt official manner. Bowen was one of those Canadians who flaunt their Englishness. He was tall and handsome in a fleshy, sallow sort of way, and he presented his soft-looking body with a certain bravado. His striped shirt and pinstriped suit bespoke their London origins. He swept an unruly swatch of gray hair away from one eye with a dramatic gesture and regarded me sharply.

"Defense? Ex-Canadian? Perhaps you have some sentimental attachment to your mother country that Canada should exploit." He looked at me in alarm. "My God man, just a little joke, a little sport. You look as if I offered you a bribe. Do wipe that look of horror from your face. Denby, is everyone in this city so serious?"

I avoided meeting Gardner's eyes.

"John and I met in Paris," Gardner said. "He was at the Canadian embassy for a short while, but he was reassigned before you got to Paris."

That was all it took. My carefully constructed autonomous identity melted away and I heard myself say: "Do you remember that Canadian intelligence officer who was stationed in Paris, the one with the red hair, what was his name?"

"You mean Jack McGowan?" Gardner said. "I had forgotten completely about him."

"Of course I remember him from Paris," Bowen said. "He was quite a character."

"Did you ever run into him in Canada?"

"It seems to me someone mentioned his name not so long ago but I can't recall the circumstance. We move in different circles, thank God." He looked at me inquiringly.

"Can't think of why he suddenly sprang to mind," I said.

Late that evening, when I was curled up in bed next to the wall between our houses, I felt a tremor as the Boyers' front door slammed behind Larry. I drifted off to sleep picturing Larry in his family room as he debated if it was too late to call me about the satellite. Over the last several months, I had begun to see more of the Boyer family. Once or twice a week I would accept Larry's invitation to come over for a drink before dinner while we watched the evening news together. There was a determination to my visits, an effort to add some domestic color to my Washington life, even if it meant subjecting myself to the Boyers' household entropy of spilled milk, misplaced scissors, moldy bread, burned rice, and missed appointments.

I awoke well before seven. As my coffee percolated, I glanced out of my kitchen window and saw Larry walk out on his patio and look up at my porch. He glanced at his watch: still too early to call me. At seven thirty little Mark streaked out onto the patio followed by Deborah. She stood there benignly while he climbed up on and fell off each piece of patio furniture. I came out on my porch and Mark spotted me. He pointed up to me and chortled his rough approximation of my name. Mark had become extremely fond of me without the least encouragement on my part. Perhaps I made an impression on him because I was the only person who didn't try to grab him or engage him. More likely my nervous stiffening whenever he appeared only goaded him. A month ago I had attended a barbecue at the Boyers' at which Mark spurned a patio full of guests clamoring to fondle him and perversely insisted on occupying my lap for most of the afternoon. Larry took Mark's affinity for me as a demonstration of my amazing innate talent for entertaining children, but Deborah saw my reluctance and was amused by Mark's devotion. As Mark sat astride me, eructing joyfully and smearing ketchup on my pants, I wondered if my enlistment in the family of man had gone too far.

"Winston!" Larry had come back out on the patio. "You're home. I was afraid you were in New York. It's important that we talk. Soon. Maybe this morning?"

I invited him up for a cup of coffee and within ten seconds I heard him clumping up my stairs. We seated ourselves on the porch while Mark screamed from below for his own invitation. Tossing a scowl in our direction, Deborah swept the boy up in her arms and carried him inside.

"You read the papers?" Larry said. "This satellite thing . . ."

"Is everyone excited over at the Pentagon? About the satellite, that is. They should be happy. You saw how the newspapers handled it this morning. A black eye for America. We're falling behind the Russians. This will mean lots more money for the Pentagon. Especially the Air Force, I should imagine."

"Do you know that for sure, Winston? That would be great. The thing of it is . . ." He twisted awkwardly in his seat. "The thing is we've just managed to get this photo reconnaissance project going. Our own satellite program."

"We? Meaning the Air Force?"

He nodded. "It's called the WS-117L. And it looks a lot more promising than the Navy's Vanguard."

"And you didn't tell me anything about it!" As usual, when Larry had something he wanted to tell me, he was afraid to do it. Dragging it out of him was like getting a lying child to confess the truth.

"Well, it's sort of hidden."

"How could you hide the cost of developing a new rocket from me?"

"Because it's not a new rocket. We're using the Atlas missile to launch a recoverable satellite. I just didn't think you'd be that interested."

"Oh come on, Larry," I chided him.

"We wanted to wait and spring it on people when we were further along. You don't know how paranoid they are at the Pentagon. When Bissell came around a few months ago asking what we had going on in satellite recon, we didn't even tell him."

"And he was the reason you kept it a secret from me."

Larry nodded. "He's going to find out now, isn't he?"

"You'll be lucky he doesn't take it over. If your program's any good he will take it over. He's not stupid. After all, this might replace his precious U-2."

"Can you help us?" Once more, Larry was getting into bed with me.

"'Us'? You, I'll help if I can. But you have to start helping me, beginning with telling me about any new U-2 missions."

"All I know is that Twining is always ranting because Ike is so cautious about approving these missions."

"Bissell is also frustrated he can't play with his toy. But they should be cautious. If one of those planes goes down in the Soviet Union it's an act of war."

"Don't worry. I'm on a Pentagon study group that tracks Russian antiaircraft capability. We're sure the Russians aren't close to being able to shoot down the U-2."

"They weren't close to putting a satellite in orbit either. But now that they've got the satellite up, the U-2 is going to be flying again. We're going to have to see all over again if there's a missile gap. Maybe you can let me know if your group changes its mind. Just in case the CIA isn't paying attention."

It was very satisfying to know a secret that the CIA didn't. And to know the U-2 would be flying again. The U-2! It was if a bell had rung in my mind, setting off a series of speculations having to do with the consequences of a U-2 going down. Things were beginning to add up in the mysterious intuitive way they had over Suez. I didn't have as specific a sense of the future as I had with Suez, but from that moment I was alert to the possibility of making an imaginative contribution to the way things unfolded.

For several weeks, Bissell had his aide, the dutifully unhelpful Jim Flannery, return my numerous phone calls and tell me nothing. It wasn't politic to complain to Russell, though he kept asking me if I was on the case. Russell, with an eye to advancing Lyndon Johnson for the 1960 presidential nomination, declined to chair the new round of Armed Services preparedness hearings in favor of Johnson. Russell didn't even object when Johnson, who knew better, took up the so-called missile gap as his issue. I was watching the news with Larry and Deborah when Johnson was interviewed about the Pentagon's lagging satellite program. "And when they do get a satellite developed, it will probably have chrome trim and automatic windshield wipers," Johnson pronounced, thrusting his big mutt's face forward to smirk at us.

Four weeks after the Russians launched their first satellite, they launched a second one, the one carrying Laika the dog, which gave America a second black eye. And at last Bissell returned my call, to tell me to arrange for him and Dulles to meet with Russell and Lyndon Johnson. The CIA wanted to discuss limiting the agenda for the intelligence portion of the upcoming preparedness hearings.

When we assembled in Russell's office, I could see that Bissell wasn't happy with my presence. If they couldn't own me, they didn't want me in the way. Dulles was full of false sympathy for the military's predicament. "We're in this together," he repeated several times while shaking his head slowly, as if he didn't understand how those idiots at the Pentagon could have failed to have a decent satellite program in the works.

"Who would have thought the Russians had a rocket that could put a thousand-pound satellite with a dog up in the sky?" I said.

Bissell looked at me venomously but Dulles replied: "As usual, Mr. Bates gets to the heart of the problem. You recall the U-2 image Dick showed us of that big rocket at Tyuratam? We suspected it might be a prototype of a new family of rockets."

" 'Course it was," Johnson said. "They've probably got hundreds built by now. If we don't get moving, we're going to be sucking hind tit."

There were several agendas in conflict. Dulles wanted Russell and Johnson to understand that the United States had an overwhelming military superiority; though we couldn't let the world know, since that would be admitting to our U-2 spying. Johnson was interested in claiming a lack of military superiority, with which to beat up on the Republicans. Russell didn't want the emphasis on rocketry to divert attention and money from conventional forces because the more we had to rely on nuclear deterrence, the more likely we were to use it. And I wanted Dulles and Bissell to at least acknowledge the technical brilliance of Russia's achievement. I was sure the Russians were going to try for more spectacular coups, since this was their only way to compete with the United States in the eyes of the world.

Dulles made clear his disapproval of my presence at the meeting by a condescending concern for my sensibilities. Bissell's disapproval was more overt. I understood: I had refused their overtures, and this meeting was just the kind of thing they had in mind for me to support them. Bissell scoffed at my respect for Russian rocketry. "The dog is irrelevant. It's just there for show. They've probably launched twenty-five failures just to get two satellites into orbit."

"So we're ahead because we've only had one failure," I said, referring to a recent Navy Vanguard rocket that had exploded on the launchpad. "Sooner or later, we're going to need a satellite to take over reconnaissance from the U-2. We all know Ike is so afraid of one of the planes crashing or getting shot down that he's reluctant to approve new missions, even though the U-2 has been a gold mine of information."

Bissell ignored the compliment. "The Russians have zero ground-to-air capabilities," he blustered. "And their air-to-air missiles are primi-

Richard Bissell, the architect of the U-2 spy plane project, was deputy director of Plans for the CIA from 1958 to 1962. We did not have a constructive relationship. *Copyright Unknown, Courtesy of Harry S. Truman Library*

tive. They've failed so miserably to nail the U-2 that they've stopped complaining about the flights. And we're not just sitting still. The U-2's altitude is being improved."

"But the Russians can improve their ground-to-air and air-to-air rockets as well. The future is going to be in satellite surveillance, no?" I said. "Maybe we've put too many eggs into the Navy's basket. You know the Air Force has a promising satellite reconnaissance project in development."

Dulles turned and looked sharply at Bissell.

"They've tried to keep it under wraps," I went on. "It's called the WS-117L. It's a recoverable satellite, launched by an Atlas missile. So it won't require a lot of new rocket technology."

"I'm sorry we haven't known about this," Dulles said. "After all, we're still the ones who will have to evaluate any intelligence it gathers." The accusation hung in the air: Either Bissell or I had been derelict in not informing him.

I looked at Bissell apologetically. "I'm sorry you haven't had time to speak to me lately. It was something I found out inadvertently, an Air Force secret. I felt I couldn't tell Jim Flannery, only you." I couldn't resist the thrust at Bissell yet I was also appalled at myself: I had sold out Larry and embarrassed Bissell in front of his boss. "But I agree with Allen," I went on in an attempt to placate Bissell, "the CIA should be running this. The Air Force may figure out how to get the satellite up and recover it when it comes back to Earth, but they don't have a clue about building a camera."

Bissell sat there stonily, his arms folded over his chest.

"We'll have to look into this, Dick, won't we?" Dulles said. "Orbital satellites are a lot safer than planes."

"Unless the thing comes down in Moscow," Bissell grumbled.

"That's why the CIA should be in charge," I said. "Those Air Force cowboys need to be controlled." The more I tried to suck up to Bissell, the more he glowered.

Russell wanted to know whether the Russian satellite could spy on the United States.

"We're confident they don't have the imaging capability of our U-2," Dulles said pulling on his pipe and nodding reassuringly. I noted Dulles's clever use of the pseudotechnical term, "imaging capability"; it sounded as if there had been countless CIA study groups on the subject.

"Just to control a sophisticated camera from that distance is almost impossible," Bissell added. "We use a panoramic camera with a thirty-six-inch focal length on the U-2. It shoots from seven different positions. That's why we use pilots and not robot planes."

"Maybe that's why the Russians sent up a dog," I said. "They've trained it to move the camera and snap the shutter."

Bissell glared at me but Johnson thought this was hilarious. "Laika the Kodak dog! Woof woof, snap the picture! Woof woof, snap the picture!"

The meeting ended, as so many did, in indecision and unexpressed bad feelings. But that was appropriate to the general sense of dissonance and drift. Washington was in its late Eisenhower era, lurching from issue to issue, crisis to crisis; no one wanted to alter the image of the good life by connecting the new dots. As for me, I felt a growing excitement. The intensifying obsession with the Soviet Union's missile and military capabilities would surely provide an opportunity for me to make a creative impression sooner or later. I may have irritated Bissell, but I was confident Russell would protect me—overconfident as it turned out.

15

More and more I felt like the entrepreneurial Robinson Crusoe, whose ingenious improvements made a livable world out of his island. Instead of scavenging a scrappy sustenance from work and Washington social events, I foraged more widely now. There were my evenings in the Boyer Museum of the Quotidian. And rather than flinch inwardly every time I saw Gardner Denby, I tried to embrace my relationship with him. This led to my having dinner at his home, where I cooed over his two charming children and exercised my rusty French with his rather severe wife. Accompanied by Fay, I still popped in on one or two of the more civilized hospitality suites.

My sister, Alice, had been unhappy with me because I brushed off Simon's attempt to reconcile, but after a short interlude I resumed visiting her in Manhattan—at least once a month during the opera season. Now that Robert Cage had become her friend and I had become her boyfriend Stanley's friend, I felt I was implicated in her life and an interesting life it was. With the encouragement of her therapist, she had begun to let her inner Lillian emerge. She never let her emotions get ragged with me, but on several occasions I got to see her temper when Stanley or Robert got in the way of one of her tidal dissatisfactions. I recall a stormy night in the late spring, after an interminable performance of *Meistersinger* at the Met, when I returned to Alice's place to find her flaying Stanley. They were in the living room, where I slept, so I retreated to the kitchen and listened, hoping to pick up some leads to the elusive nub of need and desire. She was goading Stanley to re-gard his generosity, his sensitivity, his impeccable attentiveness, as self-ish and controlling.

"You're always mocking me, mocking me with your phony con-cern!" she kept shouting. Stanley's ameliorating murmurs only added fuel to her fire. Periodically she would come into the kitchen and sit down at the table with me, pour herself a drink and brood ruminatively until, seized by a new wave of rancor, she would stalk out to rejoin the battle with Stanley. Finally Stanley lost his temper and there was lots of shouting and noise and breaking of glass, and then she screamed for him to get out. After the door slammed she came back to the kitchen, a defiant, satisfied glint in her eyes.

It seemed ridiculous to pretend I had witnessed nothing, so I said: "Why don't you plan a similar scene for Dad when he visits you in the fall?"

She grinned at me crookedly. "Is that why you never visit when he's here? You're afraid I'll throw the family fat in the fire."

"It's him, not you," I muttered.

"A little family drama would be good for the two of you."

I also was present for a disagreeable episode with Robert, where she picked apart his prickly defenses as if they were so much colorful fluff on the surface of his inconsequence. On each occasion, Alice's coruscating tirades seemed to eat at the edge of her friends' racial and sexual identi-ties, harshly insisting that the one's dramatic self-possession, the other's easy graciousness, was the result of some repugnant accommodation with being homosexual or black. This corrosive climate appeared to be the way of the world in their circles. I remember being dragged to what Alice euphemistically referred to as a "literary party" in a barren little flat in the West Village. Everyone stood around in a blue haze of cigarette smoke, wearing grubby tweed jackets or dowdy skirts and blouses, drinking like fish and deriding each other's horrible poems and novels. In the kitchen they pawed and licked each other's spouses and lovers, then returned to the living room to slap and berate their own loved ones.

*

Over the next eighteen months, I relied on Larry to keep me up to date on the U-2. Afraid of a U-2 crash, Eisenhower refused to approve any U-2 flights over Russia. Instead, U-2 flights skittered along Russia's borders, bringing back relatively low-grade intelligence. In the meantime, Bissell efficiently hijacked the Air Force's satellite program and renamed it Corona, but its fitful development was everything the U-2 was not. It crashed on launch repeatedly; when it did get off the ground, the camera malfunctioned or the film self-destructed in the high altitude. But such was the faith in Bissell's brilliance that he was made the CIA's deputy director for Plans, in charge of covert action, clandestine intelligence gathering, and counterintelligence. Now he was even more inaccessible to me. Once in a while Jim Flannery would give me a little good news about Corona to pass on to Russell. I relied on Larry to tell me the bad news.

The pressure on Eisenhower to approve more U-2 flights over Russia increased early in 1959, when the Soviets began testing what appeared to be a new class of long-range missiles. It was the cautious Eisenhower against everybody—Allen Dulles, the new defense secretary, Neil McElroy, the Joint Chiefs of Staff, and Christian Herter, who had replaced the dying John Foster Dulles as secretary of state.

Allen Dulles asked Russell to persuade Ike to approve new U-2 missions. Russell came back from his meeting with Eisenhower quite concerned about Ike's yearning to get a peace process started. "I don't understand it. Every time Khrushchev pulls some nasty stunt like his Berlin ultimatum, Ike wants to make peace with him. I never thought I'd say this about the man who won the war, but he needs someone like Foster to stiffen his backbone."

With foreign ministers meeting in Geneva to try to resolve the Berlin issue*, Eisenhower invited Khrushchev to meet with him in the United States and tour the country. The invitation was contingent on progress at Geneva, but Khrushchev accepted as if there were no conditions.

---

* Khrushchev had demanded that the Western powers sign a German peace treaty and turn Berlin into a demilitarized zone. If they didn't in the next six months, he threatened to let East Germany control access to the city.

Russell was apoplectic when he heard about it. I had just spent a damp, diplomatic weekend on the Eastern Shore with the Fervers, and I passed on to Russell the gossip that the State Department envoy to Khrushchev had blundered by not making the conditions for the visit explicitly clear. I told Russell that I wouldn't put it past Khrushchev to have put Eisenhower in a corner by pretending there were no conditions mentioned, no matter what the envoy said. "Khrushchev has a kind of crude cleverness. Two weeks ago, when Ike finally allowed the first deep penetration of Russia by a U-2 in over a year, Khrushchev didn't say a word about it. It would have been a good excuse to indignantly refuse Ike's invitation."

"What cleverness does that prove?" Russell said. "It shows he wants to come here. He probably figures he can outsmart Ike."

Despite the flubbed invitation, Eisenhower decided to make the best of Khrushchev's visit; perhaps they could advance the agenda for the upcoming Paris summit conference on which Ike was staking his reputation as a soldier of peace.

I had a new theory: Khrushchev hadn't condemned the last U-2 flight publicly because he wanted to encourage the United States to fly more missions. A spectacular feat such as shooting down a U-2 over Russian soil just before his arrival in the United States would allow him to scuttle the peace process and blame it on the United States. It was just a theory, a fantasy really, of how things could work out. Yet what are our idle fantasies but rehearsals for our impulsive indiscretions?

In the event, Ike didn't permit any U-2 flights before Khrushchev's visit. But I was correct about Khrushchev's desire to pull off a spectacular feat: Just before his arrival in the United States, the Russians landed a rocket on the moon. It was enough to prompt Bissell to call me directly.

"We hope your senators know this event is purely a public relations stunt connected with Khrushchev's visit."

"You're calling it a stunt? Why not an achievement?"

"Come on. They didn't land the goddamn rocket, they crash-landed it."

"So we're winning the missile war but losing the public relations war. What will we do?"

"We're doing our best. We've primed Nixon to talk about the Soviet failures—all their other rockets that have blown up on the pad, how other attempts have missed the moon and gone into Earth orbit. People have to understand, the Russian rocket program is like some drunk in a bar playing darts. Sooner or later he hits the bull's-eye because there's nowhere else to go. But there's no missile gap. Senator Russell knows that. Lyndon Johnson knows it too, even though he's making it an election issue."

"Eisenhower can't convincingly deny the gap without admitting the existence of the U-2."

Bissell snorted. "And Russell's letting Johnson get away with it because he wants Johnson to be president. What a racket!"

On September 15, 1959, Nikita Khrushchev's airplane touched down at Andrews Air Force Base in Maryland. I watched the elaborate reception ceremony for Khrushchev on my television at home, carefully attuned for any mention of the U-2. I now expected him to exploit it sometime while he was in the United States.

At the office, everyone was buzzing about Khrushchev's arrival. In less than a day the pudgy, earthy premier had made his presence in America into a captivating circus. His impulsive and splenetic reactions were almost bizarre by current diplomatic standards. No one had expected the enemy to have such a human face.

When Russell arrived he headed directly for my office. I had asked if I could be a fly on the wall at the Foreign Relations Committee tea that afternoon with Khrushchev.

"There's no way I can get you into the meeting. The pressures were enormous. Since we're calling it 'afternoon tea,' several senators thought they could bring their wives. Fulbright finally said no outsiders could come." Russell looked at me sharply. "Allen Dulles called me on your behalf. He also wanted me to bring you to the tea."

"Dulles himself?" I asked. "He probably assumed I could give him a word-for-word account. But I never asked him to call you for me."

Russell nodded, a little too sternly for my comfort. "Then it's forgotten," he said with firm reassurance, which mainly assured me that some doubt about me had been raised in his mind. The idea that I would get Dulles to put pressure on Russell on my behalf would surely annoy Russell. What could Dulles have said about me? After regarding me thoughtfully, Russell said: "But I'd like to know, Winston, do you have a particular reason for wanting to go?"

"Yes, though I'd never confide in Dulles. Do you think I could talk to you after the meeting?"

"I'll be going straight home. Do you want to stop by? Seven should be about right. Unless our tea produces fireworks."

I arrived at 6:59. I had visited Russell's suite at the Woodner several times since my first visit three years ago, when I warned him about Suez. By now he didn't bother to ask what or if I wanted to drink, and I had never managed to tell him I would have preferred scotch to bourbon. He toasted me with a little gesture as he raised the glass to his lips.

After Russell described the meeting with Khrushchev, I asked, "Are you sure he objected only to 'subversion' by the CIA? Was that the word he used?"

"I'm sure, though of course it was being translated. I replied that I was the one who appropriated the money for the CIA and I knew of no appropriation for subversion."

"How did that go over?"

"He sort of sniffed, like he was both amused and irritated at the same time." Russell twisted his thin lips, scowling at the insistence of my interrogation. "What's your point?"

"What I really want to know is whether Khrushchev objected to the U-2 flights over Russia. Or even alluded to them indirectly."

"Not that I noticed. But why would he? There hasn't been one for a while and besides, it must be an embarrassment to him that he can't do anything about it."

"Well yes, precisely, an embarrassment. And his generals probably like it a lot less than he does."

"But as I said, he didn't mention it," Russell said. He sounded impatient.

"Would you mind if I'm in New York the day after tomorrow? I managed to wangle a ticket to the Economic Club dinner where Khrushchev is speaking."

"Khrushchev again? I wouldn't imagine he's going to bring up the U-2 there, but if you've got a bee in your bonnet, by all means go." There had been a note of peevish sarcasm in Russell's voice, and now he produced a sigh of exasperation. "You know, Bates, there are more things going on around here than the U-2. Giving you the CIA subcommittee wasn't meant to turn you into an intelligence officer."

I was under attack again. It was Bissell and Dulles I decided; they had deliberately made me a complication in Russell's mind because I had refused to be their errand boy. And now I had provoked Russell to recall all the times I had brought up the U-2 in his presence. With an assist from the CIA, my persistent interest in the U-2 had placed me in a new frame of reference for Russell, one that reconstructed me as a bit of a zealot, someone who had lost his perspective, his sense of proportion, over a private idée fixe. Hardly the sort of reputation one wants in Washington.

I went to New York anyway, changing into my tuxedo at the airport and going directly to the Waldorf-Astoria where the Economic Club was meeting. This was very much a New York event. Business leaders filled the huge ballroom; I hardly recognized anyone from Washington. Khrushchev occupied the stage with robust assurance, full of basso bluster and buffo peasant humor.

I stayed over at Alice's and caught the first plane from LaGuardia Airport to Washington. I managed to beat Russell to the office in a craven attempt to demonstrate my dedication. I saw him come in shortly after nine, but he went directly to his own office. An hour later he appeared in my doorway.

"Didn't expect to see you here this morning. What's the latest on the U-2 front? Did it land in New York?" Russell's patronizing tone was hardly a relief.

I waved my hand airily, as if this minor issue had vaporized. "Not a word. Not a word about anything, really. It was useless. There we all were—us in our tuxes, him in his proletarian suit—exchanging gibes with the second-most powerful man on earth."

"Ike never should have invited him. If Dulles were alive it never would have happened. I mean what's the point? What is he here for?"

"Well, there are still the talks at Camp David next week."

"You think he's going to bring up the flights with Ike in private?"

"Oh no, that's not what I meant. I was trying to say maybe that's what he's here for, to get something done at Camp David so the summit in Paris can be successful." My flustered attempt to make myself clear only made matters worse. Russell now had a tic about the U-2 and me, planted in his mind by Allen Dulles. Just when I thought I had everything under control, my perilous balance was upset. If I hoped to restore Russell's respect for me I would have to discipline myself never to mention the U-2 to Russell again. But what could I do about Dulles and Bissell?

A few days later, as I left the office early to go to Walter Lippmann's seventieth birthday cocktail party, I felt Russell's eyes boring into me disapprovingly. Elizabeth and I had successfully ascended most of Washington's social Himalayas, but Lippmann's party was Mount Everest as far as the 1950s were concerned. Elizabeth looked like a young girl in her big new limousine. Her feet barely reached the floor and she was practically bouncing on the backseat. "This party is bigger than anything done for Khrushchev. I called Helen yesterday. Walter is positively staggering under all his honors. Phil Graham gave him a *car*! And the Phillipses gave him lunch and a private afternoon in the collection. Earlier today he was the guest of honor at the National Press Club. It's like an inauguration! He was even the Russians' guest for Khrushchev's UN speech, though I don't think that had anything to do with his birthday. There are going to be over five hundred people here tonight. Five hundred!"

I should have found some way to excuse myself because I was primed to behave badly. There I was, at once a member of the Five Hundred yet, with Russell, Dulles, and Bissell aligned against me, my standing was shaky. Scores of cars and limousines were descending simultaneously on the Lippmanns. Still a block away, Elizabeth insisted we jump ship before we missed all the excitement. We wormed our way through the mob at the door, the press of the crowd squeezing us slowly toward the shrilling cicada buzz of chatter until we burst into the living room. I turned away for a moment and when I looked back Elizabeth had vanished. I was on my own. Below me the sunken living room was packed solidly. I skirted the periphery, avoiding conversation until I had a supportive drink in hand.

After a good deal of slithering, I edged up to a bar that was surrounded by the ambassadors of Sweden, Norway, Iran, Holland, and Portugal. Because it was nearly impossible to move anywhere else, they had become happily stranded in a genteel drinking frenzy. I elbowed my way through them and ordered a prescription for disaster: two drinks, which I gulped down while standing at the bar, and then two more to take with me. With my head and shoulders hunched protectively over my drinks I shoved off. At a less crowded party, I would have circulated, tossing off frivolous and gossipy banter along the way. All I could do here was to stumble along the path of least resistance and slurp at my drinks when I had a chance. I finally fetched up at a table of hors d'oeuvres where I unluckily encountered Allen Dulles who was also holding two drinks. Though I felt resentment acidly eating at me, I forced myself to smile. He grinned back.

"One of these drinks belongs to her," I said, tossing my head in the general direction of the party.

"She'll never miss it," Dulles said. "One of my drinks belongs to him."

Dulles nodded toward his feet and I noticed a man kneeling on the floor between us. "Is he all right?"

"I'm fine," the man said looking up. It was Walter Lippmann. "I just had to say hello to Panache here." Panache, a black poodle, was cowering beneath the table. Lippmann stood up and said with breathless giddiness, "Panache loves parties."

I was trapped. We looked to one another waiting for a conversation to ensue. Loy Henderson, the deputy undersecretary of State, appeared. He congratulated Lippmann while I berated myself for neglecting this obvious formality.

"How did you ever get to be the Russians' guest at the UN?" Henderson asked Lippmann.

"You'll remember I interviewed Khrushchev in Moscow only last year. Menshikov told me Khrushchev was very pleased with my reports. I sat right next to Marshall Zhukov at the UN."

"Did he say anything about spy planes to you?" I blurted out.

"Zhukov? Why would he say anything about spy planes?" Lippmann looked uncertainly at Dulles who had turned slightly green. Henderson stared intently at his cracker and cheese. All of them surely knew about the U-2. People had been gossiping about it for months. Though Allen himself had probably been indiscreet, it was in theory a top secret and I was embarrassing him in front of a journalist and a diplomat.* I might as well have brought up one of Allen's girlfriends with his wife present. I had gone too far, yet some sort of diminished mental capacity now prevented me from turning back.

"Of course he didn't mention spy planes!" I said triumphantly. "And Khrushchev didn't mention the plane either. Not at the UN, not at the Economic Club, not when he was taunted at the National Press Club, not at the Senate Foreign Relations Committee, not face-to-face with Ike."

"Well, there's still Camp David. But why should he mention it?" Dulles was beginning to sound cranky.

"Why shouldn't he? That's the question. He gets pissed off every other day, but he never mentions the U-2."

My message wasn't getting across. I saw a cautious smile pass between Henderson and Dulles. They had decided to regard me as irrational or drunk or both. I began to berate them. "The whole thing is ridiculous. Thanks to the U-2, we know the Russians don't have enough ballistic missiles to destroy Finland, much less the U.S. But we can't say we know it because we would have to admit we've been spying on them. But they know we know. Khrushchev's generals are so angry about being

---

* Some secret! In 1958 Allen Dulles had appealed to Arthur Sulzberger, the publisher of *The New York Times*, to censor Harrison Baldwin, *The Times* military correspondent, who was writing a U-2 story.

spied on from the sky that Khrushchev has screwed up the pressure on Berlin to placate them, because unless we're prepared to wage nuclear war, they're far better prepared to fight a land war. Yet their sputniks and rockets to the moon make them look like the kings of the missile age. Not only that, Lyndon Johnson, who knows better, and now Kennedy, who probably doesn't know any better, are both running for president on the basis of a missile gap that doesn't exist. We've created this unbalanced, upside-down pyramid of policy whose point rests on this tiny little airplane. And it's all because our secret is that we know their secret and they know we know it."

"It doesn't appear to be such a big secret tonight," Dulles said drily.

It was hard to think of a way to make matters worse or I probably would have. I drew myself up to my full five feet seven inches, raised one of my empty glasses to Lippmann, toasted his health, and stumbled out of the party. Two hours later Elizabeth found me sound asleep in the backseat of her limousine.

16

By all accounts, Khrushchev never brought up the U-2 at Camp David. Eisenhower and his advisors took that as evidence of Khrushchev's positive attitude as they laid plans for their extraordinary Paris summit in the spring, the one that was going to end the Cold War. Meanwhile, I was under siege. Though my outburst at Lippmann's party was never referred to again by anyone, people began to avoid me and to patronize me when I was unavoidable. Weeks went by without a call from Gardner Denby. If I ran into him, he was friendly and formal. Jim Flannery only called with secretarial matters. Russell withdrew from me almost entirely. The other legislative assistants, their noses raised to the bureaucratic winds, smelled my impairment and drove me from their hyena pack. My name was dropped from routing slips; I was cut out of casual lunches; and no one used me anymore as a conduit for getting messages across to Russell.

I told myself it was all in my imagination. On the surface, life went on much as always. I visited New York regularly and Elizabeth continued to gallivant around Washington with me as if she were oblivious to my exclusion. But in March I inadvertently learned of a little dinner Elizabeth had held for Walter and Helen Lippmann's anniversary. Had Lippmann asked Elizabeth to omit me?

Larry Boyer was the only Washington acquaintance of mine who failed to recognize my isolation. He was now chairing the Pentagon study group on Soviet antiaircraft capabilities. In March he came to me in great excitement. A new, more powerful generation of SA-2 antiair-craft missiles was being placed around Soviet cities. Though the Pentagon didn't have a precise estimate of their range, the previous generation was estimated at fifty to sixty thousand feet, so it was reasonable to assume these missiles might go as high as seventy thousand feet, while the U-2's maximum height was also seventy thousand feet. Larry's group wanted to recommend new routes for the U-2 over Russia as a precaution, should there be any new flights. But General Twining, a strong advocate for more flights, was afraid to even show such a report to the White House.

"What should I do, Winston? You know how jumpy Ike is. If I come on too strongly the whole U-2 program could be scrapped, just at the time everyone is desperate for more information. The generals will hate me and so will the CIA. They want some really good flights over the main Soviet missile bases before the Paris peace conference so Ike will at least know what the Soviets have in their arsenal. If you ask me, Twining's really hoping to find a vast arsenal of Soviet rockets so Ike will have to be very cautious in Paris."

I barely listened to Larry at first because I resented him so much. Thanks to me, the hapless dodo had moved to the inner circles of the Pentagon while I was in exile! But when he mentioned the possibility of U-2 flights across the heart of the Soviet Union he got my full attention. As at a signal, the oppressive fog that had eclipsed my mind's eye lifted, and the future of the world appeared to me in hyperrealistic clarity. I knew exactly what to do.

"Look, Larry, the problem is not how high the antiaircraft rockets go as long as the U-2 goes higher. Based on what I know from the CIA, you don't have to worry that much. Just say in your report that once the U-2s are all fitted with new engines, the possibility of shooting them down is as remote as it was before. And that's really true. The pilots themselves say the new engines are even better than they expected. The U-2 should get another ten or twenty thousand feet." I was making these numbers up, though my contact at Pratt & Whitney had claimed greater power for the new engines. "You can also say in a definitive way that there is no evidence that the new Soviet rockets can *accurately* exceed sixty thousand feet. That gives you a cushion of at least twenty thousand feet."

"But why would they deploy the new missiles if they weren't better than the previous ones?"

"For the same reason that we go cranking out new military equipment that is no better than the stuff it replaces. Also you can say that improved methods of making the U-2 undetectable to Soviet radar give an added margin of security."

"But I thought Project Rainbow was discontinued."* Larry's objections were rendered so weakly, I could tell he wanted to be convinced.

"But we learned from its failure. The point of your report is to keep the U-2 flying."

Larry nodded slowly, still hesitant.

"I understand, Larry. You have your professional integrity and you also have to cover yourself. Here's what you should do: Take a definitively positive tone in the executive summary of your report, then a more measured but still positive tone in the body of the report, and bury the worst-case scenario in the notes. That way, you will cover yourself and everyone will be happy."

It took some more persuading, but Larry did as I told him. He reported that his Pentagon superiors had embraced his encouraging estimates of Soviet antiaircraft capabilities enthusiastically. Bissell too was pleased with his recommendations. "Bissell thinks it's all a matter of risks and rewards. And in this case, the reward of knowing what the Russians are up to is very large, so it makes the risk look small by comparison. LeMay even wants me to take out the disclaimer in my footnotes, which says that our estimates of the SA-2 as well as air-to-air capabilities must be constantly reviewed. I refused. It's at least an out for me if something goes wrong."

"It sounds like LeMay is really eager for more flights."

---

* Project Rainbow was an attempt to disguise or reduce the U-2's radar footprint by attaching wires and high-frequency reflective material to the plane. It only succeeded in reducing the plane's performance. To be frank, the only improvement after Rainbow's termination was that the plane's range and altitude returned to their original levels.

"And he may be getting his way. The one last week was the first deep penetration in six months."

"You didn't tell me there was a flight."

"I'm telling you now. Once my report was accepted they jumped right into it. No one wants to take a chance that the Soviets will get an operational ICBM ready without our knowing about it. The mission was a big success. Not a peep from Khrushchev and no sign the Russians have their ICBM program working. Now we all want to try to squeeze one more flight in before the summit starts week after next."

I could have warned Larry then to cover himself. I should have. But I resented his success. I still picture him that evening, grinning with doltish pride at being one of the big boys at the Pentagon.

Each time I saw Larry over the next week, he shook his head. "No flight yet. The weather's horrible over Plesetsk."

A few days later, I came home from a bridge game on a Friday evening. As I put my key in my door, Larry popped out of his.

"Thank God you're home at last. I've been waiting here all night. We have to talk. The weather is lifting. They're ready to take off this weekend!"

"That's exciting," I said. And I was excited.

Larry followed me up the stairs. "It's not just exciting. It's scary. I'm really worried. I need your help. I got to thinking about that last flight. It was less than three weeks ago and it was tracked all the way on Soviet radar."

"So what, Larry?"

"The Russians are going to be ready for us. The U-2's been sitting on the ground in Pakistan for a week waiting for the cloud cover to lift. Plenty of time for our security there to be breached. If they pick up the flight path early, or guess right about the path and get a missile into place quickly, they just might shoot it down."

"I thought we agreed it was a pretty remote chance, thanks to the new engine."

"Well yes . . . and while I didn't exactly fudge our data, I wrote my report to make it seem really remote. Just as you told me. That's what everybody wanted. And when we briefed Bissell and the others on the report, we all just discussed the executive summary. The unlikely possibilities are buried in the notes."

"But now you're worried."

He nodded. "I asked myself, 'What if I tried to slant my report for someone who *didn't* want the mission to happen?' And you know what, the evidence for that point of view is much stronger. So I've revised the report. But I'm afraid to show it to anyone at the Pentagon, even though I've left it in a file to protect myself. Bissell doesn't want to hear anything that would abort the mission. But you can show it to Russell who can get to Ike. It won't take much to get Ike to cancel the flight."

Larry's interest in taking independent action was as surprising as it was worrying. "That's a really bad idea. It will look like you are just covering yourself, and if Russell gets involved it will look to Dulles and the Pentagon that you went over their heads directly to a senator."

"If you don't do it, I'll find someone who will listen. At the White House. Or I'll go to a newspaper." He sounded frantic.

I spoke to him sternly. "That would be the worst thing you could do. You would lose your job for sure."

"That's why I need you to get the word to Ike."

To keep Larry from doing something rash, I agreed to try to warn Russell, though I had no intention of doing so. I wanted events to unfold according to my enabling anticipation. I had come to understand why I was able to see the future so clearly. Without belief, power, obligation, or patriotic compunction, there was nothing to blur my vision. I might have lots of opinions, but I had no convictions to get in the way of clear thinking. During Suez, I had felt history flowing through me; now I felt it flowing from me. The presidents and premiers who were going to the summit conference in Paris thought they were making history, but I was the one who was artfully shaping it. I should have warned Larry to destroy any evidence of his new, more conservative estimates. The poor guy thought he was covering himself by being right, but it is better to be wrong and share the guilt with others than to be the only one who is right but fails to warn anyone. He was also unaware of the effect of the delayed schedule: The U-2 would be flying over Russia on

Sunday, which was May Day, the Communist national holiday. The Russians would be wild with fury.

On Saturday afternoon I saw Larry come out on his patio and begin to fire up his barbecue. I went out on my porch and called down to him. With a helpless shrug, I indicated to Larry that I had been unable to contact Russell. "Don't worry. I'm sure it will be okay," he reassured me, as if I shared his anxieties. On Sunday I waited for Monday.

On Monday I waited in my office for the phone to ring. Unexpectedly, it was Gardner Denby who called at ten thirty from his office. "Listen, I thought you'd want to know, there's a bit of a flap going on over here. There's a weather plane missing over Russia, and some NSA technician picked up Russian pilot transmissions about trying to intercept an enemy plane."

I said nothing at first.

"Did you hear me? I said there's a weather plane missing."

"I heard you. Are you telling me something or asking me something?"

"The thing is, people have been racing in and out of Hugh Cumming's office all morning." Cumming was head of the Bureau of Intelligence and Research, State's liaison with the CIA.

I was impressed with Denby's ability to nose out where the action was. "If I were you, Gardner, I'd keep my mouth shut and my head low. That's what I'm going to do."

"I guess so." He sounded disappointed. The nerve of him! He had barely spoken to me for weeks and now he expected a confidence from me. I hung up firmly. When Larry called at noon I didn't take the call. I expected he would be waiting on my doorstep when I got home. But he wasn't there and he didn't call. He was probably staying the night at the Pentagon, where they had to be in crisis management mode.

On Tuesday the cover story was released, appearing in a very few newspapers as a minor squib about a missing NASA weather plane and its pilot who must have perished. By then Russell had been briefed. Late in the afternoon he walked into my office. To his credit, he didn't pretend there had been no change in our relationship.

"I owe you an apology Winston. I realize now you were trying to tell me something and I shut you up."

"Tell you something?" I said innocently.

"You may not have heard yet, but there's an announcement about a weather plane out of Turkey that's gone missing."

"Not by any chance a U-2 weather plane?"

"You know already, don't you?"

I nodded.

Russell shook his head slowly. "How could they do this? Ike is about to leave for the Paris summit. He's going to look like an idiot."

"Can't you see there isn't going to be a summit?" I said, unable to hide my impatience with Russell's deliberate thought process. "Ike would be better off canceling the whole thing."

Russell stared off into space for a moment while he went through the steps. "You've got it all figured out, haven't you?"

On Thursday Khrushchev told the Supreme Soviet how an extraordinary Russian rocket had shot down an American spy plane. I was already focused on what wasn't said rather than what was, so when Khrushchev made no mention of the pilot I immediately assumed he was alive. I am sure there would have been enough time for me to have told Russell, for Russell to have told the White House, and for the White House to have come up with a policy of frankness and honesty. But I kept my thoughts to myself. When I read the next NASA press release, still insisting on the weather mission and the poor dead pilot who had trouble with his oxygen and became so disoriented that his plane strayed into Russian territory, I pictured Khrushchev and his colleagues howling with laughter over its earnest disingenuities. They were waiting for the administration's lies to accumulate before revealing that the pilot was still alive. Yet this was a schoolboy trick; how could Allen Dulles and Bissell fall for it and not protect Ike?*

There was still time to warn Larry. I debated whether to tell him that the pilot was alive as I walked home on Thursday evening. It could

---

* In Moscow, Llewellyn Thompson, the U.S. ambassador, learned that the pilot was still alive and tried to warn the White House but it was too late.

help him at the Pentagon to appear to be a savant. And it would help me if Larry were still respected at the Pentagon. But I was also reveling in the private triumph of being the only person in America to know the ending of this comedy. I believed in myself again and so did Russell. My drunken rant at Lippmann's party would now be redefined as another brilliant, admonitory bulletin from Winston Bates. I felt better than I had in months. It was a beautiful evening. The air was soft and sensuous. As I approached my home, I decided I would sit with my drink on my porch for a short while and enjoy the moment before giving Larry a call.

Mrs. Trinker placed my mail on a small table at the foot of the stairs. On the bottom of the stack I found a large manila envelope with my name scrawled on its front. Inside the envelope was a copy of *The Toronto Globe and Mail* and a smaller envelope. Inside the smaller envelope was a sheet of notepaper whose letterhead read THE JEFFERSON HOTEL. The unsigned message read, "Please come to Room 504."

Canada calling.

I didn't try to think constructively until my second drink was in me and night had fallen. My neighbors' lights glowed warmly. The air was filled with a gentle din—the buzz of insects, distant shouts and laughter, the faint background hum of automobiles. I should have expected this, I thought; the perfect moment for them and the worst moment for me. I had learned to live as if I had no Canadian ties; now I was supposed to give up my independent sense of myself. After Suez they had left me to my own devices and I had recreated myself. Yes, I was still a fraudulent, counterfeit person, but at least I was my own invention.

On the way to the Jefferson, my taxi passed the White House. Eisenhower, Dulles, Bissell, and Herter were surely all there, fumbling for the light switch in a dark room. I realized it was the last small moment of selfish pleasure I would take in having orchestrated this fiasco. When I got to the Jefferson, I floated through the lobby in a stupor. In the elevator I suddenly understood that Jack McGowan himself would be there to greet me. I knocked at Room 504.

"It's unlocked," said a muffled voice from inside.

He was sitting primly on the bed, his hands folded in his lap. He rose as I took several steps toward him. "I think it's time we cleared the air between us, Winston," my father said. He looked at me uncertainly, searching my face for a sign of acceptance or rejection. Then a huge smile spread over his face. "Look at you! You *are* glad to see me." He rushed toward me and embraced me. Over his shoulder, I caught a glimpse of my face in a mirror. I smiled at myself in disbelieving delight; I had been reprieved. When Simon released me I sat down on the bed and held my head, as if it was going to burst from confusion.

He looked at me anxiously. "Really, Winston, I just wanted to know something about your life. Alice was always urging me to call you but I assure you, she had no idea of my plan to approach you face-to-face, father to son, if you know what I mean. I only wanted to tell you how proud I was that you had made your way in America, but now that I'm with you . . ."

He sat down next to me on the bed and reached out to touch my arm. The poor man had mistaken my relief that he was not Jack McGowan for my joy at our reconciliation. He was dressed nattily, with black tasseled loafers, a richly patterned silk tie, and a black and gray-checked wool suit that was much too heavy for May in Washington. His hair had thinned considerably since I had last seen him, and his slightness of build and tentative gestures made him seem fragile and uncertain. He spoke softly, each hesitant sentence a request for approval. As Simon went on, all I could manage to say to him was, "Of course, Father. Thank you, Father, thank you," as if he had given me a great gift.

"You know, Winston, when I ask myself why you've avoided me all these years, I wonder if you're still angry with me for living apart from Lillian. Or perhaps you feel you've failed to live up to your promise after your brilliant college career. But from what Alice tells me, you have an important position and a wonderful life here in Washington."

He explained how he had first come to Washington to see me. "You mustn't think Alice was a party to all this. I came on my own. I was so nervous that first time three years ago, but I finally went right up to your door and rang the bell. You weren't home. I returned the next day intending to announce myself. I waited for you in a taxi. But when I saw you, I panicked again and drove away. I was so afraid of your rejection. Later, in my hotel room, I tried to summon up the courage to go back to see you. I called Alice for advice but the first thing she told me was that Lillian had died. At that point it all seemed too complicated to contact you and tell you I was in Washington. I returned to Winnipeg."

"Of course you had left your little sign for me."

"Sign?" he squeaked innocently.

"The claim check. At the Willard."

"I don't recall that," he said quickly, not wanting to seem too ridiculous. When he peeked at me shyly I knew he was lying. It was just like him to leave tantalizing signals so he wouldn't have to put himself on the line. He had tried to stage it as one of his practical jokes and now he was embarrassed by the idea. "And you even snuck into my room at the Willard that night."

He feigned indignation. "Absolutely not, Winston. I would never go into your room. I went right back to Alice in New York when she told me that Lillian had died." He peeked at me again to see if I was buying his story. What a ridiculous man!

"Why didn't you simply call me, or write to me?"

"The truth is, Winston, I was afraid of you. But when I returned to Washington this time I did leave you a note with my hotel and room number. I didn't sign it but I hoped you would call and say, 'Is that you, Father?'"

"And if I didn't call and didn't come here, you could still pretend to yourself that I hadn't rejected you since I hadn't realized it was you."

He winced. "I didn't think you'd come straightaway. As I sat here waiting for your call, I realized how foolish this whole scheme was. I took a deep breath and called you at home. No one answered. I was devastated. But then came your knock on the door. You did understand! We were at last speaking the same language."

Just as I was beginning to get angry with him, I thought again of my good fortune. No one was out there, no watcher, no control, no McGowan. I closed my eyes and tried to retrieve the triumphant, independent Winston Bates who had sent a U-2 crashing to the earth. Simon thought I had been overcome with emotion again and he embraced me with joyful consolation. "Now now, there you go, there you go now."

At one in the morning my father and I bid each other good-bye. I saw no reason to disabuse him of the pleasure he took in our reconciliation. He apologized for shocking me, though he was really pleased by my emotional reaction to his appearance. Half an hour later, I crawled happily into my own bed at home. Before I could sink into sleep, I heard the Boyers' front door slam. After several silent minutes, Deborah's voice pierced the wall. "How could you let this happen, Larry? What could you have been thinking of? Don't you have a brain? Oh you fool! You stupid ridiculous fool!"

17

After Suez, I went forward *as if* there were no control, though I still thought he was out there somewhere. Now I was certain: No one was hovering on the outskirts of my life, watching and waiting for the perfect moment to tap me on the shoulder. Sometimes I suspected an intentional abandonment: Canada was afraid of me; I was a mistake, an error in judgment. Not knowing what to do with me, they continued to pay my salary. Other times I thought I had simply fallen into the cracks. In my mind, "they" were no longer personified by an all-powerful control, but by a harassed bureaucrat in Ottawa, as likely to misfile and lose me as to sit in his office wringing his hands and praying that I keep my mouth shut.

As for my U-2 intervention, I hadn't expected it to have such wide-ranging consequences. Khrushchev wrecked the Paris summit, though it was difficult to tell whether he was incited or enabled by the U-2 crash. In the months that followed, hardly a week went by without him threatening or denouncing the United States. Was this my doing? Had I set the Cold War on a more dangerous path? It was the scale of it all that let me off the hook, I concluded. How could we go from a modest ten- or twenty-thousand-foot inaccuracy in Larry's report to Khrushchev flailing his shoe in the UN General Assembly? Many other missteps, for which I bore no responsibility, had to happen in between. The world stage was so vast and I was so insignificant. Was I any more responsible than Bissell, Dulles, Eisenhower, the Joint Chiefs, Khrushchev himself, or even the thousands of minor analysts and functionaries in Washington and Moscow, whose small and large decisions defined the Cold War? There was no moral dimension to what they did; it was all about self-interest. My own contribution simply highlighted the failures of policy and diplomacy that were already in place. Meanwhile, I couldn't help myself: Every time someone muttered about the state of the world, I shivered with private pleasure.

I no longer thought of myself as castaway on a distant island; it seemed more convenient to think of myself as a small sovereign state enclosed within a larger country, like Monaco, or the Vatican, or San Marino. As would any state, I had defended myself against threats to my independence. And now I had evolved a foreign policy whose general approach could be defined as oppositional and stylishly opportunistic, rather like France's come to think of it.

There was nothing more likely to bring out the oppositional in me than the effervescent giddiness with which the Kennedy campaign celebrated its own election as it planned for its coronation in Washington. Awakening from the last desultory years of the Eisenhower administration, Washington was in a condition of blissful expectation. The sovereign state of Winston Bates, basking in the success of its U-2 venture, saw great opportunities ahead for more creative interventions.

Richard Helms, now Bissell's number two in clandestine operations, called me one Friday afternoon shortly after Kennedy's election. Allen Dulles was out of town, Helms told me, but scheduled to appear next week before my subcommittee for a friendly chat and he wanted a heads-up on any questions. It was just like Dulles to assume my job was to make sure he was briefed. It was too late in the day for me to go to Helms or for him to come to our offices. He was seeing Dulles on Monday morning to brief him. "Would you mind dropping by my home over the weekend, if it's not a terrible imposition? Saturday afternoon, on the early side?"

In 1958, Helms had expected to become the CIA's deputy director for Plans, in charge of all clandestine action, but Bissell got the job.

Helms had run the department efficiently without the title for almost two years after Frank Wisner, the previous DDP, suffered a mental and physical meltdown as the Hungarian Revolution collapsed. But Dulles was smitten with Bissell and gave him the position. When I called to congratulate Bissell, I said, "I thought you liked running operations, not huge bureaucracies," implying he lacked experience.

"Helms has agreed to stay on and work for me. He knows where the pencils are kept and where the bodies are buried. And he's a superb administrator. It will be a famous matchup."

I had been introduced to Helms on a number of social occasions over the years. He was a tall, youthful-looking man, whose slicked-back hair and self-assured bearing gave him a kind of continental demeanor. He always acknowledged me with bland but friendly greetings. Smiling easily, nodding thoughtfully to indicate he knew I was part of the intelligence community, he would then glide off, leaving the impression that he was too professionally correct to engage me without a brief to do so. Everyone had a strong and positive impression of him, though no one could tell me very much about him. His correctness seemed to set him at a distance yet people were drawn to him. Though he was not extremely wealthy, Helms had enough social credentials to make Dulles comfortable. But he wasn't part of the Georgetown set—the Bissell, Dulles, Barnes, Wisner, Alsop, Graham crowd. He led a well-to-do suburban life: a wife and two children and a nice house in Chevy Chase.

It was a warm mid-November day shortly after the election. The lawns of Chevy Chase, still lush and green, were stippled with brilliant, brittle leaves. Helms's house, part of the original Chevy Chase Village project of the early twentieth century, was a commodious, wood-framed exercise in easy gentility. He opened the door as I left the taxi and walked toward me, an elegant figure dressed in white from head to foot. "No car? I would have been happy to come to your place. Excuse the outfit. I've got a tennis game on later. The club's right around in back of the house."

He insisted on feeding me. A plate of little sandwiches, the crusts neatly trimmed, had already been prepared and we set ourselves up in his study at a small coffee table.

"It's so good to get a chance to really talk. Of course we've met many times but . . ." He smiled contritely, regretting the previous impediments to our conversation.

I agreed that I had wanted to get to know him for some time. "I used to go over this sort of testimony with Bissell."

"To be frank, when Allen mentioned the testimony, I told him I would like to call you. Dick is so busy now with his projects. Besides he's out of town right now with Allen. They're down in Florida with the president-elect. But I'm sure it's fine with him too. You know, Dick and I have managed to sort out our separate spheres almost intuitively. Dick took over the overnight cable traffic. No problem. I suppose he felt he needed a daily dose of everything going on out there. On the other hand, espionage doesn't interest Dick—except of course for eye-in-the-sky projects. So I'm still in the business of running agents. At a great remove now, but unless you've had the hands-on experience you can't really assess the information you get from them. I've also been allowed to retain what you might call the housekeeping responsibilities—personnel appointments, that sort of thing."

"I should think Dick would be fascinated by espionage."

"Not really and you know, maybe he's right. It takes so much time, so much patience to run an agent. And when you hook a big fish you have to be so cautious. Only dull plodders like me really enjoy it. And sooner or later the source makes a mistake. They all do. Your man in Moscow . . . we took him on, we thought we had a live one, and then he was gone."

That put me on my guard; he had said it so casually but now I knew he had kept up with me, or was there a CIA file on me?

"Dick likes to take bold action," Helms went on. "I don't have the appetite for it. Look at me. Do I look that old? God knows I feel sometimes as if I've been around forever. I suppose after a while you just get too cautious. I'm sure if I had come into the CIA the way Dick did, at the top, as Allen's special assistant, I'd have a much different point of view. Especially if the first thing Allen asked of me was to stick my nose into the Guatemalan operation."

Six years earlier, the CIA had managed to depose the left-leaning

I found Richard Helms to be an attractive and compelling personality, though we tended to circle each other in a friendly but cautious manner. *LBJ Library photo by Yoichi Okamoto*

government of Jacobo Árbenz with hardly a shot being fired. It was a dual triumph for Tracy Barnes, the agent in charge, and Bissell, whom Dulles had placed at Barnes's side.

"Bissell was right at home," Helms went on. "He had gone to Gro ton and Yale with Tracy. I didn't quite see how their plan was going to work. And Frank Wisner was especially worried. But it was almost magical the way they pulled it off, like a rabbit out of a hat. A rabbit out of a hat . . . ," he mused. "I imagine it's quite an encouraging example when you start to think about Cuba. Another sandwich?"

When we got around to Allen's testimony, I informed Helms that it was mostly about the costs for the U-2's successors, the SR-71 and the satellite program. "All Dick's projects," Helms mused. "Oh well, I'll have a word with him before I talk to Allen."

I took a chance. "As for Cuba . . ."

"Jay Mark?" he inquired, as if I had said the words. "I shouldn't think Allen would want to discuss Jay Mark."

Helms insisted on driving me home in his dinged-up old Cadillac.

"You're right in the thick of things," he said with mild amusement as he dropped me off. "Tracy Barnes a few blocks away. Poor Frank down the street. And isn't Allen himself just around the corner?"

It was hard not to feel the attraction of Helms. He wouldn't have left me out in the cold if he were the one running me. Compared to the strident self-confidence of Bissell, he was secure enough to be self-effacing. Without his uttering so much as a word of complaint, I knew that Bissell had marginalized him, that he thought Bissell lacked experience and had a taste for flashy, risky operations, and that Jay Mark might be one of them. I didn't know what "JMARK" stood for, but "JM" usually meant "Joint Military" and, come to think of it, the last letter was probably not "K" but "C" for "Cuba" or "Castro." It would be untrue to say that at that very early moment I was already alert to Cuba's potential for fiasco, but a thought had been planted. On reflection, Helms had quite intentionally planted the thought. Perhaps I *was* now being run by Helms, but if so what did he want me to do? Warn Russell most likely.

For months after the U-2 crashed, when Larry Boyer and I happened to encounter each other, he would avoid my eyes and ask after my health with muttering awkwardness. There were no more invitations for drinks with the Boyers, no more afternoons in the Boyer patio dandling little Mark on my knee. I could hardly blame Larry for resenting me. To my surprise, Deborah Boyer called me one Saturday morning in December. After a few awkward apologies about how inaccessible she and Larry had been, she said: "We're having a baby sitter crisis. Do you think you could mind Mark for a little while in the afternoon? He really misses you, you know."

I was mystified by Mark's adoration of me. He was a serious, dark-eyed little boy, now five years old, who always lingered in my presence when I was in his home. If I stayed for dinner, Mark would draft me to read his bedtime story. If I encountered him walking with Deborah in the neighborhood, he would insist that I take his hand. He seemed to derive some deep satisfaction from my proximity yet I was slightly embarrassed by his attention. I decided Mark had imprinted on me in some mysterious, psychobiological manner.

I took Mark downtown to see *Cinderfella*. After the movie, we took one of Washington's soon-to-be extinct trolleys back to Wisconsin Avenue. As we were walking along Dumbarton Street, Mark holding my hand contentedly, I saw Joe Alsop approaching us. With his prosecutorial gaze and his thick, round-framed glasses, he resembled a small owl. To encounter Alsop these days was to encounter an apotheosized version of himself. A few days after the election, at a dinner party at David and Evangeline Bruce's home, he had regaled Elizabeth and me with the story of how he and Phil Graham watched the election returns together, drinking and cheering. "They all talk about Illinois, but Phil and I knew the key was Texas. And I don't mind telling you, after all the work we had to do to convince the Kennedys to take on Johnson as VP, we felt a keen sense of satisfaction when the Texas return came in."

Alsop liked to take breaks from work with brief, seigniorial strolls along Dumbarton Street, on which he had lived in one house or another since 1937. I had run into him twice before. On each occasion, Alsop had swept me up, insisting I accompany him, but I expected Mark's presence would let me off the hook this afternoon.

"Well who do we have here?" Alsop said. "Mr. Bates and Mr. . . . ?

"Mark Boyer."

Alsop was one of those people who think small children are amused if you speak to them with exaggerated formality. He bowed to Mark and shook his hand. "The honor is mine, Mr. Mark Boyer. May I have your permission to accompany you for a short distance?"

Mark looked at me quizzically.

"Okay if he walks with us?" I said.

Mark shrugged.

"How kind of you," Alsop said. As we walked, he shared with me his profound satisfaction with the way the new administration was shaping up; it seemed they were following his instructions to the letter. "McNamara, Bundy, Doug Dillon . . . serious, accomplished, thoughtful men. We haven't seen their ilk since the Lovett, Acheson, Bohlen crowd."

"What do you suppose Kennedy will do about Cuba?" I ventured. I was suddenly nervous. What if I was revealing something to him?

Alsop didn't blink. "I applaud the intention of removing that bearded despot. Don't you?"

"But at what cost?" I said, trying to hide my lack of any information.

Alsop snorted. "You of all people should know exactly the cost. I suspect you do, to the penny. You needn't be concerned about my discretion. I kept silent about Árbenz, and before that Mossadegh in Iran. And I have said nothing since. It is not my job to blow the CIA's cover. In Iran and Guatemala I was actually informed in advance—in strict confidence of course. This Cuba thing I discovered on my own before worming the story out of Dick Bissell. But if I found out, so can others. And that's the trouble with this thing. How can you recruit and train a guerrilla force on the sly?"

That did it. The words "guerrilla force on the sly" married to "Cuba" gave me an almost erotic tingle of prescience and opportunity. "Maybe it really should be a military operation," I ventured, trying to keep Alsop talking.

"Oh my God! Don't let the military get their hands on it. This is a local problem. They'll turn it into a world war before we know it. Jack will get it right. You know, he's all for building up the military, but McNamara is going to figure out what they really need. Jack's not going to be cowed by those generals the way Ike was." He turned to Mark. "And what, young man, is your take on the new administration?"

Mark, who had been walking placidly, turned to me in confusion, looking for permission to ignore Alsop, which I granted with a helpless shrug.

My irritation with the Kennedy coronation overcame me. "We haven't heard much about the missile gap lately, have we?"

Alsop gave me a crooked grin as we rounded the third corner of what was shaping up to be a round-the-block saunter. "Jack's a realist. After the election, when Dick and Allen briefed him, he took the news quite well. I should imagine it's quite encouraging for a new president to discover he has an unexpectedly huge advantage over the Soviets."

"You don't suppose he got a little inkling of that even before he became president, back in August perhaps, when rumor has it you introduced him to Bissell? Perhaps you knew too by then?"

Alsop reddened. He had been warning about the missile gap for much of Eisenhower's last term. "Now now, Bates. Politics is politics. And I have publicly admitted my error." We were nearing Alsop's house. He worked in an office at the rear of his rather ugly cinderblock home, which he had designed himself. Its squat, bunkerlike form, painted yellow, had incensed his Georgetown neighbors but he said it was the only way he could afford the space he needed for entertaining, writing, and displaying his rich but eclectic collection of fine furniture and objets d'art. "I expect we'll be bumping into one another rather frequently over the next several weeks. It's going to be a strenuous social program what with saying good-bye to one administration and embracing the next."

Indeed it was a demanding social season. Elizabeth worked feverishly to polish up her old progressive and Democratic credentials. I was at her side at least two or three times a week during this period. She was like a shrew, her metabolism running at such a pitch she needed to consume at least four times her own social weight a day just to stay alive. She was especially pleased to snag Clark Clifford, who was managing the transition for Kennedy. It was widely believed he had given Kennedy the crucial advice on handling the allegations that Kennedy had not written *Profiles in Courage,* which was the beginning of their relationship. When the subject of Cuba was raised at the dinner table, as it seemed to be on almost every serious occasion, Clifford had so little to contribute that I was sure he knew nothing. Neither did Fulbright and Albert Gore. But when Douglas Dillon, currently undersecretary of State and recruited by Clifford as the token Republican to be secretary of the Treasury, spoke up, I couldn't help but hear a JMARC reverberation. "All over Latin America, they are convinced that an attack on Cuba by the U.S. is imminent," he said. "It's not. But I am confident any approach to Cuba will be carefully reviewed by the new administration."

As the days went by it was fascinating to learn how many people knew and how many people didn't know about JMARC. You could be at a reception at the Mexican embassy and some utterly obscure third secretary would upbraid you for training an army in the jungles of

Nicaragua; while the following night, at Elizabeth's good-bye dinner for Eisenhower's press secretary, Jim Hagerty, most of the drunken journalists didn't know a thing about any organized anti-Cuban activity.

On another evening, at Joan and Tom Braden's brawl of a cocktail party, everyone was in a preinauguration frenzy. They all knew things were going to be different; as they tried to define the elusive difference to each other, their canapés and drinks disappeared at an alarming rate. In the midst of the hubbub I spotted the CIA's Tracy Barnes, standing as if in a spotlight. Despite being introduced to him at least nine times over the years, I had never managed to penetrate his self-absorption. An extremely handsome man with an extremely attractive wife, he moved with the grace of an actor impersonating an athlete. Many people regarded him as a dashing, romantic figure and the pleasure he took in their regard was transparent. I edged my way over in his direction, but just before my presence was unavoidable, he avoided me. I tried again later, and again he moved away. I became convinced that Bissell, who was also at the party, had warned him about me. Richard Helms had connected Bissell and Barnes to JMARC and now I saw Bissell and Barnes as opposed to me. At that moment, the seed that Helms had planted in me about JMARC began to grow; now JMARC looked like a creative opportunity for me to be in opposition to Bissell and Barnes.

Two weeks before the inauguration, Elizabeth called me. "Have you heard?" she gasped. "They are adding two more balls. At this date! Two more inaugural balls plus the three that are already planned. Just imagine the nonentities who will be there!"

"I'm sure all the best people will be with us at the Mayflower."

"Any of the first three are fine, I'm sure. But what you must do, dear Winnie, is find out for me which ball the Kennedys are going to attend *last*. Will you? That's where we'll want to end up too. My guess is the one at the Armory. Meyer Davis is playing there and he played for Jackie at her debut and also at her wedding."

About the only joy I took in the inauguration was the petty pleasure of being the only person from Russell's office besides Russell to be on the shortlist for the first round of the choicest inaugural ball tickets.

As the inauguration approached, Washington worked itself into a lather of expectation and excitement. The Kennedys' ability to confer an alluring glow on every social function well before the event was extraordinary. Elizabeth and I, along with an awful lot of other people, were not invited to the party that Stephen and Jean Kennedy Smith planned to throw in their new Georgetown home for her brother and sister-in-law, but all of us knew that Frank Sinatra and Oleg Cassini were to be in attendance. The whole Kennedy family seemed to be moving into Georgetown; the area had always been central to Washington social life, but now it was becoming a theatrical setting for the Kennedy extravaganza.

Elizabeth managed to snag a second set of inaugural ball tickets. "It's going to be so perfect, Winston," she said triumphantly. "The Kennedys will hit the Mayflower first. We'll be there. We'll circulate, meet people, et cetera. Why we might, dear boy, even take a turn or two on the dance floor?" she added, mischievously alluding to my status as a clumsy, reluctant dancer. "Then, after they leave, we can go back to my place, have a quiet dinner and go on to the Statler at midnight. Yes it's the Statler that's last on their schedule, but at least we won't have to stay long and I'm betting the Kennedys won't either. We just have to make sure we get there before the Kennedys leave."

Snow had begun to fall for the second day in a row as I arrived at Elizabeth's house on the evening of January 20. I offered to tell her about Kennedy's inaugural address, but she was too busy making some last-minute adjustments to her burgundy silk gown, with its fragile swirl of sculpted epaulets. On our way to the Mayflower, I discovered my own fashion problem for the evening: my black patent shoes, purchased to accompany my new wide-lapelled satin tuxedo, were already blistering my toes. To make it worse, Elizabeth had refused to disclose the motive for her careering from one ball to another so I was feeling more than usual like the pendant on her necklace.

Elizabeth's purpose in attending two balls, I decided, was to increase the odds of meeting the golden couple. She was very aware there were other Georgetown hostesses who were ahead of her in their access to the Kennedys. But as the Kennedy entourage surged into the May-flower ballroom, Elizabeth made no effort to get close. When the Ken-nedys did not take the dance floor, everyone else rushed forward to perform for the royal couple's pleasure. Out of respect for my feeble abilities, we remained seated while Elizabeth gazed hungrily at the Kennedys. An hour later the Kennedy tide swept out of the hall. After a discreet pause, we followed. In the hallway, a damp, bedraggled woman was berating her husband for having missed the president. Their limou-sine had skidded off an icy road and they'd had to walk some distance in the snow. Elizabeth sighed. "We can't drive all over Washington in this weather. You better find Bud and tell him that we'll stay at the Mayflower until it's time to go to the Statler. It's only a few blocks away."

At least three times an hour Elizabeth forced me to go to the lobby to call the hotels on the list and track the Kennedys. When I told her

On a freezing night in January 1961, the new president and First Lady arrive at the Inaugural Ball at the National Guard Armory. It is the third of five inaugural balls, and Jackie is already looking a little wan. *Abbie Rowe. White House Photographs. John F. Kennedy Presidential Library and Museum, Boston*

that the Kennedy caravan had gone directly to the Statler from the Mayflower she grimaced angrily, as if the Kennedys had betrayed her. A little while later I spoke to the Sheraton Park Hotel who told me that the Kennedys were now at the National Guard Armory and that the Sheraton would be the next stop.

"Then we'll go to the Sheraton now," Elizabeth declared. "I can't take the chance on losing them."

Our limousine crawled through the snow and it was approaching midnight when we arrived. Elizabeth was in a panic. "What if they don't come because of the snow? What will we do then?"

Up the street I saw the cordon of limousines and Secret Service vehicles. "Look, they're just arriving now. Do you have tickets for this ball?"

"It doesn't matter. We'll show them our Statler tickets. They'll let us in."

We had to park down the block and shuffle awkwardly through wet, ankle-high snow. I was now hungry, cold, and wet but Elizabeth, consumed by the hunt, was unfazed. As we approached, Kennedy was exiting his limousine. The Secret Service forced us back from the entrance, but we could see Kennedy turn back and speak briefly into the limousine. Then he entered the hotel along with his retinue. The limousine began to pull away. Two other cars from the caravan followed.

"My God! Jackie's going on by herself. Back! Back!" Elizabeth began running to our car.

I could barely keep up with her. "What are you trying to do?"

"I'll tell you in the car. Now find Bud. He should be nearby."

Bud wasn't nearby. We had to run a long way down the sidewalk because the Kennedy cars occupied all the area around the entrance.

When we were finally in the car, she told Bud to catch up to Jackie's limo.

"Are you crazy?" I said. "They'll arrest us."

"They'll never notice us."

I took off my wet shoes. My feet were numb. "What is going on?" I demanded. "I refuse to be abducted."

"You don't have any choice, unless you want to get out and walk.

Don't you see? There's got to be a postinaugural party. Something private and informal. Somewhere. I've even heard rumors but no one will talk. That's surely where Jackie's headed."

"You mean we're going to crash the party?"

"You bet," she said.

I was aghast. "We'll never be invited anywhere again."

"Don't be silly. We'll march right in as if the Kennedys invited us, as if we're part of their party. Just act like you belong. Hmmm . . ." She pressed her face against the steamy window. "Where *are* they headed?"

It didn't take me long to have a good idea where we were headed but I kept my mouth shut. Every time we fell behind Elizabeth would rap forcefully on the partition. "Keep up, Bud. You keep up!" It went on like this for quite a while.

Finally Elizabeth said, "Doesn't the White House look lovely in the snow? Oh no! She's not returning to the White House is she? Bud, why are you stopping?"

A car was blocking the street. We came to a stop. A man approached our car, identified himself as a Secret Service agent, and demanded to know where we were going. After our awkward explanation about being lost in the snow, he made us turn around and drive away as Jackie's car drove up to her new home. Elizabeth was shaking with frustration.

"I'm sorry, Elizabeth. The party must be back at the White House. Jackie's probably gone ahead to check on the arrangements. We can't crash the White House. Let's just go home. It's after one o'clock. I could use some dry socks and some sleep."

"You don't have to sound so happy about it, Winnie."

In all the years I had known Elizabeth, I had never gotten around to telling her how much I detested being called Winnie, but tonight it pushed me over the edge. "Happy? I'm overjoyed! You've dragged me all over Washington on some wild-goose chase. The first ball was bearable for about forty-five minutes. But we had to spend two hours there. Then we started driving like maniacs. We've barely spoken to a single person we know all evening. I'm starving. My feet are frozen. All so you could elbow your way into some mythical party where you weren't wanted. Why shouldn't I be happy to go home?"

"Oh, you're the most ungrateful person! I can't believe you're speaking to me this way! Excuse me for even inviting you!"

We spent the rest of the trip in angry silence. As we entered Georgetown, Elizabeth told Bud to drop her off first and then take me home.

"I'll walk, thank you." I painfully wedged my feet back into my shoes. When we paused at a red light, I got out of the car.

"Oh you ridiculous man. You'll freeze to death. Please stop behaving like an idiot."

I tramped off into the night and Elizabeth drove away. The snow was coming down quite heavily. My feet felt like dead stumps, which was sort of a blessing, but I could tell it was going to be a real slog to get home. As I walked down Wisconsin Avenue I saw a line of double halos coming toward me through the snow. When it drew closer, I recognized a somewhat abbreviated edition of the presidential motorcade. They turned on Dumbarton Street. Though my legs could barely move, I began to stumble after the motorcade with growing excitement. Sure enough, up ahead the cars had stopped in front of Alsop's home, which sat invitingly above the street. Light was pouring out from all the windows; the snow reflected its golden radiance. As Kennedy walked up the stairs, alone, to the front door, Alsop's neighbors leaned out of their windows, applauding and cheering. Kennedy turned, waved, and disappeared into the house. For a brief moment I was transfixed and then I marched right up to the door. A Secret Service officer stepped in front of me. Behind him Peter Duchin opened the door. "Joe asked me . . . ," I said.

"Winston! You too! How wonderful!" Alsop had appeared. The Secret Service man stepped aside and I entered the house. Alsop was ebullient. "This is surely the most unusual party that has ever happened to me. I told a few people to come by for a late drink, and they asked a few other people, who must have asked a few more and now the president himself is here! I had to wake up José and Maria to get some food ready. Terrapin soup and champagne! That's not a half-bad way to end an evening like this. Leave your coat here. You look like you could use some hot soup."

The huge fire roaring in Joe's fireplace and the steaming tureen of soup imparted a warm, smoky fragrance to the room. I had come to an oasis. I got myself a bowl of soup and plopped down in one of Alsop's comfortable chairs. It was all I could do to resist drinking directly from the bowl. When I finally felt somewhat thawed I looked up. There were a number of people I knew and some I only recognized, such as Peter Lawford. There was a sense of subdued contentment. People spoke quietly, delighted to have a chance to prolong this evening in the presence of the new president.

I looked around for Kennedy, whom I wanted to see up close. I noticed George Smathers, one of Kennedy's better friends, speaking to John Sherman Cooper, another Kennedy friend. I decided to attach myself to Smathers; sooner or later he and Kennedy would find each other. I stood up and nearly fell over. My feet were paralyzed. I was alarmed—what if I had frostbite?—but I could hardly remove my shoes and socks right there in front of everybody. With both hands on the armrests, I pushed myself to my feet again. I managed to shuffle my way down a long corridor toward Alsop's private rooms. I came to a closed door. As I hesitantly tried the handle I felt a hand on my arm. It was Lawford. "The president is in there. He'll be out in a moment. He just needs to refresh himself." I shuffled on until I came to another door and entered what was clearly Alsop's bedroom. I closed the door behind me and sat down on the bed to inspect the damage. My feet looked like raw meat. The tops of several toes were scraped and bleeding. After some vigorous rubbing, feeling began to return. Fifteen minutes later, wearing a pair of silk socks I had stolen from Joe's dresser, I returned to the party. Kennedy had appeared in the drawing room. He was speaking to Smathers, but so many people were edging toward them it was impossible to get close. I was speaking to the third wife of Henry Fonda when Lawford returned to the room with a striking young woman—lush figure, creamy skin, golden hair, and barely wearing something that resembled a gossamer skein of spun sugar.

It was well after three in the morning when Kennedy finally left. The rest of us departed soon after. I had consumed enough champagne to feel anesthetized as I walked home. The next day I washed Joe's socks and returned them by mail, anonymously.

18

A few days after the inauguration, Larry Boyer called me at the office to ask if he could drop by in the evening. He said he had some U-2 news for me. I was startled by his appearance when he arrived. His small face seemed to have contracted around his sharp features, giving him a look of anguished exhaustion. He sat down and stood up several times, as if preparing to make an announcement and then thinking better of it. I tried to make him feel relaxed, bustling around making drinks, chattering about the Kennedys, carefully avoiding anything about his job.

Larry replied mechanically, his agitation suppressed, until he blurted out, "Do you know where the U-2 is headed these days?"

"I could guess, but you tell me."

"Cuba. They're searching for Russian MIG fighters. Thought you might want to know . . . a last little secret . . . before I leave."

"You're leaving the Pentagon?"

He gulped. "Yes. I'm taking the fall for the U-2 being shot down."

"I'm sorry, Larry. I feel terrible that my bad advice—"

"It's not your fault. You were only trying to help me. Just before that last flight Eisenhower got cold feet and Lemnitzer showed him my original report, which calmed him down. That made me a hero for a few hours. I never should have changed my mind after that, or told people that I had changed my mind. I should have listened to your advice. I did try to get my retraction to the White House at the last minute, but Lemnitzer got wind of it and had it buried at the Pentagon. But because that retraction turned out to be correct in the end, it was like *I* was the one who caused the plane to crash."

Tears suddenly tumbled from his eyes. He stood up abruptly and clenched his fists, trembling in frustration. "And I'm leaving Washington too. Deborah says we should try to live apart for a while. You get what I'm saying? I'm going to leave and she's going to stay." He moved a few paces away, standing with his back to me while he shuddered silently. "I'm losing *my* job and she sees it as a chance to get rid of me!"

"I'm sure Deborah's just as sorry and disappointed as you are."

"Oh sure she's sorry! You know what she told the marriage counselor? She said I overwhelmed her with *niceness* in college. Niceness! That's her reason she married me. 'Mr. Goody' she used to call me. Who wants to be called *that*?"

"But Mark . . ."

"Mark!" he wailed. "Even *he* likes you better than me."

I must have looked shaken because he looked at me with sudden concern. "Sorry, Winston, that's not your problem. I didn't come over here to blame you or anything. I need you to keep an eye on them for me. Please?"

"Larry, Deborah would never trust me if I—"

"I don't mean like *spy* on them, exactly. Just help them. Let me know if they need help."

"Where are you going?"

"Back to California. I couldn't find a job in Washington. Deb's father gave me a job in his PR office. He doesn't know yet that she's not coming with me. But maybe, if I'm in California, maybe Deb will want to come out there too. Maybe."

First the Paris summit crashes; then Larry loses his job and family. That was a local effect I hadn't anticipated. Globally, my sense of responsibility for bringing mankind closer to nuclear armageddon was more notional than remorseful. But when Larry burst into tears, the sudden pang of guilt was unexpected as well as unfamiliar.

*

As the new administration took office, Russell told me the Pentagon wanted me to have my personal high-level liaison. I could see why the Pentagon wanted to stay close to Russell's office. For years the Joint Chiefs had flaunted their barely resistible itch to get it on with the Russians and Chinese while Russell encouraged them. Not that Russell was ever eager for war, but it was a way of pressuring Eisenhower to keep the defense budget growing. When Russell began declaring how impressed he was by Robert McNamara, the new secretary of Defense, and his legion of cost-cutting technocrats, the military was concerned they were losing their champion.

My new liaison was Colonel Henry Hess of the U.S. Army. Hess was an aide to David Gray, a brigadier general whose assignment on the Joint Subsidiary Activities Committee of the Joint Chiefs of Staff made him the coordinator of all secret paramilitary operations between the Joint Chiefs and the CIA. Socializing with the likes of me didn't come naturally to Hess, who was more dogged than ingratiating. His idea of an amiable encounter was lunch or dinner at the Army and Navy Club, with its oversolicitous black waiters and its blockhouse portions of mushy beef. Happily the drinks were massive too, and after a couple of martinis I could let my mind drift contentedly as Hess instructed me in the ways of the military. Trained as a logistics expert, Hess was also a logistics enthusiast, full of mind-numbing anecdotes about supplying horses to the Assyrian army's cavalry squadrons, or the Egyptian "revolution" of the ox-drawn cart, or the Persian army's brilliant system of naval resupply of ground operations. My first impression of him, probably influenced by the uniform, had been of a muscularly bulky man, but on second, third, and fourth encounters I began to see that his was a more doughy physique, which went along with his baleful, flabby face and an ample second chin. He jerked his head as he spoke, tossing his words out of the corner of his mouth. "Laos is where I learned what a force for peace the Joint Chiefs could be. When I told them it would take two hundred and seventy-five thousand troops to win in Laos, they thought that was great. But when they told Ike, he backed right off. Maybe with a little assist from Senator Russell?" He cocked his head expectantly.

"A land war in Asia is one of Russell's big fears. It sounds like you stacked the deck to save us from a blunder."

"Let's say I did my part to ensure no one went into this with any illusions. Besides, Allen Dulles was only too happy to take a whack at running a covert operation in Laos, not that he knows any better than the military how to fight an insurgency."

His Laotian experience had inspired Hess to reinvent himself as an expert on guerrilla warfare. It made him somewhat of a lonely prophet in a Pentagon obsessed with its big-bang arsenal. He fancied himself as something of an intellectual and he had studied some of the texts associated with revolutionary insurgency. I found it disconcerting to hear Hess quote Chairman Mao as we dined in the Army and Navy Club, surrounded by battalion insignias and portraits of venerable generals.

To establish a rapport with me, Hess displayed an exasperated amusement at the foibles of the military culture, attempting to entertain me with accounts of the byzantine structure of the military's administrative organization—committees and study groups reporting to coordinating committees reporting to joint committees. "Us in the military, we've forgotten about Korea. We're still puffed up on our victory in World War II. The way the Joint Chiefs look at it, sooner or later they're gonna have to pull America's fat out of the fire again. But the Kennedy people, they don't give a flying fuck what the Joint Chiefs think. And between you, me, and the gatepost, I don't exactly blame them. War heroes and bureaucratic survivors, that's what you get at the top of the military heap. And they sit around like a bunch of old maids and gossip and bitch about McNamara and the Kennedys. But the military system is bigger than your individual idiot. Not too many of us are brilliant, but get us all hitched together, each one doing his part, and you get some serious light. Cumbersome? Sure. But when we're minding our own business it works. My message to you: Let's not screw up the part that works."

Hess must have found me as unlikely a dining companion as I did him. He often matched and sometimes exceeded my martini consumption. One evening in late January at the Army and Navy Club, when we were postprandially collapsed in huge leather club chairs, side by side, watching the smoke drift up from our chimney-sized cigars, I heard Hess mutter something about Cuba. An exasperated tone in his voice grabbed my vagrant attention. With a jaded sigh I said, "Oh that JMARC thing, is that still on?" Hess sat up rigidly, looking around the cavernous room as if there were a hidden microphone in every corner.

"You and Russell, you know what's going on?"

"Of course we've been informed," I lied. "But to be honest, Bissell hasn't been very forthcoming about the details."

Hess was relieved to find something substantive to discuss with me—or was this where he was headed from the start? He lay back and then shifted over onto his shoulder so he could face me, grunting at the effort. I rolled toward him, facilitating a kind of chair-to-chair pillow talk.

"Here's what I can tell you. General Gray recently briefed the new administration—meaning Kennedy, Rusk, and McNamara—on the six options for getting rid of Castro, which run from feeble economic sanctions all the way up to a full-out military invasion. But right in the middle of the list is the one that attracts Kennedy's attention because it seems like the perfect compromise: guerrilla infiltration by Cuban rebels with U.S. support. Then, to almost no one's surprise, Allen Dulles pipes up: 'Gentlemen, that's just what the CIA has in the works already!' A few weeks later, Dulles and Richard Bissell presented the CIA plan to the whole National Security Council."

As Hess described the operation, my miscellaneous collection of remarks, rumors, and suspicions at last resolved into a coherent picture. Beginning a year before Kennedy's election, a machine had been conceived, designed, assembled, redesigned, reassembled, improved, and expanded in Washington, Panama, Miami, Guatemala, and Nicaragua. There was no single inventor, though Allen Dulles could be regarded as the blind watchmaker. He was present at the machine's conception, representing the CIA when Eisenhower and the National Security Council first agreed that something should be done about Cuba—a something that in its preliminary, experimental model was a twenty-five-man guerrilla force of Cuban exiles, trained in Panama and parachuted into Cuba. Dulles knew just the people to make the model into a bigger and better machine. There was Richard Bissell, his brilliant protégé and heir apparent, and Tracy Barnes, in whom the canon of an intrepid CIA officer was so sleekly aggregated. Dulles reserved for himself the role of avuncular patron.

From Operation Pluto to JMARC to JMATE, its latest name, the low horsepower, twenty-five-man infiltration machine was retrofitted with spare parts borrowed from the military to be a four-hundred-man amphibian-landing machine whose short excursion on the high seas, courtesy of the Navy, would be called Operation Bumpy Road. Marine Colonel Jack Hawkins and Jacob Esterline of the CIA were Bissell's choices to actually manufacture the machine. Continually evolving, the machine's manpower grew to seven hundred Cuban exiles, now training at a secret base in Guatemala. As new features, such as a supporting air force made up of war surplus B-25 and B-26 planes, made its operation more complicated, Bissell and Barnes pointed to its fail-safe mechanism: If, by some remote possibility, the Cuban people were not inspired to rise up against their Communist oppressors when the machine spewed out the Cuban patriots on Trinidad Beach, the fighters could melt away into the nearby Escambray Mountains and begin a guerrilla insurgency.

Hess went on. "When Dulles and Bissell finished presenting the plan to the NSC, Kennedy looks around at the Joint Chiefs and says, 'What do you think of the plan?' Silence reigns. Admiral Burke finally pipes up and says there should be a formal military review and approval of the CIA plan. To which Dulles, in his clever way replies, 'I agree. Military evaluation is crucial.' So we get assigned to evaluate but not approve."

It was close to midnight. The club was quiet, though I could hear the occasional murmur of conversation from other clusters of club chairs. "Why don't I give you a lift home?" Hess offered.

He took an indirect route back to Georgetown. When we neared the Lincoln Memorial he pointed to Quarters Eye, the ramshackle World War II barracks, now one of several CIA buildings around Washington. "That's the JMATE headquarters now. It's where we went to evaluate the CIA plan—me, Colonel Tarwater from the Air Force, General Gray, and three other colonels."

"Was the CIA cooperative?"

"At first I thought they were hiding their plans from us. But then we realized *there are no plans*. Oh they think they have a plan—which is train a bunch of soldiers and dump them into Cuba. But there's no plan for amphibian training, no plan for tactical support, no manpower assessment, no maps, no logistics. But they're spending a hundred thousand dollars a month to support the Cuban government-in-exile!"

"Who briefed you?" There was hardly a need to pry; Hess was letting it all pour out.

"Tracy Barnes. He danced around and waved his hands. I never met anyone who could talk more and say less. It was like a beautiful fog—nothing you could hold on to. Our report to the Joint Chiefs gave the operation a fifteen percent chance of success, but the Chiefs told us to find a way to be more supportive before we reported to Kennedy. So we pushed for a massive air strike to destroy the Cuban air force on the day of the landing. That got us up to a thirty percent chance of success."

"That's still not good is it? What did the CIA say?"

Hess snorted. "They were happy enough. Long odds seem to excite them. But the number didn't come up when we met with Kennedy. Bissell commandeered our report and presented it himself. All he did was read the executive summary where we say the plan has a fair chance of ultimate success as long as the CIA is right about the political situation in Cuba and there are mass uprisings in support of the operation."

"'Fair chance of success' sounds much more positive than thirty percent. What did Kennedy say?"

Hess took a thoughtful puff on his cigar. "The president said to carry on with the operation but he reserved the right to cancel it at any time. Not exactly an endorsement."

"'Reserved the right to cancel it . . .' That sounds so *very* presidential," I mocked. "How would he know if it is a good plan or not? He must have been trying out his voice of authority."

"It's just a little country, Cuba. The Joint Chiefs will probably back anything that has even a slight chance of getting rid of Castro on the theory that once it gets rolling, they'll be asked to make it better. We have a chance to pull it off if the Navy and the Air Force can go all the way in support of a full-fledged military operation, not a back-alley intelligence operation."

At last I understood what Hess was after. "Is that what we're facing, another territorial battle? Who owns the operation? Is that what you're after here? You guys want to run it and you want Russell to help you get it away from the CIA."

Hess looked genuinely hurt. "Did I say that? Let's make sure we've got a plan that will work. That's my goal."

"Russell doesn't like to interfere in turf wars."

"What if you could speak to him more authoritatively? Maybe I can let you see for yourself how things are going."

"You know I don't like this kind of clandestine operation," Russell said to me when I described JMATE to him. "When it gets that big, too much can go wrong. It really should be a military operation. But I can't undermine Allen at this point. Even if he hasn't briefed me about the operation, I've always supported him on the big issues. And I don't think Kennedy would start anything unless he was dead certain he could finish it. I remember what I said to Ike when Lyndon and I tried to talk him out of supporting the French at Dien Bien Phu: 'When you commit the flag you commit the country.' "

"And that means . . ."

"Be darn sure you're right, because you're going to have to do whatever it takes to win."

"Do we think Ike passed the message on to Kennedy?"

Russell looked at me sourly. I sounded flippant, a tone I usually tried to repress in his sober presence. "Now you listen to me carefully, Winston. I want you to keep up with this operation. I didn't pay enough attention to you on the U-2 and I'm not going to make that mistake again. If you think there's something I can do, something I *should* do, I want you to tell me directly. If this goes wrong, my committee is going to be sorting it out for years to come. If Bissell needs more firepower, even if he doesn't know he does, you have to tell me. I'm always ready to do the right thing, even if it means going in to see the president."

I didn't yet see how I could play a creative role in JMATE but it looked as if there would be opportunities for intervention. My ambitions, unfortunately, had been inflated by my success with the U-2. In the meantime, I couldn't afford another breach with Russell. While I looked for the perfect opportunity, I would also have to convince Russell I was looking for the "right thing" to do.

"Just remember, you can always come to me," Russell repeated. "I had a call the other day from your Colonel Hess that sounds like it might be connected to this Cuba thing. He wanted to know if I could spare you for a couple of days. They're inspecting some training facility and he thought you'd like to go along. See what you can find out, but don't worry, son, I've been assured you'll be in no danger."

19

Our CIA contact, identifiable by his briarwood pipe, was supposed to meet us at the arrival gate after our commercial flight to Miami landed in the late afternoon of February 24. We had been instructed to look like tourists and each of the three colonels sported an exuberantly colored Hawaiian shirt and white linen trousers. Hess's shirt in particular stood out, with its constellation of neon-red pineapples against a black background. Standing next to the colonels in my summery seersucker suit, I felt like the manager of a tropical barbershop trio. Not only were the colonels conspicuous, their disguises weren't very thorough: each of them carried an identical, military-issue duffel bag.

I had met one of them, an Air Force colonel named Tarwater, at the 1955 manpower hearings. The other colonel, the expert in paramilitary training, appeared to be profoundly hungover. His eyes were bloodshot and during the plane trip to Miami he had stumbled to the bathroom three times. His deeply lined, weather-beaten face suggested that he was in this condition fairly frequently. Despite the fact that he had aged thirty years in the twelve years since I last saw him, I recognized him as soon as I shook his hand at the airport in Washington. He said, "Nice to meetcha, kid," and took a drag on his cigarette, just as he had twelve years ago. He was a major then, Major Matthew Mason from Army Intelligence, the man in Frankfurt to whom I had handed the cash during my career as a courier.

I spent the entire flight in a terrorized debate with myself. Should I remind him who I was? If I said nothing and he recalled me later, would that seem extra suspicious? How many times had he seen me anyway? Eight, as I remembered, each time for no more than a few perfunctory minutes. Our entire conversation would consist of him saying "Thanks, kid." And then, after counting the money: "It's all there. You can go." And it *was* twelve years ago, though he still called me "kid." But he was an intelligence officer, possibly trained to remember faces. Was he waiting to see how I behaved before he turned me in? A connection to Canadian intelligence in the past was just the thing to excite CIA counterintelligence; they were convinced that Canada's intelligence service was crawling with Communists.

By the time we landed I had persuaded myself to say nothing to Mason. If he belatedly recognized me, I would pretend I hadn't recognized him but be innocently overjoyed to see him. But what if he was pretending not to recognize me? I would have to wait for him to make the first move. The last thing I wanted was for this man to become curious about me.

A slim, sunburned man, who had been waiting at the opposite arrival gate, approached us. He wore a white shirt and khaki pants. A pipe was clenched in the corner of his mouth, which he removed theatrically. He regarded us with a turned-down smile, as if he was barely suppressing an amusing remark at our expense. "Harold?" he inquired.

Hess stepped forward, hand outstretched. "Do you mean Hen—"

"Harold will do," the man said taking his hand. "We're all going to be on a first-name basis. And you," he said to Tarwater, "you're Ted, and you," he surveyed Mason, "you look like a George." The operative turned to me, his snide amusement no longer repressed. "You are definitely a Max. Short for Maximilian. As for me, call me Eduardo." No one could have looked less like an Eduardo.

We walked through the parking lot. In the late-afternoon sun, the palm trees threw off jaunty, serrated shadows. We squeezed into Eduardo's dingy black Ford and set off, the cloying stench of his pipe filling the car. "We're going to stop first at the *Frente* headquarters—that's the 'Front' in English. That's where most of the recruiting for the brigade is

This is the man I knew as "Eduardo" on my trip to Guatemala, until I encountered him a number of years later. ©*AP Photo/Henry Griffin*

done," Eduardo said. "Then, when it's dark, you'll take off for Guatemala. There's one thing I must stress, gentlemen. When you're in contact with any Cuban, either here in Miami or in Guatemala, no matter how high up he might be in the brigade hierarchy, you're not, I repeat, you're *not* a group of Pentagon big shots who have come here at the behest of the Joint Chiefs of Staff to assess the training and readiness of the brigade." Sandwiched between "Harold" and "George," I could feel them stiffen at Eduardo's tone. He sounded at once preemptory and dismissive, a sophisticated adept speaking to clumsy beginners.

"Two reasons," Eduardo continued. "First of all, most of the brigadistas have been training for months. As far as they're concerned, they *are* ready for action. Any suggestion that they are still being assessed, or that there is a chance that the mission could be postponed again or even canceled, and I've got a tropical storm on my hands. Second, the extent of our American commitment is a secret, even from our brigadistas. Our Cubans are passionately dedicated to the cause. But they have an excitable, expressive nature that often overcomes discretion.

Bissell wants us to keep the operation buttoned-down. Deniability is crucial."

"'U.S. Helps Train an Anti-Castro Force at Secret Guatemalan Air-Ground Base,'" I said, impertinently referring to a *New York Times* article from early January, just before Kennedy arrived in the White House.

"Well we denied it, didn't we?" Eduardo said with a snort. He nodded toward me. "I've been briefed on *you*."

Never one to miss an opportunity to annoy Bissell, I had let Jim Flannery know that I was going down to the Guatemala base at the invitation of the Joint Chiefs.

"And what was the upshot of that article?" Eduardo pressed me accusingly. "Nothing! No one cared—except for the usual hand-wringing in the left-wing press. *Everyone* wants Castro removed. Publicity can only help. We were flooded with new volunteers. Now, with the Kennedy people running things, even deniability is not enough. They want it to be a *real* secret. Get rid of Castro but don't let any shit stick to us."

"Good luck," Mason said.

"When we get to Frente headquarters, and while we're in Guatemala, you gentlemen are simply experts on various aspects of guerrilla warfare and insurgency. Technical advisors. Not—I repeat, *not*—emissaries of doubt. No one at Retalhuleu must know the purpose of this visit. That includes any other CIA operatives you may run into at the camp. As for you, Max, shall we say you're the expert on hand-to-hand combat?"

"No thanks," I said, realizing with some satisfaction that I had made an enemy.

"The Frente is pretty much my invention. I've put it together in just a few months. My job is to persuade all these separate Cuban exile groups, most of whom hate each other, to support a common purpose."

"One hundred thousand dollars a month can be powerfully persuasive," I said.

The Frente headquarters, in a big rambling house in southwest Miami, was a hubbub of men streaming up and down the stairs, popping in and out of rooms, milling about in the halls. Several of them interrupted their fervent discussions to greet Eduardo affectionately in

Spanish as he escorted us through the building. He led us upstairs to a stuffy little room, barren except for a few small chairs and an unused desk. He returned in a few minutes with another man; they were carrying four heaping plates of rice and beans.

"Eat up, gentlemen. It's a seven-hour flight and there's no more food until we land. I'll be back for you in an hour."

While we waited, the colonels went over the plan for the next two days, deciding who would review which training exercises. When night had fallen, Eduardo shepherded us back into his car. We took a long, evasive route to the abandoned Opa-locka naval airfield. Once we were at the base, Eduardo killed the headlights. There were no lights on the base but Eduardo knew his way on the endless expanse of apron and runway. When I stepped out of the car I was in a vast, amorphous blackness. I heard a voice and turned. I could just discern the shape of the airplane.

In the C-54, the seating choices were bench or floor. The compartment was crowded with crates and cartons as well as a group of new recruits, seven young men who managed to look at once resolute and apprehensive. The small portholes had been painted black and ringed with black tape. The pilot, who had a deep southern accent, introduced himself as Riley. "Just 'cause we're taking off without lights, there's no need to worry, gentlemen. There's nothing for us to hit out here."

I slept on the floor of the plane in a sleeping bag. When I awoke, I stiffly uncurled myself and stumbled to a window. Through a gap in the black paint I could make out daylight; a carpet of green jungle streamed across my peephole.

"Sleep well?" Eduardo inquired brightly as I stretched. "We'll be there soon. Both the air base and the infantry training camp were carved out of a coffee plantation, a finca called La Helvetia. A pal of Ydígoras, Guatemala's very obliging *el presidente,* owns it. Ted's the lucky one. He gets to inspect the air base, which is where the finca residence is. We call it the Hilton. Things are more primitive up the mountain at the training camp."

The landing was bone rattling. When we left the plane, I saw we had stopped just short of a jungle mountainside jutting up vertically before us. It had rained recently. The leaves were wet and the steamy air was suffused with the musty sweetness of fertility and decay. Two men met us, one of whom, a lithe, handsome Cuban, introduced himself as José San Román, the brigade's commander. The other, solid and confident, stepped forward. "Roberto Alejos. Welcome to my finca."

"Alejos?" I said. "The Guatemalan ambassador in Washington is—"

"My brother Carlos," Alejos said.

Two jeeps took us on a terrifying ride up the mountain. As we swung around a sharp switchback at the edge of a cliff, Eduardo noticed my desperate grip on the door. "You know why they've named it the 2506 Brigade, don't you? Recruit number 2506 was the first brigadista to die. He fell off the mountain during training."

At the camp, Hess and Mason hoisted their duffels, Mason staggering under the weight of his. He looked ravaged after the bumpy ride. Despite his costume, Hess looked ready for action. And there I was, clutching my alligator-skin suitcase like a life raft as my exquisitely pliant Italian leather shoes sank into the mud. We were taken to our quarters. Hess and I shared a small shack furnished with two grimy canvas cots and a broken chair with two legs. I had not packed well; instructed to look like a tourist, I outfitted myself with Bermuda shorts and tennis sneakers. Hess and Mason knew enough to bring boots and old fatigues.

On the first day, I trailed after Hess as he observed various training exercises and spoke to the instructors, who seemed to be mainly Americans. Hess was so attentive to me that half of the officers and instructors assumed I was an important person and the other half assumed I was a helpless idiot. I did my best to take it all in, disguising my boredom with a look of intense scrutiny as groups of soldiers demonstrated their ability to break down machine guns and grenade launchers and to swing on ropes over obstacle courses. No matter how hard I tried to seem professional, there was something about me that inspired solicitous warnings about biting insects and poisonous snakes. As I wilted in the sticky heat, I grew irritable. I sidled up to Hess and said: "I don't understand how watching a lot of sweaty men do calisthenics would give anyone a clue as to their performance under fire." Eduardo overheard me, as he was intended to, and frowned.

Hess answered patiently. "It's talking to the instructors and officers that's the most help. You want to see if the officers are realistic about the abilities of their troops."

"Are they?"

"I'm afraid so. It's the brigadista troops who could use a dose of reality. They all believe that when they land in Cuba their American instructors are going to be just offstage, along with thousands of other American troops, ready and waiting to pitch in."

As we spoke, we strolled to the edge of a steep drop. The entire valley stretched out before us. Beyond the valley, a line of mountains disappeared into the vaporous haze. The panorama was otherworldly in its green vastness. Behind me, I heard Mason shout, "Look out!" and then felt a blow on my back. I started to tumble down the slick, muddy mountainside. I screamed and fetched up against a small tree, which kept me from going all the way down. I looked back up to see several startled faces leaning over the edge. "Hang on!" Hess shouted. "We'll get a rope."

They lowered a brigadista on a rope who got another rope around me and we scratched and scrambled back up as they pulled from above.

"Are you okay?" Hess said, as I sprawled on the muddy ground trying to catch my breath. "We better get you cleaned up. You don't want those scratches to fester in the jungle."

I nodded. I was trying to figure out what had happened to me.

Mason appeared, looking down at me with great distress. "Thank God that tree was there," Mason said. "I saw you starting to slip and reached out to grab you, but I think I shoved you instead."

Was that how it happened? Did the blow come *after* I started to fall? It happened so fast I wasn't sure.

There was no shower. I poured several buckets of murky water over me and then tortured myself by swabbing alcohol on my scrapes and scratches. I stayed back at the shack for the rest of the day, and joined the colonels for dinner. We ate beans and rice as a sudden downpour leaked through the canvas canopy that covered the mess area. Mason sat next to me and kept apologizing for nearly killing me.

I was soaked by the time dinner was over. Hess and I made our way back to our shack. I changed my clothes again. It was not very late but I was exhausted. Our cots had been covered with grimy rumpled sheets and there were no pillows, but I was too tired to care. As I moved to my cot I noticed one of the rumples in my sheet move of its own accord, like a wave moving through my cot. Startled, I jerked back, grabbed at Hess, and pointed to the cot. "Don't move," Hess said. He pulled one of the legs off the broken chair and brought it down several times on the sheet as hard as he could. For a moment the sheet writhed violently and then blood began to seep into the sheets. Hess stepped back, watching intently with his club raised, but the sheet was still. He finally pulled back the sheet so we could see the dead snake. "Fer-de-lance," Hess said, "you don't want to be sleeping with that."

Hess carried the snake from the shack, dangling it from the end of his club. Everyone was quite impressed. When Eduardo learned it had been in my bed, he snickered mischievously. "Two close calls in one day. I'm not sure I should fly with you."

Two new grimy sheets were found for me. I lay on top of the sheets, uncomfortably conscious of the slightly damp bloodstain on the cot beneath. I remembered that Mason had excused himself during dinner to have a pee. It was unlikely he could have found a fer-de-lance and slipped it into my bed in just a few minutes . . . unless he had an accomplice. I told myself I was being paranoid.

The next day, having soiled most of my clothes, I had to wear the seersucker pants and dress shirt I had worn from Washington. In the morning, while Mason and Hess met with the brigade's commanders, I stationed myself outside their tent, determined to keep Mason in my sight all day. After lunch, Hess, Mason, and I approached a group of men who were gathered in a large circle. They were observing an American trainer who was standing behind a brigadista, positioning him and his knife for the correct stance for a fight.

"Right," the trainer said, stepping away. "Now I need a couple more volunteers."

Mason stepped forward and the trainer gave him a knife.

"Isn't knife-fighting your territory, Max?" Eduardo said, loudly enough for the American instructor to overhear.

"Yeah," Mason chimed in, suddenly invigorated, "show me your stuff, kid."

Someone pushed me and I stumbled into the center of the circle.

"Here, hold my knife so it looks realistic," the trainer said to me. "You're right-handed?"

I nodded blankly.

"You guys are going to do this in slow motion. *Slow.* We don't want any injuries here." He adjusted my stance and said to me, "You are going to make the first move with your knife hand. Then he will counter in the way I just demonstrated." The trainer glanced at Mason, who was standing lightly on the balls of his feet, the knife in his right hand weaving sinuously like the head of a snake. "You seem to know what you're doing," the instructor said to him.

Mason looked at me intently, taking in my ruined shoes, my muddy seersucker trousers, my crumpled blue dress shirt with its circles of sweat expanding from my armpits, and the huge knife in my right hand.

With a rush of inescapable logic, it came to me as I stood there: *This is it. I've been set up. This is how I'm going to die, in front of everyone as if it's an accident.*

"Okay, move towards each other slowly," the trainer said.

I didn't move but Mason did. Then, over a twelve-year divide, Jack McGowan spoke to me and I shuffled forward myself. When I was close to Mason I lunged at him, thrusting my left arm toward his knife. He reacted spontaneously, flicking his knife out and cutting my left arm and then I stepped forward and plunged my knife into his chest.

An hour later, Hess entered our shack. "How's your arm? It doesn't look too bad. You'll be relieved to know you didn't manage to kill Mason, but his shoulder's sliced up pretty good. He's embarrassed and he's also pissed off because he's out of booze. You looked pretty professional out there."

"I didn't know what I was doing," I said. "When he cut me, I had this instinctive reaction."

"And they were worried at the Pentagon about *your* safety!"

The drive down the mountain was much rougher than the way up. Mason rode in the back of my jeep, his shoulder heavily bandaged and his arm in a sling. He winced and grunted as the jeep lurched from bump to bump. At the end of the trip, he mumbled something to me about the fault being entirely his.

I had a chance to shower at the finca residence before putting my fetid clothes on again for the flight to Miami. In contrast to their good cheer three days ago, the colonels' sober demeanor suggested they had already come to a tacit assessment. Colonel Tarwater, who had remained at the air base, looked particularly grim. Eduardo encouraged them to open up during the flight to Miami but the colonels kept their opinions to themselves. When we landed, a car was waiting for Mason to take him to a hospital. Eduardo drove us straight from Opa-locka to the Miami airport. When he pulled up at the terminal he challenged us. "Well, you can't say we're not ready and eager for battle."

There was an awkward silence until Tarwater spoke. "Oh you're eager all right."

When Eduardo was finally out of sight, the colonels looked at each other and shook their heads hopelessly. I spent the flight to Washington waiting for Mason to turn around in his seat and say, "Haven't we met before?" But he kept himself busy organizing a steady supply of drinks from the flight attendants. By the time we landed, I had persuaded myself that it was all a terrible coincidence. There was no reason he should try to kill me even if he did recognize me. Unfortunately I had now given him a reason to think about me.

Hess drove me home from the airport. He was silent in a distant, reflective way. When he pulled up at my home in Georgetown he finally spoke. "Fifteen percent likelihood of success. Unless . . ."

"Unless?"

". . . every single one of Castro's planes is destroyed on the ground and there is an immediate, massive uprising by Cubans after the landing. There's still a chance to pull this operation together."

I limped into the office the following afternoon, having spent the morning getting my left arm stitched up. Russell summoned me immediately. "My goodness, what a sorry looking sight you are," he said. I did look awful. There were scratches on my hands, a big red splotch of indeterminate origin ran up my neck, and the lump on my forehead was beginning to turn purple. Hess had called Russell in the morning to apologize for the damage to me and he told Russell about my knife incident. I tried to pass it off as an accident, which Russell accepted with a skeptical shrug. I wasn't sure I liked Hess being in direct communication with Russell, but he seemed to have kept his thoughts about JMATE to himself. As rumors of my ability with a knife spread in the office, I enjoyed a new, uneasy respect.

Hess called me at the end of the day. In disbelief and outrage, he told me that while we were away, a new engineer had stepped forward to tinker with the JMATE machine, the president himself, proposing a series of cosmetic changes to camouflage its operation. The Trinidad region of Cuba was too populated, too exposed; the machine was too "noisy." Some forty miles down the coast, on the Zapata Peninsula, the accommodating Bissell found the lonely Bahía de Cochinos, the Bay of Pigs, with a small beach surrounded by swamps and a nearby airstrip. According to Hess, Colonel Hawkins and Jacob Esterline were unhappy with the new location. The Escambray Mountains would be inaccessible, the airstrip was pot-holed, and there were fewer Cubans nearby to rise up in sympathy. But the machine, now renamed Operation Zapata, would be concealed, or at least its made-in-the-USA label would not be so visible. With the machine scheduled for operation in less than a month, it was a major change, but Bissell was sure he could pull it off. The president had a couple of further suggestions: Couldn't both the inland parachute drops and the beach landings come at night instead of the day so the U.S. Navy support would be well away before things heated up? And the air strikes, perhaps they could be modified from an all-out, D-day strike on Cuba's airfields to a couple of smaller, earlier strikes. Further strikes would have to come *after* the Bay of Pigs airstrip was secured so we could pretend they were brigadista planes, not American. Hess worked himself up into a lather. "Who is going to tell Kennedy the operation is screwed up? There's no review system at the White House now. It's all ad hoc task forces. For JMATE, Barnes is the liaison with the White House, and Bissell steps in there to pitch when he wants as well. And who is he pitching to? Bundy. Do you think Bundy is going to tell Kennedy that Bissell is fucking up? He was Bissell's student at Yale! So was his brother Bill. So was Rostow.* Ike's way was deliberate, but at least everything got reviewed."

When Hess finally calmed down I said, "It sounds like Kennedy is whittling it away until there's nothing left and he has to cancel."

"Not likely. First of all, he got elected promising to do something about Castro. Secondly, if he cancels now there are going to be a lot of armed and pissed-off Cuban guerrillas on the loose. And Khrushchev, who already believes he can bully Kennedy, will know that he backed down. If we can't turn this thing into a serious military operation, it's not going to work. I've given you all the ammunition you need, but I can't get exposed here. Most of the generals want to ditch Zapata in favor of a full-scale military assault. A few want to improve the operation so that it works as a guerrilla insurgency, which is what I'm in favor of. But one way or the other, the CIA needs more military support, not less."

This was where Hess had been pointing me all the time: I was supposed to march in to Russell and get him to take the operation away from the CIA and give it to the military. I could now see the endgame for Operation Zapata as clearly as I had seen Suez and the U-2. If things went along as currently planned, Zapata would be a disaster without any creative help from me. But until the machine was turned on, it was a just a scheme, a huge bureaucratic chimera that could, with an assist from me via Russell, flame out in Washington before it ever rumbled onto a beach in Cuba. The repercussions of a Bay of Pigs operation, canceled at the last minute, could turn into a wonderful Washington imbroglio. I pictured the finger-pointing aftermath of the aborted invasion: the ragtag Cuban brigade romanticized as a magnificent fighting machine that never got its chance; the CIA claiming their brilliant plan was squandered by a weak president; the U.S. military command insisting that if they had planned the operation the president would have been willing to act on it. I could not yet see how I could

---

* McGeorge Bundy was Kennedy's special assistant for National Security and Walt Rostow was Bundy's deputy.

accomplish this without leaving my fingerprints all over it, but I was sure an opportunity would present itself. In hindsight, it was reckless of me to think about intervening in JMATE in any manner when all that stood between me and my unveiling as a Canadian operative was the rum-soaked brain of Matthew Mason. But at the time, the danger seemed like part of the creative challenge to pulling off another brilliant coup.

I was confident I could talk Russell into my way of thinking. This was the kind of operation he disliked instinctively. And he trusted me now; at times he was almost fondly paternalistic toward me. I was also pretty confident Russell could convince Kennedy to call off the invasion. Kennedy was wavering. With Russell's support of aborting the operation, Kennedy would feel he could oppose the military and the CIA. Many people expected Russell's White House influence to wane with the new president, given his distaste for Kennedy's domestic policies. But Kennedy had been quite solicitous of Russell in the early days of his administration because it was Russell who gave Kennedy the final boost into the White House. In the last weeks before the election, despite Johnson's place on the ticket, the South had swung toward Nixon. Johnson turned to Russell who had refused to campaign because he disapproved of Kennedy's platform. According to Johnson, only Russell had enough credibility as a racist to get southerners to back Kennedy. If he didn't get out there and campaign for Kennedy, the election was lost. Johnson took to calling Russell's staff, imploring us to intercede with Russell. He called me late one night: "He'll listen to you, boy. Dick thinks the world of you. And don't think I can't help you. I'm not going to be some useless VP who wipes the president's ass." The next day Russell relented and agreed to campaign in Texas. Though I had not said a word on his behalf to Russell, Johnson decided that I was the one who finally persuaded Russell. When Johnson pledged eternal gratitude to me, I did not disabuse him.

Kennedy's retooling of the invasion plan provoked Hess to give up all discretion. He began to treat me like a cousin with whom I shared a demented relative named Zapata, and he called me at all hours of the day and night to inform me of new absurdities. The Navy carrier and destroyers escorting the brigade's landing had been ordered to paint out their hull numbers. "What are they hiding?" Hess exclaimed. "Where else is a fleet of warships in the Caribbean going to come from besides the U.S.? And they have to stay twenty miles offshore, their guns muzzled unless directly attacked. And no Navy planes can be involved, even to protect the brigade's B-26s."

Hess asked me daily when I was going to march in and confront Russell with the bad news. Occasionally he would barge into my office unannounced and I wondered if he was trying to stage an encounter with Russell on his own. I tried to put him off. "You know how Kennedy is wavering. If we do this too soon, he just might cancel the operation instead of letting you guys beef it up."

Hess looked shocked. "That would be the end of me if I got blamed. They're all for getting rid of Castro at the Pentagon. Some of them want to be absolutely sure it happens, even if it means taking out half the Cuban population as well. Which is not what I want. The original plan for a true guerrilla insurgency was the right way to go. It can still work but without more military support we won't get the brigadistas off the beach and into the mountains."

I saw Hess more clearly now as one of those lone wolves, devoted to the military as an ideal and himself as its conscience. To him, the insurgency was the intellectually correct approach and he couldn't resist nudging things his way.

"Russell and I are working on it. Russell already told Kennedy that when you commit the flag, you commit the country."

Hess gave me a fishy look. I realized this was the third time I had used this phrase to encourage him. To change the subject I asked after Mason. Hess told me he wasn't doing so well. Some tendons in his shoulder had been severed, and he wasn't sure he would regain the full use of his arm.

I felt obliged to say, "I'd like to call him. I hadn't realized he was having a tough recovery."

Hess fixed me with an inquiring look. "I wondered when you were going to ask."

"I've wanted to call . . ."

"Maybe it would be good for you to talk to him. You'll see what I'm up against. He really hates Zapata. He agrees with General LeMay, just throw the whole fucking arsenal at Cuba and fry the island. Also, Mason's not too happy with you. Sitting around at home with nothing to do except drink and brood isn't doing him any good. He thinks you had it in for him because he pushed you down the cliff."

"But I never blamed him. It was an accident."

"Sure, but from a certain point of view that's how it looks—first he tries to kill you then you try to kill him." Hess paused. When I made no answer, Hess burst into laughter. "Boy, did your eyes get big at that idea!"

Jim Flannery, Bissell's aide, called me a week after my return from Guatemala. I was immediately on my guard as he asked me for my impressions of the training camp. Whatever I said would go directly to Bissell. "I'm not really qualified to judge the military preparedness."

"Well what did the colonels say?"

"They didn't confide in me."

Flannery was silent.

"All right," I said, "they weren't too impressed. But what do you expect? They'd like to run the show. I'm sure Bissell will get their report. Tell me this—are you confident the president knows how important the air support is?"

"We'll make sure he does. Tracy is supposed to give the president a special briefing on air support well before we launch. Now I'd like to ask you something in strictest confidence: Would you mind telling Helms what you saw in Guatemala?"

"Helms?"

"I've asked him twice to get involved with Zapata. He hasn't exactly refused. It's more like he demurred. Obstinately. But his organizational skills, his experience, could make all the difference. And it's not just Helms himself. A lot of the old hands around here, guys with plenty of experience, take their cues from him. If he's staying out of it, they figure they should too. Dick's overall plan is great; this can be a brilliant operation. But there's a certain level of tradecraft he just doesn't have."

"He'd be the last person to admit that. Didn't Bissell try to get rid of Helms recently, send him off to the London bureau?"

"Oh, Dick just got unhappy with the way Helms holds himself apart," Flannery said. "But if Helms volunteered . . ."

"And I'm supposed to talk Helms into volunteering?"

"I can't do it. If Dick knew I was saying this to you, he'd slice me up. But he won't know. I'll mention to Helms that you were in Guatemala. He's too curious not to bite."

Helms called before the afternoon was out. At seven the following evening my taxi dropped me off in Chevy Chase again. Helms, in a crisp white dress shirt and pinstriped pants, appeared to be preparing for an evening outing. As he ushered me into the library, I heard muffled voices and laughter, a distant domestic medley.

"I took the liberty of making a pitcher of my famous martinis. If I call them 'famous,' people are usually too polite to refuse." Helms grinned at me and poured. "I appreciate your coming out here to see me again, but I know what Jim Flannery is up to. I've told him that I'm not going to get involved. Unless of course, I'm formally asked."

"I'm not here to ask. I don't even understand what's going on, exactly."

"Neither do I." He held up his hands helplessly. "*Aber keiner sagt mir was.*"

It took a moment to realize he was speaking German, another moment to figure out what he was saying, and a distressing third moment to wonder why he was trying out his German on me. I attempted a look of vague perplexity, as if I didn't understand German. When he shrugged and translated, "Nobody tells me anything," I decided it was an innocent reference.

As I described my three days at the training camp, I watched Helms attentively. What if I could engineer a meeting between Helms and Russell? He would be the perfect witness to the folly of Zapata and my fingerprints wouldn't be so obvious. Helms didn't give much away as I told my tale. My mention of Eduardo elicited a derisive grunt. And when I brought up the brigadistas' belief in a supporting cast of thousands of American soldiers, he was first startled and then briefly vexed before controlling himself. He smiled when I described the knife incident as a stupid accident.

Helms's penetrating concentration had a way of encouraging my imprudence, and I disclosed several of Hess's revelations. Helms didn't appear to react, but when my account was over he took a deep breath and said: "Well JMARC seems to have come a long way," as if he had heard nothing about the operation since we last spoke. That couldn't be true, yet I had a sudden uncomfortable sense of Helms, having hooked me four months ago, now reeling me in for my report. I stopped speaking and waited for Helms to react. Finally, I said, "It doesn't sound good."

"It's not for me to judge," Helms said carefully. "Dick probably thinks he's got several extra arrows in his quiver. I'm sure he *believes* in the likelihood of a mass uprising by the Cuban people. Another drink?" He replenished our glasses.

"It still doesn't sound good."

"There's always the in-for-a-dime-in-for-a-dollar theory. That worked so well for them in the Guatemalan operation."

"I thought the Guatemala revolt was a perfect operation," I countered.

Helms raised a cautionary finger. "Early on there was a moment of . . . let's call it uncertainty. And Allen asked Ike to permit a little more firepower on our side, a couple of ancient Honduran P-51s to replace three rebel planes that had been shot down. Ike didn't believe in quitting halfway and authorized the planes. Ironic, don't you think? The man who threw vast armies onto the beach at Normandy is sitting in the White House worrying about two rickety fighter planes. But the planes gave the rebels an edge. There were a few more anxious moments but then the Guatemalan army panicked. And the rest is glorious history."

"In for a dime, in for a dollar . . . that sounds like a variation of Senator Russell's watchword: 'If you commit the flag, you commit the country.' So Bissell got Kennedy to put down his dime and if things don't go well he'll ask him to throw some more money on the table. And then some more . . ."

Helms looked at me inquiringly. I seemed to be leading him somewhere. And I was. I was getting ready to ask him to see Russell. "I don't know Senator Russell well," Helms said, "but I think Russell's precept is meant to inhibit one from committing the flag in the first place, not encourage it. I suppose that's why I'm such a fan of old-fashioned espionage. I can't think of an easier government to penetrate and undermine than Castro's. It would take time, but it would lessen the risks of any direct confrontation with the Soviets. Dick has almost no idea of what Havana is thinking. He's too impatient. Why I've learned more about Castro from a source in Moscow over the last few months than Dick has learned from a year of organizing his war on Cuba."

It was the first time he had been overtly critical of Bissell. This wasn't quite what Flannery had in mind. "Tell me about your source in the Kremlin," I asked.

He looked at me reproachfully: "I can't say any more and you can't even repeat the little I've said. To *anyone*. Let's just hope he survives longer than the one you found for us."

"Didn't you tell me they all make mistakes sooner or later?"

"Mistakes . . . sometimes I wonder," Helms reflected. "It happens so frequently it's almost predictable. Think of them, these spies and moles we recruit. Once they make the choice to help us, they must be shocked to discover how their secret has separated them from their families, their friends, their fellow workers. No one really *sees* you anymore; you've become invisible. There you are in the midst of your life, yet the life around you has become ridiculous in its blind ignorance of who you really are. After a while, you don't even know if you have a true self.

"Some of these actors fall apart. For others, the urge to make a private gesture becomes irresistible. They don't want to be caught but they want to affirm their authenticity. So they pursue an unlikely sexual adventure, or suddenly insult one of their bosses, or try to impress their handler with a few lies, their handler being the last person with whom they have an honest relationship. It's like scratching graffiti on a wall or sending anonymous hate mail. It gets a reaction, recognition, even if there's only private satisfaction. And there's the guilt. Sometimes these obscure hints are a kind of substitute confession. But once you start making private gestures, you're eventually going to go too far."

Was that what I wanted to do, scratch graffiti on the wall of history? I didn't exactly panic. I was sure he was speaking about an impersonal "you." Yet Helms had innocently uncovered my secret self—at least I hoped he was speaking innocently. As a precaution, I would have to give up on the idea of enlisting Helms to speak to Russell, though in my reckless way I still clung to my fantasy of aborting Zapata. Russell expected me to figure out the right thing to do and I was now sure that canceling Zapata was the right thing to do. Kennedy would never approve an all-out bombing and military invasion of the whole island. He might relent and let Zapata have a little more firepower but it seemed to me it was already compromised fatally. I was pleased to see it so clearly; when you're invested in nothing but your own survival and self-interest, determining the right thing to do can be a challenge, whereas seeing the future is not. Now I would get to savor the delicious aftermath of cancellation, but doing the right thing as well would be like having my cake and eating it too.

20

The prospect of Zapata hung over Washington like a vague, disturbing odor. As I made my social rounds in Washington, people who had heard about my trip to Guatemala would sidle up to me and ask with a disapproving scowl if this Cuban "thing" was really going to happen. The ones from the military and defense world were mainly worried about the mission failing. I encouraged them with the prospect of Kennedy as an "in for a dime, in for a dollar" kind of president. Others—diplomats, journalists, and many legislators—simply disapproved of using the military to overthrow a government. To them I suggested that Kennedy was imposing such restraints and conditions that I wouldn't be surprised if he scaled the mission back until it disappeared. To whomever I spoke, I always added, "I'm just speculating of course . . ." or "This is only my opinion . . ." or "I don't know this for a fact . . ." but spoken with such mock ingenuousness that people assumed I did know what I was talking about. Appearing to take each side of the issue without taking any side was my way of hiding in plain sight.

Early in April, I ran into Senator William Fulbright at Gwen and Morris Cafritz's annual Easter party. It was a freezing day and we clustered indoors while the daffodils shivered along the Potomac. When I tried my "uninformed" speculations out on Fulbright, he furrowed his brow and drew himself portentously up to about my height. "If you have the slightest shred of evidence that we are not on our way to a strategic and ethical blunder, you must tell me now before I speak to the president in two days."

His intensity startled me. I backed off, mumbling something about trying to make sense of a few stray rumors.

"Stray rumors!" He scowled and marched away. Fulbright, I learned a few days later, was about to take advantage of a courtesy ride to Florida on Air Force One with Kennedy to buttonhole the president with a passionate argument and memorandum about why an invasion of Cuba would be a huge mistake.

If Fulbright succeeded there would be no need for my intercession with Russell. I doubted, though, that Fulbright could have as much influence as Russell: Fulbright's opposition was based on the unfortunate consequences of *success*—the moral and political fallout from the violent overthrow of the Castro regime. But Russell, after I pointed him in the right direction, would speak to Kennedy about the consequences of failure—a military disaster perhaps followed by a protracted civil war in Cuba that the United States would be obliged to support.

One morning in early April, I arrived at the office later than usual. Russell's door was closed. On my desk were three messages from Hess. Each one said, "Call me as soon as you get in."

When I reached Hess he said, "That's LeMay in with Russell. You've got to do something."

I knocked on Russell's door and opened it. "I'm sorry, I didn't realize . . ." I started to back out.

"Please come in, Winston," Russell said. "You know General LeMay. We were just winding up."

LeMay was sitting at Russell's conference table, chomping on his unlit cigar while tapping on the table rapidly, his square face a dull, glowering red. "We've been talking about military oversight," Russell said. "I was just saying how much I agree with General LeMay—it is unfortunate that the Pentagon has been excluded from the approval process." He looked at him regretfully. "But it's not my place to give it to you, General. The president is a bright young man and he's trying to accomplish a lot while he's still figuring out how to get things done. I can tell him what I think of his legislative agenda for the military, but organizing the executive branch, that's not my prerogative. Eisenhower did it his way and President Kennedy has to do it his way. It would take a national emergency for this creaky old constitutionalist to feel he could speak to such an issue."

LeMay could not restrain himself. "*Somebody* has to point out to the president that Cuba is a pissant little island. If Zapata doesn't work—ha! *when* Zapata doesn't work—he'll have to let the Navy's support planes loose or Khrushchev will think he's a complete pussy. So why shouldn't my bombers go in and fry the place right off the bat? One round of saturation bombing and we stroll into Havana."

Russell's lips tightened as he stood up; the meeting was over. He had affection and patience for military brass, but LeMay always pushed too far.

I met Hess for a drink at the end of the day. He apologized for LeMay's sudden appearance. "LeMay cornered me this morning and asked why I hadn't been able to get in to see Russell. I told him we've been waiting for the right moment. I tried to placate him with your line about committing the flag, and he said 'Kennedy's barely waving the fucking flag as it is.' Then he picked up the phone and called Russell. Were you able to calm things down?"

"I kept my mouth shut. I think LeMay's extremism may have helped us. We'll sound reasonable when we go to Russell and tell him that he's got to make sure there is air support and that the Navy should do whatever is needed to make the landing a success."

"'We'? I can't expose myself. All Russell has to do is pick up the phone and mention my name and I'm going to be cleaning latrines in Arkansas." Hess began to shout. "*You've* got to do this. Maybe you've fallen for this 'in for a dime' shit too. Listen to me: Kennedy's shaved his bet down to a nickel, but unless Russell speaks to him, he'll never raise his bet. And if Kennedy takes his money off the table and cancels, my ass will be fried." The pasty ring of fat that spilled over Hess's collar quivered as he flung his words at me.

"I have to choose the right moment with Russell. If you're not with me, he will be harder to convince. But I'll do my best."

Hess looked at me with distaste and then looked away, wrinkling his brow as if searching for some distant connection. "When you were in Europe . . . did you spend much time in Germany?"

"Germany? I was in Paris after the war. Who would want to go to Germany then?"

"It's funny . . . Matt Mason now thinks he met you somewhere. I told him you were in Europe when he was."

"Thanks for feeding his obsession," I said testily. "Anyway, not *Europe*. Just Paris. I hoped Mason would get over me by now."

"Don't worry. It's not like he's mad at you anymore. He's just got too much time on his hands. And he's somebody who really doesn't need time on his hands. If you guys got to know each other better, he'd relax. How about this weekend, the three of us? Dinner? Maybe we can bring him around to our point of view about Zapata. He's the one who designed the training program for the brigadistas. If we got him on our side . . ."

Just what I wanted, a face-to-face dinner with Mason while we reminisced about postwar Europe! Yet every time the risk to me wound up another notch, it only excited me. I had a good excuse for not dining with Hess and Mason. Alice had invited me to New York for the weekend to celebrate our birthday. If I absented myself from Washington for a few days and avoided Hess and Mason, I could return just before Zapata launched and launch my own a preemptive attempt to convince Russell that the inevitable failure of the Zapata mission would cause a national emergency. If I didn't convince him, or he couldn't convince Kennedy, at least I'd be remembered as a prophet.

Early Saturday morning, April 8, I took a taxi to National Airport. The terminal was quiet. I was standing in line at the Eastern Airlines boarding gate when a figure rushed past, his flapping overcoat brushing me as he shouldered his way to the front of the line. A tall man who was on line ahead of me called out to him, "Tracy!"

It was Tracy Barnes. He showed his CIA identification to the gate agent and motioned for the tall man to come to the head of the line too. They were immediately escorted onto the airplane. When I finally boarded, they were too engrossed in conversation to notice me. The other man was Harlan Cleveland, an assistant secretary of state.

By the time we landed at LaGuardia Airport I had finished *The Washington Post* and *The New York Times*. According to *The Post*, CBS was about to broadcast a story on an impending invasion of Cuba by an exile army. *The Times* had a front-page story about mysterious activity in Miami, with local Cuban exiles departing at night and rumors of an imminent general revolt in Cuba. Why would Tracy Barnes be leaving Washington almost on the eve of his operation?

The terminal in LaGuardia Airport was nearly deserted on this sleepy Saturday morning. I trailed some distance behind Barnes and Cleveland, keeping them in sight as they hurried out of the terminal. They boarded the first taxi in line. I slipped into the next one. "Follow that cab, please," I said, shocked at my recklessness.

The driver turned slowly, a look of disbelief on his face.

Rather than invent a flimsy pretext, I gave him twenty dollars. "That's on top of the fare."

He took the money unenthusiastically. There were few cars on the road and it was not a difficult task to keep their taxi in sight. Emerging from the Midtown Tunnel, we traveled a few blocks in Manhattan. When they turned onto Park Avenue at Thirty-fourth Street and pulled over, I knew all I needed to know. They were at the U.S. mission to the UN. This was probably the final briefing for Adlai Stevenson, the UN ambassador. Zapata could not be more than a few days away from launching. I told my driver to drive me to my sister's new apartment in Greenwich Village.

With every other person in my life, my nagging sense of spuriousness was always in the back of my mind. But Alice and I had constructed a protective intimacy, a relaxed affection that never threatened and never criticized. Alice's attempts to repair my relationship with our father ended after my encounter with him in the Jefferson Hotel. He must have told her how happy I was at his appearance, but when I told her that it hadn't gone well, she finally let it rest.

A year ago Alice had decided to move from her semi-slum on the Lower East Side. When I saw the small apartment she wanted to rent, I insisted on giving her enough money for the down payment on a large two-bedroom apartment on Perry Street in Greenwich Village. It was a relief to spend some of my accumulating hoard. I claimed it was a selfish gesture so I could continue to stay with her in New York, but she was deeply touched. Alice had mellowed; pleasure now seemed to be as important to her as confrontation.

To celebrate our birthday, Alice asked Robert Cage to come along with Stanley Wright, who seemed to have emerged as her sole and steady boyfriend. After a number of fringe jobs in New York, Robert had learned of an opening with a public relations firm that specialized in Broadway theater. He enlisted me to write a letter of recommendation on official Senate stationery in which I praised his abilities as a public information officer for the Library of Congress. In those days people rarely checked references; a good letterhead was all it took. His deadpan style went over wonderfully well in his new profession. He could utter show business banalities and hyperbolize about the most egregious celebrities with poker-faced earnestness. Yet there was hardly a celebrity in New York about whom he did not have some scandalous episode to relate.

For the celebration, Robert had organized a campy evening at the Stork Club, which would allow us to be at once titillated yet smugly repelled. Stanley was reluctant. The club had a bad reputation where blacks were concerned. A few years ago there had been an infamous incident with Josephine Baker, who waited over an hour after ordering dinner before storming out and calling the newspapers.

"Not to worry," Robert said. "Billingsley's going to fawn over us. I told him the other night I was bringing someone from the New York City government who has the power to suspend the cabaret license of any club. That would be you, Stanley."

The maître d' greeted Robert warmly. On the way to our table, Alice muttered indignantly: "It doesn't seem that full."

"It's still a place to be seen," Robert said, "but no longer the absolute top place."

Our table gave us a decent vantage point from which Robert was able to point out a number of tableside attractions—Abe Burrows, Hermione Gingold, Irving Berlin, Salvador Dalí—scattered across the club like an archipelago of preening islands.

"Robert Cage, is it not?" A homely little man with an ingratiating smile had materialized before us.

"Leonard Lyons!" Robert said quite loudly, ensuring we all caught the name of the gossip columnist for the *New York Post*. When Robert mentioned our birthday, Lyons insisted on bringing over the brutish owner of the club, Sherman Billingsley, who acknowledged Robert with a curt nod.

Robert wasn't fazed. "This is Alice Bates, the noted sociologist and downtown heartbreaker, and Stanley Wright, the always suave deputy commissioner in the city's Division of Licenses. To my right sits Winston Bates, brother of Alice, key Washington insider and special counsel to the Senate Armed Services Committee." He was enjoying showing off.

Billingsley greeted us with a perfunctory smile. "This place must be getting too high toned if your type is showing up." He smirked grossly, pretending it was a compliment. With a feral instinct for the crude truth, he said: "You probably think you're slumming, right? Let me know if there's anything I can do for you," he offered indifferently as he moved on.

"If that's fawning," Stanley said, "I don't want to get on his bad side."

"Oh look!" Alice said. "Isn't that Roy Cohn sitting over there? And who's he with, that man on his right? He looks like a movie star."

"No, he's definitely not a movie star," Lyons said, practically vibrating with knowingness. "That's just one of Cohn's boyfriends."

"Would you like me to introduce you? It would be my very great pleasure."

"No thanks," I said quickly.

Lyons bowed deferentially and left us.

"Tell me something," Alice said to Robert and me. "Did either of you know before the McCarthy hearings that Cohn was homosexual? Or is that the sort of thing that everyone knew in Washington?" *

"Not everyone," Robert said. "But I was always happy to spread the rumor. Speaking of secret homosexuals, I hear that Joe Alsop has gotten married."

I was dumbfounded. "Alsop, homosexual? You know this for a fact?"

"Are you sure intelligence is the right line of work for you, Winston? Alsop had a boyfriend in Washington, a stalwart young sailor who's now in New York living with Tennessee Williams."

"Why didn't you tell me?" I burst out accusingly.

"Don't be miffed. I only found out recently, when I met the boyfriend with Williams at a party."

"Do you suppose a lot of people in Washington know about Alsop?" I was disconcerted to have been so oblivious.

"I wouldn't be surprised if J. Edgar's spiderweb caught a few juicy tidbits." Robert's eyes widened. "Speaking of secret lives . . . one approaches."

Cohn was moving in our direction. The young man, who looked much too beautiful to be a movie star, was just behind him. As Cohn passed our table he paused.

"How are you doing?" he said to me. "It has been a long time." His eyes bulged and he was breathing heavily, like someone engorged.

I may have looked familiar but I couldn't believe he remembered who I was. To show off, I said: "Yes, it has been exactly eight years minus twenty days. These are my friends—"

Cohn spun on his heel and walked away. I looked around the table and grinned. "You see what a key insider I am."

Suddenly Cohn was back at the table. His dark face had turned maroon in anger. "You think I don't remember you but I never forget. I thought you were fishy when I met you at that party and I still think you're fishy. You know, I tried to have you checked out but Saltonstall

---

* It wasn't until Joseph Welch's pointed reference to pixies and fairies during the Army-McCarthy hearings that Cohn's homosexuality became a subject of widespread gossip.

called it off. But I'm never wrong about these things. Are you still working for Armed Services? If you are, what are you doing here? Shouldn't you be in Florida?" His voice was getting louder. The young man came back to the table and pulled at Cohn's arm but he jerked his arm away. "Leave me alone. You know what, Bates? I'm going to have you checked out all over again. You think I can't, you little queer? You'll see." Then he was gone.

After a moment, Stanley spoke up: "Helluva party, Robert."

Alice glared at him and patted my arm. "Odious man. What was he talking about?"

I was unable to speak. I spread my arms widely in innocent bafflement.

"And Florida?" she continued. "What was that all about?"

"I can't talk about it," I said.

"Cuba," Robert said. He was staring at me curiously. "I take back what I said about you."

Cohn's attack hung over the rest of the evening. Alice, Stanley, and Robert now held me in a new, disoriented regard. The gossipy tales of Washington with which I entertained them had never featured me as an actor, only an amused observer. In the taxi on the way back to Alice's, I said: "I can't imagine what I could have done eight years ago to even interest him." I sounded hollow and defensive.

But I knew exactly what Cohn had seen in me: He had seen himself. We were members of the same tribe, the People of the Living Lie. There must be thousands of us living out our solitary secrets but only someone with Cohn's malign intuition could recognize a fellow member. The rest of us recognize a living liar the way everyone else does: when his house of cards collapses into a pack of naked lies. And there he is, exposed for what he isn't: the man who escapes from jail and for twenty years leads an exemplary life, a fond husband and father, a pillar of the community; the CEO, nineteen years with the company, whose original job application was accompanied by forged letters of recommendation; the high school principal who never graduated from high school; the homosexual with a public career who lived to flaunt the lie and died swearing by it even as his death betrayed him.

*

I returned to Washington in a chastened, nervous mood. It was just sadistic bullying, I told myself. Cohn was angry because he was out of Washington and I wasn't. He enjoyed intimidating me though I doubted he would follow through. But how did Cohn know that I had moved to the Armed Services Committee? No, *why* did he know? That was the worry. Was he right now calling his contacts, telling them to take a look at my security file?

From Mason to Helms to Hess to Cohn, the sovereign state of Winston Bates had been repeatedly threatened. The only place these threats meant something was in my own mind. But they seemed to surround me, an invisible circle of implication. If some harsh light of scrutiny were turned on me, the circle would magically appear, revealing me for all that I wasn't. I could not afford any more to be known as the man who aborted Zapata. Nor did I want to be known as the man who put Zapata on the right track at the last minute. The main thing was not to be known at all. It was a matter of survival. With a sense of resignation I surrendered my ambition to play a creative role with Zapata.

I did not know when, exactly, Zapata was going to lumber into motion, but it had to be any day now. I was surprised not to hear from Hess immediately on my return to Washington. I wasn't exactly sure how I would play it with him, but I was prepared to say that Russell had refused to get involved. At 3:00 A.M. on April 12, I was awakened by the telephone. Though the connection was bad, through the static I could tell it was Hess.

"I can't hear you," I kept saying. "Speak up. Where've I been? New York. Where are you calling from?"

I finally determined he was calling from Nicaragua, was due back the next day, and wanted to see me as soon as he returned. He called again at the office, late in the afternoon.

"I'm back. I'm calling from Bolling air base. I was sent to Puerto Cabezas to check on the loading of the invasion ships. You can't believe the disorganization. They've stowed gasoline drums next to explosives. There aren't enough landing craft to get all the fighters onto the beach with their supplies and there isn't enough equipment to unload the supplies. Even if they secure the airstrip, there isn't enough fuel to run air support from it. We need to talk to Russell now. And yes, I'm willing to go in there with you. And guess what, so is Mason. He can't believe how unprepared the brigadistas are. We can be there in half an hour."

When I didn't reply, he said, "All right then, listen to this: Esterline and Hawkins, the two men who put the operation together, went to Bissell's home this weekend and told him they were quitting but Bissell managed to talk them out of it. And General Gray just told me he rode over to Quarters Eye with Tracy Barnes earlier today. Barnes admitted he still hasn't briefed the president on how crucial air supremacy is to the operation. Gray went crazy. Barnes has been promising to do that for weeks now. Even if Barnes does brief him, Kennedy probably won't get it. You know what Barnes is like. *Now* will you get us in to see Russell?"

"I can't meet you anywhere today and neither can he," I said firmly. "Don't you read the papers? The Russians have just orbited a man in space. Kennedy was on the phone this morning. He wants the space budget to get a boost and he wants to announce it immediately. I've been with Russell all day and we're just about to go over to see Senator Hayden."

"Look, if we can't get him to endorse more firepower then I'm willing to go for cancellation. I'll probably be thrown out of the Army but this can't happen."

He sounded sincere, but I didn't believe him. I wasn't going to go with him and Mason to see Russell and give Mason another chance to recognize me. "I can't help you now. The Washington Opera opens tonight. I've got to be at a preopening dinner at the Robert Richmonds in two hours and I don't know when I'm going to get out of the space budget meeting here. I'll call you in the morning when I know what the day is looking like."

"What? Don't you get it? We've got less than forty-eight hours and then it's too late. If we can't get Russell to act we'll have to go to the newspapers. This is your chance to be a hero!" he shouted as I hung up.

Just before I left the office, Russell's secretary came in to see me. "That

Colonel Hess, the one who calls you all the time, he called to speak to Senator Russell. He said it was an emergency. Senator Russell is at the Woodner. And he'll be working there tomorrow. I wasn't sure I should disturb him."

"Give me the message. I'll get back to Hess and see if it's worth bothering the senator." It would be difficult for Hess and Mason to contact Russell at the Woodner over the weekend. But I would still have to find some way of keeping Hess and Mason from getting to Russell over the next few days.

The dinner for forty-eight at the Richmonds' had lots of buzz to it. There was a Russian astronaut in outer space and the not so secret Cuban "something" was about to launch. Before dinner we circulated with our cocktails and our gossip. I was with Elizabeth in the drawing room when I noticed Arthur Schlesinger heading my way. According to rumor he had opposed the Cuban invasion. Did he have something to say to me? Stewart Udall intercepted Schlesinger and led him off to the library and I followed. As I was edging toward them, I noticed a large, familiar figure pass through the foyer on his way to the drawing room. It was Hess, out of uniform in a business suit and very out of place at this kind of social occasion. It took several beats of shocked reflection before I realized he must have crashed the party as a civilian in order to track me down. But when I spotted someone in uniform just behind him, his arm in a sling, I was struck with a dreadful certainty: *Mason and Hess are going to abduct me and make me take them to Russell.*

Before Hess found his way to the library, I circled around to the front door where I encountered Bob Richmond. "Winston! There's someone here looking for you."

"I know. There's an emergency. Will you tell Elizabeth I'll try to be back before dinner is over? Otherwise I'll meet her at the opera." I rushed out into the night. I knew what I had to do.

Half an hour later I was at Russell's apartment at the Woodner Hotel. He wasn't so much surprised as nonplussed by my appearance. He stood in the open door, blinking in the hall's bright light before ushering me into the gloom. His apartment had taken on the appearance of a recluse's lair. Books were piled on windowsills, radiators, and tables. I navigated around more volumes on the floor. The stacks of files on his writing table teetered precariously. He gave a little embarrassed chuckle as he cleared a few books from the sofa. His courtliness was reassuring as he went about settling us in for a serious conversation, pouring drinks and pulling up a chair so he could face me. I fumbled for a way into the awkward subject, until he impatiently said: "Okay, let's have the bad news."

I tried hard not to cast Hess and Mason as villains. I described them as passionate patriots who were making things difficult for me in their efforts to ensure that the full might of the U.S. military was unleashed on Cuba. With a look of pained bewilderment I said: "Hess wanted me to persuade you to intercede with Kennedy. He wouldn't leave me alone. And to be honest, I probably led him on a bit about that possibility in order to find out what was happening. Now he's threatening me, telling me he'll go public and sic journalists on me because I am protecting the CIA's flawed plan. He wants the U.S. involvement to be undeniable. He thinks once the news is out there, Kennedy will have nothing to lose by unleashing the military. I'm afraid he's going to put me in the spotlight, which will also focus attention on you. That would be unfair, because the CIA has never officially briefed us, but it won't look good for us to have allowed the CIA to leave us out of the loop since we're their oversight." Russell shrugged phlegmatically; he could take the heat. It was the idea of Hess going public that he regarded with horror. "I don't know how I got myself into this mess," I said.

He looked at me sympathetically. "Just tell me, is there something you think I should do at this point about Cuba?"

There it was. I could have told him about Esterline and Hawkins's attempt to quit; about Tracy Barnes's failure to brief the president on air support; about Kennedy still reserving the right to cancel the operation up to twenty-four hours before the landing. I might have made a case compelling enough for Russell to act. As for Kennedy, Russell was the one person who could shield him from the wrath of the Joint Chiefs. But I would be exposed if Kennedy canceled the invasion at Russell's urging. Afterward, Hess and Mason would still be out there, ready to point the Joint Chiefs in my direction. And sooner or later Mason would sober up enough to remember me.

I said, "No matter what happens, it's going to be a mess. Anything you might do at this point would have as much potential for making things worse as better."

"Then we'll have to live with it. Don't you be concerned. Nobody from the CIA briefed us about their plan. We weren't obliged to act. Things that go wrong, they sometimes come out for the best in the long run." I must have looked quite abject because he reached over and patted me on the shoulder. "Now about these two guys. I know how to handle them. I'll call Lemnitzer. And don't worry; I'll leave you out of it. What are their names again?"

I left Russell's suite feeling reassured. I had relied on my own wits for so long I couldn't remember the last time someone else had protected or defended me. I don't know how Russell pulled it off, but whatever he did, it was effective: Hess went silent.

On Friday, April 14, the president told Bissell to reduce the force of the Saturday air strike by the brigade's B-26s on Cuba's airfields. On Saturday afternoon, shortly after the air strike created uproar at the UN, I watched Adlai Stevenson's televised performance before the General Assembly. Holding up pictures of a bullet-riddled plane with Cuban air force markings that had landed at Miami, he made an impassioned case for a rebellion by Castro's air force with no U.S. involvement.* I hadn't thought such persuasive dissembling was in Stevenson's repertoire but then I remembered his briefer was Tracy Barnes. Poor Adlai had probably been left in the dark about how and when the CIA was going to accomplish its goal. On Sunday afternoon Kennedy gave the final go-ahead for the landing. A few hours later, Dean Rusk, nervous about the reaction at the UN, persuaded the president to cancel the Monday air strike. The brigade wouldn't be allowed to bomb Cuban airfields again until the Zapata airstrip was secured.

In agonizing slow motion, the wheels came off the machine. Without the Monday air strike, the Cuban planes that survived the feeble Saturday strike were free to shoot down the brigade's B-26s, which were flying support over the beach, and then bomb and strafe the brigadistas.

---

* The plane was actually a clumsy CIA hoax that was soon exposed by a sharp-eyed journalist.

Once on the beach, the brigade encountered a swamp; on the other side of the swamp the Cuban army awaited, unthreatened by the brigade's bombers. There were no mountains to disappear into for eighty miles. Finally, despite the Frente press bulletin about "the Cuban patriots in the cities and the hills" who were rising up to throw off "the despotic rule of Castro" (ghosted by Eduardo, I suspect), there was no popular rebellion.

For months afterward, I lived a cowering life—going about my business cautiously, afraid to become problematical in Russell's eyes, half expecting Roy Cohn to follow through on his threats, and apprehensive that Hess or Mason might turn up. When the Pentagon appointed a young Navy Intelligence analyst to be my new liaison, I asked him if he had been in touch with Colonel Hess. I said I hoped Hess hadn't been censured in the fallout from the Bay of Pigs. He told me Hess had received an emergency transfer to Laos on the eve of the Bay of Pigs. It

After the debacle of the Bay of Pigs, President Kennedy forced Allen Dulles to retire from the CIA. Here, at a farewell ceremony at CIA headquarters in Langley, Virginia, in November 1961, Kennedy gives Dulles the National Security Medal. *Cecil Stoughton. White House Photographs. John F. Kennedy Presidential Library and Museum, Boston*

was a relief to know he was far away. Russell might have kept my name out of it but Hess would still have gotten the message. I never heard again from Mason either but I imagined he too had been deposited into some distant military rat hole.

Aside from the addition of President Kennedy, the cast of guilty actors was pretty much the same as in the U-2 crash, though the failure was more inexcusable. But Kennedy couldn't fire himself. After he fired Allen Dulles and replaced him with John McCone, Bissell was first demoted and then pushed to resign.

I don't know who put me on the guest list for Bissell's farewell dinner at the Alibi Club. Perhaps Richard Helms, Bissell's successor as deputy director for Plans, overestimated our friendship. But any awkwardness that I, along with several others in attendance, might have felt was relieved by a lot of good wine and cigars. When the time came round for toasts, Helms made some especially graceful remarks. I could see that Bissell was touched.

PART THREE

THE FOOL

21

In the aftermath of the Bay of Pigs invasion, there were charges, countercharges, recriminations, and, finally, secret hearings. In my subterranean world, I conducted a kind of shadow hearing with myself. The U-2 crash was so easy and the consequences—lots of posturing and pontificating by statesmen—only served to remind me of how deftly I had pulled it off. But the immediate consequences of the Bay of Pigs—114 dead brigadistas—were much more insistent. I had meant well, at least at the beginning. Was I any worse than Helms, who also sat on his hands, or worse than all the characters who actually created Zapata? I told myself that I been intimidated by Helms, Cohn, Mason, a knife and a snake; I told myself that in the end I had really done nothing. But my usually dependable moral agility let me down and I couldn't shake a stubborn and unfamiliar sense of guilt. What should I have done differently? Since I had known early on, with absolute certainty, that Zapata was a disaster in the making, I could have acted to derail the plan; instead I saw it as an opportunity to make my own impression. Of course, my clear-eyed ability to see the future derived from my complete lack of implication in the world. That was the trouble: Without an identity, I wasn't *armed* with a moral vision to tell me what I should or shouldn't do. I seemed, however, in my chastened state, to have discovered a retrospective moral vision. What was it good for? If nothing else, I recognized that my project to paint graffiti on the wall of history had failed. And so I resigned myself to live out of sight; I would no longer try to make an impression on the world.

On a Sunday afternoon in October 1962, I glanced out my kitchen window and saw my CIA neighbor, Mr. Cleary, the genius from Scientific Intelligence. He appeared to be cleaning out his bomb shelter. From inside the shelter, he was tossing out a steady stream of baseball bats, deflated inflatables, stuffed animals, folded lawn furniture, croquet mallets, volleyballs, and golf clubs. When it became dark, the activity subsided. Later that evening the swaying beam of a flashlight in the yard caught my eye. Now my neighbor was bearing two large canteens. While his wife held the flashlight, he carried them down into the shelter. They made several more trips, bringing several cartons and two suitcases into the shelter.

Russell was in Georgia and mysteriously inaccessible the next morning. No one from the CIA or the Pentagon returned any of my calls. A short time later I learned that Kennedy was going to address the nation on television about a matter of extreme urgency. A sense of catastrophe was in the air. That afternoon Russell appeared in the office unexpectedly. All he would say to his staff was that he had a meeting with the president later in the afternoon. He retreated to his office and closed the door.

I couldn't resist. I opened his door and leaned in. "Can I help you? I know something big is in the works."

"What do you mean?" he said, looking away and mumbling. He was a terrible liar.

"Something unpleasant. Like nuclear war."

He pointed to the door. When I had closed it he said, "I truly don't know. The president sent Air Force One to pick up a few of us so I estimate it's pretty big. Bill Fulbright was on the flight too and we guessed it would have to be Cuba again. After we see the president at five, I'll let you know."

But Russell didn't return after the meeting and I learned about the Cuban Missile Crisis and the standoff with Russia the way most people did, on television. I watched Kennedy's speech to the nation with Deborah Boyer. She asked me to come over because she was too frightened to watch it alone. As Kennedy laid out the terrifying situation, Mark blithely assembled the Erector Set I had given him for his birthday, oblivious to Deborah's succession of little gasps. I couldn't avoid thinking this crisis was a consequence of the Bay of Pigs. As I contemplated my new culpability, I imagined Kennedy's next appearance, when he would tell us the missiles were flying. I pictured myself leading Deborah and Mark downstairs and forcing our way into the bomb shelter next door.

After that evening with Deborah and Mark, when the world did not come to an end, I became again a frequent visitor next door. With Mark now in school, Deborah had found a part-time job as a proofreader at Ashford Abelow, the downtown law firm, and began to take courses at George Washington University to finish her undergraduate degree. She often drafted me to baby-sit, slyly saying I was the only sitter Mark liked. If I didn't have another event on, I always obliged. I had once made fun of their day-to-day disarray; now it seemed like a way for me to slip into their world.

When he was very young, I had tried to dismiss Mark's attachment to me as a childhood quirk since I neither encouraged it nor thought I possessed any attributes that would be of interest to a child. But something about me suited Mark: He was a cautious, apprehensive child who cringed when teased or joshed, and my wary awkwardness around him seemed to encourage him. He was also a child with many questions and I was the one with the answers. As I explained why atomic bombs explode, how television works, or why Chinese people look the way they do, he would listen intently, clenching his small, dark face. Deborah encouraged him to call me whenever she couldn't answer one of his questions; after three calls one evening, I began to wonder if he wasn't trying to stump her in order to call me. As I became more comfortable with Mark, it was a relief to drop my prickly guard at last, even if it was with a seven-year-old boy.

I found Mark remarkably compliant. Any activity I suggested was fine with him including chess, bird-watching, and visiting the National Arboretum—not the usual menu for a young boy but I was hardly equipped to be a Little League coach. I even took him to the National Gallery to see the touring Mona Lisa, for which he waited patiently in line for an hour.

Believing that I should share more "normal" activities with Mark, I persuaded Gardner Denby to bring his son, Antoine, for a playdate. We took them to the Georgetown Playground at Q and Thirty-fourth Street. The children hit it off and I rediscovered the amusing, enthusiastic friend I had known in Paris. Gardner was delighted to be my docent in the mysteries of childhood. We began to have frequent playdates. At least once a week in the spring and summer we would hurry from our offices, pick up the children, and meet at one of the many parks in Washington for a couple of hours. Sometimes Gardner would bring his daughter as well. As the sun set and the lush lawns exhaled their fragrant grassiness into the humid air, Gardner and I would sit on a nearby bench, dazed with satisfaction, gossiping and passing a bottle of wine between us like two happy bums while the children frolicked.

Mark was a worrier and a brooder, but I learned not to pry. If I gave him enough room, sooner or later he revealed what was on his mind. Once while we were playing chess at my apartment, he asked, without looking at me directly, "Are you going to move soon, Winston?"

"Give me a minute to think. You have me trapped."

With his eyes still on the chessboard, he shook his head impatiently. "No, I mean are you planning to move from here. *From this place.*"

What had brought this on? I recalled the last time he came over to play chess, when I had complained to him about how small and hot my apartment was. I realized I had unsettled him. I assured him that I was planning to stay and he nodded gravely, his eyes still fixed on the chessboard.

On another occasion, as Mark and I were having lunch after visiting the Smithsonian, he abruptly interrupted my explanation of how airplane wings provide lift. "There's a story we read in school. Actually we didn't read it. We heard a record of it, but the teacher said we could borrow the book to take home. It's hard to read."

Ten minutes after I brought him home, he was at my door with the book. He was amazed that I had never heard of Edward Everett Hale's *The Man Without a Country*.*

"Do you want me to read it to you?"

He nodded emphatically.

It is the story of Philip Nolan, a rash young Army officer who becomes unfortunately entangled with Aaron Burr's rebellion. At his court-martial in 1807, Nolan angrily blurts out his desire to "never hear of the United States again." The court grants his wish; he is sentenced to live out his days on a succession of Navy ships where he is forbidden to hear, read, or learn of any aspect of the United States. As the years pass, Philip Nolan comports himself with dignity and courage. He develops into a sympathetic character whose love for the United States is palpable as he yearns to know more about the country he spurned. On his deathbed, still aboard a ship, he begs a Navy officer to tell him of everything that has happened to his now beloved country. The officer looks around and sees the secret shrine to America that Nolan has made out of his little room, with an out-of-date flag, a picture of George Washington, and a magnificent eagle he has painted on the wall, its wings spread, its talons grasping the whole globe. The officer relents and tells him of the growth and prosperity of America. In the face of Nolan's joy, the officer doesn't have the heart to tell him about the Civil War.

It took three sessions over two days for me to finish reading it to Mark, who kept his eyes fixed on my face the entire time. When we finished the story, I uncharacteristically confronted him. "Why did you want me to read the book?"

"You know," he said uncomfortably.

"Can you tell me?" I was making it hard for him, but I wanted him to say it.

---

* Hale, a minister, abolitionist, and distant cousin of Nathan Hale, wrote the story in 1863 to rally the country to the national cause. It was a huge success in its time and is still incorporated into the patriotic curricula of many American schools.

He winced and sighed. "Because you're not really an American."

Mark was going through an intense patriotic phase, which did not please Deborah, who was becoming more politically outspoken in an undergraduate sort of way. But for children in Washington, the continuous pomp and ceremony, the omnipresent monuments, the incessant flag-waving, must have been hard to resist. I had once told him how Saltonstall engineered my citizenship and Mark was bothered by the idea that I was simply declared an American, more or less at the stroke of a pen. I pointed out all the other Americans who have become citizens, but having studied immigration at school—including a speaking role in the school's Statue of Liberty pageant—Mark believed it was the sweat and toil of forging lives and making families in a new country that Americanized even exotic peoples. I was not authentic.

"So you think the man without a country is like me?"

"He's very sad."

I shuddered at my insensitivity: It was not the dishonesty of my American identity that bothered the poor boy; he was concerned for *me*, for my sorry life without a true national identity. "Am I so sad? Look at it this way. I work for the American government. Doesn't that help make me more American?"

"I guess."

"Besides, do you think that not having a country is the worst thing in the world?"

He regarded me suspiciously.

"Look at it this way, Mark, it's not just a country he doesn't have. This guy is on a boat his whole life. He doesn't have a home, he doesn't have a wife or family, he doesn't have a job. Even if he makes a friend on a ship, there's always a wall between them because the friend isn't allowed to say anything about America. Sooner or later Nolan moves to another ship and the friend is lost to him. The friend can't even send him a letter because it would have an American stamp on it. Nolan never really gets to have a life. Only once does he even mention not having a family. The rest of the time he worries about what the borders of the U.S. look like. He doesn't seem to realize how much he has really lost. It's like he agrees that what he said was so awful that he deserves to live without a life."

After a moment of deliberation Mark said, "He believes in God."

"There's that," I conceded, "but he doesn't have a church. And it doesn't make him happy."

"Do you miss Canada?"

I realized my explanation had only disquieted him further. Perhaps he was hoping I had a secret shrine of maple leafs. I told him I felt like an American now (one of the few times I was not straightforward with him) and, as evidence of my wider circle of American life, I mentioned my sister, and Gardner, and his children. I told him he would always be my friend and so would Deborah.

After our conversation, I felt a strange mixture of melancholy and elation. Yes, I could see the analogy to my life, but I had spoken meaningfully, if not directly, about my life to one of the very few people in this world who cared about me. I had in a sense confessed—not exactly to being a spy, of course, but still, I had confessed. And in some way, Mark had understood. If I hadn't been in one of my more hopeful phases then, if I had not been seeking some sort of pardon from a small, anxious child, I'm sure I wouldn't have spoken so close to the bone.

For almost a year, the only aspect of my life in which I might be said to have acted with spylike insincerity was in my monthly conversations with Larry. He called regularly to check up on his family and seemed satisfied with my perfunctory reports. Should I have told him that his son had adopted me? If he was unaware of my presence in his son's life, then Deborah too was hiding its extent from him.

I didn't offer Larry many details about Deborah's life, especially along the lines of how she often didn't arrive home until ten or eleven in the evening, even when her classes ended in the late afternoon, nor did I mention a few occasions when she had shaken me awake on her couch at three in the morning, with hardly an apology. And what would Larry have made of his neat little Georgian brick home now that books, papers, and clothes were scattered here and there? A congealed blob of toothpaste had survived for weeks on the bathroom faucet and there were always dirty dishes in the kitchen sink. Mark's toys were permanently strewn across the floor of Larry's family room. I especially didn't describe how breathlessly happy Deborah seemed, even when she was harried and behind schedule. Larry said little about his life out on the West Coast except to insist that things were "going great" for him. He often ended our conversations with a vow: "Just don't you forget—they'll all be surprised when Larry comes back." There was something redemptive to him about his exile in California. He nursed a fantasy of returning to Washington in triumph, reclaiming his wife and family, and putting right all the injustices of his time in Washington.

This period after the missile crisis was a unique hiatus in my life, when my sense of falseness was usually no more than an afterthought, when an entire day could pass without a reminder of my indefinitely indentured status. I sedulously minded my business at the office, while my playdates with Mark and Gardner and my quieter social calendar gave my life a relaxing rhythm. Elizabeth Boudreau wasn't up to competing with the new breed of Kennedy-era hostesses, who flaunted their accomplishments in the arts and politics. She avoided parties where she might be expected to scintillate culturally. As far as her own entertaining was concerned, snaring the likes of Lyndon Johnson for dinner, which Elizabeth did six times in that year, was hardly a coup in the Kennedy years, but now that Johnson traveled with an entourage, it was the easiest way for her to see him. I didn't mind; I was free to baby-sit and to see Gardner. I also visited Alice more frequently, who noticed the difference in me and gently tried to pry from me the name of the woman I must have fallen in love with. But as I say, this hiatus was unique in my life and it came to an abrupt end. . . .

Senator Russell was stepping into the Marble Room behind the Senate chamber to check the news ticker when Edward Kennedy rushed past him. A moment later Russell saw the news come across on the AP ticker: President Kennedy had been shot. Russell called his office from the Senate and personally broke the news to each member of the staff. When he spoke to me, he was somberly deliberate. "No one knows how large this thing is. Lyndon may be injured too. I want you to get in touch with McCone or Helms. Make sure they check all their international contacts."

McCone wasn't available but Helms was on the job. He was already three-quarters of the way through the CIA station list and all was quiet. I went out into the office's reception area where the rest of Russell's staff had gathered around a radio while they prayed and consoled each other. As I approached the small group of devastated secretaries and legislative assistants, my own emotions—bewilderment, anxiety—seemed inadequate. All I could summon was a look of bleak futility as I hovered awkwardly, a barren planet on the outer orbit of the human constellation. Did I feel cast out because I was Canadian? Or a spy? Or without religion? Or was it because I was wondering whether Kennedy's shooting was somehow connected to the Bay of Pigs, which was somehow connected to me? An hour later, after we had heard that Kennedy was dead, Russell called again and told us all to go home.

The streets were streaming with weeping federal workers who had poured from their offices. I walked home, avoiding the crowds around the White House by walking along the Mall and then up Virginia Avenue. In Georgetown the streets were deserted. Occasionally a car pulled up at a home and the driver rushed inside. At the little bookstore on Twenty-eighth Street, Victor Lasky's anti-Kennedy diatribe, *JFK: The Man and the Myth,* was being removed from the window. Soon after I arrived home, Deborah called and asked me to come over and watch the news with her. "I'm upsetting Mark, sitting here sobbing while I watch the news. Both of us could use some company . . ."

After the assassination I would have no time or energy for the simple life I had so recently led. I saw Mark only infrequently and Gardner not at all. Deborah was exasperated by my unavailability and Gardner became sulky, like a spurned lover. I tried to explain to each of them how I had lost control of my life but none of them could understand how difficult and hateful it was to work in Lyndon Johnson's White House.

When Lyndon Johnson wanted something, he got very close and became very insistent, even with Senator Russell. *LBJ Library photo by Yoichi Okamoto*

Seven days after the assassination, Johnson conscripted Russell to serve on the Warren Commission to investigate the assassination, even though Russell detested Earl Warren, was not very healthy, and couldn't spare the time. According to Russell, Johnson leaned and leaned on him and then told him he was going to announce Russell's appointment to the commission no matter what Russell said. A week later I was the prize and Russell surrendered me. "When your president says it's in the national interest, you just can't say no. I want you to go over there and do your best for Lyndon. I'll take you back if it doesn't work out."

My photographic memory had made an impression on Johnson. He wanted me to serve the national interest as a kind of personal defense encyclopedia to help him manage the Joint Chiefs of Staff and "that McNamara and his bunch." His agendas with the two groups were different. He didn't trust or respect the JCS and my job was to provide the ammunition to bully them. As for McNamara, whose dazzling competence made Johnson insecure, I was there to help Johnson keep up with him. I knew all of the defense appropriation bills along with the accompanying testimony for the last several years. I could recite the specifications of every important weapons system and the projected troop levels of all branches of the military.

From my subterranean office in the Executive Building, I would be summoned three or four times a day to meetings or conferences where Johnson would force me to tell some recalcitrant admiral exactly how overdue and overbudget his favorite new aircraft carrier was, and how the plug could be pulled on the next one if he didn't get out there and lobby with the public for its necessity. Or I would be called to the Oval Office where McNamara and a couple of his clever minions were calculating for Johnson how much money could be saved by closing a group of military bases and installations. Johnson would make me do the political calculation—the quid pro quos that went into appropriating the bases' construction and their annual budgets, the size of their civilian workforce, the relative power of the congressmen and senators in whose districts they were located—to figure the most dollars that could be saved for the least political fallout. Other times I would be required to resolve some minor point of information such as the name of the second longest river in South Vietnam.

The worst aspect of the job was Johnson's delight in showing me off, like a poodle who could walk on his hind legs. If I knew there was a ruler, premier, or president from some obscure country coming in for a visit, I would browse through a few almanacs and State Department background sheets. It's appalling how impressed these people were to hear me quote their constitutions (those few who had them) or to narrate the blood-soaked chronicles of their royal descents. The demeaning pleasure Johnson took in trotting me out to perform made me wonder if Elizabeth had told him of our relationship, though our sexual relationship had grown even more sporadic and perfunctory of late. Between my job, Elizabeth's revival as a hostess in the Johnson era, and Johnson's closeness to Russell, there was too much Johnson in my life.

My talents did not endear me to anyone else in the White House. Not only was I seemingly free of responsibility, but also Johnson never abused me except in his guffawing regard for me as his court jester. He could explode at almost anyone else, drenching his victims in a tidal wave of obscene vituperation, or else he would humiliate members of his staff by forcing them to converse with him while he sat on the toilet. Every detail received the same feverish attention, whether he was brooding about strategy in Vietnam or trying to get the chairman of the Haggar clothing corporation, Joseph Haggar Jr. himself, to make a few pairs of pants for him with extra room in the crotch, his crotch being a subject of large and public interest to him. It was rare to have a conversation with him that wasn't interrupted by one or two telephone calls during the course of which he would place his hand over the receiver while he mocked whomever was on the line—"Hubert wouldn't know how to pour piss out of a boot if the instructions were written on the heel"—before returning to the call without missing a beat.

He had an extensive collection of metaphorical vulgarities: "You're as useless as tits on a bull"; "he's gonna feel like he's shitting a squealing worm"; or, my personal favorite, "that's the worst thing to happen to America since pantyhose ruined finger-fucking." For all that he was abusive and domineering, there was something faintly ridiculous about his oversized approach to everything. His heedless, humorless charging ahead, his willingness to make a spectacle of himself, was like throwing down a gauntlet: Anyone who could abuse propriety so excessively had to have the biggest pecker in the room, as he would have proudly put it.

Johnson's filial relationship with Russell protected me from his tirades. One of my duties was to help manage Russell. They were in frequent contact—Russell often dined with Johnson and Lady Bird at the White House—but there were profound areas of disagreement between them now. I couldn't do much about their growing divide over civil rights and the rest of Johnson's Great Society agenda, where they were resigned to disagree, but Johnson still regarded Russell as a key mentor on foreign and military affairs, and he spoke to him almost daily. Johnson also depended on Russell to keep the Senate in line, a task Russell was no longer quite up to, as well as the Joint Chiefs, who resented Johnson's adulation of McNamara.

When Johnson wanted to relay bad news to Russell, such as an increase in advisors in Vietnam, he often chose me to soften him up. "You've got to tell him that there are American boys that are in trouble in Vietnam. We're in there like it or not and we've got to support our boys. He's got to hear it from you so it's not just ol' Lyndon trying to hornswaggle him." We both knew which buttons to push with Russell. He supported a powerful military in general and the safety of the individual fighting man in particular; and he believed we could not allow the dignity of the United States to be insulted. But he also opposed overseas military adventures unless the national interest was compellingly at stake. The point of power was to keep you out of military conflicts and to get you in and out of them quickly when you couldn't avoid them. To Russell, fighting a land war in Asia had always been a prescription for disaster. When Eisenhower sent the first group of two hundred "advisors" to South Vietnam after the Geneva Accords in 1954, Russell had privately called it a terrible mistake, but he would not publicly criticize Eisenhower.

Vietnam had lurched into my life soon after the Bay of Pigs, in late April 1961, when I attended a dinner at General Maxwell Taylor's home. It was a farewell dinner for Taylor, chairman of the JCS, and Walt Rostow, the deputy National Security advisor. They were setting off on a fact-finding trip to Vietnam. They were strong advocates of sending several more American combat units to help the South Vietnamese, and now they were going to find some facts to support the idea. "I don't know why they're bothering to go to Vietnam," I told Russell. "Rostow is absolutely confident these troops are going to make all the difference. Here we are, barely two weeks after the Bay of Pigs, and he's ready for action."

Johnson's White House was a demanding place to work. He regularly put in twelve-to-fourteen-hour days and expected everyone else to do so too, including me. I never had any explicit duties or even a job description aside from my title—Military Affairs Liaison. The second- and third-tier bureaucrats, who had little direct contact with Johnson, observed my access to him. Hoping that I would convey to Johnson the brilliance of their confabulations, they swept me up into a nonstop round of meetings in obscure corners of the Executive Office Building and the Pentagon. There I would be, half listening to some soporific

report on the 57 mm recoilless rifles on the PT boats that we were co-
vertly supplying to the South Vietnamese under OPLAN 34A when a
secretary would enter with a summons for me from the president. As
envy fretted the room, I made my apologies. A short time later I was
reciting a list of my forty-three favorite French cheeses, with notes on
their provenance, to Georges Pompidou. "Well how about that?"
Lyndon Johnson said. "And his French ain't bad either, right?" Pompidou smiled weakly, unsure if he was the victim of an obscure practical
joke. "Now let's get down to some horse trading," Johnson went on,
"you know that part of the trade treaty, where we talk about . . . ?"
Johnson nodded in my direction and I rattled off the clause word for
word. The president of the United States had become my organ grinder.

With my pleasant personal life replaced by the numbing boredom of
my White House job, I felt trapped and my old concerns resurfaced. I
began to wonder if my presence in the White House, at the very center
of power, would at last inspire Canada to contact me. These thoughts
were more on the order of self-pitying fantasy than serious expectation:
*Now that I'm stuck in this awful job, it would be just my luck if Canada
came after me too.*

And so, with an inevitability that felt derisive, just my luck began to
come my way in late May 1964, when President Johnson dragged me
into a cabal whose agenda was Canada. The main actors were Assistant Secretary of Defense John McNaughton; McGeorge Bundy, re-
tained from the Kennedy administration as the special assistant for
National Security; McGeorge's brother William, who had segued from
the CIA to Defense and now to the State Department as assistant secretary for Far Eastern Affairs; and Michael Forrestal, a White House special assistant. Johnson stayed long enough at the meeting to describe a
conversation that he and McGeorge Bundy had had with Lester Pearson,
now the Canadian prime minister, in New York several nights before.
"Pearson can't wait to get his oar in the water," Johnson said. "But the
mission has to be a secret. And his fellow can't be seen as directly threatening Hanoi. After all, Canada's supposed to be an impartial member of

A luncheon meeting at the White House. During such meetings, President Johnson expected me to be on call. Once, when I corrected Secretary of Defense Robert McNamara about an obscure and meaningless fact, Johnson could not disguise his pleasure. From the left are George Christian, Walt Rostow, Robert McNamara, Tom Johnson, Richard Helms, Dean Rusk, and President Johnson. *LBJ Library photo by Yoichi Okamoto*

the ICC.* We told Pearson what the stakes are—bombing is a last resort if we're pushed. But we don't want his man to throw that in their face. Now you fellows work out the details."

McGeorge Bundy pursed his lips in an approving smile, like a proud teacher. After Johnson departed, they began to discuss the brief to be given to Blair Seaborn, the Canadian member of the ICC in Saigon. He was to go to Hanoi to reassure the North Vietnamese that the United States only desired the maintenance of the status quo as defined by the Geneva Accords, but would respond harshly if the tide of battle swung too far in the North's favor. As a member of the commission, which had been set up in 1954 to monitor the Geneva Accords, Seaborn

---

* The International Control Commission had been set up in 1954 to monitor the Geneva Accords that separated North and South Vietnam. India and Poland were the other members.

shouldn't have been representing one side's interests, but Lester Pearson, unable to resist getting into the game, had authorized it. To allay Pearson's qualms about threatening Hanoi, Seaborn was also going to dangle the promise of U.S. economic aid if the North cooperated.

William Bundy stressed how Seaborn could not speak *for* the United States. "He can say: 'It is my *belief* that the U.S. would be favorably disposed to give economic aid to the North if they would back off from the South'; or 'If you abide by the Geneva Accords, I am *convinced* the U.S. will be very supportive.' "

They discussed whether "convinced" was a strong enough promise; perhaps "given to understand" would show more sincere commitment on the part of the United States. But it couldn't be too explicit; the hazards of sincerity required escape hatches. Abruptly, McGeorge Bundy switched the conversation around to a completely contradictory problem: how to make sure this peaceful gesture was accompanied by the threat of serious consequences if the North did not back off.

Forrestal said, "Seaborn could appear to be motivated by a personal fear that if Hanoi doesn't cooperate, who knows how far those crazy Americans will go."

McGeorge Bundy objected. "He has to say, in so many words, that U.S. patience is growing thin, that he is convinced the U.S. will escalate, *radically* escalate, if they don't stop their incursions."

McNaughton looked concerned. "How much detail did you give Pearson about our plans in case we have to escalate?"

"We didn't tell him we have a list of ninety-four bombing targets," Bundy said dismissively. "And bombing being a disagreeable subject for Pearson, he didn't press for details, though I think he gets the idea. Seaborn *can't* mention bombing."

"Could he allude to the draft resolution?" Forrestal asked.

McGeorge was shocked. "That's even worse. The idea that we've drafted a war resolution to have in the ready for Congress must be kept absolutely secret. Not only would North Vietnam draw the wrong conclusion but so would American voters. After all, Barry Goldwater's the one who wants to escalate and he's getting ready to run against Johnson in the election. And if the Canadians knew we had already drafted a war resolution, they'd never help."

"Then perhaps we should make the point in the way that Lodge suggests," William Bundy said. The ambassador to South Vietnam, Henry Cabot Lodge, wanted to precede Seaborn's visit with an emphatic attack on a large target in North Vietnam to underscore America's determination.

"We can't seem eager to stride into war," McNaughton declared. "Any attack has to be a response to a provocation. And our response must always seem strong but measured. Otherwise they won't get the correct message. And they won't know how to send messages back to us."

"Rostow would say we should be increasing the level of our reactions exponentially, without any regard for the provocation," William Bundy replied, cleverly attributing the objection to someone else. "We shouldn't be bringing a message *about* war. The only message they'll understand *is* war. They won't get the message unless we bomb a major facility. He even thinks that OPLAN 34A is too mild. Let me be clear—that's what *Rostow* would say." *

There was a moment of silence while they considered the notorious belligerency of their colleague and then, in an unspoken compact of shudders, sighs, and grimaces, decided that they weren't ready to go that far . . . *just yet*. That would be an unfortunately noisy sort of message—to China and Russia, whom we wished to keep out of the war, and to the American voting public, whose choice in six months would be framed as the strong but sensibly restrained Johnson versus the reckless, bombs-away approach of Barry Goldwater.

Speaking with clipped, Kennedyesque succinctness, McGeorge

---

* OPLAN 34A was a program of guerrilla warfare and raids on North Vietnam. The naval component included a small fleet of heavily armored, Norwegian-built, Nasty-class PT boats under the nominal command of South Vietnam. The operation was run by a U.S. group of Navy SEALs, Marine Intelligence, and CIA advisors. As for Walter Rostow, he would succeed McGeorge Bundy as National Security advisor when Bundy decamped for the sanitizing embrace of the Ford Foundation.

summed up their strategy agreement: "We'll add a few emphatic nuances to Seaborn's message. Nothing too strong. But when the DRV offers an opportunity to respond forcefully to one of their provocations right before Seaborn's visit, we shall respond . . . a little excessively."

Forrestal pointed out that the Canadians had insisted on the right to vet Seaborn's message.

William Bundy said: "So we'll let them add a few peaceful nuances. Pearson must think there's another Nobel Peace Prize in it for him."

McGeorge snorted derisively. "He doesn't see it now, but with this he's allowing himself to become our partner. If Hanoi doesn't come around, Pearson is going to have to support our stronger measures, ICC member or not. He's invested in the process. Well, Bates, does this seem like a coherent plan?"

Everyone stared at me with sudden curiosity, though I doubt anyone knew of my Canadian origins. I could have pointed out how most of their brilliant diplomacy had been expended on reconciling their own views; the reactions of Pham Van Dong, North Vietnam's foreign minister, to Seaborn's visit had hardly been considered. But uppermost in my mind was how appalled Pearson would be to know of his cynical exploitation. I finally said, "Let's hope this gets us on the road to a peaceful resolution in Vietnam."

With that their curiosity turned to puzzled frowns. I'm sure they were merely disconcerted by my earnestness but to me it felt as if a giant maple leaf had been branded on my chest. It reminded me of my conversation with Helms before the Bay of Pigs, when he'd innocently described the life of a mole and I quaked inwardly.

22

A few days after the Seaborn meeting, Gardner Denby called. I was surprised to hear from him. Over the last months he had become quite irritated with me as I kept canceling playdates and lunch dates. He finally gave up trying to set up dates.

"I've missed you, Winston. We must try harder to see each other. If it's too difficult to organize the children, we'll have to try something on the spur of the minute, just the two of us." Gardner lowered his voice. "I hear things are pretty awful these days at the White House."

I was disappointed by his suggestive, "entre nous" tone. All he wanted was for me to manifest the awfulness with a few pungent revelations and then we could go on to bat some good gossip back and forth. Without children as intermediaries, we ceased to be friends and reverted to the usefully acquainted. I guessed there was something he needed from me, some marker of White House intrigue that he could negotiate at the State Department for recognition.

"It's tolerable," I said coldly.

Gardner was not discouraged. "Speaking of spur of the minute, I could get away from the office tomorrow afternoon. How about a drink? Why don't we meet in Georgetown for a stroll first? The weather's lovely. Along the canal? We can always find a place for a drink when we get thirsty."

He paused. I didn't answer.

"I've got something juicy for you," he offered in a seductive singsong.

This was even more offensive but also effective. At four thirty the next afternoon I stood on the overgrown banks of the C&O Canal, which reeked in the ninety-degree heat. In those days, before its rehabilitation as a national park, the Georgetown section of the Chesapeake and Ohio Canal was more like a stagnant drain pit. I spotted Gardner hurrying along the towpath toward me.

"What a pleasure to see you again, sport! Such a delight!" he chortled artificially. "You can't imagine how sorry I've felt not to be in touch with you lately."

When people dissemble, they don't look away; they look you straight in the eye, anxious to see if their lies are working. As Gardner searched my face, I saw him anew. Though his blandly handsome face was still youthful, a flurry of thin red veins had etched his cheeks; incipient jowls puckered at the corners of his mouth; and his sturdy, compact torso was beginning to sink softly over his belt.

"Shall we walk awhile?" he suggested. "They say the humidity is wonderful for the complexion. We'll just give ourselves over to it. At least we won't be interrupted." He cackled, trying to turn it all into a joke. He didn't look comfortable. He removed his jacket and tugged at his damp collar.

We walked along the canal while Gardner exclaimed over the scrubby trees and tangled weeds as if we were in paradise. He began to pepper me with questions. "What's going on over there at the White House? Is McNamara really in charge of everything? We're all afraid at State that he's setting our agendas too. Is Rusk just tolerated or does he have any influence?" He sounded slightly manic; no one usually admits to such ignorance. Everything about his manner was forced and false. Could he be this desperate for inside information? Or, it suddenly occurred to me, was he was dying to tell *me* something?

"I'll show you mine if you'll show me yours," I said.

He looked puzzled for a moment—a contrived expression it seemed to me—and then said, "I nearly forgot. Do you remember John Bowen, the Canadian trade official you met at Elizabeth's?"

I suppressed a gasp as my knees went weak. "Yes, yes, I remember him. He knew . . ."

"That's right, old man, he knew Jack McGowan."

"And . . . ?"

"So you haven't heard."

"Why would I hear about McGowan?" I said quickly.

"Bowen called me the other day because he remembered we knew McGowan. He told me McGowan's dead."

I thought: *I'm free!* "When did he die?"

"Several months ago, it seems."

No, not free: The money hadn't stopped.

"He killed himself," Gardner went on. "He was out alone in some godforsaken Yukon wilderness. He was climbing into his bush plane while holding his gun. No one knows why. He must have stumbled or tripped. Somehow he shot himself in the stomach. It doesn't look like suicide because they figure it took a while for him to bleed out. A lonely way to die out there."

In that millisecond of hope, when I thought I might be free, an explosion of joy had gathered in me. When I quashed it, I sensed how efficiently I had managed to ignore the remorseless burden of my life as a mole all these years. The immediate residue of this disappointment was spiteful anger. "Is that what you lured me out here for in this suppurating weather, to tell me this? And how many confidences do you expect me to supply in return?"

I stared at Gardner's expression of gaping torment. What had I said to upset him so?

"I admit it, I did lure you here, Winston. But you must believe me; I don't want your confidences." He moaned softly. "I need your help."

And then I saw it, unfurling from present to past before my mind's eye: Gardner had told me of McGowan's death just when Canada was on the agenda at the White House; eight years ago I encountered Gardner at the Canadian embassy in Washington when Suez was on the boil, whereupon he vigilantly kept up with me; nine years before that I met Gardner at the Canadian embassy in Paris. Was this coincidence or contact? Perhaps I was leaping to conclusions but there it was, a resurgent expectation, long buried but still alive in me. Yes, it was difficult to imagine how an American diplomat could become trapped in Canada's coils, but no less difficult to imagine than a failed Canadian poet rein-vented as a mole and situated at the center of power in the United States.

Gardner had buried his face in his hands.

"Gardner! Gardner!" I couldn't get his attention. I sensed he was inviting me to wring a confession from him. "Don't you think we'll attract too much attention out here? Two men in suits, sweating like pigs . . . This is a clandestine meeting that unfortunately looks like a clandestine meeting."

"Clandestine?" He looked at me hesitantly, almost hopefully.

There was no turning back. "Oh come on, Gardner, I *know*."

It was as if I had struck him. He slumped helplessly and raised his hands in resignation.

We walked silently, each of us wondering or fearing what he was get-ting into, until we found a shabby bar on Thirty-third Street. It was dark, cool, and deserted, except for the bartender and two men seated in symmetrical glumness at either end of the bar. We ordered supplies—two martinis for me, a double scotch for Gardner—and took them to an unoccupied area in the rear where there were a few booths. Gardner stared down at his drink.

"You're not exactly practiced at this, are you?" I said. I was fishing for an outright confirmation from Gardner of his role as my contact before committing myself.

"Sorry to disappoint you," he muttered, avoiding my gaze. "I'm a complete amateur . . . a *victim* really. How long have you known?"

"I've suspected for quite some time," I lied, attempting to sound pro-fessional. I hadn't expected my contact would be a master spy, but I wasn't happy about dealing with a fellow amateur.

He took several deep, tremulous breaths. "But all this time, you really never told anyone of your suspicions?"

"Why would I? We go back a long ways. And it might have drawn attention to me. I had already kept one secret for you."

"You see the connection between those secrets, don't you?"

I hadn't until he asked the question. "It's the Hiss thing, isn't it? That's what they've held over your head."

"Yes. They told me my 'Communist past' was safe with them. But they didn't want me to be a spy, just someone to turn to for background occasionally, a consultant really, like others they used in Washington."

"That seems to be the Canadian style," I said wryly, as if we were gossiping about our boss. "It's a network of amateurs. They let you pretend you're not a spy, just a casual source."

He looked at me strangely. "You seem to know a lot about the way they operate."

"It was McGowan who recruited you, right? Now that he's dead you figured it was safe to talk to me."

He lifted his head for a moment, looking beyond me into the distant past. Then, shaking his head in sad distress, he said: "You are the only person I ever told about Hiss."

He had figured it all out: For me to know he was a Canadian operative meant I had to be the one who had passed on his Hiss connection to Canadian intelligence. But I hadn't. Or had I? I tried to remember what I had actually said to McGowan so many years ago. We had been quite drunk but I was sure I had only vaguely alluded to Gardner's secret. Was that all it took for someone like McGowan? If I was responsible, it no longer seemed like such a strange coincidence for us both to be Canadian spies.

"It wasn't McGowan himself. They came after me when I was working for the Marshall Plan. I was sitting in the Place des Vosges one day. A stranger struck up a conversation with me about anti-Communist witch hunts in the U.S. I thought he was an American. Then he asked if I was still in contact with Hiss."

I tried to seem all knowing. "You probably should have resisted the first time they held Hiss over you. Others have survived such minor transgressions without losing their jobs."

"I should have. But they rushed me into a very minor indiscretion and then, to show their gratitude, they gave me some money, which I was foolish enough to accept. Once I realized how stupid I was, I refused to take any more. But they told me they would continue to deposit it for me in a special account."

"I know the problem. It was the money that trapped me too," I said, underlining our close bond.

Again he stared at me strangely. "Not you—"

I had a sudden intuition he didn't know I was a fellow spy. He had so far acknowledged only his role, not mine. I realized that he was, in tradecraft terms, a cutout, set up to shield his handler from me. I was merely a source of information to him. I thought of all the conversations and gossip I had supplied to Gardner over the years. Had I been very careless? I couldn't remember Gardner actually prying any secrets from me.

I should have confessed to my own life as a spy right then and there. But I could not get the words out. I had been on my guard for nearly fifteen years; inhibition had become a reflex. I quickly said: "I meant the money and gratuities the lobbyists used to throw at me. I can't say I didn't succumb a couple of times. And then I was obliged to them."

"Hardly the same thing. But you must believe me; I've done nothing for them. At most, I pass on a little gossip about who's up and who's down at the State Department. Don't you see why I've had such a lousy career? I've maneuvered myself into dead-end jobs so I *wouldn't* know any secrets. I could have moved up at the State Department. Instead I became a trade officer in Lyons and a salmon negotiator with the Canadians. *That* was a perfect dead end! And then representative to the Geophysical Year. Having a French wife has also kept me out of a few assignments."

"But she did help you once, didn't she? You were able to tell them where Suez was headed."

"That was the only big secret I ever knew and I found out about it from my wife right after I met you at the Canadian chancery. When I told my contact I had met you, he forced me to get in touch with you. He told me I should allude to my Suez secret to see if you would be indiscreet with me." He looked at me sheepishly. "Sorry, Winston. I really didn't want to know your secrets."

"What do you know about your handler? How do you contact him?"
He drew back and stared at me for several seconds.

"I don't *need* to know," I said. "Just curious." More than curious: I needed to know why I had been left in the dark all these years, why Gardner or the handler couldn't have just approached me directly, spy to fellow spy.

"I once referred to my current contact as my handler and he got very indignant. 'I'm not your handler,' he said. 'I'm just an acquaintance. A contact.' Some acquaintance! I don't even know his last name. In fifteen years I've had two contact people. Well three if you include the man who laid it all out for me in Paris. But there's always been one person at a time, only one, and I don't contact him. He contacts me."

"He isn't your handler. You are a cutout and so is your contact probably. He insulates you from the handler or principal, who is back there pulling the strings. I doubt if your contact knows much more about the handler than you do."

My use of tradecraft jargon impressed Gardner. He nodded deferentially and continued: "It's all so natural. No skulking about. He just calls me up for a little chat every so often. We lunch openly. Lately though he's been much more interested in you. I keep telling him you don't have time for me now that you're in the White House. But of course that's why he's interested."

"Have I been so loose-lipped with you over the years?"

"Just enough to keep them intrigued. But I don't tell them everything you tell me. I just pass on the more innocuous information and even that makes me feel terrible."

"Well, it is only Canada. But they've never asked you to go further with me, to try to compromise me?" Perhaps the Canadians thought that I had been turned by American Intelligence.

"No. I get the feeling they're afraid of you. I have to be totally cautious with you. No direct questions about what you're up to. My contact says they want me to keep in touch with you but they don't trust you. They've suggested you're dangerous. The only way you'll tell me anything is out of innocence. Once in a while, when I've met my contact, I got the feeling that he had been watching me while I met with you."

"'Dangerous'!" I was puzzled. "You don't think I'm dangerous, do you?"

He shook his head. "Obviously not. I want you to know, I came here with the idea of confessing to you, though I wasn't sure I would go through with it. There have been other times when I've been on the verge of confessing—to my wife, to a State Department security officer I met—but I could never bring myself to do it. You don't know what it's like, living with something like this—always alone and always on guard. When the two of us started having our playdates, I realized it was the only natural, friendly relationship I've had in fifteen years aside from my family. I forgot I was supposed to be *using* you. It was just like when we first met, only with children instead of movies. But when you went to the White House, things got quite scary with my contact. He kept pressing me to see you and you kept breaking dates with me. He began to sound almost desperate and he tried to threaten me. For the first time he gave me a way of contacting him, in case you told me anything important. I couldn't pretend to myself any longer that it was all just a harmless transgression. I stopped calling you. I told them you were getting suspicious of me. But I also began to think you might be able to help me escape this . . . somehow . . . I just thought, hoped, with your connections, you might figure out some way to finesse it. Maybe in exchange for catching my contact, I could be allowed to resign quietly. I never passed any big secrets or caused any harm. I mean they were interested in your gossip about weapons and the Defense budget, but I always said you were quite careful. I may have passed on a few little tidbits, but nothing important. And as you say, it's only Canada!"

I patted him reassuringly on the shoulder and went for another round of drinks.

When I returned, Gardner sighed. "Where do we go from here?"

I knew where. "I've learned something recently that will be of enormous interest to your contact and his handler. And the more important the information, the higher up the network we can go."

"Are you sure we want to go up the ladder? We'll only get me in more trouble. Now that I've confessed to you, I feel so much better. Maybe we should just drop it."

"I'm trying to get you off the hook. But it's not your contact we want to reach; it is the *handler* who is crucial. He will be in our power if we can identify him. He can't afford to be identified running a Canadian spy network because the U.S. would be furious. The Russians are supposed to spy on us, but not the Canadians. That's our leverage. Then we can force him to let go of you. I'm not entirely noble. I've been seen quite often with you. If you were found out, the trail would lead to me. If the FBI got their hands on you, I'd be next. Just the suspicion that I was indiscreet would do me in."

My lies had been leaping out so spontaneously that it took a moment to realize this last concern was probably true; there was a risk for me. But this was my break: the first and probably last chance to contact my hands-off handler. I sensed I was coming to the end of a long journey. I pressed on. "This is what you're going to tell your contact: In a few weeks a Canadian envoy named Blair Seaborn is traveling to Hanoi on a mission of peace and fair warning on behalf of the United States. That's not such big news; your control will know that already. Seaborn is supposed to say that the U.S. so desires peace they will provide economic assistance to the North. He's also supposed to say the U.S. will be angry and respond harshly if the incursions continue in the South, but the basic emphasis is on peace. The thing is, this is nonsense. The U.S. is utterly cynical about this visit; regards it as a warning, not a peace feeler. To make sure Hanoi gets the point, they are going to stage a whacking good attack just before Seaborn arrives."

His eyes widened. "Isn't my contact going to wonder why you're telling me this?"

"You must make him think it's all innocent gossip. Tell him I sounded indignant, that I have some leftover Canadian patriotism. After all, this could seriously embarrass Lester Pearson." I spoke rapidly in an attempt to sound competent. "Wait for your contact to get in touch with you. When you tell him, act as if neither of us realizes how big a deal this is. To you and me it's just another stupid American ploy. But you must also say that I alluded to a true secret, something so big that I wouldn't tell you. Something that will scandalize Canada if Seaborn goes through with this." I had in mind the list of ninety-four bombing targets and the draft war resolution. These were the lures with which I intended to expose our control.

"I don't know if I can do all this. He'll see I'm nervous."

"That's okay. He knows you're an amateur. If he seems suspicious, ask him to tell you why his masters are afraid of me. Tell him you're worried. Ask him if *you* should be afraid." I laughed again at the thought. "Why would anyone think I'm dangerous?"

23

Unlike my other interventions, my plan was not a self-indulgent gesture; I was treasonously ready to pass real secrets on to Canada. The meeting where I learned of Seaborn's trip had been cynical and misguided; I could see that Vietnam was on its way to being another fiasco. Wasn't I doing the right thing to warn Canada? Wasn't treason trumped by such a principled gesture? And Gardner would benefit as well, though I wasn't exactly sure how I would work that part of it out. But mainly I plunged ahead because I was two cut-outs away from Gardner's handler, and I was unable to restrain myself.

For several weeks I heard nothing. No word from Gardner and no information about Seaborn's mission. I was afraid to make overt inquiries about Seaborn at the White House. A meeting at the beginning of June with McNaughton, McNamara, and President Johnson about OPLAN 34A seemed a promising opportunity. A big OPLAN 34A operation would have been the perfect way to send a harsh message to the North Vietnamese in conjunction with Seaborn's mission. After I performed a tour-de-force recollection of the secret defense appropriation for OPLAN 34A, I tried to turn the conversation around to recent developments. But McNamara, speaking with exaggerated courtesy, said: "Thank you, Mr. Bates, for unraveling these complex technical details." Johnson took the hint and excused me from the meeting.

*

The queen's birthday was celebrated on a beautiful June afternoon. The extensive grounds of the British embassy were lush, the roses were in bloom, and the strawberries, caressed in sweet cream, were succulent. Hundreds of the most important Washingtonians traipsed about the lawn and politely competed for the tiny garden tables and frail chairs that had been scattered about. I spotted Joe Alsop, splendidly outfitted in British bespoke, and I was reminded he had recently returned from Vietnam. Surely he owed me a confidence or two. Several months ago a column of his had begun: "An anonymous source at the White House, one of those indispensable, behind-the-scenes players who make things happen, told me in confidence . . ." That would be me, though my anonymity was more impressive than my indispensability.

Alsop was not a White House favorite. His manner epitomized the Georgetown social world that Johnson resented. And his columns about Vietnam were not simply critical; they presumed to tell the president what he ought to be doing if he only understood the history and political culture of Southeast Asia. But Alsop still had good contacts in the military and State Department and he was close to Henry Cabot Lodge. He could have heard something about the warning attack. As we shoveled our strawberries into our mouths, I brought up Vietnam. Alsop immediately began to say that Johnson was too restrained, too weak in Vietnam. "Oh, I know what the president is up to. And I agree—Goldwater's too far over the top. He scares people. But the president is running the risk of looking weak. One good offensive by North Vietnam and Goldwater will have control of the issue. It's not just politics. If we take the offensive now we can prevail. Shoring up these gimcrack South Vietnamese governments is a useless exercise. You only need to spend a few days in Saigon to know how hopeless they are. But you have to be there, talk to the people on the ground, experience the weather in the streets."

"But we have launched a couple of especially strong retaliatory strikes lately," I said invitingly.

"Oh indeed?" Alsop reared back, taking my measure. "Do tell."

Rather than eliciting information, I had put myself in the position of offering it. Casting about for a life ring, I spotted a lean, familiar figure striding across the lawn. "Look! There's Dick Helms." I grabbed Alsop by the arm and propelled him along until we intercepted Helms as he was passing an unoccupied table.

Once we were seated and had negotiated the initial pleasantries, the dogged Alsop said: "Winston was just about to tell me—"

"Joe!" It was his wife, Susan Mary, effervescently dressed in the French manner, topped off with a wide-brimmed, cream-colored straw hat. "The Harlechs are asking for you. You must say hello."

Joe made one of those exasperated "these women!" gestures and off he went.

"But you weren't going to tell him much, I assume," Helms said with a smile.

I had forgotten how disarming Helms could be. "He was about to tell me something about the weather in the streets . . . the streets of Saigon that is."

Helms laughed genially. "When Joe travels, there's an umbrella over him at all times. He stays with the ambassador or the local USIA head. He meets with the highest military command levels. He gets to talk to the top South Vietnamese leaders. Once in a while he'll even go on a nice, safe training exercise. He loves climbing into helicopters and roaring over the countryside. But he's never exactly in the field or in the street."

"Speaking of the field, how are those new Norwegian PT boats working out, the Nasty-class PTFs we've purchased for 34A activities?"

"Marriage seems to suit Joe," he replied firmly, ready to move on to another subject.

"And Susan Mary too." If he wanted chitchat, I would give him chitchat.

He shot me a quick glance to see if we were sidling up to the same delicate subject. I concurred by looking about to see if we were out of earshot. We leaned conspiratorially toward each other. I was ready for this; I had done some homework since Robert informed me of Joe's homosexuality.

"You know," I said, "I'm told that Joe stayed with Susan Mary and her late husband in Paris many times, over many years. Yet after her husband died, and Joe proposed marriage by letter, telling her in all frankness he was homosexual, it was the first she had heard of it."

"Many people in Washington still have no idea. You can imagine how his friends felt when the photographs arrived."

"Photographs?"

"You don't know about the Moscow pictures?" Helms said ingenuously. He proceeded to tell me how Alsop, on a trip to Russia in 1957, met a very attractive young man at a party in Moscow. The next day the KGB confronted him with a number of photographs. Sexual perversion is a crime in Russia, he was told sternly. He could be arrested. But if he would do his best to further Soviet-American relations back in the U.S., he could avoid trouble. Helms had a humorous tone to his voice as he narrated the story; this was a curious tale, not a prurient one. "Luckily for Joe, his old pal Chip Bohlen was the ambassador. Joe told the whole story to Chip, who immediately got him on a plane and out of the country. Unfortunately, the KGB believes you have to follow through on your threats. If you're in the blackmail business, your reputation for pitilessness is everything. Back in Washington, the photographs were mailed to a number of his friends and a few journalists. Joe has his faults but a lack of courage is not one of them. He spoke frankly to each and every person who got the pictures and that appeared to put out the fire."

"So you think there's nothing hanging over him anymore?"

"There's an epilogue. Somewhat later, the Russians got fed up with Joe's splenetic anti-Communism and started to circulate the pictures again, out of spite I suppose. This time Joe decided to make a public confession. It would have been a terrible blow to his career, but he was damned if he'd let the KGB push him around. He came to me for advice and I advised him to hold his fire and let me try to get the KGB off his back. The agency has back-channel access to the KGB—fellow professionals and all that. I let them know that we could respond in kind if they persisted in torturing Joe. There was nothing in it for them and they backed off."

From a certain perspective, mine, this story could be seen as having a moral about secret lives. I remembered Helms's disquisition on the lonely lives of moles and informants at our meeting after my Guatemala trip.

"Joe must be very grateful."

"Unfortunately, I couldn't protect him completely. J. Edgar Hoover got his hands on the pictures. God knows what he's done with them. I know he showed them to Ike." Helms abruptly stood up. "Time to circulate. Delightful to see you, Winston, as always. Let's try to manage a lunch sometime."

Helms's exemplary tale did not encourage me to contact Gardner, who appeared to be in no hurry to contact me. I was in a quandary: afraid to go forward with Gardner yet, having come close to the mystery of my conception as a spy, unable to let go of the connection.

As June gave way to July, a stubborn sense of destiny kept me on the alert for any news about Seaborn's trip, which must already have taken place, but I heard nothing about it or about a big strike against North Vietnam. The closest I could get was to learn something more about OPLAN 34A operations, which had been stepped up lately. I called Dave Camwell. He was the Navy Intelligence analyst who had been appointed as my Pentagon liaison after Hess disappeared. After I went to the White House, we no longer had any official connection, but my closeness to Lyndon Johnson made him eager to please me. "You should know that the Norwegian PTF crews have all gone home and we're using Taiwanese operatives now, along with the South Vietnamese, on covert operations. And I wouldn't be surprised if the occasional SEAL goes on these raids, only to observe, of course." Though he said it offhandedly, the information about the Navy SEALs was his real leak to me—direct U.S. involvement was forbidden and denied at the highest level. The leak was supposed to impress me but it wasn't what I was after. When I asked him about any large, excessive actions in North Vietnam, the kind that might have presaged the Canadian peace initiative, he said, "Nothing big really. Just a lot of quick strikes along the Tonkin Gulf."

I finally took the initiative with Gardner in mid-July and proposed a get-together with children. He was not delighted to hear from me but he agreed. On a windy, sunny Saturday afternoon, Mark and I met Gardner, Solange, and Antoine at the Norfolk and Washington Steamboat Company. In the company of a church group from Bemidji, Minnesota, we set out on a Potomac excursion. Gardner looked quite dashing in his billowy white casuals. While on the boat, he ensured there was always a child between us when I drew close to him. When the excursion was over, he marched his children determinedly over to Maine Avenue and looked for a taxi. Desperate to prolong the encounter, I suggested to his children that they come over to my place for ice cream. Before Gardner could object, I had crammed the five of us into a taxi. As I had hoped, Deborah was home and happy to take over. I brought Gardner next door and took him out on my porch. The wind had died down and the air felt heavy and sullen. Below us, the children sprawled on the Boyer patio.

I offered him a drink.

"Don't even try. It all looked too easy last month when we were both half drunk. But I've changed my mind. I'm sorry I ever confessed to you. You made me think you were going to help me escape. But exactly how is that supposed to work? I don't see that we've gotten anywhere. I just wanted to confess and get it over with. But now I've changed my mind."

"Just tell me what happened. What scared you off?"

According to Gardner, my description of the hidden, cynical attitude of the Americans was enormously gripping to his contact, as was my hint of a big secret. "However, there's one slight problem," Gardner said reproachfully. "There wasn't any big attack by the U.S. before Seaborn's visit. It was almost too quiet in the period before his trip. As you might imagine, this cast some doubt on what you said. But they know Seaborn is going back in August. Now they want to know if the big strike is being planned before that visit. They're more fascinated with you than ever. And more suspicious."

"What do you mean 'they'? Have you seen somebody new?"

"No, but it's clear my contact is checking with someone else and then getting back to me. He's very hesitant and never volunteers information. If I ask a question he says he'll have to think about it and give me the answer the next time."

Our handler seemed to be getting closer, hovering just offstage now. "Did you get a chance to inquire why they're afraid of me?"

"It's the CIA. You were so close to them while you worked for Russell. They can't imagine they didn't get their hooks into you."

"Do *you* think I'm part of a CIA counterintelligence operation? It was you who approached me."

"You have to understand: For fifteen years I've mostly been useless to my masters aside from the occasional indiscretion from you. And even with you, I never told them everything you told me. My contact and I have been able to pretend to each other that our meetings are innocent. And they were! At least compared to the way it is now. I think my contact was as relieved as I was to have nothing much to report. I've decided I can live with that. Now I really want to have done with you, Winston. If you can possibly find it within your vast powers to keep your mouth shut, I would deeply appreciate it. Soon I will be of no interest to my contact. I've taken a new assignment to teach social protocol to State Department trainees. We start at table settings and go on to thank-you notes."

"Please hear me out."

He clenched his teeth and stared fixedly away from me.

"I am going to resign from my White House job."

That got his suspicious attention.

"I mean it. Russell has said he'll take me back. If we play it right, we can draw your contact out with one last big White House secret before I leave. I might get you off the hook completely."

"No! Don't try to get me off the hook. No playing! Just quit. If you do, if you actually leave the White House, that's what will make them lose interest—in you as well as me." He was very agitated now. "I don't think you've considered the consequences for either of us. Just get out of it!" He stood up and abruptly headed into the house. A few moments later I saw him rush out on the patio below, frantically gather his children, and flee.

The word "resign" had just popped out of my mouth as a tactic to get Gardner's attention, but after Gardner was gone it got my attention too. Something had happened to scare Gardner. I knew he wasn't being entirely frank with me, but I did sense that he was trying to caution me. If he was warning me off, I was easily warned. What good would it do me now to confront my control? Gardner seemed to believe that if I left the White House and he went on to teach table settings, it would be enough to lower the level of Canadian interest in each of us.

*

Two weeks later, on Monday, August 3, Lyndon Johnson called me directly. "Dick Russell's nephew Bobby and his wife are going to be staying with us for a couple of days at the White House and Dick's coming to have dinner with us tonight. You come too, for a drink before we sit down. Now I want you to take Dick aside. Make sure he understands there's no connection between those South Vietnamese raids and our destroyer being there. There's no case for provocation on our part. And tell him the North Vietnamese should damn well know it too."

Destroyer? I had no idea what he was talking about, but I knew where to find out. Dave Camwell, my Navy Intelligence friend at the Pentagon, was enthralled by his role as a source. All I had to say was, "The president needs to know if he's been given the whole story about the destroyer," and he was mine.

"All I know is there's been an attack on one of our destroyers in the Tonkin Gulf. But I don't have to go far to find out more. Just down the hall." An hour later he called back. Three North Vietnam torpedo boats had attacked the USS *Maddox,* a destroyer on an intelligence mission, code-named DESOTO, to monitor North Vietnam's radar capabilities. The attacks were unsuccessful and fighter planes from a nearby aircraft carrier had damaged or destroyed the torpedo boats. "Here's the tricky part—there's no direct connection between the DESOTO patrol and OPLAN 34A, though the North Vietnamese wouldn't know that. Just three days ago, four 34A PTF boats shelled several islands off the coast of North Vietnam. Now those PTFs are, at least nominally, South Vietnamese. But on the way back to base, the PTFs passed within sight of the *Maddox,* which was just entering the gulf. So you see, the North Vietnamese torpedo-boat commanders might honestly think the destroyer was connected to the raids." Before I could react, Camwell continued: "But there's another possibility. What if this attack is a 'message' as the McNamaras like to say around here, not local at all but sent straight from Hanoi? The *Maddox* was well away at sea and it wasn't doing anything overtly hostile at the time. Attacking an innocent U.S. destroyer on the high seas is a significant escalation if the order really came from

Hanoi. Can we let such a provocation pass without a response? That's the question of the moment." The officer was enjoying spouting off.

"Do you think the White House has been fully briefed?"

"You tell me. I'm not in on the policy side. I know McNamara is trying to get up to speed on this. He's got to brief the president again this afternoon."

When I arrived that evening, the Johnsons and the Bobby Russells had already assembled. I had met Bobby several times over the years. He was a great favorite of Russell's, a kind of surrogate son and a frequent visitor to the office. Back in Georgia, he monitored local politics for Russell.

"I sent a car for Dick," Johnson said to me. "Why don't you meet him when he arrives?"

When alone with Russell, I always alluded to the difficulties of working for Johnson, and occasionally Russell would take the hint and reaffirm his pledge to take me back at some time in the future. I was at the White House door when the car pulled up. Russell extricated himself from the car gingerly, scowling at the effort, but he greeted me fondly. I launched right into it. "I'm supposed to tell you there's no connection between the South Vietnamese commando boat raids and the *Maddox*."

Russell looked at me in surprise. "I got briefed this afternoon by McNamara. He said the same thing. But even if there wasn't a connection, we have got to strike back. I've been telling the president we're beginning to look weak and indecisive in the eyes of the world, which is just going to invite more incidents. And we're also going to play right into Goldwater's hands in the election."

As we neared the dining room, I couldn't hold it in any longer. I grasped Russell's arm. In a low voice I said, "I can't take it anymore around here. I'm just a glorified errand boy. I want to come back to work for you."

I must have looked desperate because he patted my hand comfortingly. "Don't you worry yourself. I'll see what I can do."

Russell called the next morning. "I told the president last night I wanted you back. I said to him if he wants me to help him out, I need you to take a load off me. And it was all right with Lyndon, though he said he never met anyone who can remember things the way you can. He thinks you're better at it than McNamara. I want you to know I'm not just doing you a favor. I really do need you. We're headed down a slippery slope in Asia and it's going to get worse before it gets better. This morning at the congressional breakfast the president told me there's some evidence that North Vietnamese torpedo boats are going to go back after the *Maddox* again. If they attack, he's going all out in retaliation. Something he should have done already."

Johnson himself called a few minutes later to tell me he had reluctantly agreed to my return to Russell's office. "But don't you forget, you'll be able to do for me as well as for Dick over there." It sounded like a threat, but I didn't mind. I told Johnson I could be out of the White House at the end of the week, a tacit admission of my expendability. I was immensely relieved to be out of there. Did I really need to flush out my control? I had begun to feel like the target rather than the hunter.

To celebrate my escape, I took off for the rest of the day. I went to the Corcoran Gallery, just down the street from the Executive Office Building, and spent several pleasant hours. I returned home in the early afternoon with the idea of taking Mark out for a walk or a snack when he came home from school. I had a glass of wine, which made me dozy. As I drifted in my armchair, I told myself I should drink more, indulge myself more . . .

Gardner's call jerked me awake. "You're not at the office!" he screamed accusingly. "What are you doing at home? I've called three times."

It was nearly six o'clock. "I've quit as of yesterday."

"Oh no!"

"I'm still there for a few days. What's wrong?"

"I can't believe this!" he wailed. "They're after me again. I'm supposed to talk to you. Something big is going on."

"I thought you were out of it."

"Well I might have been if you had quit when you promised. I told my contact two weeks ago I'd accepted a job teaching social protocol to trainees and that you were quitting the White House. I announced I would be useless to them in the future."

He was disintegrating, but I finally pieced together the whole story.

After being left alone for a while, he had been contacted today by a much tougher and more aggressive man than the regular contact. This man knew I was still at the White House and he insisted Gardner contact me. When Gardner demurred, he read passages to him from his old fawning letter to Alger Hiss and told him it would be mailed to J. Edgar Hoover. There was something big going on right now and he had to know the details. The Gulf of Tonkin attack must have excited Canada's interest. But why would they put such extreme pressure on Gardner? Couldn't Pearson just call up Johnson and get the real story? I wondered if Seaborn and Pearson had not been entirely frank with the United States on Seaborn's return. Or perhaps Seaborn was due to visit Hanoi again and they didn't trust the United States to tell them how things stood. Because I was untrustworthy, the handler insisted that Gardner meet me in a public place. He wanted to see and hear for himself that I was just a big gossip, that I wasn't playing some deep game. Gardner was dangling the possibility of getting the handler out in the open, but it would also get me out in the open.

"Let me find out what I can," I said. "I'll call you at home."

I tried to get hold of Russell. His secretary told me he was back at the White House for another briefing, after which Lyndon Johnson was preempting the TV networks for an announcement of major national importance. I got hold of Dave Camwell, who had been on the job for twenty-four straight hours. After an edifying talk, I called Gardner back.

"They've been after me again," Gardner moaned. "Someone actually came to the house this afternoon. My own house! He left a message with my wife!"

I told Gardner what I had learned: The *Maddox* had reported being under continuous attack for about two hours this morning, along with another destroyer, the *Turner Joy*. "If you tell them this," I suggested, "they probably won't insist on our having a public meeting."

"Thanks for the big news," he said sarcastically. "Chet Huntley just announced that on television. The report came from the AP."

"Did they say that Johnson's going to announce a major retaliation? A series of bombing strikes based on a list of targets that they've had at the ready for months? And then Johnson's going to ask Congress to back him with a resolution of support, a war resolution for all practical purposes—also something they prepared months ago."

"Not yet. But once it's announced, there's no big secret anymore."

And then I made a huge mistake. I told him the most interesting thing I had learned from Dave Camwell: There was a strong possibility that the second round of attacks never took place. Soon after the "action" ceased, Captain Herrick of the *Maddox* cabled a message expressing his "doubts" about many of the reported sightings of attack boats and torpedoes. Freakish weather, skittish sonar men, and ghostlike radar images may have contributed to an exaggerated report.

"And Johnson knows this?" Gardner asked.

"If he doesn't, he soon will. McNamara knows. That should satisfy your handler. Tell your contact what I've told you and say I was unusually loquacious because I'm on the way out. But there's no possibility I'm going to meet you."

That evening, as U.S. planes bombed North Vietnam, Johnson delivered his speech without the slightest mention of any doubts about the attack. The next morning, before I left for work, Gardner was back at me in a complete panic. "They have to hear it from you that Johnson knew the attack did not happen and went ahead anyway."

"Why?"

"Canada is getting ready to break with the U.S. over this. They have to be sure."

"I'm not going to talk to them."

"Just meet me. Just let them see you with me. You have to. You got me into this."

"This is what I'll do. I was planning on going to the Corcoran tomorrow. Meet me on the sidewalk in front at eleven thirty. We'll have a very short conversation and then go our separate ways."

On a high floor of the Executive Office Building, there was an airless, little-used conference room. From its window one had a clear view down Seventeenth Street where the splendid Corcoran Gallery stood, its entrance guarded by two stone lions. At ten o'clock I taped an IN

USE sign to the door, which I wedged shut behind me. I seated myself at the window and adjusted the bird-watching binoculars I had borrowed from Mark Boyer.

Along with the usual stream of tourists entering the Corcoran, I noticed several solitary men with bad haircuts and ill-fitting business suits who went in at ten-minute intervals. They could have been art lovers, or they could have been intelligence agents. At ten thirty a car pulled up across the street from the gallery but no one got out. At eleven twenty, Gardner appeared on the sidewalk before the entrance. Standing on the steps above Gardner, next to one of the two stone lions that flanked the doorway, was a man dressed in a loud shirt and silly sun hat. He appeared to be an exceptionally typical tourist as he studied his map and brandished his little Kodak camera. I scanned the area around the entrance but saw nothing suspicious. Except for an occasional sideways glance, Gardner ignored the tourist.

By noontime, Gardner was agitated. He began to look at his watch impatiently. He shot a quick glance at the tourist who, looking irritably up and down Seventeenth Street, appeared to have been stood up as well. They both inspected their watches on and off for another twenty minutes, occasionally folding their arms in stagy exasperation. I happened to be focused on the tourist when I saw him jerk his head in Gardner's direction and Gardner obediently and hurriedly departed. A few moments later, the car that had parked across from the Corcoran pulled away.

I stayed at my post for another fifteen minutes, hoping the tourist would lift his head—one good look and I would remember him forever. Finally the tourist descended the steps from the Corcoran and turned up Seventeenth Street. His face still hidden under his hat, he scampered diagonally across Seventeenth Street where he intercepted a tall, lean man who was walking up the street toward the Executive Office Building. The lean man looked oddly familiar. I realized I had seen him from the back about ten minutes before, walking away from me on Seventeenth Street. As they stood at the corner of Seventeenth and F Streets, almost beneath my gaze, the tourist opened a map as if asking the tall man for directions. They spoke for a few moments. The tall man was not wearing a hat and he had only to look up slightly as he took an impatient drag on his cigarette for me to recognize him. He had lost weight and looked even more lupine than he had seven years ago but there was no mistaking him. It was Sergei Striganov, the KGB operative from the Russian embassy, whom I had met just once, when I visited the embassy on my clandestine mission for the CIA. I had heard he had left the United States some time ago for a post in South America. Had he returned just for this operation? For me? Without knowing exactly what I had done and how I had done it, I could see the unfortunate consequences of my debacle.

In an attempt to make amends, I informed Russell in advance of the war resolution vote that there was little evidence for the attack in the gulf. Though he had been all for retaliation, he had misgivings about an open-ended commitment to allow the president to wage war. In the end he voted for the resolution but he added language to it allowing Congress to cancel the grant of power to the president.*

I avoided Gardner for several months and he avoided me. As best as I could tell, the Russians avoided me too, though my level of tradecraft here was limited to looking over my shoulder frequently. I knew I would have to confront Gardner sooner or later. I wondered if he would have the nerve to show up at Elizabeth's postelection Thanksgiving cocktail party, which promised to have a celebratory tone after Johnson's landslide victory over Goldwater—thanks in large part to Johnson's show of strength over the Tonkin Gulf incident.

Gardner was there, very much his old self in his well-cut, slimming suit, his explosive laugh audible above the din. He waved to me eagerly. He was talking to the resplendently florid Jack Valenti and the hesitant Katherine Graham, now on her own since her husband had killed himself. Valenti certainly recognized me, though it was clear he could not summon my name immediately. Gardner, socially agile as ever, said, "Winston Bates! It's been months. You must excuse us, Winston and I

---

* Only two senators voted against the resolution, one of whom, Wayne Morse, had received a tip from a Pentagon source that the "attack" on the *Maddox* and the *Turner Joy* was questionable. In 1967 Russell introduced a motion to cancel the Gulf of Tonkin Resolution, but his power had declined by then and the motion was tabled.

have a little business to settle." He took me by the elbow and escorted me out of the ballroom. "You know this house, Winston. Where can we talk?"

It was startling to encounter this decisive, confident Gardner. I led him into the library. Behind a set of sliding doors at one end of the room was a little pocket study with a desk and two uncomfortable horn chairs that Elizabeth's decorator had acquired to signify her love for America.

Gardner jumped right in. "Winston, four months have gone by without any contact. I think you've succeeded in scaring them off. I'm still not sure how you pulled it off, but it looks like I'm free. When you didn't show up at the Corcoran, I was ready to kill either you or myself. But since then, nothing! The Canadians have left me alone."

I was ready for him. "You can drop the Canadian pretense. I want to know one thing. How long have you been working for the Russians?"

He didn't even try to deny it. Instead he made a little performance of applauding me. "So you finally figured it out. Where did I slip up?"

"I realized you weren't being honest with me when you said your contact read sections of your letter to Hiss. How could Canadian intelligence have gotten their hands on the actual letter? Hiss would have given it to the Russians, not Canada. And then I watched your performance in front of the Corcoran from a safe distance."

"Oops!" He grinned winsomely. "At least I can be honest now. You must understand, I was never told who was holding my Alger Hiss past over my head. There was no reason they had to. I always *assumed* it was the Russians because who else would know about it? Over the years, whenever there was another attempt by Hiss to prove his innocence, I would think that I was one of the few people in Washington who knew for sure that Hiss was a Russian spy." He laughed, but I found it difficult to join in.

"Then you told me I was a Canadian spy. A strange idea but when I thought about it I realized you must have told some Canadian back in Paris about my Hiss problem. That idiot McGowan, right? So I believed you at first. And it was *nicer* to think of myself as a Canadian spy. And it was encouraging to think that you were obliged to help me because you entangled me with the Canadians. But when I had a chance to reflect, it just didn't seem to make sense. Canada? Running a spy operation against the U.S.? I couldn't accept it. But now I had to know. I couldn't tell my contact I had confessed to you, so I came up with what I thought was a clever ploy. I told him you had accused me of being a Canadian spy when I asked you about the Seaborn mission."

"Oh no!" What would Russian intelligence make of this?

"He didn't take me seriously. He told me you were playing some deep game, just as they suspected you had before."

"Before when?"

Gardner shook his head slowly, dumbfounded by my inability to put the whole story together. "They were interested in you even before we met again at the Canadian chancery, but they were keeping their distance. I was just a casual and not very useful contact for them until you showed up with your fancy job. I told them that it was *you* who told *me* about the Suez conspiracy of the French, British, and Israelis. That got them very excited. They started to follow you around Washington, probably looking for an opportunity to recruit you. But you began to behave weirdly. They weren't sure whether you had spotted them or what you were up to. At one point, either intentionally or foolishly, they were never sure, you left some top-secret photographs out for them to see. In a hotel room? Do you know what I'm talking about?"

With a sickly shudder, I saw the bed in the Willard Hotel and my box of U-2 photographs of the Sinai.

He looked at me sharply. "What were you thinking?"

I could only shrug helplessly.

"Well never mind," Gardner said. "I'm probably better off not knowing. Whatever those pictures showed, it made them very suspicious. But evidently it was a big help to them in the end."

"What they saw was—"

"Really, you don't have to tell me. I'd rather not know at this point."

What they saw on my bed was the very beginning of the Suez action. Thanks to me, they had the comfort level they needed to send in the tanks in Budapest. They knew they could behave like imperialist thugs in Eastern Europe because the old colonial powers of Europe were doing the same in the Middle East, and the United States was too implicated to seriously oppose the Russians. I recalled that first abortive appearance of my father. He had denied sneaking into my room. That must have been the Russians. Perhaps there was one less thing to not forgive my father for.

"I see you remember. Don't worry—you can trust me. Especially if you don't tell me anything." He laughed theatrically, all too pleased with himself. "After that, my worst fear came true. I was finally of real use to the Russians. My contact was always after me to keep up with you, but because they didn't trust you or understand you, I had to handle you with kid gloves. Believe me, I didn't want to know any of your secrets. I always tried to change the subject any time you came close to saying something that would interest the Russians. I actually felt like a secret patriot! But it wasn't until this Tonkin Gulf thing that it was made explicitly clear to me that I was working for the Russians. But then there were no more friendly meetings with my contact. This new, very tough guy was on my case. As long as you were in the White House, I was to either get Tonkin Gulf information out of you or trap you or both. I had to tell them everything. That day at the Corcoran, I was wearing a microphone. They had cameras. But then you didn't show up. They freaked out and decided you might be thinking of turning me in. As long as you were giving me information innocently, I was of use to them. Now I'm not. Your turn, sport."

Four months with no contact and he was acting as if he had been released. I knew better. Sooner or later the Russians would be back on his case. "I can't believe you tried to trap me."

"I'm sorry, Winston. Don't you see? I really had no choice." Remorse was not his strong suit.

"Have you thought about what *you* did?" I charged. "The North Vietnamese already knew there was no second round of attacks in the Tonkin Gulf. Now, thanks to the two of us, the Russians have surely told them the U.S. knew it too, went ahead and bombed them anyway, and then adopted a war resolution that had been drafted months in advance. Why should they ever trust us again? They'll never negotiate with us in good faith."

"Winston, it was all you," he said with exasperated resignation. "You did it. You have to live with it. I don't. I'll give you credit for this—you blundered your way into scaring them off me. If the Russians weren't so afraid of you for turning one of their agents years ago, it would have been a lot worse for us."

Finally I knew why I appeared dangerous to them, why I was treated with kid gloves. It was the KGB "writer" I found at the Russian embassy party who became a Moscow source for the CIA. Once the poor man was captured, a good intelligence officer like Striganov would have put a microscope to the agent's movements in the United States. When he checked out the party's guest list, he would have discovered I had hidden my real job with Armed Services. That, plus my bragging to Gardner about my contacts with Helms, Bissell, and Dulles, made me a CIA operative in their eyes. And if I had accepted Bissell and Dulles's overture so many years ago, that's what I would have become. My bizarre behavior was only further evidence to the Russians. Of course, none of this explained why the Canadians had never contacted me.

Gardner stood up. "Good-bye Winston. Have a nice life."

I didn't understand why he was so sanguine about his prospects until a month later, when I received a note from him. Françoise's parents were now both deceased; he was resigning from the State Department and moving to France where a large inheritance awaited. I never saw Gardner again.

A year later Helms called me. Johnson had just appointed him to be director of the CIA. In the course of their interview the president mentioned how highly Richard Russell thought of him and how much that counted with Johnson. Helms decided I was the one who had supported him with Russell. "I'm deeply appreciative, Winston. You're one of those people who make things happen behind the scenes. Do not hesitate to call on me."

PART FOUR

THE HERO

24

The first thing I saw when I awoke on June 16, 1972, was the red ceramic, pseudo-Mayan deity on Deborah Boyer's coffee table, its upraised arm poised to thrust a spear at me. It was 5:30 A.M., and I had a crick in my neck because I had slept with my head propped up against the armrest of Deborah's couch. She had called yesterday afternoon to ask me to drop by after work, but Elizabeth Boudreau and I were attending the Opera Ball that evening at L'Enfant Plaza. Insisting she had to see me, Deborah persuaded me to come by after the ball. She was not home when I arrived at eleven and I fell asleep on her couch, as I had so many times in the past.

I heard a distant strain, more a faint emanation than music. It was unlikely to be from Mark's room—Deborah had said he was sleeping at a friend's house—so I padded up the stairs in my socks, the tails of my wrinkled formal shirt hanging over my droopy tuxedo pants. I pursued the delicate sound past the family room where Mark's dusty drum set resided, up past Mark's bedroom to Deborah's bedroom on the top floor.

She wore a flowery silk robe as she knelt on her bed and brushed out her damp blond hair. The bed was a great raft of a mattress floating in the center of the richly patterned oriental rug that I had given to her in 1969. Arrayed around the mattress were several neat stacks of books, a spindly avocado plant, a collection of lacquered boxes and trays, and a tape player from which emerged a soothing quasi-musical hum.

"Winston!" she said, smiling with such radiant pleasure that I nearly whimpered. "You look like a decadent aristocrat stumbling home after a depraved evening on the town. I came home later than I expected— only a couple of hours ago—and there you were, just the way it used to be when you baby-sat. You looked so comfortable I didn't have the heart to wake you. But I wanted to stay up for you so I took a shower to revive myself. Would you like to revive yourself too?" Her languid stream of observations, which flowed with a serene sense of pleasure in her own performance, beguiled me as it always did when I hadn't seen her recently.

In the bathroom, still humid from her shower, a familiar fragrance of scented soap and shampoo hung thickly. As the water coursed over my slightly rounded torso, my wiry skein of body hair writhed and twisted. The purple soap had a verdant bouquet, and I emerged feeling like a moist perfumed pear. I returned to the bedroom wrapped in the voluminous pale green bathrobe with ruffled collar that I had given to Deborah in 1967. Sitting back on her heels, she reached out to me, inviting me aboard the mattress. I gathered the robe up around my thighs and stumped toward her on my knees. When I was facing her she said: "You *do* remember, don't you? You *do* remember." As I nodded, she pushed me lightly on the shoulders and I fell backward. With calm deliberation she unknotted the belt, unfurled the robe, and ran her hands over my fuzzy body, periodically fondling my penis and scrotum as she regarded me with affectionate amusement. Soon she shrugged off her robe and collapsed in slow motion next to me. Then I was on her, crouching crablike above her, my body stroking hers like a soft brush. She moved beneath me fluidly, her head tilted back and her eyes scrunched shut as though in search of an elusive thought. She came the way she spoke, in a flutelike succession of little cries. "Your turn," she said apologetically. "I don't think I can stay awake much longer."

She fell asleep curled away from me, a drool of semen drying on the back of her thigh. We hadn't made love in nearly two years but of course I remembered. Our lovemaking this morning was a close replication of the first time we made love in 1966. There were differences: I had been baby-sitting for Mark. Instead of waiting for me to awaken, she shook me at three thirty in the morning and led me upstairs. Half an hour later she told me she had smoked marijuana just before coming home or she never would have had the inspiration to seduce me. That was how it began and it set a pattern. I don't mean we repeated the same steps each time we made love, but with my encouragement she frequently smoked marijuana before we had sex. I almost never used marijuana, but when Deborah was stoned, her slack accessibility allowed me to abandon myself.

But the memory of sleeping with Deborah that first time would be forever linked in my mind to another event that occurred almost simultaneously: once, and only once, the monthly stipend from Canada did not get posted to my account. In the aftermath of the mess with Gardner and the Russians, I had given up, telling myself if I lived hopelessly, without expectation, I would never again create havoc. But still, when the money didn't appear I wondered if a door had opened. Though the money impassively resumed the next month, by then I had slept with Deborah several times. I *had* stepped through a door and I knew exactly what to do—something I could have done, should have done, years before. I went to the bank, withdrew all the money, and closed the account. Why had I never thought of this before? I suppose because ever since enlisting with McGowan, my life had been arrested by a sense of diminished possibility. Now, with Deborah imaginably in my life, my sense of possibility had been enlarged. I didn't expect my gesture to be acknowledged by Canada, nor did I expect to feel I had forever discarded my sense of myself as a spy. It wasn't and I hadn't, but for the time being I had closed the door behind me.

We became a couple. Deborah had made new friends while finishing her degree at George Washington University and I joined her in a social circle of consultants, academics, arts and foundation administrators, and obscure but brilliant government bureaucrats. A number of them had arrived in Washington during the Kennedy-Johnson years and had hung on with Nixon's accession. Others brought specialized talents to the Bureau of Standards or the World Bank. Most were married, a few had small children, and they all liked to have a good time at the parties they held in their rambling homes in offbeat neighborhoods. At their parties they smoked marijuana, played rock and roll, and danced with giddy self-consciousness. Though I couldn't exactly *throw* myself into dancing, Deborah was satisfied to sweep and swirl around me as I marched rigidly in place, my clenched fists pumping like pistons. I was almost the oldest person in this circle but I tried hard to keep up by affecting a new look—fat, floral neckties, exuberantly striped shirts, and longish sideburns extending down from my flourishing frisée of graying hair. I felt I was appositely poised at the side of the youngest person in this circle, the blond, long-limbed young woman who, a hint of maturity refining the bland evenness of her features, had become so striking.

I expected antagonism from this crowd—they were all quite antiwar and I was still working with Armed Services—but it never came up. Many of them felt demoralized by their own employment. There was an NSA analyst—a skittish cryptographer and failed poet with a memory as good as mine—who always greeted me with a look of anguished empathy, as if we shared some awful secret. I often kidded around with a fat and funny mathematician who had been hired by the judiciary department in the Kennedy era to make economic models for predicting social unrest. He was surprised to be kept on in the Nixon era until he realized his models were as useful for repression as for amelioration. As for the couple Deborah and I were friendliest with, the Schifts, Roger was a State Department specialist in Latin America whose wife, Sheila, a lobbyist for the Environmental Defense Fund, liked to tax him with her moral purity. Even those with the most tenuous of ties to government—a curator at the National Gallery, an anthropologist at the Smithsonian—expressed their sentiments about the war with a kind of compromised irony. And there was Alvin Meers, the epicene professor of diplomatic history at George Washington, whose twee tea and sherry seminars at the State Department had begun to focus exclusively on diplomatic failure. His brief affair with Deborah, then his student, had introduced her to this set.

My private pursuits that I had cultivated all these years—the museums, the chamber music, the opera—stood me in good stead with this crowd. And once my new friends realized that I had a wide range of social contacts at the top of the Washington food chain, they greeted me with eager delight. They were as hungry for gossip as anyone in Washington, though they regarded the peccadilloes of the elect and the appointed with amused exasperation.

My new affect aroused some suspicion at Russell's office, but I ignored the chiding comments about my clothes and the length of my hair. Russell himself was oblivious, too intent on husbanding his waning strength and power to give much personal attention to the office. My own position was threatened in 1969 when Russell, looking for a less demanding schedule, resigned his chairmanship of Armed Services and became head of Appropriations. But he stayed on the committee, and Senator John Stennis, his successor, deferred to Russell on most important questions, including keeping my assignment on the CIA subcommittee. The members of the CIA subcommittee remained grateful to me for my stewardship.

I continued to move about Washington at Elizabeth Boudreau's side. It wasn't unusual for me to go to a sedate dinner in Foggy Bottom with Elizabeth and then meet Deborah later at a raucous bash in Adams Morgan. Elizabeth took a twisted satisfaction in the fact that I was seeing a younger woman: It made her feel younger too. "Have your fun with her," she told me, "but don't you embarrass me," which meant I shouldn't bring Deborah anywhere I might encounter Elizabeth. By the late 1960s Elizabeth had become an institution, outlasting many of the social warhorses of the forties and fifties, while the crowd that rolled in on the Kennedy tide rolled out again. Her access to the southern bloc, which was increasingly looking like a Republican bloc, kept her at the top of her game in the Nixon era.

I began to bring Deborah to New York with me. Alice was delighted to see me in a relationship. At Alice's request, and to demonstrate to myself that I had at last joined the human race, I went to see my dying father in 1967. He recognized me but appeared to have forgotten our encounter in the Jefferson Hotel. In 1966 Alice had married Stanley Wright, who was becoming a very successful record producer, and they resided in a state of haute bohemian bliss with their two striking children. With the fervor of a religious convert, Alice wished for nothing less than the same for me. Mark adored Alice's children, and Deborah and I would leave him with Alice and Stanley while we wallowed in the slutty poshness of fancy hotels and attended the opera, concerts, and museums.

For four years Deborah played an eager Galatea to my indulgent Pygmalion. She could sit attentively for two hours of the Budapest String Quartet and then expect a discourse on Beethoven's late quartets. As we explored Renaissance frescos, or attended Marilyn Horne's debut in Norma, I unpacked my years of solitary pursuits for her benefit. I had the contents of innumerable programs and museum catalogs stashed away in my mind, and I gave Deborah a talking points survey of Western artistic culture. I didn't have anything original to teach her because the pleasure I took in art and music was all sensation and distraction. It was my goal to be overwhelmed by a work's power and beauty, or else possessed by its exquisite logic.

My relationship with Mark became one of unspoken but mutual satisfaction. He grew up as a slight, serious child who worked hard at being a kid. He was as unathletic as I, so together we became fans. Almost every morning I would come over from next door to have breakfast and pore over the sports pages with him. If I had slept with Deborah, I had to stumble back to my place at five in the morning before returning to have breakfast with Mark, a convention I am sure he saw through, though he never alluded to it. Real sports fans—such as the good old boys who worked for various southern senators—would have mocked the innocent delight Mark and I took in ephemera, the nicknames and anecdotal humor of sports. We always referred with mock solemnity to Earl Weaver as the "Earl of Baltimore" and we treasured the rumors of Sonny Jurgensen's carousing in the watering holes of Washington. My major sports coup, as far as Mark was concerned, was to prevail on Richard Helms, who often attended Washington Redskins games with the team owner, to twice get us into the owner's box when Edward Bennett Williams was out of town.

Though I felt Mark and I were close, it was nothing like his powerful attachment to Deborah, which was a survivor's bond. It had been a struggle for the two of them during the first years after Larry left. Deborah was determined to finish her undergraduate degree but the job her father gave Larry in California didn't pay very well and her father refused to help her directly because he blamed her for the separation. Deborah dropped out of school for a while to work full-time at Ashford Abelow but she was miserable and Mark began to have problems in school. Just about the time Deborah and I started to see each other, Deborah's father unexpectedly relented and became quite generous with her. Mark was moved to an expensive, nurturing school where his difficulties eased. Meanwhile, the new flow of money allowed Deborah to resume working part-time at Ashford Abelow while keeping two baby-sitters on almost permanent standby, which made our free-wheeling social life possible.

Deborah was not faithful to me, though "faithfulness" was not a very functional term in those days. The prescriptive leniency of the counterculture had infected sympathetic members of older generations. I was even unfaithful a few times myself, though my encounters felt more like dutiful attempts to relieve Deborah of any guilt for her own indiscretions. The most pleasure I got out of the new sexual freedom was on our occasional weekends with the Schifts at their Chesapeake Bay farmhouse. It was all a bit overdetermined. Late Saturday morning, while Deborah and Roger were fucking each other in Roger's office in the barn, I would couple docilely with tiny Sheila Schift back at the house. After the four of us enjoyed a leisurely lunch, order would be restored. I would slip back into bed and Deborah would come to me, rosy and languorous.

I was finally in the messy midst of life. Like me, Deborah had evolved her affect, and I was in thrall to the amused enthusiasm with which she now regarded the world and all the things in it. Our trips to New York, the concerts and clubs, the free-floating sex, were pleasures I laid before her to entice her to expend her charm on me. I suppose I was in love with her. I say "I suppose"—that weasel term of detached acknowledgment—because I think of our relationship as the most perfect period of sensation and distraction in my life. But isn't that enough? Perhaps that's *it*.

During those years I barely gave a thought to the implications of the five hundred dollars I had received each month for almost eighteen years. If anything, I felt a sense of entitlement. The money, its interest compounding steadily, had imprisoned me all those years. It seemed a form of revenge to lavish my little hoard on Deborah. Though the war in Vietnam was a constant drumbeat—sometimes distant, sometimes pounding— I hardly gave a serious thought to the fact of my unfortunate role. Vietnam seemed to me like a huge, rudderless ship of history; I might have given it a slight push or tug, but I couldn't have changed its direction very much. The healing detachment of time, along with cutting my tie to Canada, helped me to come to terms with the consequences of my other unfortunate actions. I had always believed, expediently, that as a hostage I was imprisoned in a moral vacuum. It was only incidentally my fault that I happened to be the wrong person in the wrong place at the wrong time, several times. But now my actions had dissolved into history. My regrettable attempts to assert, protect, or extricate myself were part of the whole fractal chronicle, indistinguishable from the decisions and indecisions of generals, the judgments and misjudgments of statesmen. It was all history now, an ocean of infinite consequence.

Deborah began to express frustration with my ambiguous attitude toward the war, not to mention my participation in the war effort via the Armed Services Committee. We continued our cultural excursions, but Deborah was growing bored with my complacent cultural pleasures. The bouncy rock and roll of our dancing days was becoming rock music, with its exhortatory attitude and accusatorily whining guitars. When Deborah charged me with moral dereliction, I could barely restrain myself from charging her in turn. The air war in Vietnam had developed a ravenous hunger for her father's guidance systems for bombs and rockets. Autonomic Devices, Inc., the family firm, prospered as never before. I often saw ADI mentioned in military procurement bills. On an impulse, I once called the Pentagon to question whether similar guidance systems couldn't be sourced from another supplier. The answer was swift and definitive: Deborah's father had become a power in California Republican circles, a member of the inner circle of businessmen who had financed Richard Nixon's journey back from political oblivion. ADI had a lock on the business.

In 1967, Deborah's father gave Larry a new assignment, Governmental Relations director of ADI, to help him keep in contact with Mark and Deborah. He came to Washington every other month to consult with the company's lobbyists. Larry seemed oblivious to my relationship with Deborah, but out of a residual sense of guilt, I set up Larry and Douglas Longsdon, head of Procurement at the Pentagon, with a meeting with Senator Russell. Russell almost never did anything like this and Longsdon was very impressed with Larry's extraordinary influence. When I would lunch with Larry every so often, he would gleefully tell me tales of the obeisance paid to him by the Defense Department procurement officers. His idea of keeping in contact with his family was to plead with Deborah to take him back and then get sulky with Mark after she refused. About a year after I started sleeping with Deborah, he informed me I was responsible for getting Deborah's father to loosen the purse strings with her. "I told him that you were a good friend and neighbor of ours as well as Russell's number-one guy on the military budget. I said you were really unhappy at watching her struggle and that he could help me to score points with you and Russell by making things easier for Deborah."

Larry could not conceive of Deborah sleeping with me, but what would happen to the points if he found out? In 1969, one of the ADI lobbyists told me that Larry was no longer working for ADI. Larry's new job, we soon discovered, was working for the California Republican Party, placed there by his soon to be ex-father-in-law. To my relief, he stopped coming to Washington so frequently.

Deborah moved from antiwar indignation to activity by volunteering to man the phones for the New Mobilization Committee, organizers of the 1967 march on Washington. When Deborah first spoke of "the Mobe," I imagined a cohort of grungy student radicals, but the Washington chapter seemed to consist mainly of aging lefties whose politics had survived the 1950s. When the Mobe got wind of Deborah's nice house, they persuaded her to throw a party on the eve of the march for our local friends who would be solicited to step forward bravely during the demonstrations and denounce their government's behavior.

"I hope you didn't tell them about my job," I said when she invited me.

"I wouldn't do that to you. You might not get out of the party alive. Just joking, Winston. I'm more worried about what they'd think of me for consorting with a war criminal like you, much less the fact that my father runs ADI." She glanced at me with amusement. "Come anonymously. No one has to know what you do. I doubt if anyone we know will be persuaded to step forward publicly. But they might march. *You* might march. No one would recognize you."

I shook my head. "Not a chance."

Several of my colleagues had already speculated about the possibility of my protesting the war. Phillip Gibbs, Senator Jackson's aide, went so far as to tease me in the presence of Russell: "Marching this weekend, Bates?" It seemed to me a snide comment on my appearance rather than any serious belief that I might march. Nevertheless, I found excuses to contact Russell three times on the day of the march so he would know I was sitting it out.

Deborah and I tried to handle our Vietnam problem tactfully. I let her assume I was against the war, which wasn't difficult since I wasn't for it either, and Deborah tried not to hector me. But as her convictions about the war became more powerful, she began to spend more time at the New Mobilization offices, which were located in a semi-decrepit office building on Thomas Circle. I tried to feign interest in the Mobe's complex internecine disputes, which Deborah described with an acolyte's enthusiasm for inside gossip. A number of left-wing and countercultural groups maintained offices in the Thomas Circle building, and the place seemed to be in constant ferment. Convinced that the FBI had it under permanent surveillance, I refused to go near it. Of course, any enterprising agent who investigated Deborah would have discovered my presence in her life, but I didn't think I had much to worry about. I had cut my connection to Canada; as for my Armed Services job, I expected Russell would protect me if I got into trouble.

By the time of the big March Against Death demonstration in November 1969, Deborah had advanced to organizing bus transportation to Washington and sleeping accommodations for 250,000 marchers.

The night before the march, a group of twenty students from Chicago slept on her floors while Mark stayed with me next door.

As Deborah grew more consumed by the war, her tolerance for me and my ways declined, as did her charm, which was replaced by a brusque impatience. If I referred archly to "the Mobe cohort," she flashed an annoyed frown. Our relationship became especially strained during the run-up to the huge moratorium and mobilization in the spring of 1970. The Washington Mobilization office had evolved into the national headquarters and Deborah exuded the heady sense of being right in the thick of things. She spoke with knowing contempt of other antiwar groups whose politics were hopeless. She was at Thomas Circle much of the day and late into the evening. We stopped making plans together. She was civil enough to me in the mornings when Mark and I chewed over the sports pages, but I began to wonder if she was only going through the motions to preserve my relationship with Mark. I was often the one who packed Mark's lunch and got him off to school while she went back to bed. If we had sex, it was because she asked me over occasionally when she came home too wound up to sleep. Other times, she brought men home with her. I would hear their voices through the wall, then the wail of guitars. If I glanced out the front window at 3:00 A.M., I might see her evening's companion shamble off.

One morning, just after the invasion of eastern Cambodia, Deborah hung around in the kitchen until Mark left for school. She stirred her coffee studiously and then sighed dramatically. "I've wanted to talk to you for some time, Winston. I'm sorry there hasn't been more time for us."

At last we were going to have it out. I was almost relieved. Each of us waited for the other to take the next step. Finally Deborah spoke. "Some of the people I work with are aware of your presence in my life. They'd like to talk to you."

It took a few moments for me to realize what was happening. "They know my name? Don't you realize half of your Mobe friends are probably FBI informers?"

"I swear I haven't told them anything about you. I've just said I happen to know someone, someone with Defense Department connections who—"

"Who what? Who can tell them enough to get himself arrested? Or maybe you want me to flame out in some spectacular manner? How about if I denounce the war machine on the steps of the Pentagon?"

"You don't have to shriek," she muttered sullenly. "It was too much to expect. I knew you'd never help me. For all your antiwar talk, that's what it is, just talk."

Her sense of reality had become warped. There had been no serious antiwar talk from me, just the usual dismissive indifference with which I described my job. I had never corrected her fantasy of me as a closeted antiwar protestor, but it should have been inconceivable to her that I could openly aid the Mobilization.

She wouldn't give up. "Just come with me, please. Just to talk. Give us some idea where this horrible war is heading."

For the next several days she harangued me but I wouldn't be moved. I told her there was sure to be someone in her organization who would betray me to the FBI. She even offered to set me up with a one-on-one conversation with Dave Dellinger, one of the Mobilization's leaders. I couldn't think of someone more likely to be under surveillance since he had just been acquitted in the Chicago Seven trial.

I had often derided Deborah's paranoia about the FBI and other shadowy agencies as romantic self-importance. Yet I assumed many of her colleagues were under some sort of observation. I avoided Deborah for several days until she finally called me at the office. "I want to see you tonight. We have to talk." I prepared again to put an end to what was left of our relationship.

They were waiting for me when I entered Deborah's home, two men and a woman from the New Mobe. Deborah looked at me and shrugged. "I told them they wouldn't get anywhere with you, but they wanted to try anyway." They were in their mid- to late thirties and had a kind of stunned exhaustion about them. It was a few days before the post–Kent State demonstration and they must have been working nonstop. As soon as we sized each other up we knew our dialogue would go nowhere. They went after me doggedly nonetheless, using me as a punching bag, a feeble stand-in for the elusive "Establishment." In a pathetic attempt to please Deborah and deflect their criticism, I tried to tell them

I was "sympathetic," even anguished by my role. I suggested I could do more to mitigate things by working on the inside. When they asked for examples of what I had done on the inside, I refused to provide any details, saying it was all classified.

One of the men scolded me: "Making things better by working on the inside, that's just your way of justifying the contradictions to yourself."

In a final attempt to assuage my fears, they told me I was not alone; a number of "high-level" government workers had agreed to sign a special petition. Those who were willing would be made available to the mainstream press for interviews to appear during or immediately after the demonstration. When I asked to see their names they refused— in order to protect them they claimed.

"And what happens to me after that?" I said. "As an ex-government worker that is? Which is surely what I'll be. The only thing I'm trained to do is work for a Defense contractor or the CIA."

I could see Deborah clenching her teeth and glaring at me. My self-ish concern for earning a living was an embarrassment to her.

The woman shrugged. "You could teach. Write. It's a big world out there."

"I told you he was hopeless," Deborah snapped.

My temper got the best of me. "Deborah, why don't *you* make yourself available to the press? That would make a great story: 'Heir to the ADI Fortune Denounces Family as Agents of Death.'"

The three Mobes slowly turned to stare at Deborah, whose mouth had dropped open in shock.

Later that evening, she stormed into my apartment and castigated me with a fury I had never seen in her. Our relationship was over.

Deborah did not speak to me for a year, except for a few terse conversations when I called to arrange for outings with Mark, who now felt like a doubly divorced child. During that year I moved, after more than twenty years in Georgetown, to a new apartment house in Foggy Bottom on Virginia Avenue. I moved because Deborah asked me to; because I knew there was no chance of resurrecting my relationship with her; because being next door made it impossible to ignore her life; but mainly because I was afraid of my proximity to her. I had been reckless.

An FBI agent could have followed Deborah's little committee of Mobilization people to her house and lingered long enough to observe me approaching from next door. If Hoover found out that a security-cleared member of Richard Russell's staff had consorted with a bunch of radicals on the eve of the demonstration, I'd have been devoured. I was a hostage to fortune all over again.

I was now forty-eight years old and my lifeline had been severed. I had stepped through a door with Deborah and now I would step back and close the door behind me. The mystery of my conception as a spy no longer mattered to me. All I wanted was to cling to my job like a barnacle and let the rest of my depleted life wash over me without incident. Perhaps I still nursed some hope for a miracle in my life—it's only human—but I kept the feeling deeply suppressed.

I surprised myself by my easy accommodation to life on the margins. I had a sense of relief, as if I were giving up a burden. I didn't even decorate when I first moved to Columbia Plaza, defaulting instead to the stark white walls of my new cell. From my windows I gazed down on the traffic streaming on Virginia Avenue toward a Howard Johnson's Motor Lodge. My work on Armed Services and my social life with Elizabeth Boudreau rolled on with rotelike momentum. I stopped traveling to New York because Alice made me feel like a failure for allowing Deborah to slip through my fingers. The circle of friends Deborah and I had shared was unwinding: the Schifts were divorcing; Alvin Meers was dying of emphysema; those who could were going to ground in academia. I continued to see Mark regularly, but where I once thought my relationship with him proved my essential connection to the hub of humanity, now it seemed, in its singularity, to imply the frailty of that connection.

No neighborhood could have been less like Georgetown than the area around the Columbia Plaza Apartments. Not even a neighborhood, it featured a ponderous collection of oversized buildings—huge new hotels, offices, and apartment buildings—whose ungainly sites had been determined by the tangle of highways, overpasses, access ramps, and underpasses that converged in the area. The newest edifice, the Kennedy Center, was due to open in a few months and there was an expectation, fruitless as it turned out, that it would inspire a cultural renaissance in the neighborhood.

There was a quality of transient anonymity about Columbia Plaza, like an airline terminal. Though expensive, it wasn't hard to get an apartment, and a number of the residents seemed to have temporary or unexpected reasons for living in Washington—foreign businessmen looking for contacts; journalists on special assignments; diplomatic families awaiting more permanent housing; and probably the occasional spy. I didn't mind the scarce opportunities for social contact. A nod on the elevator, a remark about the weather—that was the satisfying limit.

It did not take long for me to notice the group of call girls operating out of Columbia Plaza since they were in my elevator line, two floors above me. I soon identified one tall, attractive woman, whose name was Cathy, as the central figure and the only one who seemed to be in residence. Cathy was often accompanied by other women, some of whom seemed to be experienced party girls from the hospitality suite circuit while other women impressed me as semiprofessionals—college students, secretaries, waitresses—who were picking up part-time income. Cathy, who had a diva's narcissism, enjoyed playing the queen bee with her worker bees clustered about her. There was also a young man, brash, sleek, and slightly seedy, whom I occasionally saw with Cathy; he seemed to be both her boyfriend and business partner.

Occasionally I saw Cathy's women arriving with clients or stepping out with them. If I shared the elevator with an unaccompanied man, it became a private game for me to guess whether he was one of Cathy's clients. One afternoon, as I was returning from work, I encountered a man whom I had seen that same morning in Russell's office, Floyd Parker, a Savannah banker who had great influence with Georgia's peanut farmers. He followed me into the elevator and consulted a piece of paper with a letterhead from the Democratic National Committee. He pressed the button for Cathy's floor. Two days later I was finally alone with Cathy in the elevator. Our relationship had evolved from the nodding stage to the nod-plus-pleasant-smile stage. I had once even ventured a compliment about Cathy's rather musky perfume.

"I was glad to see that Floyd Parker was well attended to the other day," I said.

She looked puzzled; then, as she made the connection, her eyes narrowed sharply.

"No problem," I said quickly. "I meant that sincerely. I work in Senator Russell's office. We're always glad when our constituents enjoy themselves in Washington."

She hesitated. I smiled broadly and she relaxed. "That DNC is our bread and butter," she said. "Between them up the street and the Saudis down the street, there's always somebody in the neighborhood who wants company."

"Now I understand why you're located here. I couldn't imagine it was the Kennedy Center." We grinned at each other as if partners in crime. I continued to walk along with her as we exited the elevator. "You know, there's a possibility we might need your services sometimes."

"There's a good neighbor!" She fumbled in her purse and handed me a card. "We'll take extra good care of any client you send our way."

This was an opportunity I could not pass up: "What I really meant was me personally. *I* could use your services."

If my existence from now on was going to happen at a subsistence level, I wanted some anonymous sex to go along with eating and sleeping. Cathy couldn't have been more helpful. I was hesitant in describing my requirements, but she kept assuring me that I had the right to get what I was paying for. I did not want a practiced professional. I had in mind a slightly artless semiprofessional, someone who would be grateful to have a steady assignment every other Saturday afternoon for a couple of hours. I didn't need her to pretend to be captivated or sexually overwhelmed by me: I just wanted some real enthusiasm for the job of gratifying me. Finally, I wanted someone at least five inches shorter than me.

"If I can't come up with the right person, my boyfriend Phil has an amazing collection of part-timers," Cathy assured me. After two auditions we found just the right person. Erin, a recent graduate of Catholic University, was stuck in a dreary job with the Social Security Administration but hoped to put some money away in order to live in Europe and study fashion design. She was short, with an agreeable, dumplinglike figure, and my business enabled her to turn down the DNC's small-town politicians when they called for her. According to Erin there was someone at the DNC who kept a book filled with photos and descriptions of Cathy's crew. The DNC client could browse for someone in a secure environment, and Cathy's women didn't have to hang out at bars.

My afternoons with Erin were not inexpensive, especially because Cathy had to receive her substantial cut as well. I took stock of my finances: I had used up much of my Canadian cache during the years with Deborah; my salary was quite modest; and the Columbia Plaza apartment was twice as expensive as my Georgetown studio. After four Saturday afternoons, I offered to put Erin on a retainer that would save me some money but Cathy refused to reduce her cut. Erin was reluctant to defy Cathy; she was a little afraid of Cathy as well as a little in awe of her. "There weren't any strong women in my life until Cathy," Erin said. "Besides, she's friendly with some mob guy. I have to be careful."

"Phil's a mobster?" I said, affecting some intimacy with Cathy's operation.

"Not Phil. He's a lawyer. He's got funky stuff going on all over town but he's not a mobster. He's just a guy who helps people to party. But Cathy did say she'd take my picture out of the DNC book if you continue to see me at least twice a month."

Cathy knew she had me hooked. If Erin was my only indulgence, I calculated I could manage two hours every other Saturday with her for thirty-six more months if my income stayed the same. So I lived, as the outcast of the universe, for almost a year.

In February 1972, Deborah called me in a rage. "He's back! Larry's back in Washington. He's going to live here again. Why didn't you tell me?" After I convinced her that I was surprised as well, we had our first real conversation in almost a year. As we talked I found it impossible not to try to charm Deborah and it seemed to me she was a little taken with me again. I felt bold enough to inquire how things were going with the Mobilization. "The Mobe and I have gone our separate ways, Winston. After you revealed my family secret, they put pressure on me to do just what you suggested—denounce my dad. When I wouldn't, it got unpleasant. They were vicious to me, really vicious. What did they think?

That I was supporting myself and Mark by working part-time at Ashford while volunteering full-time for them? I *need* my father's help. It wasn't enough for them that half the money he gave me went to the Mobe. After that, I could tell they didn't trust me anymore and I was fed up with them. Winston, I so wanted to murder you last year, but now I feel it was all for the best. I'm much more comfortable with myself."

A few days later she invited me over for dinner and I saw her new level of comfort. She was dressed stylishly, with well-cut hair and makeup. An attractive, grown-up woman had emerged. The house had been painted, refurnished, and tastefully decorated; fifteen years of dust, stains, and Mark's childhood detritus had been exorcised. She had evolved herself again, or perhaps it was just a reversion. "I owe you a lot, Winston. Things have opened up for me at Ashford. I've been able to advise several of our clients how to demonstrate their good intentions by supporting the arts. It's not like I'm some expert, but it's the country of the blind at the office. The partners are so impressed to have someone on the staff who can mention she was at Marilyn Horne's debut or discuss the Brandenburg Concertos, someone who can meet with the Kennedy Center people without sounding like a philistine. So I'm the culture contact now. But all I know is what I learned from you. Can I call you sometime for advice? Is it too much to hope that we could be friends again?"

We became friends again, but only friends. Besides the arts and Mark, we had the new incarnation of Larry in common. Larry's good work for the California Republican Party had earned him a promotion to work for the Committee to Reelect the President (CREEP). He was living near Dupont Circle and was insufferably pleased to have access to people like John Mitchell, who had left his post as attorney general to be the chairman of CREEP. Larry had actually shaken hands with Nixon once or twice. Though divorced from Deborah for two years, he had no compunction about calling her up to brag about his irresistible ascension at CREEP. In his short time at the committee, he had moved from the finance chairman's assistant to his deputy. He began to call me occasionally for lunch, taking me to crowded restaurants where the frenzied social scene resembled a commodities exchange. I would come away hoarse from making myself heard.

Larry's small-featured face still looked youthful, but he had developed a paunch that stuck out like a basketball from his lanky frame. He liked to sit in a sprawling, big-guy manner and pat his little belly affectionately. When he discovered I wasn't well acquainted with the Nixon crew, he became condescending, dropping names and flaunting his access as if I were a tourist. I knew the secretary of defense pretty well, the marginalized Melvin Laird, whose oleaginous sincerity I didn't mind, but I had avoided most of the other Nixonians, especially the man who marginalized Laird, Henry Kissinger. Early in the Nixon term, Kissinger sought me out at a reception. We had been introduced several times over the years without my making an impression on him. But Helms and Walter Lippmann had both told him I was someone he should get to know. He took me in—my frizzy hair, my insincere smile— with doubtful interest. "Convince me you're worth my while," his manner implied. I did my best to disappoint him.

In late May, Larry called me for a lunch date. "Only if we have it at a quieter place," I demanded.

"Got something interesting to tell me?" he asked slyly.

"No. I just can't stand the noise. And I don't want to be introduced to every third-rate lobbyist who wanders in."

"Okay, but some of them are very impressed to see me eating with you. It helps me. Your boss is head of Appropriations. Everybody knows you, even if no one knows what you do. Those Defense contractors think you're a genius and they have lots of money to give to the campaign."

We met at a dark, semi-deserted Chinese restaurant near Dupont Circle where the loudest sound was the gurgling fish tank. I asked Larry what he was working on.

"It's kind of a secret, Winston." He was begging me to pry it out of him.

"You don't *have* to tell me. But you know I'm apolitical. You can tell me anything because I don't care."

"I'm moving into security and intelligence for the campaign," he said proudly.

"Intelligence? That sounds a little dark."

"It's politics, Winston. They do it to us, we do it to them. Short of murder, all's fair." He leaned forward conspiratorially. "The Democrats have this intelligence outfit called Intertel. We have to compete."

"What does Intertel do?"

"I don't know exactly, but Larry O'Brien runs it and Howard Hughes is a client." Larry sounded as if he was repeating something he had overheard. "There's all kinds of stuff we could do at the Democratic convention in Miami. Tap their phones, screw up the air-conditioning. Maybe set up a houseboat filled with hookers near the site of the convention, a houseboat with eavesdropping equipment. We've brought in some real pros to run things for us—ex-FBI and -CIA guys."

"And you're in charge of this?"

"Not exactly. Magruder keeps things pretty close to his vest.* But he's beginning to trust me. I got Deb's dad to get five of his friends together and they pledged like fifty thousand each to the campaign. We're calling them the California Leadership Circle. When you bring in that kind of money, people are a lot more willing to listen to your ideas."

"Such as . . . ?"

He looked pained. "Most of what I suggest, Jeb just shoots down. I had this idea about a mass food poisoning at Miami that I wanted to develop."

"Remember what you said Larry—'*short* of murder'? Don't you think that's risky? Someone could die from food poisoning."

"That's what Jeb said. He said I should leave this stuff to the pros and stick to fund-raising."

"Smart idea. How is Magruder going to follow through on those other ideas?"

He looked at me suspiciously. "You're not going to let on to anyone are you?"

"You know I'm not connected to the political part of the business."

"I told you there's this bunch of CIA operatives working with us . . ."

"What! Now you've got my attention."

"Slow down. They are all *ex*-CIA and -FBI. And only a couple of them were ever *in* the CIA from what I hear. The others are contract

---

* Jeb Magruder was deputy director of CREEP.

guys. Cuban types from Miami. But you said you didn't care. I don't want you running to Helms."

"I won't. I promise. Don't mention any names to me if it makes you feel any better. And here's a piece of advice—stay away from these guys. Stick to fund-raising and keep your head down."

He sighed. "I guess you're right. I know I'm not cut out to be one of them. But if I don't seem like I'm part of the action, I won't get Magruder's attention. And the guy he's always talking to—John Dean.* If they like me, I could get a job in the White House after the election. But they spend most of their time coming up with their own schemes and my ideas always sound so stupid."

"I gave you my advice."

"I know. But you have the kind of contacts that could help me. For instance, Stans told me that Nixon's obsessed by the CIA. He thinks they're hiding some dark secret about the Bay of Pigs. But Helms wouldn't tell him. Now he's sure they're out to get him."

"That's impossible for me to address," I said sharply.

Larry was crestfallen. "You helped me once before."

"And a lot of good it did you."

"It wasn't your fault. You told me not to retract my U-2 estimates."

"All right, here's an idea for you. There's a ring of call girls who operate out of Columbia Plaza. And you know who they specialize in? Out-of-town fat cats and politicians sent over from the DNC office down the street."

He looked at me in amazement. "You know so much evil stuff, Winston. Do you think we should get the police to raid the operation and cause a big scandal? No? Why are you shaking your head? Oh I get it. Why wait until Miami? We could bug the place now."

After Larry departed I wondered if he would have been better off without knowing about the call girl ring. And if I would have been better off without telling him. But there had been a selfish point to giving the information to Larry. A few weeks ago, I learned from Erin that Cathy was thinking of closing the Columbia Plaza operation because Phil had

---

* John Dean was Richard Nixon's White House counsel.

been arrested. He was charged with blackmail, extortion, and violating the Mann Act. As yet, none of the charges had anything to do with Cathy's operation, though she was afraid he could be connected to her business at any time. If Cathy had to roll up her operation, I realized Erin and I could split Cathy's share of her fee and I could afford her almost indefinitely.

Larry called me two days later. "I can't believe it. We already know about the call girls. Magruder knows. And we just finished bugging the DNC. But Magruder was so impressed with me, he became pretty open."

"Where are you calling me from?"

"My office. You don't think—"

I hung up; there was nothing like a little paranoia to keep Larry at bay. But I could see the future for Larry and it didn't look promising. Telling him about the call girls had made things worse. Larry insisted on absolving me of responsibility for his U-2 misfortune and now I had caught him up in something again that was sure to backfire. Even I, with my vestigial sense of right and wrong, could recognize I had a moral obligation in regard to Larry. He was a helpless child and I had been a bad guardian. I had cost him his job, alienated the affections of his son, and fucked his wife. I would have to do something.

I didn't hear from Larry again until June 12 when he called and said, "I need some Chinese food. Today. At twelve thirty." I had been expecting his call. Three days ago the newspapers had finally reported Phil's indictment. *The Washington Daily News* had a colorful but straightforward story about a Washington lawyer charged with "white slavery." *The Star*'s story didn't run until a late edition, but it was a real coup, going much farther than *The Daily News*. According to *The Star,* Phillip Bailley "headed" a "high-priced call girl ring" on Capitol Hill that featured at least one White House secretary and whose clients included many highly placed Washington attorneys. By juxtaposition, the story implied that the call girl ring was part of Bailley's indictment, which had been handed down before Judge Sirica on June 9. Where could that delicious information have come from, considering the call girl ring was not even mentioned in the indictment, nor was the White House secretary and the highly placed attorneys? All I had done, in my anonymous call to a *Star* reporter in the White House press room, was to point him in the right direction, suggesting that Phillip Bailley was "associated" with a high-priced call girl ring that operated in the Capitol Hill area.

At the Chinese restaurant, morsels of egg roll dribbled out of Larry's mouth as he excitedly chattered. "They're all going nuts over there since *The Star*'s story ran. Nuts. Magruder's been to the White House twice to see Dean. He must have told Dean that I knew about the call girls because Dean called me in. To the White House! He wanted to know what I knew about this guy Bailley, which was nothing. I could tell Dean thought I used the call girls for my own pleasure. Which was okay. That way he didn't want to know who told me about the ring. He thought I was a player."

"What are they going to do now?" I asked. "Aren't they afraid their bugs will be found out?"

"The operatives who installed the bugs are coming back into town but Magruder and Dean have different ideas of what they're going to do. Either they're going to take the bugs out or they might not go back in at all. It would be very bad if they got caught. One of the bugs wasn't working too well. The one on the hookers' connection was working but there was no sex talk on it. Magruder showed me the logs. The clients could have been calling for takeout. It's like they're reading from a catalog."

"They are. There's a book somewhere in the DNC offices with pictures of the girls. I'll bet there's also some information about clients. It's probably juicier than the phone logs."

"Wait until they hear about this at the committee. They'll really want to get their hands on that book. I'll be a star. Except . . ." Larry looked troubled.

"What's wrong?"

"Deborah's father wants me to come back and work for him again in California. He says the Pentagon people tell him that when I ran Governmental Relations, ADI was always the easiest supplier to work with. He offered me a lot of money."

"Congratulations. What's wrong?"

"I'm just beginning to move up in CREEP. I might get a White House job after the election. But it's hard to say no to Deb's father. After all, he's responsible for the CREEP job. I'm thinking maybe I could get Magruder to call him and tell him how good I am at CREEP."

"Larry, listen to me very carefully. I've got some advice for you again, and this time you better follow it. Take the job with ADI. The reason you have the offer is because I called our friend Doug Longsdon at the Pentagon and told him how much Senator Russell and I regret that you're not working for ADI any longer. He called ADI."

"How could you do that?" Larry was aghast. "Just when I'm making it in Washington."

"Larry, you don't want to be working for CREEP any longer. Get out. Quit *today*."

He stared at me. "Is there something I should know?"

"There is, but I can't tell you."

He stood up and walked out.

That was four days ago. Now it was 7:30 A.M., on June 16, and Deborah was asleep next to me. If I were someone with a spiritual turn of mind, I would have thought my episode with Deborah was my reward for doing the right thing by Larry. Once more a door had opened for me.

25

At 8:30 A.M. on June 16, 1972, Deborah stirred next to me in the bed. Her eyes fluttered open. "Winston, you're here . . ." She sat up. "Oh my goodness, look at us! I asked you to come over because I had something to tell you and this happened."

"It wasn't planned?"

"No. Really. I thought I had gotten this kind of thing out of my system. As you'll realize when I tell you my news."

"Tell me."

"I'm getting married again. Please don't look so shocked, Winston. I know I picked an appalling moment to tell you, but I swear I didn't plan it."

Even more appalling was my reaction as the news sank in. In pathetic self-protection I thought suddenly of Erin. *At least I have her,* I told myself. *That's all I need.* I burst into tears. So much for a door opening again!

Deborah consoled me, holding me and stroking my face. I became aroused again, but that kind of thing did seem to be out of her system, at least for the present. As she told me about her plans, desire drained from me. She was marrying one of the partners at the law firm, a smart, suave, corporate creature who had left AT&T to spend some time on the Federal Trade Commission staff and then moved into the law firm. I had met him once or twice and knew the type. He would see his union with Deborah as a perfect Washington merger. I imagined the unfolding of the rest of our lives. I would go on encountering her at fund-raising functions for cultural institutions on whose boards she served, her husband at her side, strong and correct in his tuxedo, she in a superbly designed gown, flexing their beauty and success like magnificent butterflies. I would greet them with appropriate interest, holding within me like a spy her larval secrets.

"Have you told Larry?" I asked.

"No. I tried to, but he was in a great tizzy yesterday. He's going back to work at ADI again. I can't believe it. He was supposed to see Mark today but he's leaving right away for California. Which reminds me, Mark will be home soon . . ."

"Don't worry. I'm going. By the way, do you mind if I borrow Mark's binoculars?"

I felt spent as I rode in the taxi back to my apartment. In the elevator, I realized this was the sixth straight day with no sign of Cathy or her girls. I wondered if my afternoon with Erin would happen tomorrow or if she would be afraid to come to Columbia Plaza. I tried to imagine what her apartment might look like—probably some squalid little postgraduate studio.

Larry had called me yesterday to tell me he had taken the job at ADI. "I wasn't going to take your advice at first. I told Magruder about the book, the one with the pictures of the prostitutes. He got very excited. A little later he called me back into his office. He told me their crew was now certain to go back in tomorrow night to look for the book and maybe plant some more bugs. He said he told Dean about the book and Dean wanted to know if I had ever seen it. I said I was a Republican, what would I be doing in the DNC? Then he asked me who my source was. To protect you, I acted sheepish and said it was one of the girls. And then he said, real coldly, 'If your name comes up in Bailley's trial, you might as well resign.' And that's when I quit."

"One more piece of advice, Larry. Leave Washington today."

I got back to my apartment by ten and called the office to say I was under the weather. I tried to call Erin but she wasn't taking any calls.

Then I called the DNC and found out they were on the sixth floor of the Watergate office building, just down the street. I spent the afternoon dozing and drifting with one woozy thought in mind: Once more, something I had imagined and enabled was going to come true. At seven o'clock, I pulled a chair and table over to the window and supplied myself with binoculars, crackers and cheese, and a bottle of red wine. I could see up Virginia Avenue all the way to the Watergate office building. Once the sun had set, I was able to see that the lights on the sixth floor were still on. They remained on hour after hour. I assumed the burglars were sitting somewhere nearby, waiting impatiently, wondering if someone had left the lights on over the weekend.

At about ten o'clock, my compulsive curiosity overcame me and I took a walk. It was a sultry night. In Georgetown, the dense air would have a moist, leafy fragrance, but here the aroma was a mephitic mix of asphalt and car exhaust. A toxic halo glowered around the streetlamps.

The Watergate Complex. At the lower left is the Howard Johnson Motor Lodge and in the distance are the Columbia Plaza Apartments where I lived after moving from Georgetown.
National Archives

I stayed on the Watergate side of the street and sauntered along, not knowing what to look for. As I drew up to the lobby of the office building, I could see a security guard at a desk inside. I couldn't just stand there but I didn't want to go back to my apartment. I wasn't planning on *doing* anything—hadn't I done enough already?—but I wanted to enjoy this drama from a better seat. On the opposite side of the street was the large Howard Johnson's Motor Lodge with its all-night restaurant. I crossed the street but before entering I looked up and over my shoulder. The lights in the DNC were still on. It was about ten fifteen. I ordered a sandwich and coffee. The few patrons in the restaurant were sitting as far apart from each other as possible, suspended quietly in the muted light. Over the next forty-five minutes several men came and went, any one of whom could have been a burglar. I couldn't see the street from the restaurant so, telling the waitress I would be right back, I walked out into the noxious night again. "Taxi, sir?" the doorman asked. I looked up at the DNC, where the lights were still on, and then up and down the street impatiently, as if I was waiting for a car. "No thanks," I said. Across the street, a man entered the Watergate office building and approached the security desk. He appeared to sign in at the desk and then disappeared into the dark recesses of the lobby.

Back in the restaurant I had a momentary urge to register at the motor lodge. Some of the rooms looked directly into the sixth floor of the Watergate offices. But it would be safer if I left no record of my presence at the motor lodge. I ordered my third cup of coffee. At eleven thirty two men entered the restaurant. Each man rapidly surveyed the restaurant before they sat down at a table near the entrance and ordered food. One of the men, who had a thick mustache, was a complete stranger to me. The other one was familiar enough, though I only knew him by his pseudonym. It was Eduardo, my CIA escort in Guatemala.

The question was, had Eduardo recognized me? The folly of my curiosity hit me. From what Larry had said about the CREEP organization, I had to assume Eduardo was one of the ex-CIA operatives who were going to break into the DNC. But if he had recognized me, wouldn't he try to cover himself by coming over to say hello, pretending there was some innocent reason for him to be in this coffee shop at midnight? Although I looked less like I did in 1961 than he did, he was trained in surveillance. Or was he sure I hadn't recognized him? For a moment I considered going over and saying hello to him, then rejected the idea. I wanted to leave Howard Johnson's, but Eduardo and his companion were sitting by the entrance. I ordered another coffee.

The two men ate quickly. As they left, Eduardo cast a quick, uncertain look over his shoulder, perhaps in my direction, but I was hunched over my coffee. When I left two minutes later they had disappeared. All was quiet in the lobby across the street. Too quiet—there was no one at the security desk. "The two gentlemen who just left," I asked the doorman, "where did they go?" He thought they had walked up the street to the Watergate Hotel. I glanced up at the sixth floor of the office building where the lights were now off.

I hurried back to my apartment. Although the lights were out on the sixth floor, Eduardo had walked to the hotel. I realized there was probably an interior connection from the hotel to the office building. I had a strong feeling the burglary was just getting under way.

Eduardo's appearance had connected me to this event in a new way. I recalled how much I had disliked him, which made me feel competitive and oppositional. I wanted to give Eduardo a flutter, make him twitch, just for my own satisfaction. I thought of calling in a fire alarm, reporting flames in the Watergate offices. Then I had a better idea: I called the police and reported that a suspicious person had followed me down Virginia Avenue from the Watergate Hotel. I hung up without giving my name. Twenty minutes later a beat-up car cruised down Virginia Avenue very slowly. I was disappointed: If it was the police, an unmarked car wouldn't scare anyone. I forced myself to stay by the window for two more hours while I finished a second bottle of wine as an antidote to all the coffee. By one thirty I was nodding off. As I stood up to stumble to my bedroom, I noticed a car pull up in front of the office entrance. With my binoculars I could tell it was the same battered car that either was or wasn't a police car. Three men got out, one with long hair, and walked straight into the lobby. A few minutes later the lights on the eighth floor went on; after a short time, they were turned off again. Next, the lights on the seventh floor went on and soon were turned off. Finally the lights on the sixth floor went on and remained on. Then, from directly below my window, several police cars, emergency lights on, silently raced up Virginia Avenue and pulled up at the office building. A group of uniformed policemen hurried into the lobby, leaving their car doors open. The headlights and red rotating lights luridly illuminated the area in front of the entrance. A few passersby gathered on the sidewalk to wait for the show. A paddy wagon pulled up. I opened my window to get a better view and the sweltering air rushed in. I held the binoculars to my face until my eye sockets were slick with sweat. I was so intent on watching the office building that I barely glimpsed a tall figure, who could have been Eduardo, vanishing into the lodge. I focused back on the Watergate entrance until at last a parade of five handcuffed men in business suits trudged out under police escort. They paused for a moment, confused by the presence of bystanders and patrol cars.

The area was bright enough for me to be sure that Eduardo was not among the men as they were piled into the paddy wagon and taken away. Could he really be in the Howard Johnson's? I swung the binoculars back to the motor lodge. A few of the lodge's guests had come out on their balconies to watch the police action. I noticed one man who appeared to be lying belly down on his balcony, watching the event out of sight of the police below. I scanned back to watch the paddy wagon pull away and when I returned to the balcony it was empty.

I was quite certain Eduardo was deeply connected to the events I had witnessed, but the remote possibility of his coincidental presence was intolerable to me. If I hadn't been very tired, if I hadn't consumed two bottles of wine and a great deal of coffee, if Deborah hadn't told me twenty-one hours ago she was getting married, I doubt I would have tried one last ploy. Hadn't I done enough already by calling *The Washington Star*? Wasn't it enough I had let Magruder and Dean hear about the book of photographs of Cathy's girls? But once this new idea struck me, I was unleashed again in a dismal, pissed-off sort of way. I tried to tell myself it was damage control—I would be letting myself off the hook in case Eduardo had recognized me—but I knew it was just an impulse, a selfish urge to finish off the graffiti I had been inscribing here, a last private gesture that with some luck would endure.

It was quite late, but Richard Helms had surely had a number of dramatic late-night calls. It took several rings before he answered the phone. He didn't recognize me at first and I had to repeat my name twice. He asked me to wait so he could pick up the phone in another room. "Winston! I assumed it was the night desk at the agency. They're the ones who usually call at this hour. Cynthia and I got back quite late and we haven't been asleep all that long. What's going on? You're not in some sort of trouble, are you?"

"No, it's just that I have a very peculiar story to tell you. And you'll have to forgive me if it turns out to be pointless. As you may know, I now live in the Columbia Plaza Apartments. Over by the Watergate Complex? Well I woke up a half an hour ago and happened to notice police activity right in front of the Watergate office building. It looked to me as if several men were being arrested."

"The Watergate . . . ," Helms said thoughtfully. "Aren't the Federal Reserve Board offices there?"

"I wouldn't know."

I paused.

"So is that it?" Helms said, a note of puzzlement in his voice.

"Not exactly. You see, somewhat earlier in the evening, before midnight, I had a bite to eat at the Howard Johnson's just across the street from the office building. And who should come in but one of your agents. He was with another man. They ordered some food but then left again in no more than half an hour."

"And who was this agent?" Helms was beginning to sound impatient with me.

"The thing is, I don't know his name. I met him in Miami, when I went down before the Bay of Pigs invasion. He called himself Eduardo but I'm sure that's not his real name. A tallish man who smoked a pipe."

Helms let out an explosive sound of consternation. "Howard Hunt! Damn! What's he got himself into now?"

"Maybe there's an innocent explanation," I offered.

"Well, he's retired. Or he's supposed to be. If he had come back to work for us I would have known about it." He breathed in deeply, trying to collect his wits. "Winston, thank you for this call. It could be nothing. But if he's involved in something, at least I'll have a head start on damage control. Until then, your discretion will be appreciated."

"As will yours," I responded. We had a deal.

I walked back to the window. The squad cars had disappeared. The street was dark and empty again as if nothing had happened.

*

AFTERWORD

On November 23, 1986, the day that I was provoked to write this memoir, I walked to Elizabeth Boudreau's home from my apartment on Olive Street, where I have lived since moving back to Georgetown from Foggy Bottom in 1974. I was in a mood to be provoked. Six months previously, I had been fired from my job at the Senate Select Committee on Intelligence, the successor to my Senate Armed Services subcommittee on intelligence, and I felt old and irrelevant. After nearly twenty-five years of service, I had been rewarded with a low-paid, low-level consulting assignment with the CIA.

I was on my way to the eighteenth incarnation of Elizabeth Boudreau's biennial, postelection Thanksgiving Day buffet of which I had attended all but the first three. In the old days, the party was for the disparate few who were stranded in Washington during the holiday. Over the years, more and more of the people who work in Washington have come to think of themselves as resident Washingtonians and, along with Elizabeth herself, the party has become something of an A-list institution, although Elizabeth still casts a wide social net to fill up her hulk of a home. The 1986 edition promised to be particularly crowded because the Iran-Nicaragua arms scandal, now beginning to be called "Contragate," was unraveling and no one dared leave the city. Even those who were having family dinners at home had made plans to come to Elizabeth's for an extra course of gossip. And there I was, naked; stripped of access and power. I was a know-nothing nobody.

Rojas was at the door, greeting everyone effusively and handing the coats to the maids. He was a round little butterball with a pencil mustache that writhed as he laughed and smiled. He dropped his obsequious bonhomie when he saw me and winked conspiratorially, as if I too were a member of the household staff. "She's upstairs and she's acting so crazy," he whispered as he removed my coat.

"Do try not to misplace the scarf this time," I said sharply.

Rojas flushed, and the tall man who was blocking the entranceway in front of me as he tried to get Alton Kheel's attention, who was on line behind me, looked down at me in amusement.

"Warming up, Winston?" Senator Moynihan asked.

"How good to see you here, Pat. Have you and Elizabeth Boudreau made up?"

"I wasn't aware of a breach," said the senator.

"At that awful play, when Elizabeth told you if you didn't stop snoring she'd go deaf . . . well I just assumed. Or maybe she didn't tell you, maybe she just told me."

Moynihan laughed and patted me indulgently on the shoulder. "There, there." He reached over me and plucked at Kheel's jacket. As the two of them went off, I heard Kheel say, "Is Carlucci supposed to be here?"

I felt that I could say almost anything to Moynihan because he knew that I knew that he was the one who got me fired from my job with the intelligence committee. Or at least he was the crucial one who didn't stick up for me when Senator Durenberger wanted to give his own person the job.

Using my drink as a shuttle, I wove my way through the crowd. Most of the guests had already organized themselves into exclusive clusters as they tried to figure out where Contragate was going. There didn't seem to be any opportunity for me to insinuate myself into, say, the little cabal of Ted Solarz, Robert Novak, and William Bennett without a certain amount of pushy awkwardness. Now that I was without an institutional imprimatur, no one plucked at my jacket at parties anymore, eager to export a gossipy tidbit in the hope of importing one from me. I would have to make an effort to make my presence felt today. Next to power, gossip is the coin of the realm and I needed to eke out a living. As long as the CIA thought I was still part of the conversation, I believed I could hang on to my consulting job for a while.

I moved back toward the door, hoping a bright conversationalist would enter. Instead, Bill Bradley appeared, blinking and shifting from foot to foot. I did know him, slightly, but as far as I was concerned he was a big clumsy man whose dogged sincerity was mistaken for earnest intelligence. Clunks like him get credited with depth while people like me, nasty, shrewish, and short, are called superficial.

And then Deborah Hewitt appeared with her husband Bradford, now the suave managing partner in his prominent Washington law firm. "Winston! I knew I would see you here."

"Dearest Deborah." I gave her a little peck right on the lips while staring directly into her eyes. "And how are you, Brad?" I call him Brad because I have it from Deborah that he prefers the more portentous "Bradford." Deborah has revealed several of Brad's quirks and peccadilloes to me over the years in a form of ceremonial adultery that is consummated when I allude in his presence to one of his embarrassments and receive a sly smile from Deborah in return. I take what I can get these days.

Usually Deborah and I have a quick word about Mark, now a war photographer and a source of constant concern. But we were interrupted.

"Winnie, you must come with me!" It was Elizabeth Boudreau, wearing a rictus of determined charm. I don't know how or why she kept herself going at the age of seventy-one, but she would be in frenzied action for the next four hours. Before I could object, Elizabeth steered me away from Deborah and into her stuffy little Empire-style ballroom with its sinuous drapes and Brunschwig silk settees. The room was quite crowded, but Elizabeth piloted me past everyone interesting, past Elizabeth Dole, past Arvin Blade the landscape architect, past Lee Hamilton, and over to a Siberian corner of the room where were frozen a pleasant-looking young man and a pleasant-looking young woman. They appeared to be successfully staying out of everyone's way. On closer inspection, the young woman was actually more than pleasant looking. Along with her blond hair and even features, there was a pugnacious thrust to her jaw. Her dark, deep-set eyes measured me.

"Margaret, this is Winston Bates who is one of my oldest and dearest friends. Winston, Margaret is not only the goddaughter of my second cousin Anne from Baton Rouge, but she is also one of the most brilliant young economists at the Export-Import Bank."

A moment of desperate silence ensued and I realized that neither Elizabeth nor Margaret knew the young man who, with his red hair, red face and freckles, appeared younger than he probably was.

"Winston Bates," I said and offered my hand.

"Henry Fellows," he said. He shook Elizabeth's and Margaret's hands too.

"How good of you to come, Henry," Elizabeth said with the cautious enthusiasm one employs with the sort of person whose name one recognizes but can't exactly place.

There was another difficult, silent moment until Elizabeth declared an obligation to circulate and left me to do my duty. I surmised that Henry had been about to try to strike something up with Margaret, so I did my best to charm her, which, given my age, vastly annoyed Henry. Margaret regarded the party as a learning experience. She quizzed me about the passing parade and I tried to humor her with pithy unpleasantries about almost everyone in the room. Henry greeted each of my remarks with a little snort of disgruntlement. All too soon, politeness obliged us to make some general inquiries of Henry. He proudly informed us he was charged by the Reagan administration with dismantling a suspiciously productive subsection of HEW.

"What do you do?" Henry asked me aggressively.

"I'm a consultant."

He smiled condescendingly. "In what?"

"I'm an intelligence consultant."

That set Fellows back for several moments until he decided not to believe me. "Who do you work for?"

I shrugged helplessly, as if I were sworn to secrecy, and tried to look apologetic.

"Huh! Well, what do you *do*? Or is that a secret too?"

It was his arrogance that provoked me. "Let's say, kiddo, that one of the things I do is remember almost anything, almost exactly. Five years ago I wouldn't even have said almost." I glanced at Margaret to see if she was impressed. "Would a party trick convince you? How about if I recite the opening-night casts at the Metropolitan Opera for the last twenty-five years?"

"Who cares?" Fellows said. Margaret looked a little doubtful as well.

This was getting tedious and yet I couldn't help myself. "Last week, sonny, I was shown an old, blurry picture of Mikhail, a young technical advisor on the staff of the Soviet embassy in 1961. I was able to recall that he had a habit of poking the tip of his tongue out of the corner of his mouth when he was thinking hard. It seems that David, a recent middle-aged Russian émigré to the U.S., supposedly Jewish, is now retailing to certain intelligence elements his intimate connections with the Soviet scientific establishment. He too seems to have this tongue-in-the-corner-of-the-mouth habit."

Before I could move away, Henry came up with a new challenge. "If you're such an insider you must know who this Oliver North person is, whose name is beginning to crop up in connection with the Iran arms sales."

"I never met the man. He's attached to the NSC, which is a world unto itself."

Henry looked at me in contemptuous triumph.

"I must circulate," I said and turned on my heel and fled. With the pathetic pride of an aging, irrelevant person, I had humiliated myself before this perfect nobody by trying to validate myself. Why had I even come to this party? In my present mood, I didn't think it would be a good idea to talk to anyone else. Luckily, this was a buffet where one can come and go without attracting much attention, though I imagined Rojas would enjoy reporting my untimely departure to Elizabeth.

As I waited on line for my coat, Senator Patrick Leahy appeared beside me. We exchanged a Significant Look. There was a time he would have assumed that I *knew*, but no longer. Finally I shrugged; I had nothing to lose. "What's going on?" I jerked my head in the direction of the party.

"There's going to be an Iran announcement tomorrow." He shook his head slowly and dramatically. "And it's going to be a big one, believe me. But that's all I can say."

"Thanks," I said, in such a way as to make it unclear whether I was thanking Leahy for the measly tidbit or Rojas for my coat. I stalked out seething. How degrading, after all these years, to endure having scraps of gossip tossed to me as if to a little yapster dog!

As I walked to my apartment in Georgetown, the impulse to write this memoir occurred to me for the first time. It was one of those "that will show them!" impulses—"them" being a legion of patronizing senators and Henry Fellowses. I made myself a light supper of cold chicken and watercress salad and took it, along with a half bottle of red wine, into my study. I placed the supper on a butler's table next to my overstuffed reading chair. I settled into the chair and, as I broke my bread and ate my meal, I worked out how I would tell this story. I must have sat there for two hours as I considered this memoir. I was lost in thought when the telephone rang. It took several seconds for me to surface from the past before I could answer. The voice I heard sounded exhausted.

"Are you alone, Winston?"

"Yes, I am."

"It's Ollie. Ollie North. I'm going to have a long day tomorrow. I'll need to talk to you soon. I want to know . . . how did this happen to me?"

I hung up without saying a word. How did this happen to *him*? I'd like to know how this, this life, happened to me.

ACKNOWLEDGMENTS

You know who you are. Thank you.

INDEX